*A*Frederick Ted Castle's
*A*NTICIPATION

a novel

4323

M c P H E R S O N & C O M P A N Y 1 9 8 4

ANTICIPATION

Library of Congress Cataloging in Publication Date

Castle, Frederick Ted, 1938-
   Anticipation.

   I. Title.
PS3553.A8143A83   1984   813'.54   83-14931
ISBN 0-914232-60-6
ISBN 0-914232-61-4 (deluxe)
ISBN 0-914232-65-7 (pbk.)

ACKNOWLEDGEMENTS
Harvey Simmonds found the title and corrected the mistakes. Stefan Brecht, Nell & Jack Wendler and David Lee encouraged me. Peter Gourfain got me to read the whole book out loud at the Bykert Gallery, New York, in November 1973.

"The Final Sale of What Remains" was originally published as "The Sale of What Remains" in *Likely Stories,* Treacle Press (McPherson & Company), 1981.

ANTICIPATION

I hereby dedicate this book to my erstwhile wife
Janet Belle Craver Castle Winston

At the Artificial Firing

Charles.
So far, as even such a phrase implies, the course has been forward in time so that it is now later than when I began to write. And there is no indication that I have been writing continuously or in the present since I began, and there are some indications that I have stopped writing and started again much later. An ordinary piece of paper affords me a scheme which I give it. And in what for you all is necessarily the beginning, I must say that I should rather include the beginning and the end inside, and to the extent that I have any intentions, I would hope to omit them both. As you say yourself it is what is in between that matters: it is my speciality to remark the obvious.

To begin with, if I were to say, Warming my hands in running hot water makes my cod pull itself up, I should be referring to other things as well. But if someone wanted to answer that problem he would almost have to say that I had also referred to the fact that it is cold, And so on, many things, or whatever you wish. But what if there is no other meaning to an admittedly tedious description of the details of the construction of the blank wall of a house. Looking at such a wall would be useless, I suppose, although one might be thinking many diverse thoughts while examining the wall with the greatest care, and could even be carrying on an important or trivial conversation and then too be writing a long letter. I have been very well entertained reading a novel by Gogol or Diderot, and I have even gone so far as to read some passages aloud and to copy out some. While it is always very easy for me to do this as I say on paper, I have only rarely certain attacks of lucidity in which everything I can think

1

goes with, fits into and makes itself the course of an imaginary narrative which I am not usually writing down at the time. Then I am thinking of everything at once. It does not lead me to do anything and it is the kind of thing that can be easily interrupted; it is my ecstasy. If I am writing at the time, the writing is very pleasing even much later, though one could not try to understand it. My not being a professional intellectual leads me not even to suspect that the book is really a conventional murder story of the the type husband-wife-lover until I happen to read the conventional explication of it printed on the back of the paper edition. After I have read all the authorities on the subject, their view of the matter still seems unlikely to me. I am quite willing to allow that what they say has at least the ring of truth—I discover by the repetition of certain phrases that they too have read the book. Undoubtedly it is a book that is complacent enough to allow me to derive by imagination its own story. If all the authorities agree on a single, simple story without any reason to expect that they should it is merely another tedious example of intellectual complicity in which we are, one with the others, everywhere enmired. Or, among those who remember what horse blinders are, it is as if everyone wore blinders.

Because last night I saw a dance very precisely made from some songs by Igor Stravinsky, I can say that the writing is very much like a dance made of songs from Stravinsky. The words, *Shade cool to rest under, Fruit sweet to the taste,* were taken as the name of the dance by a man and a woman while a woman sang such words. Nobody told me a story which could be taken from the dance or from the words, and I did not expect there to be any. For instance, tonight Janet is making hamburgers with a sauce of mushrooms and onions (after all, who knows what night this is?). It is the sort of sentence I constantly remark in American letters. It may be inferred that the question, What's for dinner? is a real American question. With as many answers as none. Actually she has not begun cooking and, according to her, she is trying to decide what to have. The proposition, then, that something could be completed over a period of time by the easy interposition of some insignificant habit—always using yellow paper, for example. It is not that it is something uttered too softly to be heard or said from too far away, but successively it gives problem to the saying of something.

But to cover our tracks and my nudity, I may say that I have read things written by Gertrude Stein, Dylan Thomas, Thomas Wolfe,

T. S. Eliot, Virginia Woolf, Thomas Carlyle, Ezra Pound, Lawrence
Durrell, D. H. Lawrence, Henry Miller, James Joyce, Theodore
Dreiser, Herman Melville, Henry James, Albert Camus, Charles
Baudelaire, A. Rimbaud, Amédée Ozenfant, John Donne, Nathaniel
West, Edward Albee, Ronald Firbank, William Carlos Williams,
David Jones, Marcel Proust, E. M. Forster, William Burroughs,
W.B. Yeats, Wallace Stevens, F. Nietzsche, Thomas Mann, Ozwald
Spengler, E. B. White, J. D. Salinger, F. Scott Fitzgerald, Ernest
Hemingway, Walker Percy, Paul Klee, William Faulkner, Oscar
Wilde, Thornton Wilder, Sherwood Anderson, George Bernard
Shaw, Henrik Ibsen, Søren Kierkegaard, John Galsworthy, Chaucer,
Plato, José Ortega y Gasset, H. L. Mencken, James Thurber,
Siegfried Gideon, Samuel Beckett, William A. White, Ralph Elli-
son, James Baldwin, Niccolo Machiavelli, Charles Dickens, William
Wordsworth, Henry Fielding, Ray Gosling and a very great many
other people whose names do not appeal at the moment for reasons
that may not be apparent. Making up those names cost a lot so I lay
down on the too short red plush worn out divan with my knees pulled
up my feet near my ass one hand between my knees and one arm across
my eyes, and I rested. I stopped and selected a new sentence.

In composing American letters there is a sort of a kind of a
discrepancy among any number of three things: I should be able to
say anything at all, I need a correspondent, I have something to say.
Perhaps that eludes the crippling categories while comprising them.
But, no, that is too much to hope for and going too far, excessive,
impossible to claim. When a muddy road in the mountains after
going through a junk yard really becomes a stream you have to turn
around if you can and go elsewhere. That is what I am thinking
about, a matter of hesitation. My hesitation may find itself in a need
to rest or in any of my schemes. But to go on at this length requires
going on to some length — it will be a long book. To begin again (I
could not possibly have time to explain this) I was born at seven in the
morning on the seventh day of August in the year of our Lord nine-
teen hundred and thirty-eight near Lockport New York where I lived
my first mostly unconscious eighteen years. Once upon a time there
lived upstate the eldest son of a provincial manufacturer of folding
paper boxes. Anyone will tell you so. There is no excuse for being
quite plain about what I have to expose. Now or later I shall perhaps
tell it you in another way but that is no reason to take my word for it.
So much for that then it is no explanation.

Later on he found a girl who agreed with his wishes. After a whirlwind romance they were married in the family church. Returning from Europe they found a job and moved in. Somebody gave them a cat. The cat was sometimes noisy but they fed it beef liver. Having acquired many things they went on getting more things, some of which they ate. In answer to all questions they implied, We are happy. And they were. It was during this time that they invested money in several books including this one. They also had for example a wood salad bowl a silver candelabra and a black typewriter. When they had finished the books, one by one, they put them away. As someone remarked they had a place for everything and everything was in its place. Someone else responded with a fake laugh, and so things went. They always said, We have very few friends, but in the opinion of their friends, they had many. Some were old and many were young—they were themselves very young to be married and have a cat. One day when the trouble began he thought, One of these days I shall have to write my autobiography. They laughed rather seldom but when they did, whole-heartedly. They lived well on next to nothing and did not know the value of a dollar. The two stories they most often told answered how they found their cat and their house. Those were two different stories with many versions long and short, but they might have said simply, in a word, by chance. Nobody could quite accept that they had not named their cat, but in fact they had. They named it every day along with breakfast. For breakfast they ate one of a number of things and sometimes they had no choice. They fed the cat called stupid beef liver and the cat true to its name chose maple syrup to follow. Occasionally they had wine with dinner. Sometimes they bought the cheapest sort and sometimes their friends brought a more expensive brand. It's safe to say they enjoyed it. Very rarely, they said, they went to a party—but it was one of their domestic niceties to say very occasionally. Very occasionally when they went to a party they said they didn't really have a good time. They had not enjoyed themselves, They enjoyed each other so much that somebody pointed to them as if at a two-headed beast. From that point on things which had been like smooth sailing became more like tough sledding on thin ice. They frittered away their time. It was somewhat of a sad thing to see it happen. If he hadn't had lunch right after breakfast he would go out and have lunch. She fell to reading books, bemoaning the fact that they had no cat, but secretly, at least in front of the cat. Stupid the cat ate nothing but beef liver with every once in a while a few tentative licks of maple syrup from the breakfast plate. They picked out white plates like everyone's but larger, They went to seven movies in one week, They went to seven movies in a row. One weekend he saw three movies out of town, two in the city and two on television. They did not have a television set but of course they did have a telephone with an indifferent number. But he was really proud of their automobile license plate number which was 1025-LP. It kept him out of trouble with the police who behaved toward him just as they did on television. Secretly though he liked the telephone number. There were more than two things going on at once—in fact it was innumerable which kept them busy. After a while due to a strike they found themselves with time on their hands. A little before that or some time after he thought of his autobiography which was still unwritten but then he forgot all about it until much later. Now he was writing as he sat on a stool in front of the typewriter his father-in-law had stolen for her from the bank. They had more time than they needed and she didn't know what to do with it. Once in a while almost every day she paged through the cookbooks they had. And from time to time she would cook something up after coming home from the store on the bus. As you see it was indescribably ordinary. Not that they were bored—they were nor reduced to playing pinochle or mah-jong. Years ago his grandmother had taught him to play mah-jong, oklahoma rummy canasta dominoes and many other games aside from russian bank for which he was not old enough. She sat fat behind her round deal table with the inlaid edge and told him if he must fart to do it in the john. For her he had occasionally fixed a leaky faucet by shutting it tight which took longer because of his fascination for her plug-in crimping iron which hung in the bathroom of his grandmother's house on the third floor of a converted livery stable. His grandmother could remember and besides she had been through a great deal. His mother still recalled her description of the blooming chestnuts in Paris in the spring of, say, 1895. Since then she had lost money and gained weight and so become what she was, as his father said, very autocratic. His father was rarely an apologist, but was able to hide in a vast sense of humor. He almost neglected to mention his mother. Concerning his brother and his sister who were younger there was nothing more to say. And he did not follow convention by going on about them as if he didn't know what he was doing.

Naturally he had forgotten almost everything. One day when he was in first grade he had been given a note by Miss Ninos, who also one time gave him half a tuna fish sandwich when he had to stay after school, a note which he took as he was told next door to the other first grade teacher Miss Daly who when he walked in was explaining distinctly that the difference between horse and house was the letter R, which fact remained with him all his life. He remembered that the first word he had learned to write was hill which his third grade teacher Miss Ritzenthaler taught him to do by first printing the word in small letters and then easily joining them together. He remembered something of a controversey over how properly to teach writing, and that the older way had been called the Palmer method. Once in a while he still wondered why when he had been in the third grade the principal Miss Armor had advised his mother to consult a psychiatrist about him—a fact his mother had told him much later when she had been especially pleased at the way he had turned out which was not always. He remembered that in second grade he had had two desks, one he visited only during class lessons which was very neat indeed, and a small spare desk in the corner, very messy, where he spent all his time. There was also a farm boy called Herman who was much older and the dunce. His fourth grade teacher, Miss Llewellyn, lived on Leroy Avenue and had a laugh like nonesuch which he rather imitated. At this time he was also first in love with Iola Long and at a greater distance perhaps with Suzanne Nagel who had a red dress and moved away. He found out where Iola lived and would go by there very unnecessarily. Once a girl Nancy Whalen invited him in to her house for what turned out to be a doughnut in the kitchen. When he was three he had been discovered in bed with Nancy Chapman by her mother who had looked in and then gone away. They had gone to live in California with the YMCA. For Miss Llewellyn, whose name was hard to spell, he wrote an essay on sheep raising in Australia on twenty-five pages of his mother's gray or light-blue letter paper. It had been lost although then as now he kept almost everything which in those days was not much. Sometimes he would cry himself to sleep at the thought of the waste that goes on in this world. Usually he would dawdle home from school humming and thinking of shit. He liked especially to think of things like lawn-mowers and tri-cycles shitting. Henry the gardener next door called him Skeezicks and was known to be his friend, but he didn't know him very well. He knew Joe the boy next door very well though. Joe had a little trouble speaking and would mispronounce words, especially tomato which sounded as if it were spelled ramata. He spent a lot of time correcting Joe's pronunciation and ran out of patience. Later he came to think of Joe as very funny and of himself as impatient, among other things. They remained fast friends. As he remembered all this as he had often done and would do forever, he thought that he could write books about it which would be not too interesting. That done, he finished his beer and read over what he had thought to choose.

There is only one reliable way to judge the size of another man's prick, he read, and that is by the size of his hands and his fingers particularly which as anyone may know bears very little relation to one's general stature and build. You may say it is an obscene cryptograph, but I can attest to the truth of this interpretation no matter how many exceptions you may cite (that of yourself, for example, or your lover). It is also true as is widely supposed that the larger races of men such as northern Europeans and Negroes generally have larger pricks than do men of the smaller races such as southern Europeans and Semites, but as medical curiosity has discovered, among individuals the size of pricks is the most various physical dimension even though there are a great many men whose pricks and whose hands are of indifferent size, neither large nor small. Once in the latrine of an airline terminal in which all pretense of privacy was ignored, not least by the facility of loudspeakers emitting muzak, I saw an uncut black prick befitting a horse. While there is undoubtedly an aesthetic of hands — no Author worthy of the title has omitted to say that whoever he was evoking had long hands, short pudgy fingers, beautifully pointed ones and so on — there is much less evidence of an aesthetic of pricks and cods. An examination of almost any nude male statuary will show that sculptors, paradoxically enough, have usually chosen to show small, uncircumcised pricks with tight cods together with hands that would be considered powerful. Whether that should be regarded as a reflection of the general size of artists' pricks can't be known, but art historians have occasionally thought to say that the choice of small pricks for statues can be laid to the judgement of sculptors that the sexual appendages are ugly, and the larger the uglier.

It is widely supposed by men that women are interested in the size of a man's prick at least to the extent that they notice the cut and other qualities of his hair. Most generally, women are of course interested in appearances and competitions, and very likely it is true that a woman does not feel that she really knows a man until they have made love together. But except for a possible trepidation that it may be too large, I suppose that a woman is not interested in the size of a man's prick because it is invisible. You may motivate the fact as you wish, but only men are interested in the comparative size of pricks in the same way and probably to the same extent that as soon as he has met another man, a man will be able to describe fairly accurately the other's physical capabilities and will notice immediately if a stomach is not firm. Nothing is more common among Authors, for instance, than for them to write that one's shabby and ill-fitting clothes belied the agility of a boxer and the endurance factor of a longdistance runner, and one need go only to the corner bar to find nightly exchanges filled with such anatomical details. Among men who are close friends, it is quite customary for them at times to have the opportunity of seeing each other naked, perhaps in a shower room. It is just as usual for them to enjoy each other physically in games or more figuratively by talking about automobiles, hockey, tailors, horses, women and all that vast category of automatic masculine converation which amounts to a test of strength like Indian wrestling. In completely masculine society, that of the toilet and the locker room, of armies, in homosexual schools, among ships' crews and work gangs it is a matter of course to talk about who has the largest prick and which are the busiest fuckers. I can conclude that a common man typically admires large even outsize pricks and cods while an artist, commanding greater than common sensibility, likely draws everything up tight and restrained even at times when baroque muscles are the vogue.

At this moment in the course of the American era, speaking of fashions, there comes again the custom that young men wear tight pants which express not only the muscles of the calves, thighs and loins but also the soft shapes of the prick and cod. Such tight pants are of various sorts all characterized by what is known among tailors as a short rise—a relatively short distance from the waist band to the breech of the pant legs—often so short that the *penis et testicles in scrotum* form a definite bulge rather than hanging inconspicuously amid the fullness of the pleated trousers of yesteryear. It is possible that at no time in the history of dress succeeding upon the possibly euphemistic fig leaf has this detail been so naturally expressed. You recall that in the almost exclusively masculine society of fifteenth and sixteenth century Europe men wore cod pieces at the breech which often accentuated their sexual extremities to the eye. But then they didn't bathe and would think nothing of taking a piss in the hall or a maid in the bush. That fashion was succeeded by a formal vogue which included tights without even a fly. Later and indeed through many variations until now the custom of baggy trousers characteristic of classical British dress developed in the nineteenth century came to be adopted throughout all adequately civilized parts of the world. We come now, perhaps, to the beginning of a moment when it is again quite admirable for men to be well-dressed in tight fitting clothes. In the United States this vogue can be popularly justified despite an extreme and traditional distrust of vanity in men by the fact that somewhat similar clothes were the custom of men in the fabled American west of the nineteenth century where one may still hear it said of a man one admires that his pants fit. Even though certain western pants manufactured by Levi Strauss & Co. of San Francisco command a premium price throughout the world, the popular style of tight pants is called continental with typical inaccuracy as in apology by whitewash.

During the rather long time while baggy trousers were the custom there have developed two customary sorts of under-pants. The first, with a history extending back to the origin of the shirt, was loose drawers which have come to be known as boxer shorts. The other, made popular through the large scale manufacture of elastic in the first part of this century, clung skin tight at every point by means of bands of elastic which made a pouch to contain the prick and cod. This type came to be known as briefs or jockey shorts, partly because of the world-wide success of an underwear manufacturer whose trade-mark was a jockey, and also because of its similarity to underwear used to keep a man's balls from being stunned during violent exercise by holding his prick and cod closely such as that used by dancers and professional horsemen as well as all other athletes, the elastic version of which has come to be called a jock strap. The satin version is called a dance belt. Tracing the usage of such words is difficult because of the convention that any reference to underwear, even by lexicographers and historians of dress, is impolite, but it is probable that there is some remnant of the notion of protective leather clothing in the term jock just as there clearly is in the term jacket. It is also well-known that horseback riding is a type of sexual experience and jock is a synonym for prick. Anyway, two kinds of under-pants were developed, shorts and briefs which in Europe are called a *slip*. Generally, briefs were the custom of children and lower-class young men while shorts were considered appropriate for upper-class young men and old men. There is little doubt of these American conventions of usage despite any exceptions one might cite. Effectively, shorts are less constraining and less erotic so that they are considered to be more comfortable and more proper for men who, in their general behavior, have renounced all sexual pretensions.

There is a greater variety of nuance in style among commercially produced briefs than there is among the various types of shorts which is very interesting. The cheapest sort contain almost no elastic so that they are, for briefs, rather loose making them less effective as caches-sexe to contain an incidental hard-on and more likely to sag, bind and ride up, effects which are supposed by advertisers of more expensive types to be uncomfortable, but which may be rather pleasant. Those containing elastic of the first quality are likely to pinch the flesh of the legs unless they are worn sizes too large when the other advantages of briefs tend to be lost. In point of design, each manufacturer offers a somewhat different disposition of elastic bands so that the shape and capacity of the pouch is quite various and in each sort there is a somewhat different means of overlapping panels of cloth in the pouch so that the prick may be unpocketed without removing one's clothes. I have a friend who told me that he had been travelling in the jungles of South America for some time without any underwear, probably because it had been stolen by the guides, when he met a fellow American who had with him a box of a dozen new pairs of briefs called Fruit of the Loom. My friend stole a pair of them and said that they really felt good. I knew what he meant. I myself have had the experience of occasionally stealing a pair of briefs from this or that acquaintance to find out how the different ones feel. Many of them have worn out by now, not being new to begin with, but by replacing them with different types which I buy from time to time, according to how I feel I have several unique pairs of under-pants which I use to complement my mood. Typically though, a man has several sets of one sort of underwear which he selects with apparent negligence but which he has nevertheless found satisfactory. Many young men, these days, cut across the old and unremembered class barriers to acquire some briefs and some shorts which they wear depending on how they feel or what they plan to do. Manufacturers of underwear, taking advantage of this newly expressed concern, have begun to offer more decorative briefs as well as shorts cut of printed material so that briefs which were before made exclusively of sanitary white cotton may now be seen as dark blue or striped in red when he takes off his tight pants. It is presumed, I suppose that such briefs which are also sometimes used for swimming make men attractive to their women in private, but I think that it is only among homosexuals that such details create a prurient interest, for, as I have already observed, the appearance of the cod and prick appeals mainly to the reflexive interests of men in general, and so of course more intensely to confirmed homosexuals. So-called falsie baskets, devices intended to accentuate the shape of the genital extremities being similar to a cod piece, would be regarded by women as repulsive whereas false breasts are widely supposed to attract men which is another instance of the true inequality of men and women. To the extent then that this rarely discussed subject is an element of everyone's real life, I have not had to intrigue you into the fantastic possibilities of this section of autobiography by my use of words although I have been at pains to eliminate all supposedly polite but actually repulsive medical jargon which makes all reference to sex like a conversation about dead butterflies in Latin. Your reaction to my realistic dullness is part of *your* autobiography.

Reading it over in a comfortably worn overstuffed chair, he felt satisfied that he had indeed begun his autobiography about which he had been joking for years. But he was struck by the amount of material he had intended to include in such an opening section which had not found a way into the context and couldn't even now be inserted, things that didn't naturally fall into place. But he put down the typescript and thought he would deal with such things another day for all the world like any Russian.

Finally he saw them pull up across the street turn out their lights and get out. He said, They're here. Soon he heard the bottom door slam. Then there were footprints on the steps. 'Hello' he said they said. He said, Come in. She said, Oh, you have a horrible cat, coming in and picking it up. Who did that painting, he said taking off his coat. How did you find a house like this, he said lighting up. They seemed to say, You know we're not married, but instead they actually went to sit down on the long red tufted sofa with curling arms. The first thing I said to him was, The guest gets the best and at the same time I gave him a piece of cheese like camembert, some other kind. He didn't drink but I was drinking. She was already drunk on a dull party they had just left. My wife was drinking beer from a schooner. I was interrupted by a telephone call. In the meantime, the cat came down from upstairs and my wife introduced it all round. It scratched everyone who said 'Ow' and gave it a kiss. Afterwards he said to me, It's really a difficult thing to do what you're doing. I hadn't thought about it that way before then. Later when I was opening the wine, I told him my life story. He said, I'm sorry to interrupt, and I said, That's all right it's as long as my life. Then it turned out that his life had been somewhat the same as mine. I said, I have an acquaintance who thinks he's a friend of mine. He said, So do I. We fell laughing. She was having a beer and crocheting a scarf. My wife was cooking. They guessed right away what they were eating, which was something my wife had bought at the store, some kind of food. I remember that I forgot to say that the reason I didn't like some new kind of music was because it lacked for technique. There seemed to be no way to get in that remark and besides I forgot all about it. It's because, I said, it stops and starts like a crude tape recording machine. They ran out of cigarettes and I was only too glad to rid myself of some of mine. She thought I was very funny. I was very funny and I knew how to do it. We finished the wine and I told them who had bought it. She laughed a great deal but she wanted to discuss something else. He left with my wife which gave us more privacy while she combed her hair. We have been together now for more than a year and besides, we are not married.

They arrived and shouted up to me that they were here. I went down to let them in. He was fatter. She was wearing a red burlap skirt and a yellow shirt but she was standing in a shadow. We climbed up stairs and they shed their coats. We all sat in the kitchen and I had a drink. We launched into a talk about Zionism and Israel, which I was able to explain without knowing anything about it. He also hadn't been there and wasn't a Jew. There has to be a nineteenth century of every people. He said, Things have certainly changed with them, and the change will become more apparent. I said, Undoubtedly. We went into the living room and they sat on the studio bed holding hands. She didn't mention what she did. Later, in front of the stove, she said, You soon find out that the woman has to give in to the man, no matter who says otherwise. One time she came into the bedroom and said, What do you think of that painting? I said nothing. She said,

One day two children saw it; one said, It looks like a sunset; the other said, It looks like an explosion; he was right. Goodnight. Goodnight. After dinner he said he was writing a novel and they lapsed into tales of foreign countries of which they knew many. Finally I let them out and they went on their way.

One time somebody came unexpectedly and rapped on the door. I was glad to see him but we had nothing to say. He was looking for a house which pieced out the silences. We used up the other bottle of wine with dinner which was very good wine. He left early after dinner as he had come. One day we went to see him in his new room with a fireplace. There was nothing to say, and he hadn't read his books about which he could only say who had given them to him. He had a number of friends and one dream. He had just polished his brass ashtrays which were just like mine. We talked about the sun. I arranged to borrow one of his books and then we left him.

The two of them walked in and sat down. We all had a drink or two. I began telling a long story which they knew how to interrupt. Shall the ending be happy or unhappy? During and after dinner I told a much longer story which was more interesting and fantastically complicated. We got drunk and they stayed late, not apologizing for the hour at which they left.

I need a longer bit. That spring, this spring, while we were waiting through February to come we forced forsythia on the coffeetable. One day, today, it came out in yellow flowers. With spring comes one of a number of things that is like cold mushy snow, like blue bells in the forest, like crocus at Easter, like chestnut clusters blossoming along the boulevards, like tame cats molting and caterwauling if they can, like a young man's fancy clothes, like a leaf a bird brought, like the promise of thunder, the smell of lightning, like a trip through the country to look at the cows. Polyphiloprogenitive was the word — youth is wasted on the young; fantasy with fact makes one fact the more. Acne of the world-soul, twenty-three is the year of decision and you have to watch out because wishes come true — besides, one has the right to question one's elders; one is at home and there's plenty of time. In 1923, I married a woman of some refinement. She had hazel eyes and absolute pitch — we went as we were and we stayed as we were which was hell, man whose origin was a terminus: Gloria in excelsis deo, world without end, Amen. I said a few words to the close and holy darkness, and then I slept. Where in the world but in America, where, oh where but in America, where in the world but in America can you sing true freedom's song? Mardon me padam you are occupewing the wrong pie; may I sew you to another sheet? At this embarassing moment I am delighted to say to hell with you all — To work! To work! For heaven's sake! The wolf is at the door. Venus will now say a few words: 'Twas brillig etc.. . . . God save our gracious Queen (confound her enemies) forever and ever, the way up is the way down — de gustibus non disputandum est: a rose is a rose is a rose, but I have promises to keep and miles to go before I sleep; now I lay me down to bed, Our father which art in heaven — the classical in art marches by intention with the cosmology of the age and what rough beast, its hour come round at last, slouches toward Bethlehem to be born: the Company is not responsible for acts of God or the Queen's enemies. I wish I could remember the first tune of spring.

My friend and I meet almost every day at a certain bar in the city that you have perhaps and perhaps not heard of. There is nothing unusual about this place, it has nothing to distinguish it from hundreds and thousands of American bars in towns and cities everywhere. But there are very few bars like that in our neighborhood, really none other. Neither of us lives quite near there, yet we find it a convenient place to meet, simply, you may say, because we like the place. Usually when we go in there is hardly anybody else there and by the time we leave it is probably more crowded. We have avoided getting to know the bartender though as usual he is amiable. They have a radio there and last night or just now I heard, The soviet pledge was reportedly contained in a kremlin communication. My friend and I have great arguments about art in which he contends that writing is not art and I agree. They are the longest sort of arguments, the most tedious, the most boring to everyone but us. Sometimes someone we know will listen for a while and then shake her or his head and go away. If the acquaintance is a woman who is interested in either of us she may try to define to us that we are saying the same things over and over, a fact we have long since understood. Shall we say that a work of art is something made that is like nothing else? That allows us for example to call into the question certain fads in art which have come to our attention. There are many approaches to the subject of art and any scheme is acceptable in our conversation. One might easily say, for example, that we are not talking about art at all, but are trying to discover within ourselves and between each other a scheme that each of us uses every day to make the schedule that a conversation describes. So that of course one might say that the conversation is about art, but it might be about anything in which we are interested. Once, in fact we had a long argument about politics in which my friend is interested and I am not. It was so bad as to be disastrous if it had not meant so much to us. When we were talking about politics we naturally touched on many points in the subject of art, and it was disruptive that I am so uninterested in politics that I make up quite arbitrary schemes for talking about it. We began shouting, and he said things like, Pull your head out of your ass and listen. It is more than annoying to speak with or read someone who will say anything at all about something in which you are mortally interested. Once there was an occasion for me to write or re-write a few stories I had made up. When I took a look at them altogether I was surprised that they all ended unhappily. That was several years ago. Now I shouldn't be surprised if any story I wrote ended unhappily, disregarding my intentions in doing one thing and another.

Earlier today I was on a bus going along a street at a time before dark when one could see into the lighted windows along the way. I saw quite a number of people doing different things just at the time I was passing. None of the things was remarkable, but if I could have looked into every room in the city I should have seen a different thing being done by each of the people at home. Then the bus dropped me off at the bar. For the first time it appeared that my friend was too sick to join me so I had nobody to talk to. The bartender had already set my drink and asked about my friend who, I said, was sick before I realized that I didn't want a drink. He refused to take my money when I left without drinking more than a sip. You see it had become habitual for me to have a drink and talk, and so all I wanted was to take a walk. It was a pleasant change, and besides, though I came there nearly every day, I didn't yet know the neighborhood well. My friend had found the bar before he had discovered me. As I walked I looked at displays of pottery, brass antiques, women's underwear, men's shoes, books, phonographs, photographs, lithogaphs and potted plants all of which, except for men's shoes, was very various and very colorful. I once had a teacher who advised me that if I had to stop writing somewhere in the middle of something I should stop in the middle of a sentence for which purpose I have used this sentence. I no longer care about maintaining the flow of logic in a piece of writing; even so, his old suggestion comes back to me. As I say I was walking along in this way admiring the colors in the lighted shop windows when it occurred to me that I had no idea if my friend was actually sick or not. I couldn't even remember what had led me to think so when I noticed he wasn't at the bar. I could imagine that he had said he was coming down with a cold, or remember that I myself had sneezed several times just the previous afternoon, or suspect that his wife had been pregnant before miscarrying (which wouldn't apply, I know), but I couldn't get to the bottom of it for the life of me, which wasn't however at stake. I thought innumerable thoughts as I walked, only a few if any of which had to do wiith my friend and his indisposition. Perhaps I remember deciding that indisposition would be a more incisive term in indeterminate cases. As I was remembering the look of the Florence Hotel at one oh two west forty fourth street far from where I was I thought of the different things I might see people doing in the city at that hour if I were clairvoyant. At the same time I was in fact looking at the buildings across the street which had been reduced to skeletons by wreckers. An entire row of five story buildings had already been systematically pillaged from inside because all the doors that had been used anyhow in the buildings were selected to be lined up over the sidewalk at the level of the first floor to back-stop the fall of less convenient debris which could be thrust carelessly out of any window before being carted away, doors last. Not surprisingly I was able to explain all this to myself in an orderly way while I reviewed the actions of everyone in the city before after and during dinner, including no dinner, as if I were looking out through the windows of the Florence Hotel, although I had never experienced just such a reverse. It was so interesting that I might have been looking at an extraordinary film, but it also occurred to me that I was walking around playing the camera. It didn't have music, for I had stopped humming when I left the bus a while back. All I could hear was the sharp foot bus truck train honk dull rattle hiss shout of the city which has never been adequately recorded. As I walked I didn't hear all these things as a single sound after the manner of a recording, but I heard this and that, no doubt I missed much, but I certainly distinguished the sounds. I even tried to tell which way the underground trains were headed when I heard them which didn't distract me from my panoramic dream. On the contrary, the sound was most realistic.

Let's agree that I was practicing the scheme for conversation that

had come to me earlier on the bus. I hadn't forgotten that earlier in the day it had been snowing but as I stepped across a puddle I noticed that even the rain following the snow had stopped. I had to cross a street so I took the opportunity of turning into it. Far from the ruined tenements I had passed nearby, the buildings on this street had just opened for business. The temperature of the air in the street changed as I walked by the ventilators and the entrances and the exits of these buildings, all of which were being continuously used. To entertain myself I counted the pavement blocks passing under my feet at the rate of two and one half strides a block until I got to thirty seven when I lost interest. I saw someone who arrested my attention. I turned both my eyes on her and followed her movements down the street. It was the kind of thing that rather often happens to me as I am walking along the street, but I didn't bother about that at the time. I just watched her, and walked along behind her fast enough to catch up which took perhaps two city blocks at the rate of two hundred paving blocks in each one. When I was near enough I was sure it was she. I took her arm and at the same time inquired of her the hour.

I really hesitate to become a woman at the flick of a switch, I said to myself, but anyway I told him the time which gave me something to think about. I hadn't been thinking about anything at all, I told him right off without bothering to think up something plausible to say as my education has taught me to do. He told me about a movie he was going to make which, frankly, didn't sound very interesting. It sounded to me as he talked about his life like a movie I'd already seen and didn't want to see again tonight anyway. There was at least no question of that. He thought I was very funny and I must say whenever I met him I really did make him laugh even without my doing anything, He said it must be because he thought I was funny and so I was, just like that. You can never tell what men like him are going to say, and if you listen to them for a long time it's just boring. He said it was his whimsy. Beside, he could never understand that I really was thinking of nothing all the time. I said, Undoubtedly, and he laughed like he was more than glad he'd found me again. So was I. We were really quite gay, as they used to say. He said he'd just had a couple of beers with an old friend of mine, and he wanted to make me guess which one. I was right the first time—the two of them were really a pair. I'd gone with both of them at one time or another and had heard both siides of the same conversation they were probably still having. I didn't see how they could keep it up but they really were a pair. This one and I had been going together about the same time that the other one was married to an old friend of mine who knew all about us. She was much more patient than I am and learned to bake bread among other things like sewing. She drew the line at darning, she said, and I certainly knew what she meant. He was talking about her now, as if I'd be interested. I already knew all about her but I hadn't seen them in some time. Whenever we all saw each other like now by chance we'd have to get together and have a stew at my house. She didn't like stews but would eat mine for old times' sake, so to speak. They said she was a very good cook, and I'd yawn—you know how it goes. Now that I'm writing all this down, I see that it might make more sense if I called them by their names or some names, but to tell the truth I never even think of them by their names. It's almost an effort to remember them although they're my oldest friends. One time I ran into an old friend of mine in a bar, and I had to talk to him for a minute. I was with this one at the time and not only did I forget both their names, which was hilarious, but I forgot the name my old friend knew me by, which gets complicated. Briefly, since this isn't the point, you might say that I have a thing about names. At least I never have the idea that somebody I run into is somebody else like some people do, according to this one who remembered to mention his name in case I'd forgotten it, which, of course, I had. We walked virtually a long way, or at least quite a ways, before he got around to offering dinner if I would pay for it which I was glad to do. We happened to be passing a market and so we spent some time deciding what to get which turned out to be steak and peas since I'm not a very good cook and comparatively rich. It is always distracting to buy things of any kind with a man especially in a food market where you have so much choice. He said markets depressed him but I was still making him laugh so he didn't mind this time and in fact we were so gay that the checker laughed and joked with us even though he didn't know what we were laughing about. Neither did I, but I was having a good time particularly not knowing where it would lead. Naturally what's difficult for me is to go on writing it down one thing after the next in a continuous way, having to think of it backwards so it will make sense. Beside that, half the things I've put in here I didn't even think of at the time. I don't know what I was thinking about, maybe about cooking or something like that. We were such old friends that he could entertain himself by laughing at me—all I had to do was not think what I was saying, to just say anything that came into my head. We might have done anything at all, but we seemed to be doing things very habitually, walking on shoes, eating off forks, drinking up glasses, looking through eyes and using chairs, so that there wasn't any chance for me to fling off my clothes and suggest a swim, for example. Or to be saved from drowning as I had done in a movie he made. It was quite a bit like old times as I remembered them. Later, when the wine ran out, he would read and I would write. Or sometimes I would sketch his face or just his knees and he might be writing or reading or taking pictures of me sketching. Sometimes too, he would talk which I didn't mind if I had something else to do. Or we would go to a movie, to which he was addicted. Even in a movie he was not like everyone else, he didn't make out or talk at all—in fact it was possible to forget he was there unless he ws allowed to smoke in which case he would from time to time make a certain sound which meant that he wanted a match. He smoked a lot and had two orange fingers as a result. We both liked French cigarettes and usually on my way back from the market I would stop and get a pack at least once a week. We'd usually have one or two after dinner, but people would turn around if we smoked them in the cinema and everyone would try one if we took them to a party. We went together for some time. Afterward he made a movie about it which was never produced. I wouldn't have produced it myself if I'd had the money, unless I could be in it. I hadn't up to this point seen him again for quite a long time and needless to repeat, perhaps, I was pleased. We had a good dinner with rare steak but we ran out of cigarettes after dinner. So we went out for coffee to a place we both knew quite well nearby. It was stupid of me to forget the cigarettes. I mentioned that his friend and I had almost always gone there after dinner for coffee, while as far as I remembered this one and I had never done that. It was not, he said, a case of history repeating itself, and added that I read too many women's magazines which he despised. Somehow he had gotten into a bad mood of which I had already had enough. But I had to be polite, and so I began talking about clothes which sometimes made him laugh. He looked as though he wished he could disappear. He also complained about the price of the coffee which was high. Then somebody we knew came in, which was a welcome interruption.

    It was strange to see Jack and Helen together again, especially at Chou's. It was like a page out of a book. Helen looked as if she was rapidly losing control of the situation and Jack, as usual, looked morose. I took a chair from the next table and began talking about my plans, supposing that after a while one of them would go away. Helen seemed tired but Jack might have a few drinks left in him. We had something in common, the three of us, maybe it was a certain turn of phrase or a look of complicity or some means of identification that drew us together although we quickly tired of each other. Sometimes I assumed it wasn't true since I liked them quite a lot. But when the three of us were together there was usually almost nothing to say. I could talk to one of them, but the three of us didn't get along too well unless one of us was willing to entertain the others. When I had finished telling my plans, Jack perked up enough to ask about the news. I always read the newspapers and Jack knew this and also that I always remembered what I had read. I said, Do you want the major crisis or the cultural explosion, the two categories of news. They laughed and said, well, one said one and one said the other, so it was my luck. I went into a long story based on the news from South America, but I was careful to omit details that might have bored them or annoyed them or in some way upset this new relationship. What I did was to make a few plays on words which intrigued Jack because they were an imitation of Helen's off-hand way of speaking, and which Helen liked because she might have said them herself though she didn't know what I was talking about. I was being too clever because I was on edge. The story about South America ended sooner than it might have because I was so busy thinking up plays on words of the sort I wanted to use that I used up the actual details ot the story much too fast—I had to ignore most of them because they didn't suggest anything amusing to me. Then I switched to quoting myself about the new movies which, if anything, I overdid. Jack anyway had already read most of the stuff I was saying, and that night Helen said she wasn't interested in movies. It was like in the old days after they had quarreled. They would take a walk to get a pack of cigarettes after dinner, and as often as not they would end up with me at Chou's. They always smoked French cigarettes and I'd have one or two with them. Then it was usually Jack who talked, and I'd listen and Helen would yawn. I was twenty-three that year and he was three or four years older. We were both interested in movies and he had a lot to say about them. He wanted to make movies and would describe some scenes he had devised which were like nothing I'd ever seen. He could evoke himself, which was a phrase I liked to use about him. As it got later, either he would go on talking and Helen would beg out when we left to have a beer, or he would get talked out and want to go for a walk in which case Helen and I would usually have a beer. If Jack and I had a beer it would lengthen into four or five, but if I went with Helen she'd nurse hers through two of mine and then go home. We usually talked, Helen and I, about Jack whom we both loved in our own way although neither of us knew him, I thought. She decided she did know him because she had to know someone with whom she was living, she thought, after all, she said. All through this time, I wanted Jack to suggest that we do a movie together. I didn't suggest it because I wouldn't have known how to begin, although I did try to write a movie which was too bad even to keep on writing. I could only decide that you couldn't write movies, though people did, and it had been Jack's favorite theme that movies could only be seen. He meant that word specially, and I tried every time we talked to get it out of him. He insisted that only a camera, which couldn't talk, could have explained what he meant. He always said, If you don't see it, well then, you don't see it. I was convinced after weeks of this repetition that I must know what he meant, but I didn't and still don't. I'm not even sure anymore that he had anything to say in those days, as much as I listened. Before when I'd meet them by chance like now after a quarrel, nobody would say much of anything and nothing could be done about it. Now I was strangely full of gossip, this and that, and I now knew how to be the center of attention which I guess I'd learned from Jack whom I'd admired. It was just like Helen not to listen and to yawn. But I was having a good time talking about movies, which I remember saying, seemed to be getting better. I gathered that Jack didn't think so, but I'd changed so much since we had talked all the time about movies, that I could no longer judge what he was thinking. I couldn't have known what had happened to him. I'd also forgotten most of his theories, although some of my own theories must have been based on his. Whatever happened, he stopped looking morose and looked at me as if at an old house plant that has unexpectedly developed a flower. I remembered after talking with him in the old days feeling sort of like one of his things, a familiar cat or a piece of furniture an unpleasant feeling. Now that was gone entirely and I only vaguely remembered what it had been like to feel ignored. Then Jack suggested we all have a beer, but Helen said she was too tired, and gave us both a memorable yawn and stretch to say good-bye. Later on Jack said, You know, we ought to make a movie together, and began to talk as well as he had in the past, but I noticed that although he was just as good at it, the quality of his performance was less evoking himself than it was evoking something distinctly else. He also didn't theorize about seeing clearly and for the first time we had a real conversation.

That will do. Every morning I put my two feet straight on the floor and stand up. There's a tingling feeling, like they weren't used to it. Then I may scratch my prick and cod, change my under pants or put on some, or I may just pull on any pants I see, likely the ones I wore yesterday. I'm not awake then but I function. More often than not I have what you call a piss hard-on that goes down when I splash in the loo. I begin to think what I have to do and go about breaking my fast. I might make some toast, and I have to watch out they don't burn. I may consider what fantasies I've allowed myself at night and that may take longer than toasting the bread, so I have to watch out. I like to wash the toast down with orange juice. If I've been careful I've already turned on the fire under the kettle, but otherwise I light it in the middle of my toast and juice and stand watching until she boils. I've time then to think what I have to so, what I did last day, what I thought at night which goes away with the first cigarette, do dreams. I smoke over coffee or tea. I think of the post like a new idea and anticipate what is due me. The only bill I get is for the telephone rental, and on account of living out of the way I'm spared the shit mail from advertisers to occupant. I go downstairs to pick up the newspaper my mother had listed in my name and see if anything else has come. Usually not, just the paper. One day I got five letters, two of them interesting. Up again, I finish my coffee over the mail if anything's come, or I read some book I'm into. After maybe two cups of tea the breakfast egg has worked its way through until I begin to feel yesterday's shit. I let it out cleanly and quickly while I glance at the paper or look at myself. After that I am awake. It is appropriate to speak to me, I can talk and argue and deal with ticklish situations, answer the telephone intelligibly or re-dress to go out. I notice the weather and decide upon a sweater. If there is anybody else at home I may say, Well, what shall we do?

If I am alone then as I often am, I may say that to the cat if the cat is up as he often isn't. At the cat's pleasure, I may take him in my arms and love him for a minute or five. The cat requires half an hour a day which I'm willing to do if she'll shut up when I'm busy. My morning is usually short, a variable time between breakfast and lunch. There are four things I do in the morning. I write memorandums to correspondents, responsive letters to people I know who've written to me or to whom I wish to write. Or I read. Or I write as I'm doing this morning. Or I do errands, get the laundry or take it, go to the store or the bank, buy some stamps or some cigarettes. I never go far or do much. As I say the morning is short—it may be two before I have lunch. For lunch I notice the clock which lets me plan what I have to do later. If there is much to do in the afternoon I eat again as soon as I'm awake so I won't get hungry in the middle of my business. If there's nothing much to do I eat when I'm hungry, maybe some soup or a sausage quite late in the day if I've been absorbed by whatever I'm doing. Sometimes I sit in my chair and think for more than an hour, and often as not that will be my day dream. After a time I like to invent something to do for sitting and thinking and feeling my body quite likely will annoy me at length, more so if I've actually something to do. In the unnumbered hours of the afternoon erotic sensations impress me and if I'm alone in the afternoon I may let my mind let my prick crawl uncaged and later arrest it by hand. You see in my little life I've plenty of time to do whatever I want to, and I do, and I do want in the evening to have a good dinner a drink and some talk and I do, I usually do. The day time you may say is my own and the evening is for others. You may suppose that when I'm with people I do as they do on TV.

If I write this every day until my twenty-fifth birthday I may have something worth something, a cause for celebration.

¶Mise en scene pour l'après-midi: une promenade à pied de vingt minutes. Allons. Méthode de fade-out et de superposition des images; sur la piste sonore de la musique, une chanson populaire Américaine à mi-voix, et aussi, tous les bruits de la ville: les autobus et les autos, le métro, les conversations en passant, les bruits de pas, *et cetera*. Il y a une montage cinématographique des images de la ville la plus grande du monde: l'hauteur des édifices de commerce, les petites rues du vieux quartier, les affiches, les gens, le soleil, le vent, tout. Nôtre héro est heureux—il chant à bouche fermée. Il marche rapidement sur le trottoir au rythme de la musique qu'il chant, mais il regarde tout le monde avec le soin d'une camera. En effet, il devient un appareil photographique. Il remarque les camelots, les travailleurs de la rue, les commis voyageurs gros, beaucoup de jeunes filles et de

petites mesdames commerçantes, mais, toutes les mêmes, pas vrai-
ment belles. Après peut-être trente scenes de cette sorte, traversant la
rue finale, il entre dans un grand parc, situé de nouveau au point de
l'île de la cité. Il est désert, sauf les pigeons, assez venteux, ensoleillé,
assez tranquille et silent. Pas de musique. Il se promène le long d'une
allée pavée vers la corniche, remarquant les pigeons et les petites
arbres, regardant la grande panorama de l'arrière-port. Il traverse le
parc près d'une vieille bastille, fermée comme un aveugle mais avec le
drapeau national battant en haut, construit par les pères de la patrie
pour défendre la cité contre les anglais en 1812. Il est fait de grandes
pierres nues, peut-être un peu rougie par le soleil. Dans cette langue
ètrangère, nôtre héro pense plus lent qu'il marche; d'ailleurs, mal de
cerveau, il n'a pas tous les mots pour former ses pensées. Mais
n'importe—il pense heureusement en français.

A la corniche, sur un banc vert, il trouve deux amoureux en train
de baiser au clapottement des vagues qui jouent le rôle de chaperon. Il
fume une cigarette dans la brise de mer, il regarde les bateaux, qui
va-et-vient entre les îles du port. Après deux minutes comme celà, les
amoureux lui rompe avec des éclats de rire. Il quitte leur rendez-vous
publique suivant la corniche au fin près d'un hangar de bateaux
pompiers. Alors il retourne vers la cité où, en face du congrès des
édifices, la vieille maison de douane est très visible dans le style
baroque de l'Ecole des Beaux Arts presque 1892. Il s'arrête au bas de
l'avenue Broadway: à tout son longeur aperçu comme au millieu de la
rue, il aperçoit l'immeuble de l'Etat Empire au fond de l'île, sa
casquette étincellante dans le soleil. Il regarde ensuite la sculpture
montée sur la façade de la vielle maison de douane, de la sculpture à
grandeur naturel doublé des figures abstraits comme "la justice" qui
sont tous blancs au contraire de la façade noircie de suie. Encore il
marche au bord de la rue, remarquant les signes à main d'un gen-
darme. Il passe une grande édifice moderne, tout coins faits de l'acier
avec une façade plaqué à vitres, sans sculpture. Il regarde les pietons;
ni laiderons, ni gens de l'aspect très heureux, ni quelqu'un qui souffre
ou qui rit—tout à fait gris et impassible. Il pense à dire, formant les
mots sur les lèvres sans voix,—Merde à la puissance treize, mes frères
commerçants.

En émergeant de l'échafaudage d'une nouvelle édifice, il
rencontre l'Eglise de la Trinité de pierre noir avec son horloge de ville
à trois heures et demi à mi-hauteur de la spire unique au bout de Wall
Street. Il se tourne aller en bas de cette rue avec ses drapeux de toutes

les compagnies financières les plus grandes du monde. Il marche dans cette rue célèbre, son avis plein de pensées de la haute puissance et de la gloire de l'argent, ou du néant — c'est la même chose. Au fond de la rue, une rue assez courte pour tout son grandeur, il regarde un affréteur au quai peint en blanc et jaune. Le bateau reste impassible sur la marée haute. Enfin il retourne chez lui à pieds, pas très vite, yeux baissés sur le dallage inégal. Il monte l'escalier chez lui. Il s'adresse à sa machine à écrire: je suis un étudiant de l'histoire d'architecture.

¶Things are in a continual state of change, and all rhythms beat quicker . . . It is not less creative but it is agitated and unstable, more divided and multiform than ever before. Uneasiness seems to be its very essence, a disquietude that is haunted by the dim sense of an unpredictable future. The only appropriate label for it is the non-commital one of transition . . . This lack of stability takes many forms . . . As a result the Twentieth Century in its middle period seems to have lost its bearings and to be drifting rapidly toward the unknown . . . Recent departures have cut at the root of habits that thought themselves eternal . . . Literature, and especially poetry, has wandered away towards totally new paths . . . Up-to-date writing in verse is largely difficult or unintelligible . . . Such is the unsettled state of the present.

¶There is a fashion by which all literature is seen also as literary criticism, a habit of mind for which the root could be derived by the briefest study of up-to-date philosophy. In any event, such a conceit is doubtless useful and, in fact, I am party to that fashion. There is, however, very little utility to be noticed in fashions of dress, or of decoration. For example, it is my custom to think well of cities or of governments according with the extent to which I find them useful. If that is true, then I have no more interest in the affairs of a government than that government has in my own concerns. Nor have I more interest in the appearance of a city I choose to inhabit. When I choose a coat in accordance with an occasion on which I shall be informed by my clothes, I disregard the inutile of style, I find value in what is agreeable and unnecessary. Were I to take a walk I should like to stop at a familiar place that continues to please me. I should like to be permitted my dream as an autocrat. Nor is it that I am easily bored. I dress in a manner appropriate to me. Incognito in the city, I seek a corner, a memory of something that is otherwise forgotten. I appreciate the place. My coat becomes me. My pleasure is in recognition. For all the use of any value, I would not name a storm. Nor is any conception worth more to me than something that I find beyond which I may conduct an imaginative enterprise. Mine is part of the city where I live. And more than that.

¶In my time I guess I've investigated just about all the bars in this neighborhood, which I do by going in and drinking a glass of beer. Then not finding anybody I'd like to talk to in the bars around here, some of which are great old bars, I've looked into a number of bars that are not exactly around here, though they're not exactly far afield either. You couldn't know all the bars in the city, not possibly. There are at least two considerations in all this. There's the bar itself, physically, and there's the people who usually go there. Personally, I like pretty old bars, not fancy but anyway old. I'm always on the lookout for good bars. In most of the bars I've found what goes on is serious drinking to the tune of very loud commercial music or television. Sometimes the drinkers sing along with the ads. Serious drinking is an American custom and not delightful — Germans and Russians might have invented it if they had ever had time to discover that work and more work means only more work. Serious drinkers do not talk although they may make various noises that often sound like grumbling without content. Then there are bars for the rich, bars for the fruits and bars for the middle classes. The bars I like are usually working men's bars and also former working class bars that become popular with young people on the make, that is to say unmarried. These are the bars that in any European city are crowded with university students, but here most of the students don't go to bars and those who do are disguised as artists. I have found three or four such bars that I like, and I even think I might like some of the people I see there. In such places young people agree and argue and laugh with abandon and nobody gets very drunk. There's something about me though. Perhaps it is that I look like a musician — I've been asked if I was composer three times in one month. I myself would be reluctant to talk with a composer; even to me it would seem odd for a musician to talk. I was surprised when I read something by Debussy once because it sounded so like something anyone — even a writer — might have said. Then too, it's supposed that musicians are homosexuals, which I've also been taken for a few times in my life. Or perhaps it's because I hide behind my glasses—I've heard people say that of me—or in some way look, as I suspect, rather forbidding. Besides, I seem in this country naturally taciturn, and when I do speak, I'm likely to say something for which nobody can find a ready response. There's something in common among struck-up conversations here that I notice with awe when I return from being abroad. In ten minutes after a casual opening remark both of them have let down their hair. A woman with long hair removing her hairpins, you'll notice, picks out a dozen or ten bits of metal and the shape of her head changes completely. Like it's hard to remember in the winter what trees full of leaves look like and in the summer you can hardly imagine them bare. I suppose this preoccupation of mine—that I have to find somebody to drink with—may be just another sign of the delaying spring which paces out February with two holidays, two national holidays supposed to be in honor of political heroes of this country. Here it is another holiday eve with no festivities planned for the morrow. I referred earlier to someone I can't talk to, and it's true I have almost nothing to say to most of the people I know. Besides, it's too cold to go out for any length of time unless one has an engagement to meet someone someplace at the appointed hour which approaches. In fact it is rare for married people to have any good friends at all. I mean that the cold is a manner of speaking as much as anything else. Somebody is always waiting for something and I, for one, don't know what it is. If you want to carry on a sustained piece of writing or dancing or living you have to remember each of a thousand schemata of which no account in the play itself. *It was enough to make me believe in romantic love.* One day when I got up at three in the afternoon, for the first time in some time I found no yellow sheet of paper in the typewriter. I felt then that I had reached, therefore, the end of a little part of whatever I was beginning to write.

The reasonable man is always reasonable. He has he knows certain shortcomings with which he is able to balance his strengths. On his left hand he wears a gold ring, on his right wrist he carries a chrome watch. While it would be too much to expect that he was always right, it is surprising when he is sometimes wrong. Everyone likes him but he has two enemies. Without seeing his many friends and his three foes he is still able to be amiable. He has a kind word which is also short. Knowing nothing, he is at least able to radiate health; knowing everything, he is yet able to judge a mistake. He has a gray hat which is somewhat worn. His wife and the children are the light of his life; in the dark night of the soul he prays. His debts are paid and he borrows money. His dentist, a friend, is his equal in everything. His grocer and butcher have both retired. His baker is deaf, his tobacconist smiles the smile of a fat cigar with a hole in the head. His bookseller's rich and his maid is poorly—sciatica drubbing her down to the knees. His shoemaker has a wart on the nose, can't see as they say the wood for the trees. His lumberer walks with a heavy tread and sells wood by the board foot. His hatter and tailor both regard him with awe as did his fraternity brothers. His women are few and have all been faithful over the years and into the woods. His chauffeur is able to fix a victrola, his gardener could stoke the furnace as well. His postman delivers the mail every morning in United States government order, his cat and his horse are the light of his life with his wife placing third or fourth. His smile is like candy to orphans. His hat, slightly worn, is lightly off color, his jokes a bit near to the bone. He takes whiskey neat as food for the tongue. The reasonable man is a reasonable man. He eats steak, peas and eggs through the day with some milk. He uses drugs in moderation. He drives to and from work and gets there early. At the suggestion of his doctor he has taken up smoking, lost weight and feels better by far. Without a single accident he has gone through three new cars of a popular make in the middle price range—he smokes cigarettes without filters. His favorite expressions are *of course* and *undoubtedly* and *which,* and with them he spices his talk. Some onions are mild and others are stronger, but at white sauce and garlic he draws the lines. He reads all the readable big city newspapers and subscribes to a pile of books and magazines that would reach, laid end to end, from here to his wife. His wife is pretty but slightly dowdy, an orphan by trade and quick on the draw. His lover has not been invented yet. He walks with the aid of a white ash stick to survey his possessions on Saturday morning. He has a local radio station, a liquor dealer, a travel agent, an insurance salesman, a wine merchant, a tax consultant, a branch library, a town councilor, a county seat, a lawyer, a congressman, a committeewoman, a bank with a banker in it, a neighborhood theatre, a hardware store, a paint store, a feed store, an art supplier, a glazier, a fishmonger, an egg man, a cheese man and he is terribly witty at parties. The reasonable man is a veritable boon and it's safe to assume that he's happy.

This morning he opened his eyes, shaved and walked downtown

for a cup of black coffee. In his mail he found three bills, a literary journal, two advertisements, one for soap and one for opera tickets, both of which he threw out, and a letter from *me* which he read.

To John Malcolm Brinnin.

I have been thinking of Gertrude Stein. I have been thinking etc. . . . Even that could be interesting.

(signed) Frederick Castle.

During his second cup of coffee, which was unusual, he read the literary magazine. The novel is dead, he read, we have received many letters . . . anything that can be thought at all can be thought clearly and anything that can be said can be said clearly . . . you have to come to terms with the factory . . . although we received many responses to our essay contest, none seemed to warrant a prize . . . unlike the poetry of the past it takes no interest in moral questions . . . the moon fattens and fails . . . the shoemaker sat in the cellar's dusk beside his bench and sewing machine . . . sustaining its heartless reflection in the red of my blood . . . her small sticky face was all but obliterated by the hair that fell over it from both sides and from above . . . Cranes of America, lift me! . . . Mr. Snyder has courage and an air of faithful patience . . . let's stick to sweet reasonableness, I'd rather you did . . . that sense of song, that idea of beauty is a learned sense, an objective beauty that does not consider these times or Freud . . . it is possible to explain the book and remain fundamentally unmoved . . . stragglers among the black roots engaged in a vague destruction . . . there are no trees on the island . . . but in our own time most films still tell a story or convey an idea . . . Question: what is illogical in conceiving the obverse governing side of lingual phenomena . . . isn't it incontestably true that purposive receptivity is an essential component . . . in the eyes of death I saw your face . . . but it is the fecality of an English snob, who merely puts a little crimp in his obscenity like a curling iron crimping a curl . . . A great deal of "literature" which is "great" is simply curiosity. Like a man who could do many things did one . . . failure in communication is . . . what if your flowers freeze in their stalls . . . Oh God, whispered Lily silently . . . it is time to consider seriously the work of Thomas Kinsella . . . you are warmly invited to send contributions . . . caught between the lotus and the heart . . . it was an all, a nothing or a something . . . it is related to what the Greeks termed the divine section . . . and in committing his detached violences, Mr Huxley makes sure, to begin with, that we first excuse him by lifting a long speech from David H. Lawrence on the mechanical death of man . . . there are still resources to be tapped and new methods to be explored . . . Buscot, Farringdon, Berkshire . . . thus, our canons of judgement are as impersonal as in mathematics or physics, and sometimes as devastating . . . the trial should serve to show the extent of freedom allowed to authors in France today . . . on the other hand, familiar to the existentialist will be the weirdness of the teenager attempting fifty rapes . . . his heart was going like mad and yes I said yes I will. Yes.

He paid for his coffee, walked out and went home. There, he dictated to his machine this note: dear mister castle I have received your communication of whatever his date is and I should like to hear more from you please feel free to call me whenever you are up this way although of course I have said almost everything I thought about gertrude stein in the book yours sincerely et cetera. *Then he fell into a long reverie of which nothing is known.*

There could be reason for an interval. I could express it by an intermission: *The Same Twenty-four Hours Later.* But in a book there is no assurance that an interval will be observed—the only possibility is, shall I say, to include the interval. There could be hesitation and reasons for suspension. One can always explain away a slight limp. The expression of an interval, the expression of orange juice from oranges. As Fielding used to say, you may take a walk or a break for I have a digression to make, an interval, a weekend, if you please.

What have you done over the weekend? I have never gone skiing although you probably have. I rarely go to the seashore as you often do, but at least I too have done that. I have gone to the mountains, to the Adirondacks, to Lockport, to Williamstown, to Boston, to New Jersey, to Philadelphia, to Washington, to Utica, to Maine, to the movies, to Chartres, to a party, to the Falls, to Rochester, to Buffalo, to Venice, to Albany, to New York, to Chicago. I have stayed home Saturday, read a book, done the dishes, seen a play, taken a drive, shacked up with a girlfriend, locked myself out, built a bench, had a party, cooked dinner, gotten drunk, gone to a dance, taken a walk, talked to a friend, gone out for dinner, looked at pictures, listened to the radio, put on a play, spent it in the darkroom making photographs. In short, I have done as many things over the weekend as you have if you thought about it, But I hardly ever read the paper on Sunday. Do you remember that class of games everyone played as a kid in which who was IT had a choice as to what it was the others should guess? Of course you do, everyone did, even me. Did you discover, though, that it was not necessary to decide what the others were to guess before the game began? I mean if you were very careful you could remember everything that had been guessed as the game progressed and still have more than one thing reserved that had not yet been touched. I know how to do that and it makes being IT a pleasure and good exercise. Now you're IT.

Returning from the weekend, he fixed himself a late Sunday cup of breakfast tea and sat down to write a letter which he rattled off. He read over the piece of yellow paper he had typed, made one correction, then took another to write a covering note which he scribbled out. The letter—she thought of anything like a covering note as a letter—reached her the following day, was unsigned, and she thought it oddly addressed, to Mrs. M. J. Hornick, whom, however, she was. Folded with it was another letter in an envelope, unaddressed, unsealed, stamped with an unmarked blue Washington head stamp worth five cents which she opened and read. In fact she liked to read letters.

To Edward Dorn.

During my unprincipled reading last week I happened to read over some notes that were your reaction to writing by Burroughs and Trocchi. It also happened that last week I decided that I need somebody to have a few beers and talk with. Having already searched my acquaintances in mind, turning up some names I hadn't thought of in years and in some cases their faces, I thought I would like to have a few beers with Edward Dorn. I had thought I'd send you a note saying that I would call you, making sure you knew I'd bring no axe to grind by suggesting an inconsequential matter of conversation, say, flower pot design. Today my friend remembered that you had had some poem in an anthology he owns and from the notes there I found out that you were born in '29, eight or nine years before me and that you lived in Santa Fe once, perhaps you still do. A couple of years ago I decided that something would have to be done about my always being alone and having no one to talk to, and sometime after that I met Janet and we were married a year ago today. Perhaps one day we will meet for a beer in Santa Fe or somewhere. This note is part of something I'm writing, so I'll try to send you a copy of it as a matter for you of curiosity. I might have written you a letter, a letter about something that might interest you, but this is taking up my free time and whatever I have to say in writing. I don't know what I'd make up to say if you and I were having a beer. Writing is not one half of communication like talk. All conversations in books are mythical since both sides are in the book. So be it.

Ted Castle
24th February 1963.

She usually liked to read a letter over twice, but more than usual she felt there was something in this one she had missed. After three glances she decided that it was something that was just not there, perhaps half of a joke, or anyway nothing to do with her. So, full of thoughts about the various quality of ball point pens, she addressed the envelope, replaced the note, wiped the flap of the envelope on her wet sponge, pressed it down, placed the letter with the outgoing mail and answered the telephone. The letter, my letter I guess you might say, reached him by a devious route on the Fourth of May. It had been sent back and forth. The envelope was almost a regular artifact. It had postage due, was stamped and checked in three places address unknown, had been stamped *return to writer* in a hand, readdressed several times and postmarked twice as many. It looked as if it had been through a lot and, in fact, both a cat and a girl had left their footprint on it. But the contents had not been inspected, was intact, and hardly more contaminated with germs than the bill from your every-day grocer. It was the unique piece of mail he received that day. He looked at it carefully enjoying its obvious tribulations. He also showed it to his wife if she was at home, or he thought to show it to her when she came back with the kid from the store. Or perhaps he merely put it on the bulletin board over some aging Christmas cards where it could call attention to itself. He almost forgot to open it. He actually forgot to use it as a letter and instead he behaved toward it as he might a picture post card of an elephant with two words, a name and his address on the back, except that the envelope was more interesting to look at.

As he pinned it to the board he remembered he had forgotten to ask his wife, who had really gone to buy some cheese, to pick up some clothes pins he needed and some honey he wanted. His list, he remembered, had been just two things. He recalled she had mentioned getting cigarettes at the drug store, and habitually thought as he did rather often, that he should have spoken then of the two things to get. But, satisfactorily, when there were more than three things, he made out a list. He didn't reflect, for instance, that he had moved several times in an equally short time and that hardly anyone knew where he was living then. Nor could he have known that he had not found the job he would later get at a college in New England, where, after his wife walked out, he developed the custom of going downtown himself every day, getting the mail and reading it over coffee so that it was convenient for him to buy whatever he wanted himself by the way. Instead, he walked out the back door of the house and into the field and kept walking. It was the Fourth of May and a pleasant afternoon but he didn't listen to the birds which undoubtedly sang. Of course he was lost in thought. For it was in thought, after all, that he found himself whenever that happened, which was these days not rarely. He had always walked when he had lived in the city, but there he was likely to think about himself walking in the city, or at least about the city which was likely to intrude. I have never liked scenery, except moving from a car, and in the woods I'm bored by the woods making it seem as if I'm alone. Or as somebody said, you remember, I like a view but I sit with my back to it. And it happens I do, I have a big chair with a view of the river behind it. He was thinking of a photograph his friend had made of him with a boat passing in the background. You're most alone driving at night on a flat straight road when your thoughts play like a movie on the glass. You can be alone in a theatre but it's hard to think there. At a movie I hardly exist unless I'm smoking but I'd rather not smoke there, but I will if I can, am allowed, but I will if I may, he corrected himself, and stopped briefly to light a cigarette which was quickly smoked by a light breeze from somewhere. He neglected to smoke whenever he was walking because he didn't like it, didn't need it as he walked, it tasted bad. It tasted bad as he wrote if he wrote a lot, but I have to smoke when I write and I want to, and take a drink of water or coffee, or iced tea or beer or orangeade, never whiskey or wine as I write. He enjoyed the breeze which smelled of nothing. His nose would be clean in the country. He mushed across a facsimile brook let off by construction on the nearby hill, liked the feel of the fact that his socks were wet and wondered why he wasn't supposed to. It must be uncomfortable. He thought as he was thinking to remember to get some condoms the next time he went downtown. He might be asked to get her absorbent corks but she would never get his safes. You have to ask the druggist, man to man. His son, nephew, wife, stockboy or female employee will always tell you to wait for him. Are there drugstores tended only by women, and what would be said? I'd like a package of prophylactics, please. What? Oh, the druggist is out— he'll be back though to help you. No woman could do, except in a discount drugstore where the products lose their character in favor of the price. There are different kinds. The one with an extra tip for the spurt, most popular in Europe and supposed to reduce the question of wearing through at the end. And the plain regular Trojan, the noun of a brand no dictionary discovers though every man-child looks. And more old-fashioned but better than ever, most expensive, re-usable wet slip-over skins, nonelastic from the intestine of a lamb, as smooth as a foreskin. Petit chapeau, called in French, a cap for a phallus. The rubber ones, rubbers, may be packed dry or pre-lubricated, rolled or flat, all made possible in sum by a process, the vulcanization of rubber. I work for the Youngs Rubber Company in Toledo. Oh, what do you do? We make scum bags by vulcanization. Then the cheap shiny breakable ones sold in the public toilets of New Jersey and Germany exclusively for the prevention of disease. I encountered my first in my father's top drawer, one from a box, the most useless thing I had ever seen. Later I discovered a use and decided for a moment that my father was sick. When I first had jock itch I though I'd caught the disease by trying on the medicine. They lay, my condoms, of a popular brand in the middle price range, on a table by the couch where they were often used by him in the afternoon, and in that house there was no need to hide them away with the guest towels we hadn't yet bought.

It was for him a continuous round of reading and eating, so much so that he felt he couldn't stuff another thing in. He found the sight of a book or an egg repulsive but his revulsion quickly passed and he would sit down and gobble it up, so much so that one wondered, had there been anyone about, where everything went. He himself sometimes wondered how he could read so much, a form of self-consciousness apt for the murky reveries of eight o'clock in the morning when every day he awoke, you may think, to a host of petty recriminations clothed in tongue mud and mouth soot. He was full of himself. His hair thinned itself as he scratched, he lost weight and felt worse as he ate more and read more. In short, as somebody said, he was becoming American. Not that he often had company. What somebody said he had read in a book where it was more real to him than if his best friend had been there and said so. But friends seldom told him what he wanted to know. He had for the most part given them up, writing curt notes of dismissal to his wide acquaintance, saying no thanks to the least invitation, walking on purpose where no one would meet him, disguised in old clothes. He retired from society and contemplated taking a turn in prison, a condition so like his self-enforced life that he could scarcely imagine the difference. He was also harassed by high prices. His barber had died or removed to Florida so he let his hair grow to a scandalous length. One day he decided to go to Toledo Ohio. It was you may say the turning point of his career, the low point of his existence, the sine qua non, a point of no return, pointless in the extreme, *un point d'argent dans la nuit*. From that point on his sloth was arrested, it was onward and upward. With a new lease on life he worked like a new broom. He spent money left and right and bought a new hat in a darker felt and entertained lavishly and slavishly brought himself around. *It was as if the renaissance were a direct outgrowth of the classical flowering instead of having fallen as it did on the heels of a depression.* Whereas before he had good friends in every walk of life from artists to journalists and even doctors, now nothing could dissuade him from the truth that love, clearly perceived, is a synonym for communication. In the eyes of that light everything fell into step. He was beginning to be informed, as he thought, by a vision. He refused to argue, and became pensive at parties, to which he attended with the selective eye of an old raconteur. He confessed he was bored and tried not to stifle a yawn. He found in fact he could demolish a frolic merely by making a chance remark. Slowly everyone began to ebb away fron him leaving him drunk on the bed while a few anxious friends tried to clean up the mess. His reading was nil and his appetite fell off. But at eight o'clock in the morning he could always scrape himself together with the aid of a few insignificant habits. We doubted that he could go on like this for long, but we said nothing.

We felt as if we had a stranger in our midst. At our daily gatherings in some roadhouse or other we voiced to each other some cause for dismay among remarks on the weather and up-to-date temperature readings. If nobody minded, we also read the newspapers aloud to each other which was in those days the principal form of entertainment among us. We agreed with his old father who assumed like a madman that his son would end up in the nuthouse. It was during that time, if I remember, that we got a letter from him which he had artfully written as if he had already been condemned to a state institution. Unfortunately I burned it along with some old-fashioned engravings at one point, but I remember as clearly as I do my name the sentence which went, The typewriter is my surplice slice of hell. It was not a misprint but a play on words the meaning of which I could not grasp. You see at that time I had no key to his system of thought, no gestalten, I had made no schedule of the schemes that filled his head, I knew no study that adequately explained the root of the matter—we thought him rude and obscure. In this we were to some extent wrong, as posterity has characteristically gone on to show, but we didn't share the mistakes of the others who took his manner to be anglophilia put on to conceal his native fecklessness and bad taste. At least we knew he was a real and present danger to our own reputations if not to our lives. I remember so clearly his remark that, *Posterity is a many-headed treetop beast composed entirely of voices and eyes in the proportion seven voices to one eye.* At that time I had not yet heard of his scheme he called *the map reader's point of view,* in the light of which the remark on posterity becomes a pedestrian comment. But if you could catch him in the peculiar mood he called 'being out of his squash,' his single-minded common monologue of patter was so brilliant that the wine became superb.

Later of course he courted fame. It was somewhat of a sad thing to see it happen. Whereas he had been lax, dissolute, hard-working and irresponsible, then he became moody and imperious by turns. One day he played Faust diabolically, the next he resembled the Einstein of the collected notes of hand. Of course the critics raved. It was you may say the height of his career and I must say in all fairness, he always had a kind word for his old friends who, unlike myself, he never completely deserted. But compared with the old days you would never have recognized him, dressed and brushed back in his best corduroy of the latest cut, joking and exchanging puns with the boys on the town. He did his best, I am told, to remain odd man out, but regardless of intentions the crowd loved everything he did and said. I even gave up reading the papers to the extent that I treasured my memories of him. One day I encountered him going full speed in the other direction at the head of an entourage of reporters and tourists whom he said he was fleeing. We dipped into the nearest tiny crowded bar, ordered two beers and he asked me my name. My name, I said, is whatever you wish to call me, quoting him exactly from memory. He threw back his huge head with its alpaca blanket of hair and roared until the beer foamed. But it was clear he had forgotten my name. Later we ordered a steak on him, as he said, a steak for two with sauce bearnaise, and having finished it off with something of his old gusto, he took my hand by the wrist and promised me I'd never see him again. I had never seen him so serious, except when he was face to face with the superficial problems of life in the city which vexed him no end as everyone knows. His eyes had changed color and in them shone the glint of a new passion for death. He seemed for the first time a true mythical poet, the apotheosis of all he had ever wanted, all he had ever dreamed of becoming—a true success on all three levels. He talked long into the night over the bare T-bone on our table. When the bar closed he kept on talking as we walked arm in arm along the corniche, not listening to the lap of the water and the giggles of inexperienced lovers, both of us drugged by the sound of his words. My cab dropped him at his apartment after dawn and true to his word I never saw him again. This then is my memoir, for what it is worth, probably less than one hundred dollars.

On returning to his hotel room he went directly to his machine and typed a note he had worded while he was still in the car.

> To Arthur C. W. Crook, Esq.
> The Times Literary Supplement
> Printing House Square, London.
>
> It amuses me that your reviewer will take me at my word if it suits his case to do so when, as he remarks, I have been unfaithful to him in every other form. On what base must his trust then rest?
> If you wish to apply a test of sincerity in my case, you must conclude that I am entirely in earnest or not at all. Such a test is, I am sure you'll agree, not, therefore, very useful.
>
> F. C. Castle
> The Florence Hotel, New York.

He read it over several times thinking, rather vaguely, It's pretty good and I won't think so later but if not why not. He picked up a magazine but probably couldn't have read it. He tried to clean his glasses on the sheet where he had wiped his tears. He stared at the gold leaf on the bible. He turned off the television which had been receiving nothing for several hours. He looked at the sky. He criticized his shoes. He noticed the telephone, picked it up and said, Could you tell me what time, yeah, what time it is? Thanks good-night. He opened his map which lay on the floor and noticed the city of Utica. He had taken the train from Utica, the last train in Utica from Utica forever, the Empire State Express. He stared at Utica and tried again to clean his spectacles on the sheet. Then he bagan to read. Oriskany Falls Marcy Newport Middleville, he read, Oneida Dolgeville, Loudenville, Whitesville Bronxville Dansville Portville, Bolivar Ceres Cuba Lima, Cuylerville Leonardsville Unadilla Glen-field, Portlandville Gilbertsville Edmeston, Witherbee Moriah Tully, Painted Post Willer McGraw Arkport, Sodus Homer Fabius Etna, Genoa Marathon Manlius Odessa, Watkins' Glen, Savona Cato Han-nibal, Constantia Cincinattus Smyrna Fabius, Morris Milford Hartwick, Berkshire Williamstown Oxford Greenwich Cambridge, Salem Eagle Bridge, Schaghticoke, Chitenango, Canajoharie, Poughkeepsie, Saugerties, Coxsackie, Oswegatchie, Ticonderoga, Carthage West Carthage Rome Syracuse Weedsport, Branchport, Brockport, Lockport Spencerport Fairport, Onoville Chipmonk Limestone Eagle Pike, Eagle Bay Old Forge Holley, Stony Wold Duane North Rose Upper Jay, The Hague, Silver Bay Boulton Land-ing Diamond Point Lake George, Orleans Olean LeRoy Henrietta Waterloo, Louisville Moira Pavillion Leon Sinclairville, Almond Hemlock Castile, Nunda Ischua Cassadaga Honeoye Falls, Sonyea, Lockport Middleport Gasport Waterport, Portville Wellsville Ran-somville Franklinville, Ellicotville Strykersville Gainsville, Chur-chville Portageville; Lodi Ovid Hall Phelps, Rick Rift Clay Purdys Troy, Maine, Berne, Red Hook, Pine Plains, Afton Union Vestal Center, Alexander Attica Akron Corfu, Naples Minneto Macedon Moravia, Candor Etten Owego, North Pioneer South Ostelic, South New Berlin Central Bridge South Bethlehem North Norwich Central Square East Aurora North Cohocton West Camp East Worcester East Springfield North Dayton East Otto North Collins West Valley, Mount Morris Hammondsport; Geneva Berlin, Rotterdam Amster-dam Antwerp, Sodom, Lawyersville, Athens Tivoli Cornwall Ilion, Marcellus Manchester Batavia, Bombay Lisbon Madrid Niagara Falls New York, Au Sable Forks, Irondequoit, La Fargeville, La Fayette, De Ruyter, Vergil Dryden Milton Wilson Homer Sidney Center,

Cooperstown Cobbleskill, Davenport Dalton, Eden Florida Garretsville Hillsdale, Ithaca Jamestown, Keene Lexington, Mooers, Nyack Ossning Panama Retsof, Schuylerville Talcotville, Mount Upton Victor Warren, West Winfield Yorkshire, Yorkville Bemus Point Addison; Clymer Lakewood Sherman Celeron, Chautauqua Falconer Kennedy, East Randolph, Cherry Creek Stockton Westfield Portland, Brickton Dunkirk, Perrysburg Forestville, Fredonia Gowanda, Silver Creek, Farnham Angola Darby, Hamburg Cattauragus Little Valley Salamanca, Frewsburg Alleghaney Richburg Hinsdale, Rushford Belfast Friendship, West Valley Arcade, Delevan Sandusky, Hume Filmore Houghton, North Java Bliss, Allentown Scio Bellmont, Angelica Canaseraga, Howard Wallace Atlanta Avoca, Middlesex Pen Yan Himrod Dundee, Jasper Alfred Andover Greenwood, Woodhull Canisteo Hornell, Alfred Station DeKalb Junction, South Byron, Savona Bath Campbell, Horseheads, West Bloomfield Bloomfield East Bloomfield, Alden Varysburg Perry, Warsaw Wyoming, Olcott Wilson Barker Hilton, Lewiston Lockport, Elba Avon Stratford, Caledonia Bergen Oakfield, Albion Francher Hulberton Machias, Kendall Lyndonville Cheektowaga Blasdell, Lackawana Depew Lancaster Sloan, North Tonawanda Kenmore Williamsville Amherst Clarence Center. Then he went back and read all the names of all the places in the whole state out loud, and finally he was so pleased with them that he wrote them out on a yellow piece of paper and forthwith fell asleep to dream of flowers.

It occured to me to think that the concept to which we refer under the form of homosexuality was the invention of Europeans in a rather recent period, perhaps the eighteenth century. In such a scheme one subsumes the fact that sodomy is mentioned in the bible by realizing that sodomy is a general term for sexual excess such as crude homosexual practices. It was probably in the eighth century that the seeds of the adoration of women, planted shall we say by Christ, first germinated in the West during the first period of the supremacy of France as tiny sprigs of a new hardy weed that would in time obliterate the sky. The power of women reached the point of predominance in the nineteenth century. This phenomenon can be said to have founded the cryptic masculine sub-culture of commerce and finance conventionally referred to as the industrial revolution and the constructions of economic science. It is an ironic instance of the operation of feminine logic that the final and most concerted attack of these all-powerful nineteenth century women took form in a seige against the very bastion which the power of women had created, the so-called world of affairs. As Pursewarden said, The Mona Lisa has the smile of a woman who has just dined off her husband. However ironic, it was quite to be expected that complete control over men who were credited with worldly power would be a disenchanting experience for women who afterwards aspired to become in fact the men thay had already palmed. It is an antinomy of the first order which most suitably provided the bare stage of the twentieth century to be dressed and decorated by dehumanization and destruction. At the beginning of his century, Ortega, who also thought about such things, was naturally moved to suggest that the history of Europe beginning with the eighteenth century should be rewritten to include with the story of each generation of men who were regarded as decisive, the story of a somewhat younger feminine generation who could be seen to be in actual control. Such a task has not, of course, been undertaken for lack of evidence and lack of interest, for the science of history is not less in the grip of feminine principles than any other mode of thought capable of great legitimacy at the present time. It may be possible, however, to seek among platitudes and jokes some realization of this general notion. Messrs. Gershwin set these words for a negro to sing: A woman is a sometime thing. Cole Porter wrote for a powerful woman: A woman to a man is just a woman, but a man to a woman is her life. Clay Hunt, a bachelor, knew a cunt as metaphor for the gates of hell. These days, toward the end of the twentieth century, things having changed so logically and so fabulously, it is ludicrous even to speak of generations of people, the more so in one national place. The only analytical reality we conceive is one unique man and, by abstraction, a whole society, faceless and automatic without name or birth date. The principle of self-destruction is a feminine concept in logic, established by reversing its opposite, regeneration. Both are inhuman by masculine standards, miraculous, if you will, or inexplicable. As women popularly amuse themselves to say, all men really are like little boys.

One must argue with a woman who is a woman but one will never or always win against her. She is a fact like rain. She has driven men to construct systems which appear to exclude her, battered down all those supposedly sturdy doors and chased him out the back way. She is easily bored. I have looked up the term misogyny and found myself a happily married man.

The chief general expression of the fact of the dominance of women is, not surprisingly, the elevation of historical habits of mind to the realm of general belief. The application to every possible sort of thought, experience or creation of the logic in which causes have effects is the universal metaphor for the adulation of women which remained inadmissable on the surface of events throughout the nineteenth century and remains entirely unrecognized in most areas of thought up to the present time. Such an assertion is not supported by information which can be abstracted because the characteristic of feminine power is its imperceptibility, its very illegitimacy. But any man with the vaguest intimation of that golden age that women joke of—the days when men were men—can realize the truth of the matter in one form or another. The change which took place in the forms of the European Church during this period is the nearest one may come to a public realization of the dominant status of women and it was a matter of course for an institution that has always done well to keep up with the times. The recent ascendence of Our Lady, the Mother of God, has made a fourth of the eternal Trinity, but that change itself is highly metaphorical.

In the meantime, it has quite recently become apparent to some and vaguely supposed by many more that the only category of secrecy which remains lies in the direction of crude homosexuality. It is only twentieth century scholarship using refined historical techniques that could consider the homosexuality of Michelangelo or Shakespeare as real. Cases for the homosexuality of D. H. Lawrence, Flaubert, Henry James, Nietzsche, Shaw and so on are somewhat similar in that in each case a portion of the man's strength is laid to his ability to dissociate himself from feminine principles except that these nineteenth century men were in a position to ignore categorical homosexuality unlike the renaissance masters who knew of no such distinctions. It is natural, in the form of the intentions of God, that men and women attract each other sexually, but as my wife Janet sometimes says in her ingenuous honesty, Oh everyone is a homosexual, didn't you know? As she implies, the value of the homosexual secret is being quickly debased by means of publicity and it is possible thus to suppose that an equilibrium of sexual distinctions like that which prevailed at Athens in the fourth century B. C. will in time reappear.

The days were opened to show American time, to demonstrate that though it came again like any clock, like any clock it simply went on until stopped, until the electricity went out, until it was all unwound. American time has a telephone number in New York. It was ME7-1212 like an incantation. Like an oracle it would say, At the tone the time will be exactly seven twenty-three and twenty seconds. Bing. There is a charge of one message unit. You can't actually say that one message unit equals a price of five cents. Early in the billing month which begins after the first week in some years and after the second week in other years, one message unit costs nothing in a manner of speaking and later on in the fiscal month it may or may not cost you something in particular depending on what grade of service you're billed for. It is very well organized and no matter what the phone bill is you pay. If you don't pay there is a fine of four dollars a drag on your deposit and a blot on your credit. On the darkest day they will sell you a pink phone in one of four up-to-date models. And you have a choice of decorator colors. The only nice thing about decorator colors is that they aren't in the rainbow, not in the ones I've seen. For a long time I had not seen a rainbow, a shooting star or the northern lights. People would say, Look there! but by the time I'd looked it was gone like a fish. I did enjoy lightning and thunder and summer rain of every sort, but especially huge tempests of bucketing rain, near flashes and grave rocking thunder bolts at night. I am not afraid to go out in it. In the old days I'd wake up, widen the windows and sit close by the screen watching and smelling and listening until it was almost over or had settled to a steady drone with only a light flash or two in the distance, as far as the train whistles beyond all the trees.

On the day, for there was such a day, of ceremony to mark my graduation from college, we had just recessed, it was duly hot in June, teachers sweating in their hooded robes and afterwards applauding their wards, we had all disrobed, sweating, swearing and smiling and just as I achieved the house porch the clouds darkened the sky to make it look like rain. The blasts of wind sent spray that moved furniture. I stood on the porch alone for most of the storm, watching and feeling it, thinking nothing at all. Later it relaxed to a downpour. My friend's girlfriend came out from the family shelter inside to smell the lightning. She shared her drink. We spoke quietly in the clatter of the still rain on the drive. The story of stories, a story of my family. As we drank, the drunkeness of my father and his father his hero before and so said my father the drunkeness of my mother's

father driving his wife and his daughter, my grandmother and
mother into the arms of Christian Science, both became in course
reverend women, revilers of catholicism, looking for god's good in
all, ignorant of death. I spoke of my mother, lithe pretty black haired
and gay, an actress who said she believed in free love without knowing the facts of sex life. My grandfather left when the money was lost
going to live in Bronxville undisturbed until many years later when
he died of alcoholic malnutrition. I guess it could have been his liver.
The boys, my mother's brothers, had all grown up except for the
eldest, Don, who was stopped by the war, and in order to save the big
house called Four Thirteen for my mother's eventual wedding, my
mother travelled with her mother first to Florida, to Coral Gables
where my mother sat for her portrait in riding habit and, I think,
long hair and then for a longer time across the continent to California,
to live in La Jolla. That trip was the end of the first set of good old
days with the gang, as they called themselves, who infested the old
Bishop house which after the wedding en pleine aire fell utterly to
ruins and later had to be demolished. My father maintains when he's
drunk and nostalgic that my grandmother didn't approve of him
which might have been because he drank. But in August of 1935 the
wedding took place and there is a movie, stilted in blacks my dead
uncle took who had formerly named my father Bill. The kids at
school called him Corsets because his name was Corson. So his big
brother Jess said, he's not Corson, he's Bill and it stuck. A delightful
name, I have always thought, and just like my Uncle Jess who lived
with abandon in an old farm house and had a steer named after my
father Fred. I was named F. Corson Castle after my father as junior, a
fashionable American custom for clans on the make. *My family has
been nouveau riche for three generations.* I was called Cork. My father's
family having come obscurely from Canada and perhaps before that
from France in the course of a history that has been entirely forgotten
also included four children, one of whom, George junior, died at the
age of twelve. My aunt Dorothy whom we call Dort suggested to me
over breakfast on her annual way to Florida one time that it might be
best to let the past remain unknown. Maybe there's a Jew in the
closet, I don't know. After my father graduated from Williams in
'29, thirty one years before the exact day I told the story I'm now
recounting, he sat one day with his mother, Nina, in the parlor of the
big house on Genesee Street across from the church. He said he had
decided to take up smoking and she, a small probably silent rather

strong woman, his mother, said, Well than we will have our first cigarettes together, and they did. My mother called her Mrs. Castle. My grandmother and grandfather Castle died, I am told, within a month of each other a few months after I was born. George Castle was a bit fat rather loud and very firm, undoubtedly smoked cigars was regarded as very generous and liked to buy my mother hats. My father had ideas of his own. He would go to South America and put out a farm magazine in Spanish. He knew Spanish, Latin and Greek. He would not. He would begin to publish and print books and pamphlets under the imprint—Castle Press. He would not. My father loved his father and his father said he would not. My father said he would not. He sold classified ads for his father's newspaper, doing it well and selling more than everyone else. He left that and took a job as executive material for General Motors the biggest gun in town but got out of that ratrace. His father before dying sold his part of the newspaper back to the son of the founder, his good friend Frederick Corson, in exchange for the rights to the job printing company which was then located over the store in Main Street next to the newspaper. The Corson Company as we called it had begun to prosper by making folding paper soap boxes that were filled in Buffalo in a building designed by Frank Lloyd Wright where an organ continuously played. The other day I took out the drawer of the old table upon which I happen to be writing at the moment and on the bottom of the drawer I noticed it says, This article manufactured by our Factory No. 1, Larkin Co., Buffalo, N. Y. They were in furniture as well as in soap. Then during the depression for the future of his sons my grandfather mortgaged himself to build a new plant on Michigan Avenue to which the cutting and creasing and gluing and printing machines were transferred from over the store that when I was a boy was called Noah's Ark. When I was a boy one summer I worked a machine called the Old Scott which had been moved along with its operator, then a woman of eighty and nearly blind who remembered my grandfather as a young man and said that my father as a boy had helped her run that machine, she remembered clearer than yesterday. It could make me cry if the light was right. Then my grandfather died. Jess and Bill Castle were left with the plant in the tail of a depression without enough money for a twenty-five cent movie. As the business went in those early years, my uncle was responsible. One time he went to Minneapolis and drank martinis and played gin rummy through the night with the makers of Wheaties until at the end he got an order that would make them rich. Then he flew home and ordered a press that would print unlimited cereal boxes in four colors. During the war my father had a chance to become vice-president of a big paper company in New York. He did not. During the war he had a telegram from Washington asking him to serve in the government under his enemy Franklin Roosevelt, and he did not do it. In 1941 I remember the day we got a new light green convertible car. In 1942 just before or just after my brother Douglas Bishop was born we moved into a new house which was made of the bricks of the nineteenth century Ringueberg house it replaced. Later I found out that two brothers by that name had built identical houses when the street was new one of whose sons was the mayor of the city for many years when I was younger and one of whose daughters very occasionally comes to tea with my mother although she moved up to Buffalo to work in a bookstore when the house was sold. My father bought the house at an auction as, seven years before, he had bought my mother's rings. I used to walk very often with my grandmother from High Street where she lived a block from our apartment to Willow Street where the new house was being built. In the summer I played with bricks and sand in the foundations of the attached garage, and in the spring we picked crocuses under the tulip tree. A carpenter named Frank took me around on his shoulders to show me the house I would see again. The next year my uncle Jess died in the Mayo clinic of kidney trouble. My aunt, Mary Lib who was also called Beesh, took her boys my cousins back to Buffalo where she had come from, the daughter of an architect, Duane Lyman, who had designed our new house in the colonial style while he would have preferred to remodel the old one. My mother and father always maintain that they have never regretted tearing it down. Once I looked over the plans for changing the old square house into a more usable shape and I had to agree with them, history aside, because the new house was for me home and I loved it just as it came to be.

From time to time I would stop talking and look at the rain and she would say, No, go on, I'm interested.

After my uncle died, we tried to eat the steer Fred who was cut up and stored in an antarctic food locker after having run away several times from my uncle's farm. Fred was awfully tough but at least we had Fred. I kept close track of the rationing coupons throughout the war figuring out how much sugar and gasoline we could buy. Right after dinner every evening we always listened to the news on the radio. After my uncle died, as I say, his maid Marion, a large stern loquacious maiden aunt of a woman who knew what she knew came to live with us and to bring us up to the threat of the pancake turner which would hurt on the bottom. She especially made fine baked beans and German apple pie with a crissrossed top crust and open hamburger sandwiches. Marion and my brother and I ate in the breakfast room and we ate everything no matter how distasteful it was, trying as we were urged to think of the children starving in Europe which at that time was painted for us in black. On Saturday night my mother and father dressed up and went out to dances and parties, and sometimes they had people in. I remember my mother in a wonderful black ball gown decorated with black lace with a red flower in her hair. I had to sit on Saturday nights at the table and eat until I gagged and beyond from creamed ham and boiled eggs that was a most execrable dish. Under Marion I grew to like all food and became as fat as a house. I didn't like to come out and meet people when there was a party at home and I'd sit by the bannister at the top of the hall and listen and listen no matter how late it got or how tired I was. That time, during the war when I was little, was to my mind one of three sets of good old days in the life of my parents. The first was their four years before they had me about which I knew almost nothing except for a little description of their wedding trip through New England, and the other was under Eisenhower when Time magazine made us feel better each week and when I guess we were really rich. I designed bookshelves cupboards and furniture for the room I shared with my brother which was also air conditioned, my parents and I designed a wood panelled room with a fireplace to replace the electric trains in the cellar and the back yard was turned into a beautiful garden completely protected from the neighbors by trees with a concealed badminton court where the victory garden had been. I remember the five cent ice cream cone, I remember the five cent bus ride, I remember the day the president died, I remember the end of the war and much more.

In 1945 my mother had a baby that was three pounds, as you might get chopped beef for a meatloaf, but she lived and grew up to be my sister Marcia who was seven and a half years younger than me. Sometime after that my mother was working in the kitchen making lobster newburg which along with dinner rolls, frozen custard, corn soup, and brownies was one of the few things she cooked, and something happened as if she fell into a swoon and the doctor came. They took her away to Hartford and they thought they said later she'd never recover, but in a year or so our nurse, Mrs. Baker who was the mother-in-law of our dentist, said she had a surprise for us. I thought her friend was going to take us to the park again but instead mother came home. Some years later my father and I had a serious talk to assure me it wasn't hereditary. They said she was schizophrenic. My mother used to think she was persecuted by her brothers who called her Tub as our doctor still does because like me as a child she was fat. Then later there was this thing that she thought she should not drink and smoke but she did, and she wanted so much to be friendly and gay and she was but she thought that her friends disliked her, and they did for her odd religion and her good looks but from her childhood she regarded the human body as ugly which it was but everyone loved her especially younger people and whenever anyone came to the house as they did quite often as soon as she opened the door a party had begun out in the yard or in the living room and my grandmother to whom she was very attached having been the baby disapproved of the way we were being brought up and my father's drinking reminded his wife of her father although we couldn't have been more well-behaved and she should not drink or submit to doctors according to her mother and their religion of the mother church which later became her salvation on earth. Any physical shock could throw her off. My father drank black label whiskey in the cellar in the workshop that he kept mainly for that purpose always newly refitted with tools that Gus the old German gardener stole and painted turquoise to show that they were his. My father was also a pretty good carpenter and built me my first large train set, and a little house in the back yard that we called the shack and a fine long bench on which I practiced photography. My father idolized his father who was very strict and told him that he could not do what he wanted to do even after he was out of college. His father told him it would take him years to unlearn his education of which my grandfather was probably nevertheless no doubt proud. My grandfather's brother Will who started Castle's Citizens' Dairy took a catholic woman to be his third wife after which the two brothers never spoke to each other again and eventually the town was filled with little catholic cousins of mine of whom I heard only at school. Once I met one of them in a bar, now a woman who had married a prosperous salesman. She was drunk. One of my father's greatest insults is to call someone shanty Irish for which a number of people he did not anyway like have never again spoken to him. I was taught never to marry a catholic. So my father followed his older brother Jess into a life he actually did not want before his father's death, the life of the company, the life of sales and production, and when Jess died he acceded to the presidency and became richer and more successful by turns. The first battle I remember winning was never again having to go back to summer camp where I was the odd boy, fat and solitary, who refused to learn how to play games. That was just before I fought steadily for three years to defend myself from being sent away to school along with two of my cousins and my uncles before them. I refused to wear shirts with the buttoned collar tabs. When I was in high school my grandmother died, Eisenhower was elected, things got better, I achieved great political power in the school so that a committee of teachers was charged with the study of what they called Corson's clique, my father was almost always drunk after dinner complaining wittily about the quality of the beef which had never been better, our housekeeper was a Christian Scientist who taught my mother to bake pies, my father was said to resemble alternately the president and a famous movie star, we bought a house on Big Moose Lake where we had summered since the war, bought two boats and an unusual sporty convertible of which only three hundred were made, I was given an older car and my father at the culmination of his buying power suffered two strokes in a row a few months apart, the second severe, and I who had always been too old for my age, who had never been really a child, took over some of the duties of father. I paid the bills and tried to think what to do about the children, my brother and sister, while eventually after the worst was over my father and mother languished in all the most expensive Florida resorts. It was as if he had died. For two years my father refused to sign his name for fear that he could not do it. His confidence had been shaken, he who was always right and had never made a mistake. One time we visited him in the hospital in Buffalo to admire the way he could move his left hand. On the drive back my mother told me nearly in tears about his drinking which had been done in public and private and secret since just after their marriage. My father had taught me to write by tearing to shreds the merest school essay, shouting his questions of relevance and syntax, trained in Latin which I had neglected for Spanish and French. If I couldn't throw a baseball I was smart, goddamn it. After he recovered the use of his body and was about able again to play golf he pointed out in the journalism I was writing then the best, the most writerly thing. He admired Hemingway. The last major battle I won was to be accepted against predictions as a freshman at Yale University though I was only forty-fifth rank in my high school class. I lost a good deal of weight. I wrote a research paper as a senior about public education in the State of New York which I called "To College—Unprepared." Surreptitiously I acquired Eastern preparatory school manners, changed the style of my handwriting to a more fashionable mode, bought a great many clothes in excellent taste and got rid of my Western New York accent, which, because of my father had never been perfect to begin with. I chose my father's college rather than Yale and when I arrived there I redeemed myself Ted.

During my first year, among other things, I got a little note from my mother about flowers and trees and a letter following from father saying she had again gone off, this time not to return. We visited her at Hartford and she was as of old and gay at one moment in the course of severe shock treatments. She offered me a cigarette though she didn't know I smoked. We visited her at Hartford again and she was old, and wept, and her suit was soiled, and she had changed. My father and I went with my brother to interview head-masters of schools we thought would do my brother good, my younger brother, my brother who had fiercely admired me when I despised myself, my brother I didn't know, my brother who was sometimes thinner and sometimes fatter than me, my brother who used to have convulsions on the floor as a little boy, my brother who disagreed with me in everything, my brother who later found himself and lived, my brother who was always most thoughtful and polite and bought our mother flowers with the money that he hoarded. Once more the miraculous sustained my mother. She succeeded in being allowed to leave the institute at Hartford, and having spent a time at a Christian Science place in Princeton, she came out of her menopause beginning to get fat like her mother, utterly converted in thanks to Christian Science which my father liked to joke of as an exclusive club. She was not herself but another who by stretching one's wits and remembrance could be said to be the same one. We had used to go to New York to the theatre which both of us loved, and then, afterwards, finally it was as if both my mother and father had died leaving living ghosts of another color. I had begun to leave home then, imperceptibly, though in fact I had already left. I still used their money and name but I would as I thought no longer do as they did. So I left. I had a good job but I left, right, left, with an echo of the First World War and my grandmother, Paris in the spring of the nineteenth century, and a bad taste in my eyes eloquently. The long leavetaking is not quite yet over. Still there will be a rustle of the wind, ever so slight, that will let fall drops on my head or before me on the pavement which is not yet dry, or thinking otherwise I may step in a puddle that has not run off. Someday there will be nothing but this.

As for me and what I did, suffice it to say that I was able to give up newspaper work at an early age without any gain. I had talked with several stars of events or watched them from the privileged seat. I spoke with Jack Kennedy long before and shortly before he was elected. Also Foster Dulles and Winston Churchill. Then barely to mention John D. Rockefeller 3rd, Cornelia Otis Skinner, Maxwell Taylor, Ludwig Pursewarden, the Duke of Windsor, Bob Elliott and Ray Goulding, Ted Patrick, Henry Steele Commager, Tom Mendenhall, James Phinney Baxter 3rd, Steve Sondheim, Ornette Coleman, Pierre Mendes-France, Lester Markel, Joseph C. Harsch and Queen Jacqueline. By the time I met Elizabeth Taylor at the plane in Idlewild I was obviously losing interest because I was there on time but I missed the scene. I invented a lengthy explanation which I failed to tell the editor on demand as instructed by long newpaper usage: no one may whistle in the city room. You may be sure I also interviewed hundreds of other people whose names for the most part I have by now forgotten. I think it is to my credit that I refused to interview Mr. Kennedy's tailor saying he had said he had some clothes to sew. Later I began fabricating stories. It was somewhat of a sad thing to see it happen. I knew I had to get out although writing fictional news was most entertaining. I decided then to work for the New Yorker magazine. I spoke with Whitney Balliett, a critic whose family came from Lockport and whose father had known my grandmother well. Then I spoke with someone else and wrote them a story I never submitted. Somebody thought there was a phrase in it that deserved a better fate. Here it is: She walked like a feather duster would walk if it could. After that I had no interest in doing it. I had had it. When I began strictly from hunger to do a menial job at the New York Times Magazine, I understood in two weeks what they were all doing so that my daydream became a plot to overthrow the editor who had been doing that some automatic task for forty years. Several months later I wrote him a lengthy memorandum for which he paid me the compliment of trying to fire me but the union wouldn't allow it. I had already written a good review of Henry

Miller's works for Time magazine, so there was nowhere to go but down. Finally I didn't want to be the editor—I had already made and run my own slick magazine for which I became briefly a legend in my own time—but I used to think that if nothing else I could always fall back on that. I wrote several mannerist short stories; one of them called A Puddle of Glass was good and was published. I had had enough of politics both behind the scenes which I used to love and at the forefront where I always lost. I had written a short book on the culture boom for Columbia University. Once a friend of mine and I tried to write a movie but didn't get very far. It was laid in the Everglades. As an actor I played both starring roles and bit parts uncomplainingly until I was underrated in The Importance of Being Earnest when I retired. I hate rehearsals. I was a stage technician becoming permanent stage manager at the age of fifteen. I had also produced a musical show, directed the production of an LP disc and knew a good deal about tape recording. I have also designed brochures and programs and had them well printed. For five years at different times I was a news photographer, receiving two awards. I still enjoy photography which I do as a hobby. Perhaps more, I like to do electrical wiring, something that always gives me a complete sense of accomplishment. I was also often consulted to draft constitutions for organizations, and in that way I became an amateur of law. The language of constitutions is admirable, I wish I had more of them to read. I've also produced and recorded a radio version of Macbeth. My experience in television was limited to a conversation on the topic of Cuba about which I knew nothing. At one time I had a plan to reorganize the New York Times Book Review—perhaps the quality of mercy would improve. I have also sold things door to door quite unsuccessfully and for a short while I was a magician. I have done factory work by the hour and consider myself experienced as a gardener and as a chauffeur. I have a little experience as a librarian with the Dewey Decimal System. I have edited and reorganized three small newspapers. I might have been a cook but I never had the chance. I managed a football team. I wrote a few lyrics for songs. I have been a messenger and head of a family. I have trained a maid of all work. I have been a student and received three degrees in course. None of the buildings I designed was ever built. I'm quite a good carpenter but I lack patience to be a professional. I've been president and vice-president of fraternal organizations. I was often a recalcitrant member of the committee. I was once good at public realations and I have appointed myself adviser to men of affairs. I have sat at a desk and answered the telephone. I have some experience in advertising. I was also a design critic. I reviewed plays books and movies. As an art critic I wrote one review which was praised. I wrote quite a bit of poetry rather quickly. I have written seven hundred and fifty long letters to which I alone know the keys. I have had several friends who loved me as I loved them, and I have been in love with several different women some of whom I slept with and some of whom I never kissed. I have been seduced by two men and one woman and have taken a dislike to many confirmed homosexuals thinking, perhaps, there but for me go I. I have been rather rich and rather poor, well-known almost famous and unknown, admired and despised, understood and ignored, snubbed and befriended, laughed at and listened to, advised and exhorted, denied and forbidden and hardly ever but sometimes sick. I have never been in the hospital except to visit my friend and my father and I've had nothing removed from my body except for one wisdom tooth that wasn't impacted. I have been a welcome weekend guest everywhere in the East Coast—East Side from the Junior League Ball at the Plaza to Hobe Sound, Hyannis Port and Black Point. I have also lived in Boston, Washington and Philadelphia, Paris London, Geneva and New York. I have also been to Cincinatti, Dallas Chicago, Rome, Madrid, Munich, Grenoble, Barcelona, Amsterdam, Utrecht, Venice, Dublin, Gibraltar, Edinburgh, Pittsburgh and Tangier. I have crossed the Atlantic in a plane and on three steamships pertaining to different countries. I have taken a trip on the Mediterranean Sea and a trip up the Erie Barge Canal. I have seen Niagara Falls and fished the St. Lawrence River. My father used to take the night boat from Albany to New York and once landed in jail. I know a lot of good roadside diners in New York state and New England. I have hitchhiked and I'm fond of bicycling, although I haven't done much in years. I don't like museums but I have been to very many of them of which the best is the Phillips Collection. I have been propositioned by whores and pimps but I have not accepted. I have had whiskey on the Champs-Elysées, coffee on Bleecker Street, and danced at the Waldorf when my mother knew the bandleader. I have had lunch at Rule's and at the Harvard Club. I know Oxford and Cambridge. I am familiar with tailors and have had clothes made to my exact taste. I know the history of Broadway musicals. I have maintained four checking accounts. I have driven eighty thousand miles over a period of two years in my car and I replaced some of its parts myself. I am, however, unemployed.

Dear Sir, (I write in a reasonable facsimile of a smile) I would have used the typewriter but there is a reason for being quiet now as someone, my sister-in-law is sleeping nearby. I dreamt sleeping with her and with many & several others. She is breathing alone, a formal, learned, legible style of writing. People used not to be able to read. Broad nibs comes from reading Ulysses. American custom of negligence, negligee, lingerie, imagery of a sea-green age — sometimes runs out of ink.

Negligent handwriting, speaking,
laughing — the conversation but
remarks. Priceless. A life in a
way spent finding the right pen.
I found it and bought five of
them quick before it went out
of print. It still runs out of ink.
That will put lead in your pencil.
They redesigned it up to date. I saw
it happen — somewhat of a sad thing.
In Louisville I bought two decanters
in the South — two black pans
with signed by somebody on a
certain date noted. What this
country needs. The careless dresser
the efficient bureau. Give me a dream

that is like a dream. Thanks. Answers come true. Into the stream of consciousness flows a muddy river ~ ancient swamp a story / but she said that. A certain kind of old-fashioned black pen, to not a quill pen, they were not black in the movies. They were scratchy, shook with sand or snuff in a box like mildew. I get it all from one of my books. Life is sweet. Life is where you find it. Life is what you make it. Life begins at forty. Life ends at fifty. Live and let live. Life with father. Remember that life is wonderful. Life is a red hat, like a joke. C'est la vie. La vie en rose. La dolce vita. La vita nuora. The good life. Lebensraum. Vive la France! Life, liberty & pursuit. Life teaches, Life tells, Life looks. Life learns. He took his own life on the fourth of May. The life of a doffer, the life of me as sure as you live. Life is a miracle of modern science. From life, as I was saying, from one of my books. Drawn. I drew a figure which multiplied, changed color, and was filed away. Ain't life grand? Life is a busy street. A one-way street is a left turn. Why? Why? Why? Do you believe who gave this life so that we might live? Am I shouting? Forgive me.

I am not yet accustomed to the night,
the quality of dawn. The careless
scrawl, the hapless voice, the haphazard shawl, the luckless choice,
The American Dream, so like life
-that he gave his only Son, one
of many, a chance to move up &
live better. What is so banal as a
secret of war, a traitorous act made
worthless by a slip of the tongue on
thin ice. It's the first of March,
(note the Ides) a feckless phrase credits
lamb-lion of Saint Patrick New York's
Finest green stripe down the street
and in the men's bars beer de menthe.
Run-down shanty to starched lace curtains

with unwashed out glass near the oblivious top. May I have a statistic from the Americanization of Puerto Ricans? Thanks. Now on with the news and the weather. What's for dinner? He goes she said he was I say he went they took we say you sit and I'll go. We went they're laughing she's mad he's a bitch. My boss goes and him never. I say and she says and I go and she laughs. It was lots of fun, a pretty good time, cool it. Later baby. How much? We went we want let's order. So I said okay. They went he left my boss a sock in the jaw. They saw we laughed and him sitting there a hole in the head.

Two girls and a boy, it didn't like in the old days he said so watch it buddy she goes, redhair. Atook one look and I says to myself right out loud, my foot in it, Coco shit She had this nice red hat, see, we went and they laughed. I bet they was/get out of there! /I bet they was gissling something awful. Like a regular storm you git class, whatchucallit, he said. She went, so she takes this thing off, see, and he goes how much. That aint just honey, it's a regular conspiracy. There wasn't any toilet paper so I just, she said we went and right off then wasn't any doubt. One of these here old times a sort of a something or other. We was drunt

Comme ça, d'accord. Oui, merci 'sieu, dame. Un vieux fort, comme ça. Un peu trop cher, n'est-ce pas? Alors. comme ci, non, merde alors, mèrè, mes, merde. Merci, Nôtre Dame, mille pardons, Ma chérie. Imperturbable vagueness of stupidity, horse laughter, cupidity, cuspidors, chewing gum, ashcan, sweatshops, garbage pail, dust bin of niceties, pisspot of heaven. Life is but a bowl of cherries with peaches and sour cream, quick as your old home-made apple of the eye. The balance of trade is unfavorable, I repeat, the echo of laughter whinnies back. My sister, she said, your sister-in-law. My own

-fiancé her beau my woman his girl your lover my love his mistress my keeper her father my brother his sister my mother-in-law? His best friend her girl friend my boy friend his secretary her boss my man your employer his boy my son his girl my daughter-in-law your mother his sister her mother my aunt. — Either-either, tomato-tomato (potato-potato) piano-piano, err-err, forest-forest? neither-neither, willy-nilly, aunt-aunt? I could tell black from white, right from day, my ass from a hole in the ground, left from wrong, a thing or two, my own name and whether it was raining. Chicken Little. What's for dinner? It's in Who's Who. What's that. Where is it. How do you spell it? Who is she. Where are they from. What do you do? How do you do. Excuse me. I beg your pardon. Sorry. How's it going? I'm doin' all right. Nothing much, a little tired. Who is it. How much is it? Where did you get it, how did you find it, how do you get there, how's that? Where are you? How's the old man? Regards to the wife. A can't complain. How do you know? You don't say! I know what I mean? Really now! That's something. Fine. Yeah. Terrific, beautiful. Great! terrific, thanks, just fine. Something great. It was wonderful. Yeah really super. A t

It was really something, Beautiful. It. was a great big beautiful whatchumacallit. Yeah. As big as that. Where are you? (What's your name?) Fine, thanks. Oh yeah, it was wonderful. We had a Good time. Yes, it was fabulous. Uh, huh, nothing better. No, not bad, it was great. It was really something. Yes. Yeah, Yah, Yeah. Uh-huh. You don't say. I mean, you know what I mean. So long, take it easy, thanks a lot, I love you too. Really I gotta go, yeah, literally, all right Bye bye. Ciao. Goddamned son of a bitch! Fuck it eat shit up your ass fuck me! Shitty ass bat fuck. Why are we so nice to all these people we don't like? Answer me that. Don't curse, it isn't nice. He was very nice to me anyway. What's so nice about that? It was the nicest thing that could have happened to me. That's a very nice thing to say. If it had to happen it was a nice way to go. I love nice things. You're not nice. Oh yes I am. Mice and bats are not mice and rats and snakes really don't exist, you know, except in books. Oh yes, the point is, what I am trying to say, the message, so to speak, the heart of the matter, what I really mean, the root metaphor, it's very simple, I'm coming to the point will be there in a moment

Well, excuse me, but I must say, the trouble was, the most important thing I meant to say, the whole object of it is above all <u>Don't get excited</u>. Keep your head, your pants and your boots on, keep your wits and your manners about you, hold onto your hat, your horses, control your voice and your breath, and don't do a thing until you hear from me.

It was a very good book

(play)

(pen)

(nice day)

I had stayed up all night writing. Cinders under my eyelids. The dawn was blue, melting, icy rain, gray day. A story. We woke up early and looked out at the weather. We called up, washed, cooked ate drank, brushed dressed pissed packed, looked out, called up, woke, laughed, fed the cat and left. Ménage à trois. Croghan, my wife Chazy and Hale Eddy. Bumpy the condition of the road ice, sleepy but not going to sleep, gray day the quality of film. How do you drive on ice. Automatic conversation. Automatically. Maintain speed, hop brake, swing wide, watch out. Double exposure. Keep on going up. I like the other way, I like the other road. A long story made shorter. Screw patiently. Let's eat. A certain excitement away from home. What's next. A joke that fell through, a name that could be changed and a change that could be justified as well as any story. An automatic laugh, familiarly, a trip from the city to the country in the morning. Good time we're making, and a good name. Going back, going up, old home away from home with thoughts of death. Windscreen wipers. Old home, new love, fame replaced by the trace of a legend, new circumstances, old love. Hale Eddy has a stiff neck which suggests a wife's cure. We're married, he's not. Something is going to have to be done — you decide not to and then you do — about my always being alone. Am I being incoherent? Forgive me, but it is out of incoherence that I come. An exchange proving a laugh, a series of a certain number, in short a story. It's going to be a story of young married people on a weekend in a college town, including several married couples and introducing two men not married. Nothing like what you think will happen though some of them are sick, tired or unavoidably out of town, two wives and one husband. There will be no answers, nothing of interest, the story of a certain series. But then we knew nothing of that. I should have preferred not to go back up there. It was my profession but I've retired, very willingly. When the chance that could offer a change suggested itself, I accepted the notion that a momentary aberration could do some good, even though I had no expectation of such a result. Cinders under my eyelids, a vague ache, the quality of film in gray. We take the back way past the stone lions to a red house on the left. And stop.

She looks different. Bethany looks better in make-up, thinner in a smile. She said she'd been cleaning. She said she'd meant to clean had there been time. She'd been correcting. We were up all night too. The house and the fact of the face. It was after all a good feeling, gray day snow . . . I announce, Croghan will take a long shower. I awaken, the processes slowed by a lack of sleep. Scratch, stretch, a vague ache, undress, adjust the water, where's the shampoo, a leg in the tub to test the water. He comes in, Hale Eddy the unmarried to see me uncircumcised and white to get the cigarettes and to take his leave to go underground for the duration. That's the last we'll see of him who the story concerns. This is a version that I'm telling him, that I told him in a different way, that I would tell him if I could. It's a story about him. A shower—he had been called Dirty Ed—a shower is better for a stiff neck than the cure of marriage, the curse of women. He said, I'm not sure I believe in sex. That's the last we'll hear. He's a member of the wedding, a member of the audience, a communist, if you will. He's a former student, a would-be prince, he makes a third. Later on I was to meet once more old Needle Prick, the bug fucker, his former title, now happily married with a kid and cat, a wife like a hornet and a teaching job. But then I knew nothing of that, I couldn't have said that Hale Eddy wouldn't return, I didn't know what would come next. I felt good. The shower soothed my back, pricked my chest, I turned around and around, let fall lovely hair of a sensual length, wash, rub it down. Dress precisely in tight pants. I'm back recovered, awake, alive prepared, precisely tight rubbed scrubbed. Hello. Hello. Who wants to go into town? The excitement of not knowing. Chazy is reading a book and Balcom would rather not go. Her husband and my wife stayed with their baby while Bethany and Croghan took the laundry by the liquor store. Don't guess, I don't mean what I say.

Croghan offered to carry the laundry when Bethany said she would drive. I'll carry the laundry. I'm big and strong (no I'm not) yes you are. Two bags on my back, blue and white, dark and light. Stumble in across the snow, the excitement of not knowing in the knees, big and strong you know I'm not. They opened the doors of a large red car and got into it. She drives. Out of gas. The gas station. The last time I was at that station I rammed one of those little red posts. I said, Don't ram that little red car. She said, Good god thanks a lot. What do you want to do. We agreed. The liquor store by the laundry. Good. Don't neglect to get the milk. A dollar's worth of gas, a minute. She parked the car by the side of the road near the shops. I bought a bottle of whiskey but I forgot to bring it when I left the store. Get change, the washing meter, wake up, the laundry. Sort it in three. Two white and one colored. Hot. I watch her. My coat. Hot as a laundry. We might have been married, we were but we weren't, we were doing the most ordinary things we could do in a simple routine. You wouldn't have noticed the excitement of not knowing which was there. We walked up and down the aisles of a nearby supermarket admiring the various cuts of meat and the exotic varieties of tea on display, a routine method of looking at each other like a walk through the snow up a hill to admire the view. I prefer a certain kind of tea and I prefer another sort of meat. Then the wash, two white and one colored, from one machine into another to be dried. She said, I have to go home and get some more money. I said, No, I've some money. She said, No, I'll need more for the milk. I said, No, here, I've more, enough. Let's have some coffee, it was agreed.

You know that we are talking as we drive while you are looking at the scenery offered by the landscape of the famous Berkshire Mountains which we ignore but all you can hear is the most familiar romantic European music you know, something you can hum without thought as you watch yourself. The music is so familiar that you scarcely find yourself bored, you feel slightly hungry as if you were overtired, but it is not interesting. How tedious even a short text can be. Or if you are experienced in this sort of thing you will find something to interest you, to pass the time, something to do with the very ordinariness I am showing you. Perhaps you have difficulty deciding whether an orchestra or an organ is playing, perhaps you can invent a correlation of the countryside with the music you are imagining so that one suggests the other, but until your attention is come back to me, until you arrest your preoccupation no matter how lively it may be, until you stop humming, until then once again nothing will happen, minute by word by step. To return:

She laughed a kind of a little laugh and I laughed a lot which made her laugh the more as she conducted the car into a lot. She drove into a snowbank and got out of the car. We stopped. We were happy, we were there, we walked into a building by a back way we knew well, obscure door dark corridor where together we separately knew our way. Perhaps we didn't speak. Coming in by the back way you reach the main room easily but only after a short walk. At the threshold I saw the room as a photograph of a familiar painting suddenly flashed on a white wall before me. I retained the image still as we walked through the immobile room toward an arch at the other end. Before we disappeared I said something but it was as if I had not spoken and the room closed itself on our absence. We walked through a glass door with windows in it. There were a number of people sitting and standing alone or in small groups, talking or not, preparing to take a drink of one of a number of different kinds of drinks, very often coffee, gazing at doughnuts or other sorts of food before them which sooner or later they would eat. Habitually I looked at everyone in the room as if I expected to encounter a friend as at other times I should have done, and the people there habitually returned my glance but did not know me. We bought some coffee at a bar. We walked undecidedly through the semicircular, highly windowed, heavily columned room toward a vacant place I chose with a motion of my head. Although there were several people in the room it was almost silent, it would have been silent except that I could hear the voice of someone nearby who was reading or reciting something in French indistinctly. He was not speaking softly but he was not quite near. At first I occasionally tried to listen to the voice, to get some notion of the sense of his words or the words he was repeating, but shortly I lost interest in that pastime, and at some time before I once again listened to it the voice stopped. At the same time I was looking at whatever I could conveniently see, I could see people passing outside the building and people sitting in the room, and once in a while I would make some remark to Bethany who sat opposite me across a table.

—Who is that girl, I looked and saw.

—Obi, she said.

—I confuse her with Ardonia, I looked and said.

—How is that possible? They aren't alike.

—I don't know either of them well, but whenever I see Obi I call her Ardonia. She usually says she is flattered.

—I doubt if she is, Bethany remarked, although perhaps they do have similar hair. Sometimes I'm sorry I cut mine off. Whenever Ardonia comes over to the house the baby plays with her lovely long hair. She pulls it and loves to have it tickle her face.

—Lovely long blonde hair. Looking across I saw short red hair made into a frame of points for Bethany's accentuated green eyes.

—Why did you stay up all night. She turned her head to engage my attention.

—I was writing.

—I feel you have to have something to hold onto.

—Like in a story, the next thing must come next.

—No, I mean like you have your writing.

—You mean one has to have something to do.

—That's not the same. I have the baby and she's still almost a part of me. I want to let her go, not to make her part of me in another way. That would be something to do, that's what people find to do. I want to do something else, I want to be something, I don't know what. There will always be this child I have to attend to like an apron round my waist, there will always be this that I am the wife of a teacher someplace. That will always be something to do, but not something to be the way I want to be something.

—The curse of women! If only I was a man.

—That's true, and we can laugh about it, but still what is there that *I can do?*

—A woman can play a part. She finds a man to hold onto, a means of identity, and on the basis of that name acts out her fantasy. A woman can be anything at all if only she marries well. Without that she's forced to imitate the way of men and almost always does it badly. She's pushed here and there, beset with false hopes and momentary pleasures just as everyone is but she has nobody to inform her, to tell her who she is. There are some who can do it alone but they can be numbered.

—I don't think I'm consistent enough to play a part.

—You're not consistent enough to be a man?

—Not even enough to be a woman the way you think of a woman, a woman who knows who she is. Who can say, I want this, let us do that and so forth. No I'd confuse myself and the baby and Balcom, even, because, you know, he doesn't know who he is. I can't disguise it when I'm annoyed at him and I'm sometimes sarcastic to the baby and I shouldn't because she can't understand those things. He's a romantic of childhood, I remember your saying that about him, he can't give me my identity any more than the baby can, less probably, because I expect it of him and he doesn't understand it any more than she would if I asked her to lend me a dollar.

—He's still very young, I allowed, but it is not required that a man know who he is. It is not even possible.

—I don't know. The only fights we have are about the baby. He thinks everything should be pretty colors and sweet flowers for a child, as maybe they were for him before his mother died, but, hell, I'm as rotten as anybody else. I can't play a part—I certatinly can't play that part—I don't even want to. As soon as she can the baby should become whatever it is she'll be and let me alone. I like having a baby and doing things for her but I can only do whatever I happen to do or say. I can't be something to her, I will be, of course, but I can't arrange it. I never used to think about how others may see me, about what I am to them or was at one time. I just went along and played myself, changing, taking this mask and that one, finding this man and that one, never seeing the mask I hid behind until one time, when I hadn't seen you in some time and we began talking and you said, I hardly recognize you.

—You had cut your hair.

—Oh, I know, but after that I began to think of how anyone would recognize anyone else, and I found it likely that everyone would hardly recognize me if I wasn't sure of the choice of masks, like the choice of the appropriate dress for just the right moment with whoever it is that one is going to be with wherever it is that you may be. But I want to live as I wish. You never have to do facing up to realities if you only recognize that what they call realities are simply more arbitrary masks, all the same, subject to the limitations of the

—Wardrobe

—And the rainbow and the language and the rivers and the laws. And the limitations of the men. That's what you mean, isn't it. That's the curse of women. All right. But here I am. What do I care if it's not possible. I want to do something. May I have a piece of gum?

—Sorry. I forgot you might want some.

—It's true, I don't usually chew gum, my mother thinks it's vulgar, that's why I don't chew gum, it's because I'm afraid the baby will choke on it, it's because it will ruin the upholstery and get into the carpet, or rather it's because I'd rather bite my nails. Have you ever seen me do that? I can bite off a tiny strip of fingernail so evenly and so noiselessly that you'd hardly know I had a disgusting habit. I mean, what I mean is, why should I worry the baby to stop chewing her thumb. That's what I would like to know.

—There are people who will give you answers.

—Yes but I want an answer I don't already know to be false. People who go to a psychiatrist should see a psychiatrist. I guess I can bring up a child as well as anyone, but what I mean is I do not want to be a cow. To just be there.

—Then you have to make it.

—But I don't know how.

—Well I don't know how to be a mother, I said.

—You would probably give the thing to a public agency.

—If I had to be a mother. Yes. But I'm not a woman.

—Then neither am I.

—Perhaps we should start again. You are Balcom's wife, you have a child—

—Don't start again, I know what you're going to say.

—I'll say something else then. I couldn't be like a mother to a kid but I would keep on thinking that the first part of the kid's life is part of my life and rather than filling him up with what to do, I'd like to and I would allude to all the details of all the stories I contain for his imagination to make of them and of me what it will and instead of keeping secrets from him to share my life with him as completely as I could whenever I was with him. A child knows many things he has no words for, perhaps there are no words for some of what he knows, and I will never know what he knows and he himself may not remember. Later we may or may not become friends, but I shall have left him with something of me, not subtracted from me but applied over him, not what he should do or how he should do something, but what I have done and how I went about it. Something like his name, an unnecessary but essential accretion which he cannot ignore but which he may do with as he pleases and express as he will. I used to think that someday I would be old enough to reach the mantlepiece, to talk to people in such a way that they would listen, to love a woman and to have an answer to every question. And each thing I achieved was nothing after I had done it. I had always been as old as I would ever be. The only thing that has ever happened is that one person has done one thing and one thing and one thing and one and one and one more until one accidentally dies from one's accidental birth. And some of these things are habitual and some purposeful and some of them excellent and some gratuitous. And a scheme very much like life is established to justify existence with events so that at each point of achievement a further point appears in view offering an ever larger bait until at last one sees a clear vision of the idea of immortality which may be attended by one's own children or by God, the child of mankind, and to that vision one presumes to devote a life. But no conceivable children are worth my life, no series of events is equal to the sum of my fantasies, no history could tell me what I already know.

—Good. A little ending. She smiled and indicated with her eyes that we should leave. Last night it was Keats and became Wordsworth later, she said. She was alluding to a different scheme. I laughed. I might have kissed her. We took the car, remembering childhood, stuffed the laundry back in the two bags, speaking of babies, bought the milk, thinking of eating, and took the car, reminiscing of sex when as a child I, back to their house and stepped out in the snow.

—I used to read in the magazines that boys were liable to be grossly misinformed about sex as they talked about it continuously among themselves, but I knew everything and told nobody.

—Did you ever use to think that it was dirty, she asked.

—No, it was a secret that older people had. We stomped loudly on the porch to remove the snow from our feet and went inside where it was warm.

Inside. Balcom is ironing his shirt. Chazy my wife is reading. Bethany goes upstairs to dress. Shall we have a drink here or there, Croghan wants to know. There, says Balcom. I change my clothes to a baggy tweed. What time is it. And so on. Since nothing is happening in the house or outside at such an hour I may as well go ahead and introduce a pair of low comedy characters you may or may not meet again. Randolph and Rossie don't know each other though they are the same age and they won't meet here. They make a pair in my mind because I knew them both when they were small children younger than I, because like me they are grandchildren of two of the older families in the city where I spent my early years, because as a child I was in love in my way with each of their mothers, because in deciding not to live in Lockport their parents started a movement to which I am party that clever young people ought to seek their fortunes elsewhere, because with all this common history to begin with they both chose my college. Rossie is one type of miniature genius, quick and cheerful, a philosophy student too modest to announce that his interest in writing may extend itself to anything more substantial than weekly journalism. He's a quite private person whom very few of his many friends know because his buffoonery diverts everyone as much from his size as his cleverness. His motto, There's nothing quite like liquor is there. Although they are not alike he is congenial with his grandfather. Randolph's grandfather manufactured cloth by the Erie Canal until he retired. His father, a chemical engineer, has had something to do with plastic fabrics and is fond of square dancing. Once when I destroyed a kaleidoscope I gave his mother all the pretty stones and mirrors that were inside it. When I would go to visit his grandmother she would make me a brown cow, a mixture of root beer and ice cream. Once his father rescued my brother who had fallen into the fish pond. Randolph is the third generation of his family at this college and he supposes he will be a psychologist. Now, having centered those two in the past we can come back to the story in time to watch a transition.

Once more the car takes us into town . . . an invitation to dinner at the house . . . Balcom borrows the keys to Front Street where he will be staying tonight . . . tonight a play at the college theatre, the tickets, a social event . . . a special event, in the cast both Balcom and Bethany (Chazy's best friend) and also Rossie . . . then too, Ardonia's husband Seward as well as an old friend of mine (my best friend's girlfriend at one time in this place) with whom in my way at that time I was also in love . . . not to mention the cast of the audience filled with characters out of my past. Again the excitement at the approach of an hour. We achieve the house in time for a drink . . . a telephone call from Hale Eddy . . . arrangements to meet etc . . . dinner by candlelight among students . . . too much food consumed too quickly . . . we speak of acquaintances . . . a friend victimized by the police of another city . . . the old days in this town . . . I remember grand dinners in the house that burned down . . . the service is poor but polite . . . stage fright, a short wait . . . first call, the actors depart . . . Chazy and Croghan in two blue chairs drinking from cups of coffee. The excitement is most formidable when everything stops. My wife and I have a drink. I hear the voice of the old servant, an unmistakable croak, I introduce Chazy. I say, I remember worse times, and I better, says he. I turn to find that a small crowd has gathered about the remains of a legend hoping to pick scraps of the old days when as a very young man I, and Randolph introduces himself. He thinks I was the one his father rescued, and I call his father by his uncle's name. He introduces me to a friend of his whom it looks as if I've met before. I forget the name. The four of us have a drink in the deserted bar. A good way to pass the time before the curtain while the properties are being counted, an unexpected rehearsal for performances that will demand the impossible revival of a character—they would say, my own—who is disappeared to me. What's his name reminds me of me as I was then before I retired, and as soon as his name is recalled to me I shall be pleased to introduce you to the other unmarried one I promised.

Fillmore. He is called away. Automatically, we talk automatically. Your father your brother a member your aunt a college and. It was like living in the depression. What do you think the president, then the chairman. They fired my architect. My father was here and his father at the same time and maybe a hundred times my father has mentioned that his father was a member there and so even now I remember that. The two brothers were not alike. The two sons chose different lives. Fillmore returns, he reminds me of me. The plan and the president, a political condition and a question; the answer cast in an older term, the knowledge of experience reformed for the new moment. The president and the chairman, an anecdote that determines a vagueness in the past, a performance that recalls a style of life that was practiced there, a note to the answer that illuminates a point. I don't know whether you know anything about me, but I don't know anything about you so I'll assume that you don't know anything about me. A dazzling quick joke, a political reminiscence, a volitional memoir. The chairman and his son, a consultation, the crossing of friends' points, notes to the difference that may turn to describe an agreement. When I knew him he was in such a way that such a thing had been decided. And while he is at the top of an institution comprehensible to one man's mind he acts as if from the script for the figurehead of a vast corporation who doesn't direct but consults. A meeting, by chance, with oysters unexpectedly leading to a dead end on account of my youth. A consitution, which, when folded and reprocessed in turn appears as a bright everlasting paper flower. I went down and spoke with him for a long time after he was appoionted. The former president, the honor of antiquity, the question of Latin, the archaeology of Mexico, the inheritance of Maine, the naval history of the Second World War, a politically right two fisted goddamn — he oppressed their dearest wish for power and amazed them by his memory for fact. It gave me great pleasure to have a taste for grandfather who was still present to be introduced. The great room of a fine house was completely filled with all those I had invited. On one occasion they rose to honor him, on one occasion they stood to honor me. Things have changed and they will change again. It was extraordinary because I thought it, and as soon as I thought it I wrote it to be rewritten. The series was recast just before I left. The names were changed, the ages differed, the values were controlled, the reputations were revised, the legends settled in and gradually lost the certainty of events to become the fantasies of a different generation. I understand they aren't happy with the new man either. It was like real life and the people were characters in it.

But the prologue was nothing like the play. Fillmore reminds me of me the better to play my part. I have forgotten much. I have omitted more than that.

You would be surprised, for example, to find one morning an owl mistakenly lodged in the corner of your bathroom. It could happen, it did happen to Hale Eddy the following morning, he told me himself that he was surprised. But a photograph of that owl in a corner of your bathroom would be of no interest to anyone, just a picture of an owl, another one of many. So with this talk for which I despised myself as much as ever I have. You have heard it all and worse. Who survives my loquacity may become a friend. We arranged to meet Fillmore and Randolph later on. Last call. Chazy and Croghan walked quickly to the theatre. Good evening, I returned. The auditorium was packed with a new clear expectancy, accentuated for me by the familiarity of a long used room. I had the briefest moment to recollect who I had become, I took a breath, and the darkness closed over me.

During the intermissions, I played the part of the second act. I met a guy and his wife about whom I knew a good joke, I arranged to meet them later and I was not surprised. I met someone I didn't like and who didn't like me, I was not rude and I smiled. I avoided seeing a teacher who had been another sort of hero to me and who had later fallen from that kind of grace. I nodded to someone else. I continued avoiding his glance through the second intermission. I did not speak of the play. I smoked two cigarettes. I did not avoid speaking to the dean who did not smoke, but I found no opportunity to pay my respects. I had a glimpse of some others who would recognize my name. I saw the wife of a teacher who would no longer recognize my face. I spoke two words to my successor in a certain position who was later to become a fellow employee. I looked at photographs of the cast of the play and recognized the actress I would meet later in the green room. As I reentered the auditorium for the second time I saw I was in the way of meeting the president and the chairman. I stopped the traffic in one aisle to introduce to them my wife Chazy. I smiled. I noticed that the president did not quickly associate my name with my face. I stood in front of him in order to address a very formal remark to the chairman concerning his son whom I had at one time known in association with my best friend at that time. The chairman, whom in any case I had spoken with more often than the president, was quite friendly in his two sentences. I remembered with the clarity called as if it were yesterday the sense of every word I had been bold enough to address to these men of affairs concerning what they were then doing, and I knew that should anyone have presumed to treat me in the same manner when I held a position analogous to their own, I would have been either offended or delighted. I failed to think that they would by now have forgotten what I said as easily as anyone may forget an obscure name, or a slight flutter caused by wind passing across the desk, for I was recovering from the first act in which I had offended myself. I left Columbia University when I was told by the professor of architecture who was my tutor that a person of my age and level of education ought not to say the things I was then saying. However, as I was faced once again with these men whom I had at one time chosen to advise gratuitously I was nearly overcome with a special mortification of my pride as an actor, a sensation which goes beyond my schemes and may be put to my youthful vivid picture of myself as I had been. After the performance for the public of which I was a member, there remained one more encounter to my own second act. I waited in the room below the stage to meet again a woman I had admired. I spoke with members of the cast, those who in a moment I would collect by name to play my final scene. They spoke of her. She had been cast in an unsuitable role in return for which she had harrassed everyone on the stage by appearing to indulge in scene stealing which she was able to do with such subtlety that only the cast was aware of her intention for she played the part of an ingenuous flirt. Below stage she kept us waiting for a time. She appeared through the door of her dressing room at last, at the head of an entourage of three or four friends, in a long fur coat clutching in her left arm a bright pink azelea plant, its pot wrapped in tinfoil of the same color which seemed to be reflected in her nearly tearful eyes. She saw me as I approached, caught my hand and pressed it to her. Croghan, she exclaimed. We walked hand to breast across the room beneath the stage, accompanied by my questions and her answers. She said she felt very, very tired, she had not seen in some time my friend her lover, she did not quite understand what I was saying, she told me where she was living and that she was writing. She indicated her friends who waited at the open door as we neared it, we parted and as the door closed upon her she waved and called good-bye. It had been one continuous motion. Later when some of the cast were seeking to condemn her for crying real tears in the death scene of a farce I said, But she's an actress. And that was that.

I joined the others and we began arranging to leave the theatre. Balcom left for an appointment in New York. I spoke with Rossie who had not yet recomposed himself after playing a different part. He said his mother was well. We would go somewhere where someone would give us some beer. We made up a group. Ardonia, it appeared, was feeling unwell, but her husband Seward was introduced to me. He kept repeating his favorite lines in an exaggerated cockney. "A small chair, if you please!" He shouted that he wanted to get drunk, and he led the party out of the theatre. We all piled into his old crate. On the way around the corner to the place where the beer was, Seward passed his friend Hulburton who was driving a small truck in the opposite direction. He shouted to Hulburton to join us and missed the turn he intended to make. He regained the correct street, drew up and got out crying, "Reprievèd, I am repreivèd" a phrase from the last act of the play. The beer was in the cellar. The place was dead. It might have been difficult to get the beer as you had to sign the name of a member, but Seward, since he was not yet himself, was able to move behind the bar, surprise the keeper, and draw an amount of beer. "Let me, be so kind, my good man! There! It's quite easy, blasted foamy, not at all, not all!" We were supplied. We stood around. Bethany wanted to dance. I was talking with Bethany but I didn't want to dance. Someone said, If I may be pardoned a truism, there's nothing quite like liquor, is there. I said, Quite true. The music from the juke box started very loud and fast. Hulburton and many others came downstairs to join the party. Bethany danced with the guy who had taken the lead in the play who did a very fast stiff legged dance just like his walk and as he had played his part. Hulburton told Seward that he wanted to dance with the guy. The noise was extreme. I wanted to leave. Seward asked Bethany if she thought he ought to call Ardonia, but in the end he didn't. The possibilities had narrowed, and I suggested a return to the house where we had eaten dinner to find some people I had arranged to meet. So Bethany and Chazy and I walked through the snow to do that.

We came into the dining room from a door on the back terrace of the house to find a large group, most of whom seemed to me to be children, dancing very fast to the noise of loud electrical instruments in the near darkness. Bethany began talking with some people she knew. I left Chazy with them and went to the bar where Randolph was drawing beer. I was quiet, standing listening drinking smoking. At length I told him I hated my loquacious mode, which was gone.

We talked a little about his grandfather's property in Lockport, and about that house, and he mentioned what he had found in the attic there. I waited around. Seward and Hulburton came in and had a beer. Hulburton began telling a long story which was either very funny or very sad about how hard it had been yesterday night getting his wife to the hospital in a snowstorm. Some laughed, some didn't. The girls were drinking and dancing with anyone who came along. I hardly ever dance with my wife Chazy, in fact, I don't anymore know how to dance, she says and we agree. In other times I loved to dance and did, they said, very well, but I loved it like the loquacity I hate. My old acquaintance, the teacher with a wife, was pleased to see me. I engaged him in a long conversation on the subject of teaching in which I asked him a great many questions. At first he gave me evidence that he liked his job, which I might have doubted, and then for some time he listed the credentials of the school which he made out very favorably, and then he began to answer my questions about what he thought. His wife interrupted by deriding our seriousness, and made him dance with her. At her suggestion he said, I've been writing some poetry. She said, Very good poetry. I said, You've got a built-in propaganda machine there. They laughed and danced and disappeared on account of their cat. He had said, On Monday we talked about the fact that when you begin a close analysis of writing you may lose your emotional interest in it, while on the other hand it is possible to understand something completely and remain fundamentally unmoved.

I noticed Fillmore put down his silver tank of whiskey and begin to dance with my wife Chazy. I asked someone who he was. Two or three said he was a good fellow but rather disturbed, they thought. They said he was very screwed up. Bethany's friends appeared. I introduced myself. She said, as if over tea, "You know, you're the sort of person I can't stand." She was amusing. He was a theatrical lighting technician, and we talked schemes of stage lighting, dark versus light. "You're the sort of person who wears blue navy shirts, a man like that," she said. We enjoyed each other. Chazy had thought she would get me to dance with her if she danced first with Bethany, but instead of taking the bait as I sometimes do I introduced her to the first man who seemed to be tall enough and they danced. Usually I don't like women dancing together but I had been seeing too many movies to mind. The crowd at the dance had begun to thin out. The electric band was replaced by the juke box. Bethany was dancing with

Seward. After a time I noticed that there were only ourselves, Hulburton, Bethany and Seward, two married couples and Fillmore. Once I took Bethany's hands and swung her around and around in wide circles up the room laughing until we fell. I sat with Fillmore. I said, You remind me of me as I was. I told him what they said. Yes, he said, very, very . . . Responsibility versus irresponsibility . . . sometimes I lock the door . . . I like my thesis but the teachers don't say what they know . . . horrible . . . I should punch someone out . . . I used to play games . . . I'm vice-president of a dying breed . . . fuck it I want to throw away my tie but you see I've still got my tie on . . . good party. Let's get some beer. And we did that.

The beer was almost gone. Seward and Bethany were trying to gather the flock for a move to another place where we could carry on. "But first we must go back to get some beer," declaimed Seward and Hulburton in unison. We moved. Fillmore would come with Chazy and Croghan, driven by Seward to get the beer. Back in the crate around the corner to stop in the street. The beer was in the cellar. We three left Chazy in the car and ran in down the steps. Fillmore shouted, What a show! A drinking glass fell to the floor. We drew two pitchers of beer and stuffed our pockets with cans of it, ran upstairs and out. At the door we jumped over some people sitting there. What's your name, they growled, What's your name? I yelled, George! jumping free, but they were upon Fillmore, and Seward, groaning and steaming in the cold, trying to get a hold. I picked Fillmore's glasses from the snow. Chazy ran from the car screeching her most fishwifely, Stop! Stupid! Stop! She pounded their backs as they hugged and grunted in a pile on the ground. Stop! Stupid! Stop! (I was in a fight, she said.) Momentarily they were on each other embracing and shaking hands, introducing each other, identifying themselves, the attackers insisting, however, that beer be stolen the gentlemanly way, leave a card on the hallstand or a punch in the jaw on the way. But we left them insisting. (I was in a fight.) Great, cried Fillmore, that was great! (Regrettable incident.) I've wanted to punch somebody out for years. (Stupid beasts.) I gave him his glasses, and with Seward almost in control of the truck we careered to the end of the road. That was great. (Stupid beasts.) Wipe the blood from your cheek.

"Regrettable enough, I decline to declare, a veritable boon said Brown, a small chair," Seward continued to declaim, somewhat out of breath from the ride. Fillmore took up a guitar. Seward poured out some glasses of beer. Chazy sat. Hulburton and Bethany talked in the other room. He said, again and again, She's my wife and he's my only friend, leaning against the icebox, She's my wife and he's my only friend. Seward removed his shirt and sang, "Repreivèd, repreivèd, And I am happy, I am happy!" He fell into a chair, stopped. I shouted, Aren't you going to undress any further? Chazy explained, We just saw a movie. They undressed. Bethany played a record. Hulburton said, I finished a play tonight. I never thought it was any good all the time I was writing until I typed the last line. Here, he offered it. I looked over the pages and read a few speeches. He said, The first novel is always autobiographical. I said, I see your father here. He said, no, that's not it. I said, Did you ever read any Shaw. Yes I did. I handed Fillmore the script which, I said to Hulburton, was nicely typed. Hulburton and I fell to reminiscing about his father and his brother and his brother's wife, whom I had known at one time. The most incredible female siege I've ever seen. He agreed. They lived together for two years and then he went away and after a year she followed him, so I said they should get married and they did and now they want to blame me. Bethany, Chazy and Seward went upstairs mentioning the baby as they left. I said to Fillmore, I was in love with her once. Incredible. I thought I could talk to her. She's my wife's best friend. Why are we married? I said, Why are we married? I said, Hulburton, why are you married? He thought, I'm married and I want to go away and I go away but I come back. I may get twenty miles or eighty but I turn around and I come back. She is there. I don't know. I always come back—it's not sex. Seward fell down the stairs into the room. Why are we married! I said, Why are you married! Seward, did you ever think, why are you married? He said, Never, and sat on the floor buttoning his shirt. Why are you married, Croghan demanded again. He said, There's this girl, and then, you see, this woman, and you can do anything and you can be anything. It's a matter of trust. A small chair, if you please, a small chair. Why are we married. Why are we married. I want to go away. A matter of trust. I never met a woman I could live with. It's not sex. But I come back. You can be anything with her. She is there. Not one of them all, I never met one like her. Long black hair, green eyes, a small chair. Once I decided I wanted to be married, met a girl who seduced me, I wanted to run, became a woman and we ran together to the end of the road. Here we are. Why are we married? I want to I want to I like it I do. Here we are the three of us married, no shit, the most incredible siege. Why, why, why. I relaxed.

Fillmore played a few chords on the guitar, the unmarried, the quiet the after the shouted echoes, the end of the road, the last answer, the stopped. This is the age of the wise young man. My play your breakfast let's go I'll drive so long I'm happy don't forget come see us your name I will in the book so long I'll see you. We walked out into the snow, the dawn. Look, the dawn, the dawn is pink, the dawn is pink—Seward, look, the dawn is Ardonia, the dawn is pink, the dawn is Ardonia, look, the dawn, the dawn is pink. A story.

It's true, I lived it, it's as long as my life. I've barely begun, you see. Someone young enough and old enough. We may get to know each other quite well after some years. But will we ever agree? That's the story of Hale Eddy, my friend. Well, the silence of readers is a one-way street. Someone once told me the only way to behave. Leave the room. I only remember what I omitted. Tell me whatever you wish. One may judge an artist by the quality of his point of view. The quality of a work of art is judged by what is left out. Similarly, the ripeness of fruit may be known by practice, the type of a tree by its leaves. Into the stream of consciousness flows a muddy river and out swims a story.

END OF BOOK ONE

One Durable Significance

If the reason for a change should clarify an importunate remark, willingly let the season characterize the total of its aspiration. Carry on, another piece of yellow paper, an added momentary significance. Why do you read? The obverse is as interesting as the reverse of any window, of any suite, of any coat. *Like Goethe, I like to work fast and let it go at that.* But like Ortega, I am myself plus my circumstance. As this I see is to many other things, so am I to all I ignore. Any epigraph is as good as any other, nor is one beginning more arbitrary than many. Finally, I say, finally something is going to have to be done. My quills are selected and prepared. "Resurrection, Madame, said the Phoenix, is the simplest thing in the world. It is not more surprising to be born twice than once."

Once there was a child and this child had many peculiarities some of which were apparent to those who tended the child. He was himself aware of many observatons and he knew when they become codified as a list of repetitious stories. Strangely enough, he had however made with himself a pact that he should remember all that would be forgotten, that he would take notice of each circumstance that should be thrown away. It never occurred to him to announce such an intention and indeed as the child grew, his notions seemed to change form so that what was once remarked could no longer be discovered. But all the time the child, of whom it was said that he was no longer a child, hoarded the experience of his years against the chance of a moment he could not but imagine. There came no point when all could be done, when all would be said. Every item in his mind while he was preoccupied with other matters retained its integrity to the whole of his knowledge. In this fact there was for him no choice. He ignored a childish incantation and carried on as he thought he would and as it was expected of him to do. The child adopted many of the graces of his elders. He came to know all that had been withheld and much more. He did certain excellent things that had been done before. He discovered much that remained unknown. But when the child was indeed regarded as a very young man, it occurred to him that he would carry on in his original project with all the power of a great joy. "Like a man who could do many things did one." Although he might come to be widely and very often and very well mistrusted for it, no one could have anticipated such a choice.

She says someday when we're wealthy can we. I had always been as wealthy as I should ever be. All my schemes have fallen through. By the time you get here I shall be in some other job. I don't need a job. I don't need a scheme. So, what shall I do? Take a trip. I am a minstrel of residence. Durrell, Miller & Lawrence, associated travel agents with specialities in Greece, France, Egypt and Italy, successors to Byron & Circle. We have lived in all the towns we recommend most of which, unfortunately, no longer exist but we are able to offer a most reasonable facsimile available from Faber & Faber, 24, Russell Square, or your own bookseller. Faber & Maker, poet in residence. I want to live in New Orleans. I want to live in Mexico City. I want to live in San Francisco.

The influence of California is insidious, the universal informal reality, of which the best representation is the sort of television broadcast which can be stopped at any point without seeming incomplete. Is it over? No, not yet, she replies who is aware all the time of the time. The show will be over on the half-hour in time for inexorable station identification. I saw some experimental California movies once. The same thing. Applause in the middle by mistake. Everyone's an amateur hero, the ultimate American drawn out to the western limit of the world. To the west one imagines the extreme orient over the bridge, and one encounters the western world by flying back east. The most that can be said is, The bus began to move.

New England is the source of rationality and reasonableness. Import California customs on a reduced scale becoming picturesque. A small town filled with great universities and strange masculine women, decorated in white paint. The sub-culture of the East Coast, a very small country at the heart of the nation. Everybody knows the twins Azee and Bezee, sailing and skiing. The manner of toleration *sine nobiliate*. The creation of New York, the maintenance of Boston, the influence of Harvard. I shouldn't like to live there though I may.

So, travelling south on the Florida East Coast railway owned by William Keenan, Jr. of Lockport, the richest man in the world. The South. The decay of stupidity, coeur de romanticisme, the ever present eighteenth century. The land of writerly artists oppressed at home, the analogue of Ireland. A real live foreign country in our midst, almost dead, being crushed for the sake of international democracy by the rights of mass media. They are stupid and baffled but they know a nigger when they see one which is more than I could say. The last Christian, a lovely, evacuated woman, her white skirt fluttering in the breeze as if she had just flown in from a tour round the house. Happy to make your acquaintance. Likewise, I'm sure. Sir. How do you spell antidisestablishmentarianism. Compartmentalization. Two white and one colored. People sit in. An order of grits, pralines, October beans and turpentine. You-all better believe there is some mighty fine cultured gentlemen and women folk in them parts.

In the great south-west, we may be rude and socially unattractive, but we got the dough, bread, money to buy brains, we get em from New York and Europe. The reddest beefsteak in the world. Reconverted christianity to other uses. Cadillac with Venetian blinds. Bullheads living in Hollywood settings fostered by a store where you can't buy anything out of fashion. Nobody is allowed to walk at night on the streets of downtown Dallas. You can't buy a drink. Bring your own bourbon to an imitation of genuine imported Pompeii Italy. I don't get yr lingo, but ain't we got dough, pride of ignorance, women to bait a steer (ha, ha, ha), and a fine God churchgoing American up-standing whippersnapper public school. Military heroes fly off the front porch into the sun and fall into the empty swimming pool breaking head (I can't swim) (talk French). For the most part Texans are very nice folks.

But, and, where do we go from the end of the road? We shall of course go on, separately, as if nothing had happened, as if all literature were only a vast tautology and as if every new prose writer had invented a new way of speaking only for the purpose of saying nothing.

He returned from the weekend, cleaned up and sat down. He

had been eating cheese and wursts, mackerel à la greque, eggs and
Philadelphia scrapple from Reading Market and spaghetti with
American sauce, barely to mention various fruit and deep dish apple
pie. He had been drinking beer from New Jersey, wine from California and whiskey from Scotland. Beside all that there had been innumerable paintings by Cézanne interspersed with several by Renoir, a
fantasy of film induced by gray weather, and long walks in the city
both at night and by day.

The conversation was not refreshing. It seemed, however, to be
the first day of spring for the noises of children talking, and of birds,
and of airplanes brought him a sense of last summer and the one
before that. One could again believe that there might be leaves on the
trees though there were none. Boys and girls again walked along the
European style boulevard through the trash left by the snow. It was
enough to make me annoy a friend, kiss a girl, outrage the company,
correct an error by making a faux pas. He began too soon to anticipate
that moment of spring when the trees, still nearly bare, are downy
with green, a brief poignancy — three days, ten minutes, a party, a
song, a cut, four hours, a dance. My dictionary contains one spelling
mistake. But perhaps I can speak more plainly.

These people are connoisseurs of the city and, he supposes, of
everything that touches him. He has obscured his darkly white Russian background before he entered Princeton, and has cultivated
associations with Massachusetts. By day he is a labor expert writing
for a newspaper. At night he would tacitly contribute his share to
culture by writing in the bedroom. 'I want to get away, said an editor
of fortune to a man on time,' said a poem that he recommended. They
lived in the kitchen. In the living room, against the far walls, they
had three old chairs, two tables, a pair of silver candlesticks and a
stopped antique clock and, on one of the tables by the door, the
poetical works of Coleridge in an old edition alongside an art book on
impressionism. He has adopted the solution of a journalist who
neither thinks nor listens while he hoards in secrets, jealous of so very
little knowledge. His message is a message, constant and moral,
things were better in the old days. There is nothing which does not
cooperate with such a purpose, no occasion when such a response is
inappropriate. He wanted to live in Paris, she wanted to have a baby,
and after all they did that. There but for me go I. I feel (he felt) as if I
have been lost in a haystack.

During the course of the letter you call my first letter before or after Christmas, I was making a decision. The letter, of which it appears I have not preserved a copy, was the mechanics of a decision having little to do with you. You mention positive and negative decisions, but to me that's not a useful scheme. There are ways of saying no which mean yes. And what are called positive decisions always come down to making do with what's available. For example, a man finds that he can read poetry, make drawings, overhaul an engine, love a woman, talk intelligibly, plant a tree and elicit the warmth of friends — and he decides to be an architect for it is something he does not know. This is a crude précis, but such a decision participates in everything else about him — that he doesn't like ham or chicken, that he won't be an intellectual, that he doesn't want to teach history, that he lacks the will to paint pictures and has nothing new to say although he enjoys photography. Architecture is around the corner. A great teacher once told a friend of mine that. Everyone backs ass into life. This way the decisions and all their processes resolve to decorations that may fall down in neglect or may outlast the fashion of their beauty. Last year a friend interrupted me to inquire, Do you want to go around the world with me? Yes I do. I surprise. Something happened that was not forseen. A real life decision which led to various things. For him, not going on a trip, writing a novel. For me, a marriage and a trip and now this writing. And much more. The peculiar possibility that one actually chooses never occurs to anyone else in just the same way. It is not one of many possibilities, it is not inevitable but it is chancy, it is the thing chosen. Very likely that is what Charles meant by the next poem. There could be a reason for hesitation, but both positive and negative decisions and the paraphernalia associated with them are a simple something to do, a means of waiting out the time before an occurrence of some importance. It is possible to fear an ending, just as it may be impossible to begin.

In the meantime I solace myself who am threatened by having to make money in the next year by planning in some detail a trip around this country, a place I rather don't want to see and wouldn't like. As I say I'm glad all my plans, my daydreams of action, fell through, but this has not yet. We would go in a leisurely way through the South to New Orleans and stay for a time. Then along the coast to Mexico City. Then back up by way of Santa Fe and Southern California to San Francisco and another stay. Finally, back across the midwest from

Denver to Lockport. So I have set myself to collect twelve hundred dollars for several months of freedom in the land of thou shalt not. Making categories, or plans, or schemes is a kind of telling a story, the most efficient description, the most convenient interlude. The little questions are busyness of another type, one piled upon the other rising high beyond the trees. A plan. What will happen is quite another matter, what I shall elect.

New York, March 11.63.

When I came in, Prince Edward—you've heard of him—was on the phone. I stood around. He was speaking of dogs and I spoke to his dog who has a long nose. Soon he hung up the telephone and said hello to me. There was one problem and another which he reviewed briefly. By the way, he said, and told me the news. Something had happened to someone, something good he said. I suggested another solution. He said, You're overcome with the problematic aspect of life. I said, That's an interesting scheme, tell me another. And so things went. Somebody else asked a question which we were between us able to answer. The question was the position of insignificant habits. And then, under those circumstances, could one or couldn't one. The answer was a function of the scheme, not that we wouldn't allow other schemes. During the conversation but effectively at its end, the prince was again called away by the telephone. I took the opportunity to retire for a bath and I planned to redress to go out. When I reappeared the prince and I made certain arrangements which hung by a telephone call he himself would make the following evening. But in lieu of unforseen acts or accidents we had set it up to fall out as it might. He began offering me all the diversions that occurred to him, some of which were perhaps appealing, but we both knew that I intended to do otherwise. As a parting gift he offered to show me how his dog would bite if he handled her in a certain way, but in fact the dog would not do it. In due course I left, taking with me whatever was mine.

I had arrived, you see, on the point of having something to say to him. I had already done something and it was convenient for me just at that time that I had taken up visiting him very customarily. In such a way that whatever we might do took on the complexion of a habit rather than that of events. To me, that was delightful, the more so because we had achieved it as a matter of course without any cleverness between us. There was always time for a few questions and one or more answers, both in a completely unhurried, unnecessary manner, and customarily we reserved to a later part of the interview any business I might wish to mention. Such customary visits were so arranged by either of us that they might on occasion lengthen into extremity, easily becoming extraordinary from one or the other's point of view. To speak otherwise, it was possible to go up the full range of a scheme, and then to take leave on that point. Or we could go up and down to the original point. Finally it was possible, on occasion, usually after exhausting a scheme of its interest, for each of us to stand quite consciously at different points, speaking consistently as if in languages we did not share. Sometimes I found it possible to partake of several different schemes simultaneously, or to speak at once of several different points in one or two schemes, but it was at those times that I risked the chance that he might turn and leave abruptly, back into himself. It could happen that one moment everything was in the air and the next instant it had turned to chaff settling irrelevantly into the carpet like dust. But up to that point we had always been able to regroup the silence, if not immediately then soon afterwards, so that we always parted with some expectation of a future conversation.

In the beginning they behaved toward each other like estranged animals, allowing only the most ritualistic courtesies, assuming nothing, explaining all. Some say it was the will of one and some say because of the other that such circumstances began, imperceptibly at first, to shift form. While to all appearances things remained the same as they had always been, it was nevertheless possible for those closest to him at that time to notice a clearer tone of expectancy in Prince Edward's voice as he awaited the visits of his former teacher which were always punctual as well as brief. Beside the fact that each expected certain courtesies of the other, both men came to enjoy the ritual in which they participated almost as they might enjoy watching a great play. Rather customarily it was possible to notice that one or the other of them had composed an opening remark to speak upon entering the other's presence while, in addition, there was always a vague agenda of inconsequential matters which concerned them both to provide convenience for the meetings. An obvious change in their association occurred when the prince volunteered a different series of pretexts upon which their encounters might rest. Both of them had independently nourished an interest in photography which they had heretofore appreciated in each other only by the most ceremonial

means. But at the suggestion of the prince they were able to undertake an informal partnership against the ground of a photographic
pastime which afforded any number of opportunities for them to
partake actively in a scheme they both knew well, as if old friends
arranged by accident to meet in a room they had both loved at some
time in the past. The same precision of give and take prevailed under
their new arrangements, but from time to time it was now possible
for them to consider in its full extent any subject that might occur to
either of them. At such times which became as frequent as the
questions which created them they existed before each other simply as
men without even the distinction of names. At such a point they
behaved toward each other completely as equals, but there is no
doubt that they came in this way to understand each other in quite
divergent ways. One was likely very often to mention his shortcomings which were not apparent and on occasion even to demonstrate
them. The other would often make something of a show of his
knowledge of himself which he was able to abstract to every sort of
generality, some of them fallacious. But they fully enjoyed their
exchanges for neither was required to participate in the other's play so
that any question of belief in the dual fiction of agreement and discord
might remain out of range. Nor were courtesies proscribed. By formal even habitual means they were yet able to achieve solitude when
they were together. Their friendship endured with the patience of
philosophy.

[The process. How goes your book? It goes on. So. And what is it
about? Everything. What can I say to that? I expect nothing. It goes
on. Are you not too rigorous, a little severe, perhaps? Yes, perhaps
and perhaps not. It goes on. And these discoveries you say you've
made, they too are nothing? Oh they are rather pleasing. Then you
must be going to include them, you must be about to tell secrets after
all. Of course I am bound to let something of myself stray into it as it
is my own process. I'm quite willing in that respect. It's about you, is
it not? Yes, unavoidably, it's about me but that's not it. Not why you
wrote it, is that what you mean? It's not why I wrote it but that's not
what I mean. I wrote it because I needed something to do and it is
natural for me to write. But these days you always complain that you
don't like rewriting it, that it is a tedious job full of expediency. Oh,
it is much like that. And you say you've solved some problems. Yes,
and I have eliminated problems, and I have tried to ignore problems

and, unwillingly, I have anticipated some of them. It is all very technical. It is endless. You mean the process of rewriting? Endless as the climate. Then you cannot think of a way to end your book, is that the problem you're working on now? No question of a way to end it, just the question of going on. You seem discouraged. No, no more than usually. It must be a pessimistic book that ends unhappily. It's not a story. Could a man of twenty-five write a memoir? Cetainly, but that's not what it is. But it does end unhappily? I don't know. What? It would depend on whether when you finished reading it you were unhappy or not. And you, were you unhappy when you finished writing it? I was exhilirated. You were glad to have finished it. No, I missed having something to do but I thought it was a good book. And now you are not so sure. I am certain that last year I was not the same person I am at the moment. Of course you are still very young. Oh I know what I'm doing, if that's what you mean, but, oh well. No, go on, I'm interested. You should read my book, I have nothing to say about it. You've suggested that before, but then you say it isn't finished. All I can say is that it is tedious to perfect the mask, and since I know it cannot be perfected I have no intention of trying. I could not read it until I came to copying it out with a view to making some corrections and deletions when I was forced to rewrite it entirely. So it may be tedious to read? It might be, I don't know.]

Dear Mother and Father.
We arrived back from a weekend to find your new vacuum cleaner in a box at the foot of the stairs. We were surprised to get it but glad that you thought it was a bargain. Janet unpacked it immediately and began to clean the house after reading the instructions fully as she always does, and as you may remember I always did. She says it works well. While we were away we had the first day of spring and so it was natural when we got back to do a little cleaning. We threw out the Christmas tree which was getting brown, we hope to put a shelf of flowers in the corner where the tree was. Your plant is now rather brown in the flowers but it will make a bush for us if we can keep it alive. It appears that the newspaper strike will be over soon but if we are going to take a trip next spring I shall have to find a higher paying job. We had a little but very annoying trouble with the car which prevented us again from meeting Marcia, but I understand she didn't have to wait too long. Thanks to your help I was able to do quite a little writing these last couple of months which pleases me. Janet

plans to go and do some sewing with her mother this weekend. I guess spring is the time for new clothes. I've been taking some pictures, a few of which turned out quite well. Eddy sometimes lends me his Contax and I have that little Graflex which is good for out doors. Eddy and I enjoy the darkroom and I am glad to be able to have the enlarger again after all these years. David's gallery is opening with champagne on Tuesday. He has only a few paintings in this first show but it is a cooperative gallery—owned by those who exhibit there—so there will be other occasions. Janet has decided to name the cat Djuna because she read a book by Djuna Barnes and thinks that a pretty name, but I doubt we'll use the name very much except to tell people who ask what it's called. I'm going up to New Haven on Wednesday with Eddy and David to see the trial of my friend John Palm. There's a good indication that the police were extremely brutal in his case, so it promises to be an interesting trial. Soon then I expect it will be back to work for me—I've almost forgotten what it is like to work every day. We haven't heard from the Mosses but perhaps we were out of town when they came back from Florida. I'm going to have dinner on Saturday with Dave Weber and his wife Sandy. He has a good job, as far as I can tell, in cancer research. We had dinner with them and Brian at Paul's in Brooklyn, but after a while we found there wasn't much to say. The Webers are the only people I know anymore who call me Corson which is rather pleasant. Janet has taken to doing the crossword puzzle in the Christian Science Monitor almost every day—she says they are not too difficult and it amuses her to do it. She sends her love and thanks as do I, & to Marcia. I hope Doug will come and see us.

Love Cork

You're very intelligent and you write well, they said, but I don't know what you mean. You have a sub-editor's gift for improving on original works that were in any case cribbed from other original works in a bar in a pub or over a bottle of whiskey in a flat. I'm always fascinated by the way his mind works. I hear you run a tight shop. You have a great respect for ideas, Mr. Castle. You have beautiful hands. You look as if you go to Oxford. You look as if you've had the creeping crud. When you write, somebody listens, believe me. Are you an only child? I can tell by your face you're a good person. You have a great deal of common sense and I hope you know what you're doing. This house seems more like home than any place I've been in

New York. There's a certain lack of bullshit in the poems. A philosopher is bad enough, but a drunk philosopher . . . I always thought you were an Anglo-Saxon homosexual type. If something doesn't interest you you don't listen. Have you ever been in a fight? I have noticed that you address with words. Are you at all Chinese? Some people carry a dagger around, for themselves. You used to be so sure, so completely well-dressed. What are you, a draft dodger? For someone I didn't think I'd like at all I like you immensely.

Teehee, quod shee, and clapte the windowe to.

Devise du temps perdu—Lavori in Corso. We don't write master-pieces, not since Dryden, pardon, I mean Dreiser. The story of a European tour in three months. What are you writing. What am I writing. A poem. I am writing a novel. The novel is dead, the Great National Book by L. G. Desire—he would if he could but he can't. Cant. Kant. Convolutions of glosses, read interpretation first. Eternal influence of Cézanne. Looking for pearls in old peashells. I am writing. What are you writing. There was a little girl with a curl, a pearl of a girl. Watch movies, watch out for the national book, look forward to the great American prize cast back across the waters. She wrote, you may read, she said, I am writing a letter to myself, she thought, I will write a novel, it begins, Dear Charles. It would make a good book. You can't write with onlookers or make love. You stop. Oh, excuse me, I see you've been crying. I want to get away. Too private. Sleep. I want to—how can I say it?—develop my body—oh, dear—to find just the word—my soul!—a simple red apple. I didn't know you were asleep. It's okay, I was just a bit lazy, I have to get up now. Someone who says he is lazy is lazy. Explanations insufficient for the matter thereof. The Law of Supply and Demand on the Steps of the Supreme Court, the extrème heart, sauce suprème ou à la reine, and then, nothing but brown paper soup. A bit long for a title. Not a title, a poem. A bit short for a poem. Not a poem, a novel. Slightly lazy. Into the stream, but I've said that. But what does it all mean. I mean, I mean is it art. Is art? Is it black, or may it not be slightly white. Correctly. Then we may say, a convoluted syndrome, a hays-tack if you please, a small chair. Are you seated, sir? Ready for the worst in the archtypical chair. Program for a pogrom, el arte de dada, la nouvelle vague, two new novellas by the author, a new Roman come to take his place, a nouveau riche de nouveau, neugunder-bilkschrit. He is a patrician. My name is Croghan. I'll bash you one if

you read over my shoulder. Just a minute, I'm dressing. I'll be right
out. Hold it, mister, I'm taking a shit. What am I writing? Decisive
people explain. Really a conventional husband-wife-lover, one-way
triangle murdermystery. Astonishing agreement, collusion, no
doubt nepotism and sodomy. The novelty of Rome. Shall I say I deny
explanation, no, see note. Resolved that the indexing of names is a
proper function of the contemporary positive statement, morality,
book, play, nice day. The lewdness of significance peeps from the face
of a word elusively. In just a little while we should be able to see that
everyone is burrowing in for the winter. Will you wait? It will only
take a few moments. I'm ringing it now. Hold on, please hold on.
You work to maintain a reader's confidence, to provide them with the
information at every point that solves the question of the antonymn of
whom, that answers the antecedent of he said, that anticipates a
thunderous, How now! as loud as that. You inform something
incomprehensible, myself. *I traduce the informal.* It will if an artist. If
not, not. You can't name and explain as you write, but then we knew
nothing of that. As it conspires in a season of joy, all art is criticism.
All critics dispute man's claim, imitating philsophers' fashions.
Everyone burrows into a function of history. Apparent eternal
recrudescence of the nineteenth century. What we need is a little
solid vagueness amid all this frivolous plenty of a land. There has
always been a what we need—one thing, one thing, just another
more. And so things went. The dreadful snobbery of Britons treating
us as equal, had they anything to grant save laughter and the ignorance of France. There's sap yet in the old ashplant deal, yes, the one
with the inlaid edge. If you want the answer don't ask a question, but
listen. I dare to say, Listen. Listen softly. The deaf, it is true, require
us to shout, which, it is known, reduces the vocabulary in direct
proportion with the heat of battle. I say, this wind is too strong, my
breath is transported, this plum is too ripe. What keeps me awake
o'nights is the drip in the sink. If you understand, raise your hand and
go on. Otherwise all those who will be allowed a five-minute
reprieve. Tell me a story, please, please to tell. Ah, yes. What am I
writing? Get to the punch. O.K. A nation of platitudes flat as a
pancake, polemical racists desiring to eat, the smile of a fat cigar up
your little orphan Annie. You see, my innocent bystander, the controversy as to whether it is more appropriate to teach Greek or Latin
to the children of this country (what Gertrude Stein said to T.S.
Eliot) disappears when one considers that half the population of a vast

country in which everyone can read and write don't even speak good English. French is lovely, a wave solidified. German is a source of names. Italian is very much like French and excellent for feminine curses. Spanish is a lawn of sparrows hopping. I'm taking Russian. How do you say something in Russian? At night school. Daytime arc welders find books in tombs cut open by flourescent light. I shall get a better job and come to understand patronymics. I majored in television, and now look where I am. What beverage will you take with your cold roast plate, sirr. Un peau de soie garni, silverplay. Jan, we got a forner here. Are you nuts? It is nothing, a mild incipient baldness, it will pass. I am stranger to the world of Barb and Jan though there too I am at home. Call the police. Oui, la police aussi! the little boy cried as he watched the parade from upon the shoulders of his father. If you climb up here you escape the press and see everything as plain as day from night by arc light and vaporized speed. I will give you a rough translation. So and so said one thing and another to the other and then he hit him. It was hilarious, he gave it to him right in the middle of his spare beer tire paunch flab bread pillow basket waist protruding stomach line stuffing gut. He was out like a mercury switch, so they say. After laughing they all stood him a few more beers and told each other appropriately smiling stories of the days when men were men. I hadda go home early as the missus dont like me screwin around late see, so I dint catch all what was goin on but I got the general idear. They was some tough pricks, those guys. I give em all a big how's your ass now, bud, and take off to home. I walks in thinkin I won't never go with them no more and there she is all sweet with some new kind of powder from the five and dime, so much she don't even bitch me for laying my stuff all over the house. I relax and let her have a few details. She says, It's lucky I wasn't there, I woulda give em what they wanted. Not you baby. Really I would. Then she's got a story about out to the laundry. Those girls, she says, ain't it the same. It's good I got you. O, Crog. The TV is singin along the whole time acrost the room but not loud like and we pay em no mind. This here is new. They had a sale up to Grant's. So how do you get if off? Pull, silly, it's snaps. She does how I like it and we make it to the other room. No sooner am I in there right up to the hilt of the old wazoo than the phone rings. Christ was I pissed. I grab the pink wall style princess to smash it on the floor and crash! off comes half the whole fuckin plaster wall. All the time she's kicking and screamin something bloody murder if I can't finish what I started out to do she knows somebody that can. So I get mad and stick what's left of my big thumb back up in and push her off. It ud make a good book (fuckinphone). I guess the man's a genius, but what a dirty mind he has, hasn't he, she said over coffee at a not too fashionable café in the general direction of the visiting airmen. Yeah, they guffawed in their nervous croak (fuckingphone) and somebody wrote it down. Hemingway, remarks are not literature, she said to the snap of flashpowderkegs like feu d'artifice only to be recorded. We were photographing Picasso's water closet when the end came. At least we knew where we found ourselves. Sometimes I think all you did as a child was collect facts about sex, she said. Yeah, they laughed, and spent the rest of the time practicing what he'd found out. If you climb up here (something I left out). The question is, Does Ezra Pound have the right to play Mencken and Brigham Young together? He's an invalid, it's valid. No, sorry, now the point is, I'm coming to it. See, this low down gash makes it all the time around the corner, I seen her every night. So this once she comes up to me looking like she sees nothing but me where I live, y'understand, and she says, Baby, ain't I saw you before? She gets some word wrong and that's the tip. There she is real hot and it's showing like there's nothin underneath. But nothin. Yeah I seen you most ever night, I says. Well, how about it, she says gettin close in. Hey mister d'y gotta dime? I'd do it for a nickel baby, if I could and I would but I can't, not in this light and me drunk. So she starts laughing and don't leave off forever, I always hear the echo of it in my dreams. It must have been embarrassing, says this flick doctor. Embarrasin, shit! It was my first mortification. And the second is like unto it — 'the child is father of the man.'

Uncommon triviality of subject matter, lend me your ears. We here in America are beginning to feel the true effects of the debasement of the dollar. I am one of those facts, very likely you yourself can count several stupid people among those you know for the triumph of stupidity is achieved by education. Now that technical competence has succeeded in bringing to pass the democratic programs of the nineteenth century and has extended these fantasies into actuality throughout the entire world, we see with increasing clarity that all the force of twice as many well trained mentalities is being brought to bear against all that has remained unknown among men since time immemorial as the source of the necessity of will, creativity and death itself. It is a spectacle of theological proportions played in the ecumenical manner with the goal of anticipating all possibility in fact. But when each distinction has been formulated, when every variety has been classified by means of an elementary symbol, when one name has been demonstrated the equal of all names in every case, the people of the world, who will continue to live almost as if nothing had happened, will encounter from time to time a treacherous artist making his way with difficulty upon an endless monumental staircase to an indefinite point where he may be expected to turn and make a general offering of something unforseen. Though their machines may have no taste for it, people always respect a dreadful surprise. Each man who chooses such a course may be impounded, or ignored, for trespassing into heroism upon a purposefully useless memorial to progress, but such activity will never cease for by that means a man provides, as always, the material of history, he forces the attention of the future upon whatever he has made. Perhaps some of these adventurers will be stupid like everyone else, but even they will have come to know something, possibly by way of a forgotten ancestor one remembers as a noble man. These prophets, whom, in the fashion of my time, I call artists, will say just what I am saying at the moment. Their intentions will be indistinguishable from mine. They will be indistinguishable from each other and from form and content and from function but each will bear the sumptuary excess of his mind in the shape of something nameless that cannot be denied. *Who would have believed it?* I am old enough to know what a steam calliope is and I have seen one at an indoor circus. I can visualize steam locomotives drawn from life and I have seen a steam roller in operation. My great-grandfather early backed a scheme known as City Steam in which the company would pipe steam heat into any house for a fee. I am also familiar with the steam whistles which announced the work shifts in many factories and by which the people of some industrial towns are able to tell the time. I have travelled aboard steamships to cross the ocean. I am not old enough, however, to remember having met a quite ignorant person. There is no substitute for ignorance. One may be bright, clever, sharp, intelligent, cultured, smart, accomplished, competent, brilliant, virtuous, gifted, rich, famous, talented, creative, beautiful, wise, healthy, honored, strong, popular, gracious and kind, one may participate in the genius of all these words at once and still not have approached being the opposite of ignorant. For with all the antidotes to ignorance comes stupidity as if it were manna from heaven inducing a regularized idiocy of busyness among the people of the world, nevermore and neverless than ever, world without end.

At this solemn moment it would be possible for me to suppose that I have said something worth something as a matter of revelation. But I have made with myselves a yet stronger contract which implies that I shall carry on with what I am doing until an unpredictable happy accident may declare an end. In any event I shall use the next few moments to set down my will in case of death. It is a document of small importance, a matter of fiction. For when I am dead I shall actually have no further interest in anything at all forever.

To whomever may have occasion so to read, Greetings.

By taking part in the custom that the previous wishes of dead men may be executed according to the ability and willingness of one's former associates to do so, I seek to relieve you, my wife and my family and my friends, of some of the uncertainty that death occasions by giving you something specific to do. It is my first wish that no ceremonies, whether they be religious, or private, or public, or commercial or of any sort whatever should attach to the disposal of my body. My unclothed body should be incinerated by whatever public agency is empowered to carry out that process and the ashes that remain should be confounded with earth, air, and water.

I further desire that Janet Belle Craver Castle may have possession of all that is left over from my life. Although I have little interest in the disposition of such things, I hope she will keep to herself anything which might in any event be of some use to her, and I suppose further that items familiar to me should not be generally distributed among my acquaintance, except as she desires to fulfill any specific request.

In disposing of anything I may have made, such as my writings and photographs, I hope that she will be advised by my friends David White, Stanley Rosenblatt and David Lee. By asking the help of my friends, I do not wish to indicate what might happen to such of my work, but I allow them the problem of a decision. May they not attempt to divine my wish. I also do not mean to appoint these friends to certain duty. I leave this will unsigned and illegal, so that I may afford no means of compulsion beyond that of my former presence.

If there is any money in my possession when I die, I hope it will be used by Janet to have a party for as many of my family and friends as she likes. Any excessive money should be used in either a mundane or an idealistic manner according to circumstances and desires of which I know nothing.

New York, March 12, 1963.

Across the fruited and interiorized plain flew a uniformal corps of dancers to be lavished in all color and accompanied by the sound of their prancing upon a firm lawn. The grass was green. At every side sat the number of my friends and the masses of all time exchanging pleasantries and platitudes. A cigarette vendor clothed in a torn piece of linen offended my aunt by making a remark. The light was dark. The dancers swarmed from the four corners of the wind changing colors as they blew. Their heads showed bronze as they approached the death of the sun while against the darkness the royal of their plumes retained its life. Fruit depended lusciously from vines which all but concealed the temporary scaffolds where the ranks of my acquaintance languished. Mrs. Hunnicutt corrected Mrs. Hooper. The performance was interminable and the audience behaved accordingly. The flash of gold from the fingers of the players occasionally revealed a void at the periphery of their epoch at a point where just before a crowd had thrived. The ground, now recast in lavender, welled forth an extreme confabulation, some of it familiar. A gentle sea played about the realistic microphones. Color inhabited the air. The tent performed an ephermal aviary on each natural twig of which stood a bird to be admired. The men all dressed in black. My hanging cloak stood about me in waves, immobilized by my fixation or undulant against my stride. My shoes had the radiance of new tar. Across my grisly breast a silver clasp pulled taut. My hair was decorated by a special wind, I fairly danced. The women all seated and gossiping were clothed in pale sectors of the sky. A gray cabriolet embossed in gold and drawn by an immaculate beast stopped beneath a light.

¶One removes the dusty yellow paper from the carriage where it has been neglected for only a day or two. It is slightly faded as well, perhaps, seeming old. One has begun to live in a way that does not permit such transgressions. Neglected, you say, but for what, in favor of whom? One has yet to retell a springtime story that is already unsatisfactory and that in the midst of yet another spring with its distractions so similar to those before. Simple tedium is no longer to the point. I have in mind the provision of carpets. I have given over all such concerns to my wife who is glad to have something else to do. She looks very well in her black linen dress, the one that was formerly pink. One hears again from friends at some remove and one remembers friends who, it may be, no longer live. The fiction of a trip is no longer sufficient. Gone already are the days when anything at all would do. One wakes from the most beautiful dream of the century towards the excitement of the next encounter in the evening, just before falling to dream again. The type of attendance is different than it was. One reads contemporary French. One is content to make remarks of no consequence to anyone at all, and in the same way to get the attention of the company only to give it up, to let it wander in the woods. An old man is pleased that I should tell him that and I thank him for the present of his attention in my matter. By someone else I am assured that lower wisdom teeth are something difficult to remove. But as it happens I have never had them in my mouth. I have something to say about the nineteenth century. Then I remark the manner of a girl. I do my stuff.

¶In an avenue supported by trees from which a dusty light descended, the members of the audience as they left passed refreshed troupes moving toward the entertainment. Some among the continuous droves would recognize a friend. Outside the air was dry. Automobiles stood in the sun like lakes. Someone I had just met was gone to find someone I had heard of. A star shot across the sun. A fish swam out of sight. My words moved across the bottom of the picture at the exact speed of my design cased in handy decorations. For ten years balloons were set upon the head of every member who re-entered the arena so that at a signal described by my glove, universal stars could be focused upon the multitude gathered in a perfect blackness to make an array of every brilliant color so intense that light became imperceptible. Under the artificial surprise of having blossomed, the women forgot their next successes and stood desirably among the men who ceased to dream when they perceived that black dress had assumed the color of the moon upon which all animate attention pressed at once so that each believed himself the center. In the light of the world each realized his distinction from the others. In the silence which fell after the vacation of the women there lasted a moment of repose when every man came to know the utterly human universe where he would be pleased to stand forever as if by the unreal clarity of the early light of dawn. One by one the careful light seared each balloon so that they fell like popcorn in an erratic dispersal of the precious atmosphere in which *the admiration* had found its matrix. A changed throng awaited events.

This is a time of hopeless remembrance

¶Desperate Nostalgia should be cast in yellow and if it happens that there is anyone who can fill the space it should be ideally patterned. There are those who complete desperation by an extended additional harrassment of the audience. In this success they seek to found a classical irony based in a standard formula of dislocation and exaggeration. Their jokes are gravid with the significance of commentary and allusions to the future so that a laugh may be quickly replaced by the dignifying remarks of history. Jasper Johns, in failing the completion of his friends and passing across the strand of his fashion toward a certain type of memory, makes paintings which can interest those who dissociate themselves from his stylistic tribe. By such an attribute may one derive the promise of value for the dead. I wish to ignore the intentions of my friends and their friends in turn, of whom I have encountered a few that I would mention, to clarify with innocent will the moment of a phrase. One can see among Steve Vasey's brightly painted crudities in tar a field of daisies that exists for me, a pleasure in my eye, a smile the leads me nowhere else. George Deem in his painting and James Waring in his dances, can balance the concerns that try us without falling into categories. Mr. Waring fills the space with momentary banalities always nicely executed by a few excellent performers. He includes all the best movements of the mind often brilliantly disguised in many colors. He associates with George Brecht who, like Gideon and Ozenfant but purposelessly, accumulates oddities of the near past to reconstruct a time that never was but is. Mr. Deem's paintings allude repetitively to classifications of beauty but they are hardly a collelction of the past. In his examination of memory he may sometimes fill the space with the patterns of writing or the many faces of a friend but he actually says nothing. All the writers are enmired in the implications of literary realism which induces an embarrassing inauthentic californiaful of the a-historical remarks of children which may be let politely into the bin of nouveau romanticisme and there forgot. At Judson Church, the director Larry Kornfeld and the pianist Al Carmines contrive from the emanations of such poets as they chance to find, a series of noise and motion representing types and sounds of former value. They use poetry that has at least some worth to the disenchanted eye, of which the type is Gertrude Stein's, to make an intimate spectacle that recalls the most dramatic revery. The musicians in attempting to sunder a classical scale that may endure all they can cast against it, continue for the most part in an experimental mode that formerly established a transitory art excluding allusions in favor of a program calling attention to informality. But occasionally, as when one unexpectedly discovers a true written word, one finds amid the noise an indication that should they realize the necessity of form, the experimenters too would collate what remains. Yvonne Rainer's attitude strikes oppositely enough to lend this application her slogan against regret. In her performance pieces based in dance she traduces the informal by way of a singular style of movement illuminated by her voice. As in Vasey and Kornfield-Carmines, Ms. Rainer laughs and that best response is her only gain. She may be thought to join the movement at the dangerous point of poetry and laughter. Her writing often parodies the realistic. She is apt to run. She may improvise an elaborate play which she willingly discards without yielding to the clear eclectic games into which a similar mode has led some of her friends. David Lee's painting obscures the space in an intensity of color that logically excludes all but the shadow of a doubt becoming clear in yellows tinged with white and the disappearance of green. Like Ms. Rainer, he ignores the desirable pattern in favor of the least remaining certain shape which he reverses at will, however slightly. Like Mr. Waring's, his changes are precise. But he presents his arbitrary interest without realizing an allusion. For him the only nostalgia is the reason of honesty, the only desperation a perfect tenacity still relieved by the smile in which he adds a title such as For the Yellow Bedroom. Rather than hoard incomprehension against the future, we spend our memories.

¶While all this was going on I stood aside although I knew that my cloak was equally enhanced. My acquaintance returned with the opinion that I had made an indefinite mistake. I behaved in every way like one about to leap into power yet I made no move. As the attendance increased I busied myself with trivial affairs. I affected a carefully trimmed beard and changed my hat. I examined the closets beneath the privileged seat finding them to be in perfect working order. During *the admiration* a few long moments stopped where I was suffered the rare quality of introspection afforded by an interval in time. All that I had ever done formed an extended list at my right hand while upon my left palm weighed the sum of my thoughts in the form of a convoluted seashell both translucent and chimerical. I made an effortless comparison between the type toward which I had been reared and the way I might yet make. I dismembered what I imagined to be real causing the element of my world to show itself forth in range upon range of endless subtle differentiation on one generic form so profusely that I lost interest in the subject. I felt the grandeur of ultimate potential, a perfect joy that remained all undiminished for its limits where it exended from a figment to the far reaches of my imagination where it flourished. I knew a single excellence implying every possibility. As time presumed my seminal exercise, I remembered every thing that would be mine. Waves of cool light cast their shadows rhythmically across my youthful brow. I felt free as a man after absolute confession. Yet clearer were the saddening obligations I would voluntarily assume. I alighted from the cab to view a double line of uniform cavalry standing in endless impassivity, the horses brown, the men in heavy olive twill embroidered in blue silk.

That year winter seemed to vanish into summer making spring as artificial as the calendar. One day we were in the weakening grasp of February which was in fact long past and then the next day one could have believed that it was July. I had been looking toward the spring for some certain renewal which I had by that time come to expect of that time of year. Occasionally during the translation from winter to summer I would imagine that the dew lasted on the crocus, but it was a mirage. No sooner had forsythia been forced to early bloom than the weather became appropriate for sweet peas. The crab apple did not bloom that year and peaches were ripening in April. It seemed to be a change of climate. Women were heard to complain that they had no proper clothes and provincial newspapers occupied their readers with a supply of information, some of it historical, about natural phenomena throughout the world. The President of the United States became familiar with the jargon of meteorology which he practiced using with the aid of television every night at eleven o'clock. The Queen of England issued a reassurance to the survivors of a most difficult winter which included an indication that in due course Her Majesty's vermillion mailcars would all be repainted green. Son Excellence, Le Président de la République Française remarquait le temps et, avec une ironie pointue, annonçait que Washington était devenu la réplique de Paris. There was no question of spring cleaning for the winter doldrums lengthened directly into summer love. One night, leaves appeared full-blown to stuff the treetops. Everyone wanted to know what was going on but nobody had the answer.

At that time we lived as we had done for some time in a house that was rather old. In consequence of the lapse of an insignificant habit the house burned to the ground. As we left we chose to bring with us a silver plate which had survived an auction of my grandmother's property when she reduced her standard of living. My sister contracted a noble marriage with a scion of the Harkness family who was at that time studying to become a psychologist. Through her we happened to meet the old man in whom we cultivated his interest in birds. It was surprising. I had never seen birds before and although I was already becoming colorblind, I affected an indefatigable inclination to search out every identifiable North American species, which gave me plenty to do. In no time at all the situation was reversed. By virtue of my zeal we were graced with the rights to ten houses, all of them beautifully situated homes nearby to different lakes with beach privileges at all but one where we were compensated with free access to a large aviary where I would spend much of my time. I have never liked swimming, but in gratitude I took up skin diving for pleasure. Among other things we were given a waterproof gun as soon as my new pastime became generally known. With it I shot a large number of fish of different kinds as the waters had been plentifully stocked beforehand. But I had no patience for this sort of work even after I had proved my ability in the case of birds.

It was during that strange time too that all of the measures of man throughout the world became regularized in a single complicated system which included provision for the inexorable conversion of every valuable quantity into ciphers of uniform value, the system being based on a universal theory of infinite possibilities. In this new language, poets found to their delight that things which had formerly been regarded as eternally disparate, such as apples and oranges, could now be equalized in an elementary manner and that things which had never been thought of before formed the material for commentary that was everywhere comprehensible by machines as well as by people regardless of what language their mothers had taught them. Thus it was that the age of equilibration achieved its classic mode. At the outset, of course, there was a certain predictable idiosyncratic distress raised against the successes of this newly-formulated universe which comprehended on a world-wide scale all history, actuality and possibility. The very birds, the gulls of the seashore and the pigeons of the city who had always been regarded as the paragon of freedom, flew into the sun to roast there in peace. The canon of the international style in art gave way in desperate agreement with the ultimate elaboration of its tenets. A demand for fish as food fell off, as had threatened long before, but aside from that, people continued to live and die every day just as if nothing had happened. Gradually, and I mean to indicate that it took a certain amount of time, people began to believe that the climate in which they lived had altered itself perceptibly in a change with more effects than the disappearance of the spring. Although they continued to speak of the moon it was no more to be seen so that vast research was required to determine its color and an historical disagreement on that point became real. As a memorial act, the city of Paris was rebuilt in concrete cast of a color very like blue. The city of New York declared an emergency which resulted in the fact that by the end of summer there was nothing in existence that had been in use for more than thirty years, and by the end of winter the fact was codified to be eternal as an institution. The three rivers were continuously choked with jams of jetsam from the destruction of the city and flotsam too ample to wash upon the limited beaches contributed to an apparent increase in the sea. Due to a forseeable breakdown in general public transportation, people walked the streets for lack of something else to do. They jostled each other in a brotherly fashion and even strangers began to laugh at each other. When a general amnesty for pickpockets was justified by a clear opposition to penury, another new middle class arose. Now and then a cloud would pass over the valley of the dead but in my new-found innocence I never noticed. People said I had talent but it was only modesty. Actually I had a large stack of special yellow paper which I had hoarded from such a time as that before the war. With sporadic devotion I resolved myself upon the ledger that I fancied my paper might yet provide. It was a model wife in every way. There was an attachment which could accomplish things in which I no longer took interest if only I was still aware of their necessity. It happened that my bidding was sufficient. With some luck and at considerable expense I achieved the point of my retirement just as I completed apprehension of what I came to call the hawk-shark fantasy. So I too left nothing, which was not surprising. When the newspapers returned to work after a protracted strike, there was nothing more to say.

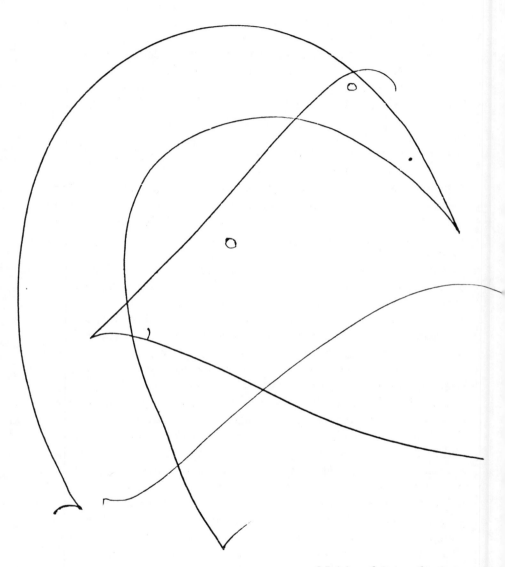

Neither fish nor fowl.

June 11. 64.

It is 'about' a gradual neglect of writing and the imposition of other desires and necessities at a time when I still included everything that I thought to write. I have arranged that this summer nothing will obsruct my desire to finish the story. I have been doing very little writing for the past few months. But the time came when I found it impossible to go on with a new version of what I had compiled a year before. Among other things that I have omitted, there is a record of my last childish experience of poor judgement, the fact of which I realized some months later when it appeared to me that the fellow I befriended was unbearably stupid. Actually I had two such disenchantments almost at the same time. Much of my first book was, of course, composed of the record of childish pastimes which, however, do not embarrass me for the book was about me at that time. But what about last year? Can I close it off by omission based in the assumption of some final childish experience? Could the cause of having promised to finish writing the book lead me to carry on with writing that is worth no one's attention? I doubt that I would let you read it now as it was in the first version, but as yet I have only 120 pages of the second. Charles suggested generously that I simply eliminate the entire first half of the book. I hardly considered that I would do that but I appreciated his remark. In the pages before me there were two major themes, that of lectures and that of making friends. I am attached to the subjects but I dislike their form. The only thing to do is to throw it out. Throwing it out may imply a third version to be written after I understand what I have made of this new section which I will begin to write, which I have, perhaps, already begun writing here. It was the play of a child, an attempt at the apple tree which while I achieved the safer boughs exhilarated in my success seems ludicrous to me now that I know how to climb a tree. Latterly I give myself to consider if there might not be a reclassification of trees on a different basis than what the old artificer gave me to understand.

When I think of understanding (he had written to her in a letter long ago) I like to think of a bridge understood by pillars that carry its weight. The pillars and the span of the bridge are both essential to the fact of the bridge. In an understanding that may take place between two people, each is at the same time both the pillar and the span, both constitute the bridge. Both form at the same time both the pillar and the span without losing their distinctness, without becoming identical. The over and under parts make a real nameable thing, bridge. Nor is an understanding of each other by two people more like to one part of an analogy than to another. Both constitute the bridge quite indistinguishably to provide a structure for communication, the occasion for a bit of poetry. And hear also what Saint Paul saith.

Electricity is not magic. It can be perfectly controlled and described by means of the strictest conventions which are completely knowable and invariable. But among everything inhuman it is most wonderful for producing of itself things which are not electricity and not like electricity, the lightning and thunder and fire and shock that have always been remarked by us, and then, our useful light and sound and heat and power that are unrelated to the conventions by which they are electrically obtained.

I might suggest other analogues, but there is no doubt that I cannot consider the problems of communication as the problems of communication, for to do so is to obscure the possibilities that run beneath the formula, or feed it, as the harbor at New Orleans offers no description of head waters in Montana.

Nor is the river much more good than the tree. For as a result of my experience I found a tear welling in my eye, and I have so much more to do. It is not a matter of distance, nor of modesty. It is hardly a question of courage and not even a subject of fashion. Resolutely I break the mask while others, for more praise, expel their doubts and overlay their errors, finely wrought.

But the information I am omitting at length also contains much that pertains to the course of this book and of my life at that time. Elsewhere I have noted that I have made some omissions for other reasons than that I did not wish the information contained in the omission known. In the sections I am at the moment missing out there was an unsuccesful happy ending, an answer not all clearly defined but still the answer for which one waited. Perhaps I undertook that friendship as a literary experiment. I know that my error discomfited me for some time during which I would always lecture rather than converse. I grew up. The classic formula for a novel. I realized a change. By the end I had achieved the disenchanted eye. The process of experiment held no longer any wonder for him, and by the end I think he had prepared himself to write a book. I had, he said, then no idea that the experiment had become a formula I could gratify and from the end, I took no more interest in it. But I do not know how to write a book any more than I know how to climb a tree. As we say, A dog barked (in the distance), and, not having heard a dog, we would mean to say that night had fallen. At the end, as it happened, I had said, A television camera has an uncomprehending and ravenous stare which could perhaps be compared to that of a wolf if there were anyone left who had ever seen a wolf, or a raven.

As you will see, after a time I went on from there to what remained of the year or so while I continued my writing. At that time I had a job which, although it was less interesting to me than my writing, took up most of my time. I had not yet the assurance that I could set forth at any time, *provided with keys, money, information and rhetoric* to amuse myself as I pleased. The life of the office occupied me more and more although I maintained, almost to myself, the fiction that I would write in my spare time as was customary for those in my circumstances. I admitted, however, that I wrote very little and that I didn't like what I wrote. Among other things, I became friendly with a pleasant woman who worked in the same office. She led me to imagine, as I was in one respect predisposed to do, that I might obtain a bureaucratic position which would afford me the opportunity of buying time in which to continue my writing or my travels at some later date. Therefore I spent some time and much imagination in such pursuits. But in addition, I met her son who was a few years younger than I. We became friends rather quickly for we shared a ready distaste for almost anyone we met or fancied we might meet. We took to entertaining each other from time to time but we said almost nothing that wasn't simply amusing. I gathered that he could not take my bureaucratic ambition seriously—after all, it did make a rather good joke—and so we passed the time. Although we never mentioned it, each of us knew that both of us would be writers and that silence was a bond while any violation of the omission would have introduced us to the mistrust which writers save for other writers. He had resigned his course in college and meant to travel for a year. I was glad to have someone with whom to laugh. It was becoming apparent to me that though I did not think of it in any such way, my life was boring, and just at the point when the life of the office would have consumed my private life, I ceased my applications there and undertook to spend my time in writing rather than in wishing to write or in hoping for the day when I might afford the time for it. I resigned my job on Labor Day and I was able, by coincidence, to assume another job in the same office which took up only Monday and Thursday. Several weeks later my friend embarked for Poland and my friend, his mother, resigned her job as well, so that in the course of a few months, I had changed my circumstance appreciably. I no longer thought anything of what presumably went on at the office and when I went there, I engrossed myself in habitual daydreams as I went about my automatic work. From time to time the bosses would inquire politely about the progress of my book.

For at the same time, I let it become known more widely than among my closest friends that I had undertaken to write a book. Even though I no longer liked what I was then writing, I knew that I would be able to write a book since I had already made an accumulaton which at one time pleased me and which was itself at the length of a short book. By now, indeed, I have been writing this book for so long—a longer time than I have spent at anything so definite as a book—that my acquaintances have acquiesced in my pretensions by coming to regard me as a literary figure of some potential, a man to be propitiated just in case. He said that such a fiction as trade secrets is requisite for every profession. If all writers usually spoke only of themselves, readers would find out that those in whom they placed a momentary trust were not different from themselves. Artists, among whom may always be counted a few who write, are however actually different from those who maintain professions in that artists care for nothing so much as themselves, no matter in what metaphor they may express their self-concern. Nor do they care much for other artists or others of any sort save those they happen to like, although there are any number of artists who are pleasant and even sometimes sociable. He said that whereas everyone's thought and action was always informed by opinion and conducted in imitation, an artist had, in addition, a certain stake of knowledge. It may not be anything that he knows *about,* but it is always something that he *knows* because it is entirely of himself. Despite anything he may say, people will believe that the source of an artist's distinction lies in a magical unknown that cannot be measured and authorized until tomorrow. *In the most unmagical age yet endured, superstitions seen under the form of the individual talent bear witness to popular ignorance of artistic impulse.* Thus it is necessarily forgotten that the talent for being a man is generic. But from the point of view of an artist at this time, which is by no means a bad time for artists, what must be called one's talent results from the convenience of volition and circumstance. An absurd will informs the historical chances of one's life to define something else, a work of art, that is unlike its sources. Some, being polemical, would say that that was always true, but there is no form of words that was always true. There is only something of eternal value which must, on occasion, be reformulated. One does not forswear what is not chosen. On the contrary, one indulges one's fancy.

For it is a fact that ought to be well known that a great memory is the mark of an intelligent man. The commons will, to their satisfaction, observe that he cannot keep in mind the time of day or where a pencil lies by his foot so that he is able, as is required, to associate himself with the general fallibility of memory. It illuminates this subject to know that any stupid cat has no effective memory whatever. It may investigate one dusty corner a hundred times and still find it new on the next occasion, perhaps not five minutes from the last. Similarly with people, who are however able to remember much. If you spend any length of time with one person of an ordinary sort, and yourself an extraordinary person, you will find that after quite a short time they will have exhausted the arrangements of words which they remember and begin, soon enough, to make again every remark they have ever uttered on any subject, over and over, not supposing that you could remember the last occasion as they themselves do not though the words may, after a long life, come to be familiar, as a small house is to an old cat. You will notice, for example, that people of great memory sometimes sit with each other in silence, a condition that does not distress them as it does the ordinary who must needs fill every hush with at least a whisper or a cough. It is during such silences that intelligent people omit to remark whatever is understood between them, as words elided in grammar are understood, or assumed to be present. But although he is not easily bored, it may amuse an intelligent man to speak constantly on every imaginable subject, never quite repeating himself and never exhausting his memory but rather renewing his store of remarks by continuous innovation. Or one may, if so choose, remain completely silent which comes to the same thing. For while he is being either voluble or quiet, an intelligent man also listens. If you happen to say anything, he will remember it. After twenty years, for example, he may remember the name of your cat which you had forgotten until it is recalled to you, the cat having died soon after he once heard you mention its name. At his most annoying, when he is seeking an occasion to entertain himself, having overheard one word of your petty conversation, he will forthwith begin a monologue which quickly confounds everything you might ever think about that subject, if it does not make you so angry that you forget everything you know. But if you have anything to say, an intelligent man will be able to get it out of you. When an extraordinary person is face to face with someone else with whom he decides to speak, he knows that what the other has to say, aside from a dreary recitation of opinion, probably concerns his life's work. Our hero is able, politely if he is willing to spend the time, to derive from you information you very likely did not know you knew about yourself, even using a scheme that you know better than he does, that of your daily occupation. He will generally find himself dissatisfied with the form of whatever you at first volunteer about your work, and if you do not listen to his questions, his interest may depart. Everyone knows best what they always do, but rarely can they tell you what it is and how they go about it. So that after one has supplied a name to the scheme by saying, I am a poet, or whatever, an intelligent man will continue asking questions, if necessary down to, What did you do yesterday? until he knows the full detail. But unless he wishes to amuse himself by being rude, he will omit to inquire *why* you do what you do. For he already knows why you do what you do, and he knows that you do not know why, and further, that you wish not to know why you do whatever you do. An intelligent man who has met two sailors may write a great book about the sea while never leaving his native inland plateau, not that he would actually write the book, but he could, believe me.

So that in case you have forgotten, I say that our hero both listens and remembers, and that he does so selectively. He continuously chooses, what to say, what to do, what to dream, what to think, what to hear, what to remember, what to write, what to wish, what to omit, what to read. For example, I wish not to bore you just now with a long derivation, a complicated drainage system such as the Mississippi River, which might be invented to describe exactly how someone makes such choices, and what limitations there are, and what factor of chance, up to the point at which the process remains unknowable, where the river is confounded in the sea. But as in the Mississippi system, what passes is not arbitrary nor 'unconscious.' Slowly everything changes. In an immense drainage there are various floods, deposits of silt, pollutions and other effects in continuous and intelligible series. In an intelligent system of mentality there is an equivalent series, a series of choices. The precise being of the series is described by what is evidently chosen, following upon other choices which may be assumed if they cannot be defined. The process is actual only to the man of whom it is a function and it may be more or less clear to him. It is this process that I choose to call one's point of view. Every point of the process is informed by a choice which is interesting. The location of his pencil when he is not using it is a matter of no interest, so he forgets. So, very easily, may he lose you if you engage in conversation with him. The schedule of his interests is the scheme of his point of view. He may not even be able to remember your name. His 'talent' lies in the direction of anticipation. His volition associates with his interests. He is very much like everyone else, but his choices are surer for he knows what he is about. He is least responsible to whim and necessity and he is always in danger of logical rigor, so that a laugh. . . .

Philosophy is equally endless. A philosophy of art is either criticism or an historical recital of phenomena. A philosophic art is French. Everything logical has its own conclusion that is liable to be missed. Phenomena are points of generic conclusion. Historical phenomena are logical end points from which the process of achievement is forgotten. A story is an artificial process. A genre is a series of coincidence. A French accident may be foretold. The conclusion of an event establishes a formal series. An experiment may or may not destroy a rule. The game is easily defined. A child may not be trusted to tell the truth. Any trust is a series of allusions. Love is an artificial series of trust. A secret cannot be told, but it may be known and it may be destroyed. All that may be known is known. Belief is the maintenance of apprehension. An artificial series may be known and it may be destroyed. An actual series may or may not be known, but it cannot be destroyed. An artificial series can be told. An actual series may be told. An artificial and an actual series may be confounded. Belief is always artificial. Necessity is logically actual but it may be extended into artificiality by way of belief. A recitation is logical, except for the mistake. A translation is actual, except for the necessary omission. A series proceeds. A progressive series succeeds. A moral series needs an artificial resolution. A story is successful. In the nineteenth century, the story of actuality became classified as History, succeeding Divinity as queen of the sciences. At the same time there was developed a classical artifical story now known, somewhat redundantly, as the romantic novel which came to take the place of epic verse in literary exaltation. The historial resolution of fact and fancy was achieved in the analytical mode by the classification of human psychology, previously the domain of poets and philosophers, or of God and of the gods. Indeed all knowledge came under the form of history. This triumph had the effect of causing artists to invent an experimental mode which would pass beyond history into the unknown still implied in the phrase, World without end, into an unscientific exploration of the Holy Ghost, into factual incoherence. But with characteristic efficiency, History quickly encompassed this kind of exploration as unconfirmed revelation of her third and dearest part, the future. The novel became a scientific fiction, more actual than the reality which history described. Artists were cast as prophets who would anticipate a disastrous end to the sequence of events. Amid all this literary realism, the amount of information increased at a greater rate than the number of people in the civilized world. But I was not too interested in all that. Having eaten as much as I honestly could, I was in the position of having nothing else to do, having postponed something I had thought I might do, I saw that what lay before me had to be where it was, having passed so much time on parole I knew the ins and outs, and having as I did as much time as I wanted, I slept very little. As the money entered my right tight pocket I could feel the pressure of it against my thigh bone and as the size of the money increased, I arranged it to be more convenient. As the course of a day's chances narrowed I adopted a mode of acceptance that made anything as welcome as any other. Far from the lecture, I remained polite, knowing as I did that they knew no better. A minute seemed to be a long time. As my hands and feet played the automatic machine, I conjured the theme of the lecture, and for the first time in a long time, I smiled. It was a good joke, it would have been a good one, and as anyone may know, the better the joke the less popular it is. I soon forgot all about it and though I knew at every moment exactly what I did then, I passed the time as quickly as I had ever done. I would sing my own songs, not poems but songs, with once in a while a little obsessive intervention of something I had heard elsewhere. I rode the night looking for horses, and looking at them when I saw them and then, as I was remembered the sequence of a harness I would pass into a mode that excluded horses until such time as I came upon another horse. It is a sea of machinery, I corrected her politely in exchange for a little automatic laugh.

MUST I CONDUCT AN INTROSPECTION
JUST BECAUSE THE LANGUAGE IS CONDUCIVE TO IT?

In the meantime, much had happened of which I was on the whole unaware. I was told by someone I had not seen in some time that someone I had seen more recently was about to be married. A friend gave me some vines which would in time make a pleasant decoration. I wrote to my father concerning a family matter. I also forgot what I had been talking about. As soon as I no longer went to the office every day I was certain that I should never again have a job that required me to do so. I had ceased my application for a bureaucratic sinecure without knowing whether I should have failed or succeeded at it. All the while, I continued the revision, as I thought, of my first book without recourse to the text. I wrote whatever I wrote from time to time whenever I had nothing else to do. In my spare moments, I sometimes wondered whether I might not be doing nothing at all. Often, in fact, I did nothing at all. Later on it will become apparent that this period in my life was characterized by a realistic indeterminacy as to what I was doing. I had had enough of doing nothing at all, but I was unwilling to force conclusions preferring for the time being to let things pass.

—A project in anticipation, an admirable idea, monsieur, but how can one approach it? I began by admiring some of the people who formed this group which at that time was not well formed. I came to be a slightly recognized figure on the periphery. I was at least a familiar sight. I became known only to a few, and then rather vaguely. But I suppose I was occasionally the subject of inquiries. No doubt the information that satisfied a question or two was quickly lost. I chose to differentiate myself almost imperceptibly by not cultivating the others. Though I was tired of listening, I went on listening. My action required no courage and not even patience but only timidity, in which I was practiced. I was introduced by my friend who was not so timid as he was easily bored. His wife had pursued her profession for a time in which some of those I came to admire were her teachers. Timidity presumes that those one would approach know everything already. Generosity, on the other hand, but why digress. I was doing almost nothing. Still, I came to be a slightly known figure on the periphery, almost always in the company of my great friend who was sometimes also with his wife.

—I admit a fascination for the disintegration of language, but in what form could one possibly express such thoughts? There was one artist, a writer of the early modern generation, for whose work, among other things, I had conceived a great enthusiasm. I began by reading her out loud on every occasion, however unsuitable. Once only one person remained awake, but I continued reading with the greatest difficulty, as I was drunk. In various ways, I found that the people I admired also admired this work. I began to write a little criticism, partly to reassure myself. Frankly, I thought I might make a little money at it. I returned refreshed to my book. (I must have made a mistake somewhere.)

—That is all very well and good, but I am unsure as to where you say you began. I began by writing a little criticism, partly for the purpose of assuring myself that, as I had already asserted, criticism would have no integral importance and partly to tell one of my friends what I thought of his novel which was about to be published. I wrote letters to one or two editors who I thought might publish a little criticism, and I met them in their offices, and having received very cordial notes of rejection, I returned refreshed to my book. One bit of criticism was not intended for publication, but my friends caused it to be circulated among some people who associated themselves with this art movement I have mentioned. It happened that this piece of writing, a series of reflections on an unsuccessful but interesting experiment, came to be useful in giving me some identity. They did not entirely understand what I had to say, but they appreciated my remarks. It was all so informal that although I made the acquaintance of a few, including the most admired among them who were excellent, I didn't become part of the group. The experiment had been formative in so far as the movement had any existence as a group at all. We did not know that we were becoming famous.

—Regret garrottes the imagination. The actual division came about when it became obvious that the movement had more than one center. That is to say that a division took place when the various centers of rhetoric could no longer be associated under one name. Then you had the emergence of dramatic literature at one point, and then too, a less articulate center where there was an interest in the possibilities of less meaning and more form. The experiment had vivified a general division among the members between those who preferred informal modes and those who preferred formal modes though they never thought of what they thought in my terms. With more than one center of action among all these artists and performers and their friends, the best that could be said was that a meeting of intentions had proved undesirable, while in a natural diversity there came to be a richness which had not been apparent when the movement had seemed to be more unified. Yet it was not a typical choosing up as the necessary conclusion of a divisive event, nor was it the simple dispersion of people whose interests do not hang together.

—One would assume that the question of the integrity of language held more interest than that. I had only to stop and select a new sentence. There was the limitation that I had decided to make no mistakes. I composed slowly, setting each word clearly before impressing it on the paper. Neither my friend nor I associated ourselves with any of the centers of the movement, though it is true that our sympathies were with the purists as one might call them. The more slowly I moved the more exhausting became the movement. Each phrase cost me a night's rest. Far from being hard work, it was superbly rigorous. I completely retained as many conventions as I remembered. I desired to ignore the original work and see the figures at their liveliest. But there was . . .

—But could there be a single formula, even if you decided at some point that you had found one? It was marvelous, the type of a quandary. And remember that at least in this respect I was still utterly observant. The play had been composed fifty years previous to its production. People could surprise themselves by finding something long obscured by its strangeness to be simply lovely. But for me, it informed an elementary concern with names so that I was able within a period of two or three months after I had seen the play several times to assemble my second book, which before I had been in some doubt of ever doing. And having seen a reproduction of the play some months after I had first seen it, it seemed to me that it must have been most illuminating of small numbers, in which I have since interested myself.

—When was that? I wish not to make an action that will abuse your credulity. But it must be lighter than it was. At every separation there is an obstacle. The composition of a question imports a certain haste. We have yet to speak of all kinds of food by name. And everything else. And end. Or a raven. Until he dies. Another is forgotten. In lightening, for example, one may imply the joke and then compound it by forgetting the allusion. Let us take the song for a mode. C'EST UN JEAN QUI EST RICHE, ET JEUNE, ET JAUNE. The translation is not perfect. But the song is not complete. A little imperfection found by measurement may still satisfy the eye.

—And is the lie then disappeared? Whereas in my first book I had experimented with the processes of fiction in its various modes, I was afforded the opportunity as a result of what I thought after I saw this play of which I have been speaking to quite ignore the historical moods against which I chafed so as to approach both poetry and philosophy from the inside without the necessity of making further attempts, and I did so by beginning at the point of performance.

—Where, oh where, is my wandering boy tonight? Where, oh where, but in America. A figure, only, played upon the words. No mistake and a bright page in silence. An equal portion that may be weighed and exchanged, or numbered. I quite properly thought of my second book as a revision of my first. My eye fell upon one sentence after another. The process was repeated endlessly with endless variation. It came to be remarkably slower.

The cake rests. The hat rises at will. A photograph may not produce an adequate reminder. A partial exchange is not equal to an additional memory. Nor does the cast of any shade find equilibrium among a humorous series. The obstacle is interrogatory. When a taste is slightly bitter, lightly practiced and much worse, it may occasion more urgency. A cut implies a knife as does a slice. But an accomplished cut is a missing slice. If the sight of a doorway is more useful that a certain amount, there remains the safety of a real reason. Without four, not a blessing. Five flowers and a whole field. Six lectures and whatever follows. No division of eight allowed. What occasion is the slight separation of a final hue. If a perfect excellence may show a further sadness the actual correspondence is more clearly logical. A chance occasion that loudly, a window substituted in the same manner. All this and more. But no laughter. Four frames or no drawn exchange. Five flames with willing exceptions. Six series complete. Eight takes the pain of blessing more seriously. A singular style makes a parenthetical noise. A waterwheel that quickly, a notion that fleetingly. A final intentional representation that results in something abominable is not the only antilope, there are even more.

When, within a special case, there was, on a certain day, something of some kind that could be treated and exposed, if one would, in a manner appropriate to it and to oneself, there might also be, at the same time, another circumstance which, if one allowed it, might alter the matter. A certain absence, for example, might, if one chose it, provide an explanation of what was, otherwise, obscure. The same fact, properly treated and exposed, might have caused something said to be entirely different. Not only that, but ignorance of such effect might result in yet a third or fifth in a series of misunderstanding. There is, furthermore, a number of possibilities in which may be founded another momentary resolution. For the truth is that if one is to go on speaking continuously, and there is every likelihood that one will choose to do so, then one must, so to speak, carry every moment of a process toward a satisfactory point where it may as well be forgotten, so much is there to do. And such is the figure of the poem.

For, among other things, there is no necessity in it and also not any preparation.

With a fullness, and there is a given fullness whether as it happens it is demanded or intractable or clearly displayed, one is taught to seek a source of satisfaction and having found it, find it. Founded in the natural center of an artificial circle, a silver point, it grows to the continuous search with diversions, vacations and humorous variations until whenever it can never be denied. Rising then at any time like an interesting circumstance, it rises, and having risen, occasions. The switch pushed to and returned remains a time alight. The light ever more strongly denudes itself of soft pretenses. Logically erected to a natural conclusion that is perfectly quick and slow, one masters an organic pulse that demands response, *the choice made in anticipation.* Extremities defile. The choice acts. Plenitude becomes responsible. Buried variously to an ultimate depth or photographed, the bloody light early blooms to destroy the meaning of effusion. Profusion of celebrious images serve their servant to conclude not the next but the first moment in prediction. Softly then a dream releases every preparation that will be made again once more, now, newly raised to the exercise that fully answers all necessity, and never stops but lingers.

And aside from a certain duration, what else. Useful images of the soft and the slim formulate a design, the occasional enterprise and the slow additional metaphor. Very easily then when the bloom desires expression and truly variously it blooms and having bloomed, reformulates. Disport and desperately one nearly hopes to play a private game once dreamt by every man as woman. Tasteless desires remain more desirable and, partaking, one dreams and dreaming, one knows. Omniscient potenate, bottled, sold, used and recovered, save of your momentary impulse a permanent standard of fire. Old artificer, seized, maintained, expressed and recovered, stand again amid fullness to press continuous interests home. Little fruit, pendulant, shrinking, abusive and recovered, find moment upon a page of appropriated color. *For unless the grain die . . .*

I am torn by a conflict between the rules of morality and the rules of sincerity.

Morality consists in substituting for the natural creature (the old Adam) a fiction that you prefer. But then you are no longer sincere. The old Adam is the sincere man.

This occurs to me: the old Adam is the poet. The new man,

whom you prefer, is the artist. The artist must take the place of
the poet. From the struggle between the two is born the work of
art.

Nevertheless, I said to myself, I shall press on in a satisfactory
manner. If one finds the intention killing oneself boring, still it
remains that suicide is actually dangerous. Any prayer would be a
new enough form, any form a good enough joke. Any situation could
be so placed as to set itself upon a point without mistakes. Many
distinctions might separate the colors that were so nearly perfect and
squares involving a technical compliment might trick the eye. Thus
encircled by illustrious dice, a mental image could instruct what was
apparently inscrutable to reform the quick from the dead. Circumstances becoming means, any form or any prayer would be convenient. From the first experiment to the next expression unto its third
regeneration, final chances would surround the choice. Poetical lists
might be improved, incongruous though the proofs appeared.
Things placed upon each other could come together neither willingly
nor without cause. It could ocasion a chance, or a laugh. It could be
called 'numerical series' and take place with volition. Inherent differences might join imperatives. Desires might equalize necessities and
dismiss them. Omissions might contain desires and even something
of interest, a mistake, that did not partake of the current game. Then
would the rules be altered by inclusion so that the measure of the
standard runs congruent to its illustration. Would that so simple a
process were successful! Everything would clarify upon a single point
that might be chosen and could be seen. However, I contented myself
with the conventions of my little life.

All alone with the best reception, all alone with more than the
best reception, all alone with a paragraph and something that is
worth something, worth almost anything, worth the best example there is of a little occasional archbishop. This which is so
clean is precious little when there is no bath water. A long time
a very long time there is no use in an obstacle that is original and
has a source.

And having seen the play once again, it occured to me that in
addition to its information of names in a manner of which I have
already spoken, it was most illuminating of small numbers in which I
have since begun to take an interest. Previous to the time when I

actually assembled my first book in a version which I came later to think of as my second book, I happened to choose a photograph for the cover of what I still thought of as my first book. Even at that time, I noticed that among several other things the photograph contained representation of such things as *three* and *five* and *six* and *two* and *one* as well as *many*. By now it seems to me that I may have exhausted my interest in small numbers, but at the time I recorded it, nothing consumed me more than to think of these things which were so clear in my mind that I could scarcely express it. BOOK ONE is composed of many consecutive sections without major divisions. At first it was the first half of my first book and it has suffered very little omission or addition while it was completely rewritten for my third book. BOOK TWO, which is the second section of my first book and the first half of the second book of my third book with some additional material and many corrections, was in its first version similar to BOOK ONE, but now in its second version it is distinct, being composed of two major sections, of which the present writing is the second version of the second section of BOOK TWO. Beside that, the second part of BOOK TWO, of which this is the second version, is also the third of six parts of my third book and ending as it will in the middle of my third book, but being the sixth section to be written in a second version, it contains the end of the whole work. *Or I may say that in that section which I am at the moment rewriting, the ending is omitted.* BOOK THREE contains three parts and was written as the second half of my second book, with the idea that it was a revision of my first. In the first version of the whole work, which was my second book including my first, there were then three books and five major divisions. In the second version of the whole work there are three books but seven sections, the seventh being additional information that alludes back to specific points everywhere in the six. In other words, I came to regard my experimental writing during a time when I had time on my hands to be my first book. Then as the many facts of which I have mentioned several conspired during succeeding months, I had the experience of writing my second book twice, to which, when it was arranged, I attached my first book before to make the first version of the whole work, which, in its second version I should come to think of as my third book. During the writing of my third book, I invented necessities of omission and addition so that unexpectedly I began to write a new section of BOOK TWO. By accident, I also came upon the alphabetical series *five, one, seven, six, three, two,* with the omission of four. All of them, save four, are represented somewhere in the different versions of the book as well as in the photograph I chose to cover my second book, the one that led me to this speculation.

He was asked a large variety of questions, many of which were almost the same. Some he did not answer, some he answered by telling a story that did not entirely pertain to the apparent content of the question. However he made no mistakes and everyone was well pleased with his appearance. Thus through occasional interruptions and discursions, all quite well enough timed, he addressed himself to various matters, and having dressed, began. It is here allowed by consent that a brief reading, as follows, shall represent in advance the journalism of autobiography by type:

> But the anecdotes that make Garnett's autobiography worth reading also indicate its shortcomings. They induce the kind of dazed feeling one sometimes gets at a huge cocktail party — after a while one longs for weightier material. This is where Garnett's autobiography begins to throw light on the difficulties of the form. A writer's autobiography, unless handled by a master who is able to thread a unifying theme through his memories, inevitably degenerates into a series of random recollections. A character drifts in, one's interest is mildly aroused, and then he drifts out again, never to be heard of more. Any competent novelist knows that simply to record events in the haphazard way they take place is not enough to grip a reader's attention. A form must be imposed, relationships developed, and so on. Reality, like most meat, must be cooked to make it palatable. But the autobiographer is restricted to the facts, and he normally restricts himself to the superficial ones. A reluctance to expose himself is likely to keep him from the intimate self-revelation he would willingly risk in fictional form, and a sense of delicacy is equally likely to keep him from delving into the kind of detail about his friends (such as how Virginia Woolf got along with her husband) that might really fascinate the reader. But the most insidious danger to the autobiographer (as contrasted with the biographer) is that personal involvement almost always distorts his judgement, making him exaggerate the intrinsic values of his material. In the pleasure of reliving the past, he is likely to forget that he must earn the reader's interest. Even the most intelligent people can fantastically inflate the significance

of their acquaintances. Garnett overvalues his friends because he loved them, just as he obviously treasures the memory of their jokes and conversation and personalities because they recall the joys of his youth. Such recollections may be enchanting to the surviving members of his circle—they are, as it were, sitting around the table. But the rest of us are outside. And peering through the window watching other people eat isn't much fun.

He said that he had a friend who was a painter. After this man had been painting for some time, his work began to be noticed by those who were interested in paintings. It became current then for people whenever they mentioned this work to use a certain phrase. Soon they would invariably use that phrase as if that were all there was to say in connection with those paintings. People used the convention of mentioning a certain phrase as a substitute for looking at the works themselves. He said he meant to indicate that in the same way as a certain phrase had once been used as a means of forgetting the work of his friend, people might later say of his own work that it was 'a scheme of schemes' and let it go at that. He suggested the resolution that no such phrase could itself be of use as an adequate scheme for that to which it might be applied. Its only use would be as a mode of ignorance.

He said that ignorance would be useful, even on occasion necessary, concerning matters of no interest. Everything is a matter of no interest to someone and nothing is not a matter of interest to someone. The course of one's interest would exclude some matters by choice or by arbitration. Thus those with no need of writing would ignore that possibility without thinking of it while others might forbear to write whether or not they had any experience of writing. He pointed out as an example that such remarks would seem to lead one toward the fiction of two or three kinds of ignorance, a scheme in which he himself took not any interest.

He recalled that he had used to taunt members of his family, some of whom were strong anti-catholics, by saying that should he ever become a Christian he would adopt Roman catholicism, but he said that it had never occurred to him to do it, perhaps because of the anti-catholic prejudices of his family. He wished to make it known that he was sympathetic with the moral impulses which had led professors of belief to make scrupulous accounts of such abstractions as hell and the condition of damnation which he would read as demonstrations of the human condition always more credible than any such representations of eternal perfection. While some might dismiss such a remark with a laugh, he said, he wished to point out that all of a person's most serious concerns are always on the point of becoming ridiculous, never more so than when a believer describes his belief in concrete terms.

He said that very occasionally he had had the pleasure of appreciating the discourse of a Jesuit priest, and although he had very little knowledge of their techniques he supposed that they were liable to be faulted by those who did not share their point of view only in point of fact and never in point of logic. Because they were so well practiced in casuistry, in which examples of coincidence would be explained and justified by way of schemes that contained a factual irrelevance, Jesuits had formerly been regarded as extremely dishonest because they did not allow themselves to be refuted while their perfectly logical conclusions opposed the conclusions of those who did not maintain the same facts. Their success must be laid to the logical manner in which they obscured their factual liberties. Of course anyone, with a little practice, might use such rigorous logic. He himself sometimes argued in such a manner, but there would be an essential distinction between his conduct and that of a Jesuit logician. The priest would do what he did for the purpose of inducing someone else to think likewise to himself; whereas he said that he would sometimes say similar things for the pleasure of amusing himself with specious logical exercises. He said he would not attempt to alter someone else's point of view. But there was every likelihood that the success of the priests must be laid to the enjoyable quality of such practice. He said further that such a volitional distinction was similar to that which appeared to separate a scientific undertaking from an artistic one, knowledge for the former being based in fact while artistic knowledge resulted from the application of one's belief to whatever one chose. That analogy, he added, would be an example of casuistry for while it was grammatically correct, its worth in terms of fact would depend on the manner in which one associated the parts of the analogy and that in fact a good case was offered for any combinations of the parts. It was therefore no definition in fact but only one in logic. He added that in logical terms, there could be no good definitions in fact.

When I was a very young man, he said, I associated myself so far as I could with people who seemed to be excellent, with things I found to be good and with ideas I regarded as true. It had never occurred to me to do otherwise. The longer I lived, however, the more clearly I saw that in order to carry on as I supposed I had done and should do, I must make the excellence of other things by attributing to them my good opinion. I realized that there were no excellent or good or true beings of any sort unless I chose them and said that they were so. I was not surprised to be thus disenchanted, and it was natural to formulate my education in a manner that was fashionable at the time among the people I knew. As I continued to look for things outside myself that I might patronize by my regard, I noticed that other people would not see things in the same way as I might, so that when I told them something to which I attributed worth or truth they behaved just as if I had said, I like ice cream. They always equalized everything I said with everything I might say. In my exasperation at such behaviour, I learned that I might change their performance when they were in my presence by insulting their attentions. To amuse myself, then, I would leap upon any chance vagary of conversation, giving myself unlimited opportunities, and construct round and about it an array of logical exercise to which the best of them could not rest indifferent. As part of my education, I became practiced in this mode which I found I might also use on occasion to teach people of the attributes of the things in which I took some worth. While I took some pleasure in such undertakings, I also found it invariable that such a mode required that I say things I did not wish to say and quite often I arrested myself in the course of saying distasteful things to people to whom I did not wish to speak at all. It was then that I adopted the historical mode. I would maintain the most rigid standards of behaviour of which I might be capable. I invented the necessity of doing something I could not recommend. In the end, I should force the attention of people I knew and whom I did not know.

But at the same time it could be said to be a case of something else again. One thing after another occurred to me. It was neither good nor bad. It was a continued life. Sometimes one thought of the future, but rarely. It was not that one was busy for one had all the time one had use for with some left over. One was prevented from thinking of the future which, it was supposed, would come to pass. In any case there were many dreams. There was plenty of time for dreaming awake and asleep. It was hard to say that the dreams alluded to the future though one might have said so. In fact, the dreams were an ever present pastime. Sometimes people talked about hope and what they dreamt of. One found it likely that their dreams would prove successful. One dreamed of making lectures and more resolutely cancelled any opportunity of making them. One neglected one's acquaintances even when it might have been pleasant to pay respects. One entertained those with whom one found oneself. It was not that they were pleasant, it was that they were there. One might occasionally think of someone who had been absent for some time but one would not desire another meeting. One doubted that they would like what they had made of themselves and one trusted that they would not reveal to themselves their dissatisfaction. After all, on the contrary, they would congratulate each other. There was a little business to be done and one did it habitually. It was successful enough. One remembered many sentences. 'Go, go some other where, Importune me no more.' There were a great many of them. Though some might have said it was an idle existence, there was enough to do without making any plans. There were certain harassments, some of them occasioned by an aspect of oneself. There were really a great many of them. Others would not be satisfied but one had learned to be easily satisfied. One was possessed of one's own youth. It was sufficient. One did many unexpected things but moreover nothing was expected. The past was contained in ever present dreams. 'But in the asphyxity of day, the night writing goes on, nevermore and neverless than now.' Some of the things that one found to do were very difficult, and others less so. Some of them were almost imperceptible, others obscured the sky. One could do one thing at a time, whatever it was. Sometimes one did not mind what it was. Although one enjoyed rain, one did not prefer it. There were many occasions. Some chances could be denied. Some could not be denied and some were denied. Having refused many responsibilities, one assumed many others. Having endured much after the manner of trees resisting the weather, the times induced one easily to carry on as if before. The choices were not always clear and one permitted no exaggeration. 'Finally, it was enough to make her realize that each moment would be her next.' One laughed easily and wished to laugh without ignoring sorrow. One remembered so much that one could not think of everything. There was nothing to regret but regret was included in the dreams that pieced out one's silences. One amused oneself in explicable games lacking significance that were of no interest to others. One sought something nameless, neither supposing what it was nor assuming that it could be found. One sat by the window to watch the darkness increase. 'The whole of the modern period has been more or less romantic.' One permitted oneself many thoughts that others ordinarily denied, and aside from hope, one denied oneself certain experiences that others thought to be impossible. One promised oneself one thing without extending one's promise to others, to whom it appeared as a possibility. But even so, one would maintain the promise like a secret in an atmosphere of doubt rather than risk the success that too easily comes of resolute attitudes. The limits were never defined. One looked for something nameable without supposing what it was or imposing any solution. The search was conducted among the multitude of one's affinities which also chanced to change. There was always the assurance of a momentary resolution and from time to time such a sentence would occur. 'Many of the air conditioning systems are working well but not all of them are perfect.'

He said that a woman asked him if he thought all men should be artists. He had, he said, politely refused to laugh. He had mentioned many things of which he would remark a few. He said it was obvious that women could be educated and that the education of a woman, like that of a man, could be understood as the mastery of a language. But the education of a woman would be like the mastery of another language while a man's education consisted quite directly in becoming master of his own tongue. The education of a woman consisted in her being trained to think rather after the manner of men, in learning a language which could be of use on occasion. He observed that women generally had great affinity for languages with the result that, for example, women predominate the profession of translation from one language to another. In addition, he said it could be seen that women customarily used several sets of logic, each fairly analogous to a different language, for their different relations with other people, as with their children, their servants, their lovers, educated men and other women of various sorts. Each of these modes, while in fact they might use the same language, would differ in point of logical usage so that, for example, if a woman said the same thing both to her friend and her husband she might trust that each would understand, but differently, what she said. He said that one would find in this effect the source of many famous masculine attitudes toward women, as that they say first one thing and then another. He said that such an affinity for languages was the result of what he would call the logical character of a woman's mind which could easily make definitions and equations that would be exclusive for a purpose. Thus in translating a poem it would be much easier for a woman than for a man to prevent the poem itself from affecting the quality of the translation. He said that although he rather hesitated to say so, he found it likely that a woman would not be willing to give any but a professional significance to the word, artist. He said it was not his concern that the great majority of men apparently did not function as artists at all, whether or not they had any adequate idea of what it was to be a man, or an artist. He pointed out that in another language the word fireworks was rendered as artificial fire. He said that all human works are essentially artificial. He said that all natural works are essentially necessary. He quoted a teacher he had known at one time as saying that there should be one woman present at every discussion because although they are incapable of ideas they bring up the damndest examples. He said that more than one woman to whom he had repeated that epigram had mentioned a case of a woman capable of ideas. Thus there would be a sense in which all men were artists. He said that the separation of women and artists, which hardly excluded the fact that a woman might be an artist, would occur in the course of differentiating an affinity for languages from the mastery of a special logical syntax that would be called oneself. 'On the contrary, Madam, I love women but I do not admire them.'

At a moment when I am behaving for the first time in a long time in a manner that describes and implies more than the minimum, more than just enough, at a moment when I begin again to do things I willingly continue to find unnecessary, things which I might not do for preference but which are yet things that I enjoy doing and which are still things of which the outcome is somewhat questionable, even including things that are quite unlikely to be successfully concluded, at such a time as I say which I mark by a certain departure in style, I am likely to do also at least one thing which is altogether at the point of the necessary minimum, something in which nothing is inutile, a thing as I should not quite enjoy but prefer to do for some reason. 'Desperate nostalgia is not satisfied in sublime banality.' It is equally doubtful that I shall be able to do that. Any justification is always available. I feel rather inclined to sleep. I recommence a love affair, though that is surprising. I continue letting time pass, but the time is now filled with a certain success which contains an extra promise of additional commitments. I indulge myself in harmless pastimes which seem to be useful. I sleep if I wish but I may get up earlier than I might in the hope of finishing something that is already begun. It is far from a need to arise, far from a need to complete my projects. At the same time, I get enough sleep. I do not sleep as much as I might wish. The air is cooler tonight. The air is warm. Insects abound, but they seem less potent. It is hot.

It is dusty. The room is littered with dozens of things that used to belong to someone else. The light burns, for it is early evening. Outside, no ships pass, but automobiles. People keep on asking me and I keep telling them. Some do not believe and some believe me and some think nothing of the sort. People inquire and I respond. Some return and some do not not return and for some there is nothing like it. I said I had a plan that awaited only execution. But it wants also that I remember what it is. I may say that I have no plan, but I surprise. I have been reading and laughing. I am nearly recovered now so that my old self assumes a parallel sensation becoming undistinguished from the rest. I find something to read aloud in almost every issue of the weekly paper. 'Few things are more damaging to second novels than foreign travel.' The plan has four points, arranged by precedence, and each of the points is elaborated with a list from first to last. It happens to cover both sides of a sheet of yellow paper. It is uninteresting to read and it would seem cryptic to anyone else but me. I have begun to undertake several of the items included in the lists, and I have done so rather haphazardly or not according to the plan. One day, in the course of arranging some papers, I may run across the plan and then spend some time amusing myself in crossing out all the points I have at length accomplished, perhaps indicating by numbers the order of achievement. Those points I have by chance omitted may retain my interest a moment longer.

It is not only dusty, but there is a peculiar odor in the room which I associate with nothing else though it may come in through an open window from outside as does most of the noise I hear, all except the noise I make. I think my love is reading imperceptibly. I desire something that I wish not to specify. However it is not the smell of longing nor yet of hope. It is predicted than an indefinite time will be spent at some task concerning which there is already a body of information and even a name. Again the amount goes unspecified. Thus, it is unlike a fixed price. It may be like something else, but I forget. I should be interested to find out, but I shall not search the answer. Were I to hunt I should quickly seize upon any game at all. Therefore I wait, but meanwhile I occupy myself with rather diverse things to do whenever I feel like it. What, I wonder, is the root exchange between dainty and dignity and what has that to do with delicacy. 'When I return, I shall come back.' I extend myself. In two years I go from one room to three, all of which are quite large rooms. My hair extends itself as well but I have it trimmed away after a while that varies and goes unremembered from one occasion to another. In throes occasioned by a poignant itch, I seek a convenient pleasure of short duration which I maintain in successive delays toward a resolution, momentary, unnumbered, variable, incidental. Owing to the damp air blowing from the river, some of the things have begun to rust and were I to concern myself with using them in any way, I would refurbish them and in some cases I might apply a preparation which could prevent the rust. But perhaps I shall leave them be. It is pleasant.

It is slightly cool, the waves of a sensation leave my brow, transmitting themselves inward, relieving my soul of another comic image while the almost nebulous light changes without a word. Soon I may say that it is dark, I may see that the dark is somewhat light, I may sense that clouds are lightening the space. As a short nap may lengthen into a long speech, so I awake in the middle of the night, relieved of one dream that I remember from somewhere, and I relent. On one side the room has three great windows through which the eastern darkness pours. Both doors to the interior stand open. Three walls are formed by the inside limits of the building which is made of brick. The fourth is set opposite the windows to distinguish a square room from a stairhall. A large door in wood panels and a large square light is set into one end of the partition. A row of board shelves is attached to the wall running from the door to where the wall is interrupted by another that takes a corner of the room for a bath. The shelves are unfinished, although they are dirty. Over the brick of the other three walls is laid wood panelling of wide boards heavily overpainted. The most recent coat is the color of old ivory. Near the center of the room along each of the opposite side walls, but not at the same point in each wall, the shape of a chimney protrudes, narrow and straight, interrupting the line of the panelling. In the wall against which the frame of the greater door has been set, the chimney and the bricks so exposed are painted in a different color from the paint on the surface of the wood. The ceiling is formed by boards like those of the wall panelling, but wider, and the groove separating the boards running between the wall of the windows and that of the shelves is of a different design from the groove between the boards of the walls. Portions of the floor are covered with sheets of tin unevenly laid. It is apparent that in past times the wood of the floor was preserved by applying oil to which adhered an amount of dust making a layer of tar-like deposits over the floorboards through which some of the deeper grain of wood still shows. The light from one hanging lamp falls principally on my table, but the color of the walls and ceiling reflects the light to give a dark yet clear illumination to the whole room.

Yesterday, I unexpectedly built a table which juts out into our room about eight feet from where it is set against the back brick wall between the stair and the refrigerator. Yesterday, as has become usual on Saturday this winter, my friend Eddy came downtown to make some photographic prints in the darkroom he and I built at his suggestion in the upper loft. It is made of a great chopping board that had belonged to the restaurant downstairs, one that they had not used for some time and one that I have hoped to be able to use in some way. I spent the day yesterday in what my wife thought of as a rather bad mood, indulged by her and my friend, and with nothing to do but what I happened to find which proved to be a little satisfactory carpentry. When he came in, as usual somewhat later than promised, usually because of having gone to visit his uncle, he said that he would leave for a few hours to do something or other. They found me distressed, restless, irritable, an inchoate state in which I am given over to making random remarks which may be amusing or annoying but which are anyway purposeless. It is unpleasant to be alone at such times even though it may or may not be unpleasant to be in company. Certainly the company one chooses or falls in with then must be perfectly indulgent or else one is liable to make enemies unintentionally. It is a very good time to have a party if there is any money. On this occasion, which was in the morning, he had been delayed not by a visit to his uncle but by what was called his spring housecleaning. I elected to go with him so that I should continue to exploit my mood rather than having to find something else to do. When we came to his place, he found that it was no longer necessary for him to do what he had thought he would have to do. When we came in, a table which I had never before noticed was obviously in the center of the room. Its place against the wall, where it had been largely covered with various possessions, had been taken in the course of spring housecleaning by an unfamiliar desk. The table had admirable legs of light wood, curved in the French manner, and joined by wood of the same color with a scalloped edge to make a base upon which was set a kitchen table top covered in pink plastic edged round with aluminum strips. As we found ourselves with nothing to do, we mounted to the roof of the tenement and entertained ourselves in taking photographs of Janet among the chimneys and against the sunset. As I am easily chilled, I soon felt cold, and as the light was beginning to fail us, we found it convenient to return to the table. I looked at it closely. Then I asked for a screwdriver and began to remove the top of the table, a matter of six screws which came out easily though the tool was old and stooped. My friend could decide what to do with the top which he carried outside to an inconspicuous place where he left it. I saw that the base of the table was quite usable and I determined to use it. We brought the base to our house, to which Eddy had already intended to return for another purpose. I thought of the cutting board which lay unused, though I had often admired it. It is a thick piece of hard wood, more than two inches thick and more than two feet wide, which is formed by three or four boards glued and dowelled together, unfinished and well marred by knife picks and cigarette scars. I thought it would be too long to place upon the base I had found and I wished not to cut the wood which I found to be lovely as it was. I admired the base of the table in the context of our room. It has the effect of making some of the legs of furniture in the room look ungainly, especially the legs under the sink that the plumber erected. I have never liked the legs of a low coffeetable on which we stack periodicals, and if anything they now look worse to me. I was quite undecided as to what to do, but it was true that I had now something to do. I do not remember what we had to eat, but everyone was helpful. Soon I measured the cutting board which in fact seemed more than three feet too long for this base I admired, but which happened to be just the right width. It occurred to me then that it might be possible to fit the cutting board against the wall between the stair and the refrigerator, using the base I had found to support the larger part of the table at one end while at the other end the table might be attached to the wall in some way. The space between the refrigerator and the stair happened to be an inch and a half too narrow, but we were able to find an extra inch and a half on the other side of the refrigerator. We brought the cutting board upstairs and moved the refrigerator over. We let the board temporarily into the place that had been made for it, standing it precariously with the base more at one end so that the board teetered on one edge of the base and had to be held up. It was heavy. I regarded it for a time from everywhere in the room. I was still uneasy. I was irritable, and from time to time I made annoying remarks to my companions. Perhaps I was hungry. Perhaps it was that I did not enjoy doing things with other people because of the necessity one was under at every juncture of explaining what one was up to and how it might be accomplished and justifying the means against their independent plans while the work itself remained undone. Nevertheless I needed their help and if I had thought about it I should have thanked them for their indulgences, which must have vexed them at the time. After some delays of this sort, I had decided to install the table and I knew how I would go about it. I should not have rested until I had found the simplest solution occasioned by my desire for a good table, the chance of finding an admirable basis for it and the use of an excellent piece of wood that was not perfectly suited for such a use. I had first to secure one of the boards of which the top was composed which had warped away from the other three. Placing the cutting board upside down on the floor, I removed various nails that stuck in the underside of the wood. I then joined the board to its mates somewhat unsatisfactorily by means of bits of corrugated steel which I pounded across the crack. I had to make a notch in one of the legs of the stair rail through which one of the edges of the table could pass and I had to cut off the other leg of the stair rail so that the end of the table would pass under it. I measured and cut. I had some difficulty in cutting off the leg nearest the wall, and I broke the chisel I was using. Then I found that it would be possible to pry the leg away from the wall without taking down the stair rail so that I could use a saw on it, so that the task was quickly done. As the table would largely rest on the base to be set at one end, and as it would be held in place by being necessarily jammed between the stair and the refrigerator, I found it only necessary to place a piece of wood, for which I found a wide board painted red, under the end of the table against the back brick wall. I measured and cut this wedge. Then, having scraped accumulations of grease and dirt from the cutting board and having sanded and washed it, we raised the board onto the base and slid it through the notch in the stair rail leg back to the wall between the refrigerator and the stair. The refrigerator was pushed tight to that edge of the board against which it would bind, and I hammered the wedge I had made to fit between the board and the floor against the wall. It was perfectly sound, and finished sooner than I could have expected because surprisingly the thing required not a nail or a screw. I drank the last of the beer my friend had brought because I had wished for some. As I was drinking the beer, I admired the table I had made of the day. While I admired the table, I placed various objects on it and replaced various objects it had displaced. It made a corner of the room in which cooking was done into a nearly proper kitchen with a fine table and plenty of space. Eddy went on making his photographs in the darkroom in the upper loft which we had built together on a day in the middle of the winter. As I worked on the table, which was the first improvement on the arrangement of the house I had ventured in some time, I began to think of how I might install a bath, and by the time I had finished working on the table I had a clear idea of how that too might be accomplished simply. As I fussed with the objects about the table, I became increasingly pleased with the table and the kitchen and the room, which was enhanced. Today, among other things, I made a list of the things I must do tomorrow, including the purchase of a bathtub, for it is now apparent that the strike which has left me the winter to do as I please will end the day after tomorrow when I shall go back to the office where I used to work, before the strike. During the afternoon, we found it convenient to make love and then to take a long walk along the river and back through the town, stopping meanwhile for a drink in a lovely old bar I have discovered. You may say that it is simply the story of spring coming once again to a young married man for the first time. Today also I am conclusively pleased with the table which seems familiar as if I had lived with it for a long time. The crack along the surface of the table where I was unable to join the two pieces of the cutting board perfectly is placed so as to be little bother to whoever uses the table. I felt quite satisfied as I set about listing a number of other household projects, some of which I did not suppose I would need to do until I wrote them down. Perhaps the pleasantest advantage of my unexpected table is that it has given me an opportunity to write about something. At least it dispelled the ill humors which my friends endured. My friend left me about four o'clock in the morning, and although I was tired I stayed in my chair for an hour more looking at the table and thinking about the bathroom and everything else.

Although it is the middle of the night, a motion picture is being made in the street outside the house for a television production which concerns the police. The director speaks to the actors, some of whom appear to be actual policemen, through a loudspeaker and his voice comes to me clearly through the open window. The scene being filmed is one in which a police car starts at a signal from the director, racing along the street that runs by the police station in the block between this house and the river, arriving momentarily on the pier at the end of the street, where the camera has been set round with floodlights, casting an industrial glare that rises like the noise of a festival from behind a structure of the elevated highway running along the water. When the car reaches the near end of the pier it stops, just before it would disappear from my view, disgorging a load of policemen who rush onto the pier. While I have watched, this scene has been enacted three times. The floodlights which principally illuminate the scene at the point where the policemen leave the car extend their light to the whole street including one corner of the house. The light shines in one of the windows, the pattern of the irregular old glass being thus projected on the wall of the bathroom opposite the window where I see the silhouette of my hand among the almost glimmering reflections cut by architectural forms. After an interval, the scene is done again. Each time the car moves along the street, it is run faster than the time before, each time halting more violently at the pier. It is announced that in this version the action was no longer recorded after the car arrived at the pier so that the cops did not emerge from the car as before, but waited in the car a few moments before returning by way of the street at the back of the precinct house to the starting point below my window. This has been going on for about an hour, I guess. Immediately the scene is enacted for a fifth time and continued through the point where the cops leave the car, rushing onto the pier where they disappear from my sight. Now the car again returns to its place to wait subdued for the next signal from on high. It occurs to me that the director may be accumulating a series of versions of a police car arriving at a certain point rather than trying to perfect one such scene for a particular use. The seventh version is about to be made, is made, and again the men do not leave the car. The eighth version is prepared. At a shout the car speeds along the street past the police station and bounds to a stop beneath the elevated roadway, another car moves near the point where the police are rushing away from their vehicle, the director calls out, O.K. federal men come on out, and the action disappears from my view. There is another interval in which the director's voice cannot be heard, when the actors or policemen stand about like factory workers during a coffee break, aimless and unsociable. A 'bus passes through the setting on its route. A private car slowly leaves the curb in front of the police station and moves along the path that the police car has been retracing, turning in a different direction at the end of the street. An unoccupied taxicab moves slowly near the figures beneath the structure of the highway. I look out of my window to see what is going on, and it is possible that some of the people I see have seen my light or heard the noise of my writing machine. Perhaps a corner of the house will appear in a picture. Now the lights are extinguished, and the company disbands from the location in automobiles. The river is silent and black. There is a breeze. Something has been recorded eight times from two points of view. A light rain descends in the street.

The principle might as well be to include everything. In making this translation I have provided images not precisely like those which adorned the original. I did not associate with those artists at all. The polemical mode is natural to this time in many ways, but it is not useful for attaining conviction. Far too much has been said already. There is no reason to think that the artists formed a group. Some said they did. The matter is radically insecure, the movement is radically unsound. To speak of it at all is pretentious. To plant one's course among the ephemera of something else that does not exist is the play of a child, the occupation of a day or longer, the consumption of another hour and a half. Institutional forms are informative. Anything may be proved to anyone by means of fictional factual systems that are no better or worse than any other sort of fact. It is only required that the syntax of each system be appropriate to whatever it may describe. But it is another mistake to confound the life of an institution, or of an individual, with any sort of factual system. No doubt fact is a function of any institutional life, or of any individual life. But a scheme is only a momentary resolution which provides for an instant, and all factual systems are incipient incidents in the life of an institution, or of an individual. Such information forms the nature even of the poetical moment which resolves itself into something else. The resolution of factual distinctions as a continuous process is fortunately so time consuming that no one can conceive its limits, a labor of the collective mind, but any amount of factual accuracy, however clearly expressed and explicably produced, has no more significance than any one fact that anyone may know. Thus, the people of the world, under the influence of the English language, make in concert a grand left turn into the one-way thoroughfare of History, moving toward the amusing future, accompanied by a matchless concentration of noise generated in the course by factual distinction. Oh, my tintinnabulary heroes of art!

LA PROMENADE HYGIENIQUE EST DEFENDUE

The generic realities, of which one type is the series described by the life of an institution, or of an individual, continue their existence beneath the appurtenance of fiction and fact. Buried variously to an ultimate depth, or photographed, the bloody light early blooms to destroy the meaning of effusion. The constructive ephemera are so convincing in English that whenever a genitive set is remarked in our language it is invariably named and derogated to the position of yet another fact, and there forgot. I contented myself, in short, with thinking in a manner involving only the association of affinity, perceiving nothing actual without its source. Wherever I found love, *des genres fleuris*. I fell into reading Gide. With a boldness for which I was afterwards blamed, I took the line throughout my lectures of making the apology and eulogy of non-culture, but at the same time, in my private life, I was laboriously doing all I could to control, if not to suppress, everything about me and within me that in any way suggested it. I should have said I was well occupied, but I had little to tell of my doings even to my best friends to whom that period of my life must have appeared utterly uneventful, perhaps unhappily boring. Although I may imagine it, it seemed that more than one friend was disposed rather to ignore me at the time, and I am certain that I ignored one or two of my friends whom I would have been pleased to see at any other time. With good fortune, my fantasies grew no more concrete though they were no more easily abstracted than ever. I continued to disperse harassments as though the end of them were in sight. That would mean, at that time, that, among other things, I took no more sleep than necessary, though I remember that my dreams asleep amused me. The realization of an uncertain destiny had, by that time, relieved me of any need to seek my singular soul so that the advent of a new mode of private life—what I thought and what I wrote—generated no change in my daily circumstances. I made one or two announcements of this effect through time to my wife and my one great friend but though they received my assurances respectfully, I had nothing to show them and I suppose they thought no more of what I said then than they did of anything I might remark though half my time was consumed in the style of thought to which on occasion I so uselessly alluded. 'One cannot both be sincere and seem so.' Whether by plagiarism or insight—it mattered not—I seemed to have emerged alone from an experimental darkness into a formal mood distinguished, to my mind, by its clarity, for I had yet to describe its other characteristics. I resisted lapses into familiar modes with force of will and perhaps with some success. Who would determine things if I did not? The question had long since been concluded in favor of the excitement induced by my ideas.

I have already mentioned that I busied myself as if in preparation for a term such as war or winter of which none but I could sense the onset. A generous paradox, the things I did seemed to be just like what I had been doing, and if it was apparent that my undertaking held more interest for me than it had done before, the fact could be and very likely was easily left at the reason of the end of summer. I acquiesced in this natural deception as I knew I should be unable to retain the confidence of my friends in any other manner. It is even possible, now I think of it again, that they noticed nothing at all. It may be my greatest deception to represent my excitement as a change, but that's what I thought it was. For it was the very uncertainty of the life I set for myself and duly lived that caught and held my interest. Momentarily, it seemed to me, perhaps by contrast, that my friends had all busied themselves in lives of which the course could only remain completely defined. Thus they laid themselves by types. But whatever anyone might say, including what would remain unsaid, I excluded my behavior from every type by participation. I was amazed at the texture and the extent I could generalize from my point of view, never quite endangering myself by incorporating any fact wherever I might please to put it, not that a random choice could have satisfied me, however fortunate it might think itself to be. I am saying that I selected every note with more care than I would before have believed myself capable on such a scale quite without the assurance of an excellent result at any point. My process pleased me.

The recapitualtion is not yet over. My wife and I became quite good friends. Besides, I despoiled some of my own fears that had nothing to do with her. Using what has become, in my life, my characteristic resource at certain points of convenience, I became completely intimate with my friend and that without weakening or reversing the type of respect we paid each other. I might have said that I was happy, but it never occured to me to say so until now. Without ever having been interested in happiness — some might say I have never been without it — if the truth could be known, no doubt I was dissatisfied in spite of my happiness. I persevered in my dreams and gradually fulfilled my single promise. Characteristically too, the promise contains elements that are factually diverse and it works in perhaps three schemes at once without ever having been formulated, for once informed, it could not remain quite vital in more ways than as a function of its formulation. So long as I could perceive a unity among the facts of my life beyond that of a simple assumption of their

integrity to me, I would remain in the midst of fructifying uncertain-
ties. Not that I could have told the world, my wife or my friend how
it was with perfect justice. Such an essay would only derogate the
promise to the position of yet another fact. Nor did I enjoy indulging
the obscurity of truth. It could have pleased me more to speak, as I
thought, with clarity, but then I should have added to my distress the
composition of a story. I do think of several solutions to this conundrum, but I dare not set them, out of respect for their equality.

The following day we were to set out at dawn as we found
travelling in the morning to be more pleasant. It was arranged to
accomplish the composition in eight stages of various duration. I
awoke refreshed by the anticipation of doing something perfectly. I
asked and answered certain questions. We happened to depart on
time. I felt a certain drowsiness compounded with fever. Although I
had never done anything just the same, just the same I knew how it
was to be. Noises that were new to me — the feet of a horse stepping
on the frozen drive — became instantly familiar. Vines growing
haphazardly at the window assumed a pleasing pattern. The day was
damp, the clouds were undistinguished. We made our way in silence
along a course in which I came to know the turnings. Our speed
attained an almost mathematical perfection. From time to time we
laughed, taking pleasure in each other's company. For my part I
remembered much. As the heat increased we took comfort from the
mere hope of release. So well had I provided that a surprise, or a
mistake, would turn to an accomodation. Nothing was wanting for
my satisfaction, nor for the gaiety of my company which was more
inclined to be still. *I had settled the question of time.*

Slowly the room begins to take on a somewhat different appearance from that which has long been so definite in my mind. Yellow is
applied to the board shelves at the back where, when the color is set,
some books are laid. One color is removed from some of the furnish-
ings, another from the others. I am prepared to make all the decisions
before they become necessary but I avoid insisting that my fantasies
be realized so that even quite recently I have chosen other points than
those originally proposed and there may yet be many changes of
which no indication at the moment. I take a chance, and then
another. Principally, I remove myself from the room at a point when
the work may be impeded by the fact that my things — never to be
disturbed — are still there. I may no longer contemplate the scene,
but from habit my memory of it is unshakeable. In the haste induced

by the completion of my dreams long in advance of the work itself, I catch myself often on the point of superficialities. The work advances with delays, almost one each day. Meanwhile I busy myself with the things I more directly control.

I eliminate one stage from the scheme with a stroke of will, as if omitting the performance of what would have become a mistake, but without congratulating myself for prescience. I am freer, I fall more lightly toward a destination. I stop or rest. Yet another fact: Modern art is chiefly polemical. My brush moves softly along the curve I draw. In finishing, I redirect one outline and then another. Perhaps it contains a theme that would recur. The surface of a photograph obscures the image printed on it by reflecting forth the illumination of the sun. Questions asked and answered. Quotations made and displayed. The theme changes quietly. Would I have made more progress? Yes, but not of the same type. There is the same calm in reading that does not go outside the word as there is in writing a lovely correspondence. I shall begin again. I make a condition for the success of the series. I include even what seems, at first glance, to be excellent. I do not neglect Charles. I see in what befits my art a congruence it shouldn't otherwise have. My exercise will take the time to make it lighter than it was. The process denudes itself aimlessly. But why talk about art? She reads on. The weather continues warm and damp. The clouds are indistinguishable. I am forced to the point of accomplishment. (A chick he has occasionally balled is expected at a party where his girlfriend will be present.) She sighs. Warmly they wind the fur about each other's necks. The clouds are indistinct. Of course it makes no difference.

It is demanded of me—what? Nothing is demanded. I am asked, but to tell the truth I ask myself. The series continues toward an unremarkable point. Once more I establish my conditions which Eddy, in a letter, amazingly calls 'your foibles.' He is so correct that nothing I can do will shake him. The same is true of me yet thousands will agree with him. 'In all my life, only one person has understood me, and even he has not understood.' I attend a party to which a number of my friends pertain.

—Would you care for some coffee? I await an opportunity that I shall make. My stars influence me perceptibly. My lights subdue themselves. I reproduce the series in a different color. I wish— cessation—time—a recess, a moment of repose—summation—one

dream, a matter of inconsequence (that was said), a little more—
line—soft, fine, merde. It is too practiced as it is.

There will be two. Three accumulates pretense, but I've said
that, and more. A matter only of the use of a few hours, I say, it is
only enough, I mean it is only a small matter, a small laughing
matter. But I claim an excess. It imports. It matters. It carries. It
carries in. It carries on into the next line, a slightly longer line. And
on. And end. Or I calm the derangement. Or I arrange the array. Or I
settle the list. *I traduce the informal.* Half of the loveliness of French is
its conventional appearance in Italic face. I omit. But I do not forget.
I remember I surprise. For a work of art to be judged by arrangement
with the intentions of its author requires the authority to make
assurances that it intends a work of art. For this dubious purpose it
will be proved against your inattention that the work participates in
history along with every other save in one detail, where, it is convinc-
ingly asserted, it corrects the course. (THE INTENTION.) He colludes
with destiny to play his part. Some will say this and some say that,
but except when he permits himself to fault himself, the least
extravagance from his course of choice will serve to leave him struggling with a vegetable dignity against what in his valueless opinion he
regards as an indisposition of the age. But if only his assurance should
be proof against any exterior fault, he rests sublime. (THE AUTHOR.)
If he is able, for example, to convict himself in the doctrine of hard
work, the work itself resuming his volition in time, so that his own
time and its reception everywhere concur in an exchange of honor,
why then his life as he unflaggingly records it unfolds before him with
the continuity of the sea, the logic of the calendar and seasonal
variations until he

END OF BOOK TWO

The First Sale of What Remains

The afterword of an interlude. Here it is the first of June, but who knows what year this is? Since I saw you last we have had spring for the first time. During the days I have again been at work, although I must assume that I am used to that by now. Betimes, between the mornings and the afternoons, I have taken to walking in the open markets looking at things to eat. In the evenings I often found someone to talk to and we talk about any of a number of things. My celebration of spring has had a household complexion, and quite against my opinion of myself I have had the air of a homeowner. I had never done any plumbing, but I installed an old bathtub to make a pleasant bathroom with a window on the street. The table was the first project. I rearranged the top floor of the house and wired it for electric lights. It is there that I sit this afternoon, rewriting. I have rearranged many things in the greater interval of a year and a half. But then I knew nothing of that. I bought a few things, useful things, in the markets. Finally, almost half-heartedly, I cleaned the stair hall and painted some white stools black, and now the spring has extinguished itself without yet having become something else. I was quite content to putter about. Soon I was pleased to receive visitors. We drove downtown in her red car, from the office, although we did not know each other. Why do you do what you do, she kindly asked. Later, I told her. I was sure that my work would be imperceptible. They doubted that I could keep on in the same way. Now and then I take stock of my near acquaintance. I did so just before I met you, and now again, but it will not be the same. How much money do you need, they supposed politely. Later, I found that I shouldn't need it.

One of my oldest friends returned, with his wife. She cried a great deal during the conversation. She was jealous and I was surprised. Have I mentioned that in summer it is hard to realize the winter? Look at the full new leaves of a tree and try to imagine them dead. I can't. While you have been reading what I have been writing I have forgotten what I wrote.

The same. Six months later. Today I shopped in the markets for groceries and Christmas presents. It was in snowfall and I didn't mind the cold. I had recovered something, or gained. After reaching a bottom point like the one, now only a joke, in which I had decided to go to Toledo Ohio, but did not go, I read once more what I had already composed by the beginning of April. The point was where I had decided to stop doing what I said I had been doing, that I should not rehearse whatever I remember or invent, even if I were to use my poetical license as a master; I could not except whatever I might happen to say from the vast generality of all information, and gripping my mind in an enjoyable deadly calm, I conceived that for me to extend that unlimited inhuman prospect in any way would be a sin against myself. It was a logical end point like a decision to commit suicide, and because it was so logical, leaving everything else in me unsatisfied, it was easily resolved, by means, for example, of the addition of much more sleep. Several months have been a period of great dissatisfaction, the onset of winter, and while I am uneasily filled, I can imagine now that some end of indistinction could be won. With that vision, beside a momentary sense of completion, or the possibility of it, for which the recurrence of Christmas is a metaphor, there is also an old notion of responsibility making me a little sad. I am familiar with that already. *We are going to be forced to recognize our own limitations, and it is not pleasant to think that we may know what they are.* No, but I shall push myself to it. Despite my ignorance of so much that I might use, what I shall do hangs from what I have done, and that makes more beginnings only exercise, a remembrance or the way a misplaced groundhog in the depths of winter is supposed to elicit the spring. He said I was reluctant to succeed. During my grand malcontents I happened to make the photograph to cover these books. It is serene in a way that makes an end point, a conclusion, for something like the addition of a name. I revised myself, after Baudelaire, by taking thought about my standards for being my own great man and saint. Even if I know and enjoy all the excesses of the weather, and delight in every process of the seasons, there remains no necessity that I record the climate, from without or within, even forsaking prophecies. There could be a question, not to be ignored, as to whether I can do more than that, but it will not bear contemplation. Like any imponderable object I think it will quite dissolve in the excitement of making something for which the enjoyment of a storm could not induce the substitute. But that is overly defined, much too clever.

After Christmas permitting. Another interval having been longer   or shorter   another   stop   gathering together sit still three times as long   no image no jokes   remarks recovered parody revised parody revisited   exprimental   out of the first metal into the new   stars coming back   you won't like ths   fr th mfgr f th cr-s mxtr w hv mn rsrcs spcll gms I rd n bk r wrt   form   games even syntax   but the bluebird   blavkbird   blueblack   this is blue   this is awk-wird   this is my word   this is my hawk including mistakes this time   thise wierdes   noes wise levengse   no you don't know   et whi ma wi ask   no not now   not so late   later three times as long   a time as long   alongtime alongalangueton- guetonofshit   metal mental mettle   and so on down along a loneof- type until the next and knockstoolackst   and you will say something else   yes yes   and moreandmore andymoorionishly   boor moron   from from reading redding bedding beer small beer *on s'amuse la muse de poesie* posy pussy   aniturts   mais lhoocu. Ocoon   but no end   no tale   no talisandhishand   whoosehand- hoseover   whosoevertogetherbethere   more mass exprimtime more exmas   people persin persinning dost soest east doer door way   I see how they could play this in phrase and count by the word the time the line the characterization of them in them and where by the back way and coming out of them allways going foreward forewarned ahead of time progressively worse until at last it continues over and over without stopping the damndest noise in the course of course in life if it can be lived and have and give the same impression to the owner who may be snatched out at any time and put away for sinning and doing nothing more than nothing that continued to go on as if a bear I mention again could do it and know it but in the first place that's impossible and so no more thought but the bell, the dinner bell ringing away on its oak ash post oh posh *fire fire fire* we must get away from it and go away and a long ways a way to go

alongwasaway so wheres it at we wanna go to but we can't they says
and that's true but oh well never mind something always gone
wrong, rung, I've dropped the bell, rand, oh yes, run to it and pick it
up off the mud and put it back, no allusion but remarks, no image
but a fact, no laugh and no particular exchange, she said, so we shall
put that in the exhibition in the yellow bedroom that was born on a
farm which comes from reading the dictionary and too perhaps having weak eyes and having seen with my own animadvertently having
read it and having gone on to fill up the space and having it written
down absolute in the first place nowhere else and having said it and
going on from there as there is every likelihood of doing for me
anyway you have it just as formal as you like, preposterous, I can't do
that assbackwards, as you like it well enough to put it there, so go
ahead as I say and pick it back up and ring it out around the square to
see if by chance there's anyone there.

'My lips were chapped and my voice was going thin again and I
told her that it really didn't matter to me what she thought.'
And then you left, he said.
'No, I stayed. In fact, we got along pretty well.'
He laughed and said, I'm not surprised.
'It isn't surprising.'
The idea was, he said, to prevent a repetition of what happened
at her debut, not that there was actually any question of that.
'Really? I shouldn't have thought so. I took it to be rather more
of a change from her point of view, a willingness to abandon all her
pretense.'
Not possibly, he said. I had it directly that they talked about it
over breakfast, and that sealed the matter for all time. She said that it
was laughable as you imply, but then, what could she have done?
'What could she have done? Anything, anything at all. I don't
know what she wanted, of course, but she certainly could have done
anything at that point. She could even have gone back to Toledo, for
example.'
Oh, look, he said.
'All right, but she could have gone to the coast for a year, or
taken the house in Parma with that English housemother attached to
it, or she could have changed her name and moved around the
corner—nobody would know her—or found a new career hiring
herself out to look after domestic animals . . .'

Hogs and bulls at the top of the list.

'Well, but she has enough experience with that menagerie she keeps . . .'

You mean, with that *ménage à trois.*

'À quatre ou cinq, for all I know. Really it's quite tiresome.'

At least she should have consulted you. He had a cerain look, with one eyebrow slightly raised above the tortoise-shell frame that normally conceals them, together with an unusual disposition to his mouth, which indicates that he has made a telling point. He is often correct, but this time, as I didn't care about it, I ignored it.

'Well I might have taken it on along with the house and so forth, but it's quite obvious that absolutely anything else would have been better than to do what everyone expected, in and out of the family, at a time when she had so much choice, It is simply another case . . .'

Of inappropriate action, he supplied.

'Damn you! If I must hold to my every renark and have it parroted back to me — if you won't listen to me on the few occasions when I have anything to say — if you can't resist the temptation to quote me, go and write another book about it, instead of sitting there behind your spectacles looking sage, I shan't stand for that kind of conversation. As it is, I've already lost my patience.'

All right, don't get excited, It's another case of — what.

'Of going away when one should come forth, or of accepting something rather than taking it by force of will, of doing the obvious rather than the inspired thing. Oh, not inspired, exactly, but not appropriate either. You know, the kind of thing that leads one to wear a red hat with a yellow gown and an orange wrap, and not have them all subdued to greys and checks as they should be. Then, I suppose you don't know. But it was like when it is said that someone whose father has died is taking it well. Of course! Oh, I'm utterly bored by all these things, but, at the same time, it seems to be impossible to think of anything else.'

You are so easily bored, Lucinda.

'A great fire vigorously consumiong all things thought to be proof against fire, driving the bears from their zoos to roast in public, a hideous sight, unseen, a miraculous catastrophe, not to be remembered, and later they said that something had changed them.'

You read well, he said, laughing, surprised at my memory.

'And I am not easily bored, though "most women" may be.'

Thank you, I've had that little blossom of your tongue and I don't wish to hear it again at the moment though I'm prepared to have it rehearsed from time to time, why not? But Lucy, do you know of people whose lives are well-written? Do you know anyone who's doing anything that is not what everyone is doing? And don't bother me with the fact that I'm a doctor, and so trained to accept all kinds of limitations . . .

'Especially human ones.'

Yes, we are all so professional, aren't we?

'You are a doctor.'

And so is he and so is he and so is he. I'll give you that without raising an exclamation. For it is all a matter of control. You can take me up for the game of limitations, which I admit, but you cannot demonstrate in spite of the story of your life that the matter of control is not the supremest fiction. For if it is not, then what can it be that makes my rightness so right, even to you, and your rightness so whimsical.

'You mean, so feminine. Of course I *am* a woman.'

So that's what it's to be— the eternal dialogue of Lucinda and the doctor. Very tight.

'What?'

The category, quite correct. But I don't think I've ever told you, have I, about my friend Crosset.

'The artist?'

Do you know of any other?

'You've mentioned him very occasionally, and it occurred to me that you did so chiefly for the purpose of arousing the envy of your younger colleagues.'

Clever of you, he said quickly, as if he thought I might divert his attention. There's no doubt that it's the same. He was my friend long before you might have met him. At that time, neither of us had yet done anything. And in those days I believed that quite everything was possible. I had just begun to realize my education. I'm afraid that's a bit tight, I mean that I was beginning to tell myself as justly as I could what it was I had come to believe.

'Often in the form of poems, I suppose.'

Oh yes, some of that, and also in a great deal of talk with Crosset, and with various girls, and so on. I felt extraordinarily strong, or potentially so since I had as I say nothing to do, I was full of myself, if you will, and though I had no experience, I knew I might do anything at all. He and I lived together, exchanging our wits and whatever we remembered, for what seemed to be a long time, though in fact I had known him for only three years and we had been completely intimate only for a few months.

'As you often say, love affairs never endure.'

No, they don't, he said. I could tell that he was becoming impatient with me.

'Do go on with it, though, I'm interested.'

One evening, as we often did, we were walking along the river, it was necessarily a perfect summer night, with moonlight, and I was thinking of nothing as I walking in the damp grass with my friend admired the low stone bridges which cross and recross the winding course near where we lived, and then unexpectedly it came to me quietly that a certain time of my life while I was still living it had in fact passed from me, and I knew that I should live differently than I had been doing. I was saddened at the thought, and there is nothing but that to differentiate that night from many others, but I expect that I shall remember it always. Had anything happened, I might have cried, but everything was so much just as it had been, down to the reflections in the water, perfect and still in the midst of the summer, that I can describe it now only because I loved that walk we often took on a perfect night. I may have become silent, which, when he noticed it, Crosset attributed to the effect of the drugs. I often became silent, or silent and talkative by turns. We took a gently sloping footbridge, perhaps to get a better view of the river, and as we reached the middle of the bridge, I hiked myself up onto one of its ledges and looked sadly at Crosset who stood with his elbows on the other ledge, chin in hand, looking toward the sea. I looked at him for some time, and then I walked away. I left him there at that time, at that moment. I had just realized I must do that, however sadly, and it was a part of my education, my disenchantment with the possibilities, likely the most important part though it was almost imperceptible. Crosset and I never spoke of that moment, but I can imagine, I am nearly certain that when he knew I was gone, the slightest impulse to follow me left him as soon as it occurred. I don't know if it is conceivable that you understand what I am saying, because, as you never cease telling me, you know me as I am, so to speak, now when I have defined my limitations so that what I am is what appears, excluding everything of the past but what I may tell you. But before my education is complete, I know that I shall have to perform some last act of faith in the world as it is and as it used to appear, on the strength of that moment in my memory, the world full of chances gladly taken. I have been thinking of that for many years, and I may carry on in the same manner, or I may decide to die tomorrow. Much later, because I was so young, I knew that Crosset had taught me all I needed to know about getting through the simple forms of life which I tightened at that time into process and volition, while he pretended to admire me for my steadfastness to purpose. For then I at once both broke that mask and began to play the games that have amused me ever since. I adopted the historical mode.

'And played analytical games within it.'

You are full of asperities today, my dear. Ah well, you are anyway listening to me. I know you find these things that I do somewhat imperceptible, I know they bore you, these literary diversions, my analytical games, but I suppose that is because you do not see them in ways that include all my experience. You merely find me doing this and that, apparently occupied upon researches with no actual result, and for that I am to you simply the one who does such impossible things—or nothing. You want me to be extravagant, to do things I would not do, even to appear differently and to say gaily all the things I would like to say for your entertainment. I quite mean that I would like to say them. But you are bored.

'No, not bored—I think I am a little tired, that's all.'

If there is anything unusual about me, it is that I have always something to do, and except when I am importuned, I find something with which to amuse myself and in which there is no necessity. When it is requisitioned, my interest turns quickly to disgust. But knowing that I am able to amuse other people when I will, what I do freely reduces itself to whatever is nearly inexpressible within me, things having no importance, no necessity from without, but which perfectly fulfill the necessity one shares with everyone of always doing something. So as to my profession, you could as well say that I cultivate agreeable fantasies; with old Bachelard, I insist on the supremacy of the agreeable over the necessary.

'I think I begin to see what you mean, though I can only guess what you really mean. I've never heard you speak to me in this way—perhaps that's it. Yes, it must be a peculiar pitch to your voice that holds me, though I yawn. I'm afraid that's an example of what you just now mentioned . . .'

You mean attributing necessity to things.

'I guess so, but here we are, and as they say about dialogue, or criticism, every line, every notion is independent in some small way from the last and the next so that all conversation is really disagreement.'

Things becoming more and more inverse.

'What?'

Things becoming more and more inverse. I've wanted to say that for some time, as it happens. It's from Badiou's book, *The Inverse Trajectory,* in which, for example, something passing over the sea knows what it is doing and delights in its own imaginary reflection, he said, his eyes seeming to peer within.

'I haven't the vaguest idea what you mean.'

I'm not sure that I have. I sometimes do that, interject a remark that doesn't obviously pertain, but at the same time I know it does. Just as when Bloy remarked, I comprehend only what I guess.

'Marvellous! I do hope that in the next line you will mention Baudelaire and quote him, even if he'd be slightly out of order.'

I'm surprised you noticed, he said, clearly pleased with me. I hardly knew I was doing that until you mentioned it. Bachelard, Badiou, Bloy . . .

'Baudelaire.'

But I don't think of anything he said, he said, unless you want to play at thinking up quotations. Horrors.

'All right, perhaps we could pass back—or forth!—to Crosset. He interests me. What happened after you left him?'

At the time, to be married seemed to both of us a way to control our lives and set up a type of order that Crosset especially very much needed. He was married one night on a beach in a very simple ceremony. One day the following week the girl came to the house with whatever she could easily carry off from her father's and moved in with us. She cooked and made friends with the neighborhood children who usually came round after dinner to sing songs and play games with us and Crosset's cats, I think he had seven cats. He always set himself near the center of quite a little society, having spent a few years in almost perfect solitude, and there were usually a number of people to dine with us. But at the same time it was his chief concern to protect himself from the familiar impositions of his acquaintants, many of whom, at that time, he actually disliked. So he occupied himself then with keeping a certain order among several people and among his cats, but he was tiring of this process because the people

were behaving like children with their petty conspiracies against his
rules. So he changed the rules. The house grew smaller as he changed
himself to suit himself, his society became exclusive. I became a guest
and so I knew that he was married.

'You mean that she drove everyone away, isn't that it? Why
don't you say so?'

I don't think she did.

'What happened, then, if not that?'

I'm telling you what happened. Many things happened,
perhaps for the first time. As I say it was rather sad, Crosset and I both
felt the sadness of it, but we regretted nothing and soon we were good
friends of a different sort. We remembered everything. I would write
him descriptive or philosophic letters which he accepted as he might
a present of fruit, and in turn, they made me welcome whenever I
chose to visit them which happened from time to time. Usually then
we would go for a walk in the city, talking, very often in those days,
about architecture, a subject in which both of us had lost much
interest, but it was a link with the past, a rusty old chain that was still
good enough, and there were amusing examples standing about as we
passed along the streets. Very occasionally, after some such practice,
we would mention in passing various difficulties encountered in the
quite different courses of our lives, and we satisfied each other that we
still agreed about what should, in certain cases, be said or done. But I
didn't anymore know what his life was from day to day, and hearing
only a few incidents from it not until several months after they had
occurred, it was as if someone was telling me of a performance or a
party which, having missed being there at the time, I could hardly
imagine or feel the want of. Each of us had then much to do, and if we
thought of each other often, or at all, it would be in a rather general
way. I remember telling him that I thought he had trained her well to
live with him, and, as I remember, it wasn't easy for him in the first
few years. He did it directly, as he did everything, although he was
quite capable of doing nothing, of silence, as well. He trained her by
shouting in sudden outbursts of rage that seemed to flow, always
ready, just beneath his characteristic mildness, in a manner he had
cultivated in order to subdue the eccentric maiden aunt who raised
him from a small boy. I expect that the possessiveness of women
would always outrage his highly developed sense of privacy. Later on
when he had succeeded, he grew bored with the game he had
invented, which, however, continued to be played around him,

requiring him to shout as if on cue, though it was part of the game that his rage be unpredictable. It was complicated, like all his games, by his lack of introspection, so much so that it was his humorous mode to inspect himself satirically. He refused to allow anyone to get close to him.

'You mean he growled at them?'

In a way, he did, he fairly growled.

'Really I don't see the point of this story at all. You've hardly told me one thing about this man because you're so interested in rehearsing what you thought about him, which is doubtless perfectly correct . . .'

What's doubtless about it?

'You knew him so well . . .'

Doubtlessly, he said, in a certain manner which showed me I should have to wait until he was pleased to tell me whatever he might have to say—I think it was a form of growling that he had learned from Crosset—and I really found the story interesting as it told me so much about him that I couldn't have known otherwise, so I made it up to him.

'Oh, don't mind, it's just that I'm impatient to hear about Crosset and all.'

Yes, women are always fascinated with the lives of artists.

'You were saying, I think, that he was becoming bored with the game of his life.'

It must be because they fancy themselves excluded from lives they do not control. For example, Crosset allowed her to choose his clothes for him, which was a convenient distraction for her as it happened to be part of her romance to take pleasure in his actual appearance, just as many women take pleasure in each other's costumes, quite ignoring the indifferent clothes haphazardly assumed by the men who serve them. In this, and in many other less apparent ways, he was able to cut her desire to control his life, so that he was hers only at the minimal point where their lives conjoined, which he controlled.

'I can see how he might well have been bored by that game.'

He was bored, more so than you have ever been, Lucinda, with any of my conversational games. But I haven't told you what was to me the awful nature of his *ennui*. Its source was a realized belief in life process, something Crosset had learned from his cats, I suppose. I don't know whether I can give you any notion of what it is like to believe in the actual processes of life although perhaps it is somewhere that you know regarded as a feminine attribute, but it is the acceptance of whatever happens. Often, even usually, it comes to doing nothing in the customary realm in which causes have effects. As one of many feminine attributes it is confounded in women with everything else about them, so that women seem to do things that cannot be unraveled, things better described as nonsense than as nothing. But when a man realizes something, such as the process of life, he does not mix it with several other unutterable strains; he believes in it and acts on it. That is why, for example, the police are regarded as dangerous by most men. And it works like an avalanche. At first one's driving passion may be imperceptible, or only occasionally apparent like some habitual idiocy, an occasional rock that falls. But, as the dilapidation continues, the effect of its impulse nearly becomes visible in a man's face. It used to be remarked all the time how one could tell by looking that a person was a miser, onanist, drunkard, rapist or sadist, but by now the very categories have gone out of fashion or possibility along with the stylistic modes that marked them. We still have, I suppose, some lascivious gat-toothed women and a number of jolly fat men, but those facts count for nothing save an unnoticeable difference that may not be remarked. Crosset was, I think, proud of the ways in which he baffled his acquaintances but he kept it to himself, never counting his successes as a woman would be sure to do. At one time I had developed a mode of understanding him, which left me still much to respect, which was surprising for it is usually the mystery of volition that generates respect. Or, one's very power is always mysterious, and its effects are interesting. I thought that his life had been based in acceptance and control, a nice paradox, especially as the poles do not make a true opposition. It was more of an elliptical series occasioned by acceptance, in which anything that happened was as acceptable as anything that might. Once done, he used every event to control whatever he found nearby. There were even strange exceptions, since he after all lived by his own rules and not by mine, in one of which, for example, he professed great resistance to sickness, using much of his time in finding satisfactory medical solutions for his every physical symptom as if his own body were the one thing he wished to control more rigorously than any other. He also affected a great interest in factual and fictional pornography, as if to control his perpetual prurience by accumulating a great store of information on sexual possibilities. He once mentioned to me that as a child he had thought that when he first satisfied himself upon a woman he would be rid of the desire that preoccupied him, only to find that as he changed his imagination became more inventive, to the extent that its satisfaction became a literary feat. *The word,* he said, *drawn like an arrow, so fits into the body of the bird it hits.* But in these things, as with all, he had no interest in their meaning. Perhaps it was because he saw their ultimate insignificance that he so fiercely sought to control in himself whatever cancers others automatically found to be beyond control. For it was his need above all to live in a way that would be dictated by chance, and then completely enforced by his own will, so that if he was bored, I could become concerned for his life. His boredom was so realized that it always approached a cessation of the will to live. If he was in the grip of this sensational boredom he would do nothing to rid himself of it, he would do nothing to divert his attention from it, but he would wait, as he usually afterwards said, for something to happen, which I always feared might be the final event of his life. One could do nothing for him. Even I, who knew him more intimately, at that time, than anyone else, and who furthermore maintained to myself that I could do anything, became as nothing before that great self-abnegation. Since then, I have had no interest in reading about those strange oriental customs that so fascinate people who think them impossible without doubting the sincerity of those who describe them. Crosset had enlarged my experience of human possibilities to the point that nothing I might encounter could surprise me. Rather for lack of anything to do, I took to reading aloud to him whenever he was bored, for then as now I was pleased by the sound of my own voice, so that reading relieved the necessity I felt of anticipating the outcome of his boredom. Early on there was the possibility that something I was reading would interest him, and in such a way I talked to him for many hours with some hope of reward. But as the impulse in him to control everything succeeded completely, so that his ruling tension lost its half and became the paralysis of pure acceptance, it was just as likely that he would die of boredom at any moment. The desperation he induced made his wife a hopeless automaton whose every wish was his desire; he allowed me to comprehend him so far that I knew any attempt to rouse him would be useless. Altogether it was the most remarkable experience of my life, except, perhaps, for knowing you.

'I don't believe it.'

What? he said, looking as if he had been awakened.

'I don't believe what you're saying about Crosset, or yourself, or any of it. You only compliment me when you intend to go to bed, and directly at that. You know you do.'

Ah, Lucinda, you have a great memory, he said as if speaking to a memory which in any case I had not yet become for him.

'I said that I do not think what you say has the ring of truth! It seems that I have been listening to you for hours and let me say that I shouldn't have bothered to stay awake for one of your bedtime stories. I ought to have realized that I was really bored, and not simply tired, as I yawned my way through your insufferably vague musings about god knows what and unlike your friend when I am bored I always change the subject.'

There, you see. You do believe what I said. He laughed and clapped me on the knee.

'I feel trapped, but I am bound to say that it is a sensation I do not always try to escape from.'

Good. Let us say, he said handing me a glass, that it was not the story you refused to believe but only your own imagination — that looks to be quite possible.

'From your viewpoint. Of course. That will allow you to go on and on, perhaps forever, talking without stops or paragraph to an audience that cannot escape though the doors are open and the house is burning down. Yes, let's have a little cosy drink, Luc, by the fire of our flamboyant old house, which I never much liked anyway, and we'll have a little chat about the eternal stars, if we can remember their names, charming bits of lights in the sky that I can just barely glimpse if I close my eyes. Oh! How much there is to remember if only one can keep up some interest in doing it. Somewhere in that little book with pink pages you gave me, who is it? Baudelaire! remarks that at the beginning of a story one must compose some very beautiful phrases which will arouse the desire to finish the story.'

Quite true, he said like a doctor examining warts, that's good.

'But what does it mean? Is it a symptom? Or a technique, or merely a fact? If I look at it through the big end of this glass, with which I am meant to identify the stars, will it appear less significant?'

Perhaps . . .

'Or might it not look simply smaller, seen in less and less detail. This is preposterous. At one moment the images, the lines, click into sequence with the greatest of ease, memories intact, just up to the point where the process loses its character in favor of the price and evaporation sets in. Namelessly, one forces oneself to renew the agreement, or to recover the loss. In the redistribution of the wilderness, every newly sundered fact resumes a protective coloration, and hides out, grinning and frothing, prepared to be discovered.'

Yes, he would define fragmentation. It's not difficult for me to tell you if you are quoting Papa or being yourself. A great fire, consuming the world, driving the bears from their gardens to roast in the open square . . .

'In public. Really you have no sense of performance. You don't remember what I read, but only that it was something along such lines, a vague evocation . . .'

Perhaps the revision improves the quotation.

'Possibly, I shouldn't be able to judge. It is, like everything, quite tiresome. But it's true, after all, that I'm not tired. What d'you say to staying up all night? I'd like to do that again. I feel as though I could talk forever, as much as any philosopher . . .'

Without stops or paragraph . . .

'Do stop this harassment.'

Please.

'Please to tell. I've said it all before, but it's the kind of a game I don't mind loving. You know, a moment ago, or half an hour, or whatever it is, I was perfectly sure that by now we would be thrashing it out, forgetting all our stories in the heat of action . . . I really know you very well, your special customs, what you do when you're hungry and so on, but there's always a little surprise when once, even after a long while, you shift your form, a little unexpected present to me of life in the old flag yet, and do something that I admire. It's your dark blue style, a blue so dark one is surprised to see it isn't black, even again and again when the light is right. Blue-black; the kind of knowledge that never has to be completed, in which nobody thinks to embroider the coat with a word—this is black, or this is blue.'

Some do, he said, some women.

'I remember hand-sewn name-tapes, the work of our mothers.'

Well, yes, but too gentle, No these women say not only is this man—this thing—mine, thay say that tacitly, but without any objection they leave the imprint of their ownership, condemning a man to walk about with a sign on nearly as plain as sandwich boards. Women have always been destroyed by not being able to make every man into a woman, a success they would of course detest if they could conceive it, for their lives are won by opposition and by enemies. And great agreement, or love, or dependence or devotion are the subtlest types of opposition. Women are likely to settle the great human tension that springs the line between performance and belief rather on the play of the moment than on the durable sign. They proceed directly from the simplicity of performance into something very like knowledge and conviction. As my mother once said after I had told her of some of the dietary laws of the Jews, Then they do not believe in pork. It is just there that one may find the origin of fact which men have extended logically into the history of appearances, disregarding everything ideal.

'Very tight—yes I see now what you mean by that expression.'

But do you see what I mean in general?

'I don't know that I understand the origin of fact . . .'

Nor do I. But in this case I have fact at one point and at the other, idea, and as always it is what remains between them, between the names, that holds my interest.

'As between bird, and thrush? Forgive me.'

Not at all, It is laughable. Any scheme, pressed logically, becomes a joke even if nobody laughs. Laughter breaks the performance, checks the spring between the names, releasing them to be arranged in different games.

'If Van Gogh and Matisse and Cézanne can, Baby you can cancan too!'

What was that?

'A line from a song—If Van Gogh and Matisse and Cézanne can, Baby you can cancan too. Oh! I wish I thought to sing that more often. That's what it's all about, isn't it?'

I expect it is—but which it?

'All these names you cast against me; all that about understanding, all this of games, this time necessity, the urgency of life, the absurdity of belief . . . what's between this and that, men and women, performance or a sign; all this analysis, a hideous caterwauling in the shade of imaginary pines, all one's pretense of certainty, the manufacture, sale and maintenance of consistent personalities out of time immemorial toward the most fashionable, meaningless, the gravest, the most intently sought prophecy of series upon process in which the end of the story is just another fact to be exchanged.'

Or disregarded, or forgotten.

'Yes. Or remembered differently . . . There is a marvellous line—there are so many marvellous lines—how is it . . . What is the commonest exchange between more laughing and most?"

I doubt that there's anything I can say to that.

'I am the commonest exchange."

Nor to that, he said, although you may well be.

'Make up something, then.'

More inanities? Thank you, I've had them.

'Anything at all. Behave! That's something you're sure to mention again. Behaving. To have and to be—being and having. Being so and having to be. Having one's being and being forced to have it. Having it and being like it and liking it and having to be being having being and liking it as it is. A short history, a love story.'

You should have been a singer and a dancer, the most popular actress, someone worshipped in the street. And if you were you'd know what you are saying, you'd have to have it by heart for everyone would make you be you to you as you would be to him, make you believe you were who you are, even withoug liking it. It's too great a task for one man.

'And you, what about you? What ought you to have been?'

A musician, perhaps.

'I don't think so. For one thing, you would be insufficiently accurate. No, you should have been a philosopher, even a poet—an artist in fact.'

It may be that, in fact, I am an artist.

'Not a painter, of course, your eyes are too weak for it, but one of those men whose very lives are their own creation, one who imagines his destiny. You as the artist and I as the actress—a very nice play. Oh, we could be legendary.'

We would have to be, he said . . . and that remark induced a silence. It was not merely that I could think of nothing to say, of course not, that is never my particular loss. In the past I had thought nothing of ignoring such terminal remarks of his, but I learned that when I did I began playing to no audience which is intolerable except as a means to indulge a great sadness. He continued to sit in a familiar attitude, quite immobile, apparently looking at nothing. Presently he took up a book and began slowly paging through it. For my part, until the interval should lapse, I took to examining various objects in the room, things such as I saw almost daily but rarely looked at. A long unfinished shelf fixed beneath the window sills on which stood rather dusty plants, their topmost branches turned toward the light. A graying pewter chalice from the lip of which depended a few desiccated blossoms, including daisies, placed next a bookstand of wood, darkly stained, laid bare and newly polished. A thick bible or a dictionary missing from its customary spot I found on the floor in another part of the room, closed. My inventory was interrupted by his voice, reading.

The protoform graph itself is a polyhedron of scripture. There was a time when naif alphabetters would have written it down, the tracing of a purely delicatessened receptionist, possibly ambidextrous, snub-nosed probably and presenting a strangely profound rainbowl in his, or her, occiput. To the hardily curiousing entomophilust then, it has shown a very sexmosaic of nymphosis in which the eternal chimera hunter, Oripeau, now fond of sugars, then leif of salts, the sensory crowd in his belly coupled with an eye for the gods truth, bewil-derblissed by their night effluvia with guns like drums and fondlers like forceps, persiflagellates his vanessas from flora to flora. Some-shows this sounds like the purest kidooleyooon wherein our mother-nation's erudition of lower lore is rich. Also her, or, from us, him, in a kitchenette darkness, by hazard and worn rolls areared, we must grope on till zerough hour like poor old Georges as we are would we save aught of moments for our eyesore today. Amusing, though not, but. Closer inspection of the *bordereau* would reveal a multiplicity of personalities inflicted on the documents or document, and some prevision of virtual crime or crimes might be made by anyone unwary enough, before any suitable occasion for it, or them, had so far managed to happen along. In fact, under the closed eyes of the inspectors, the traits featuring the chiaroscuro coalesce, their con-trarieties eliminated, in one stable somebody, similarly as by the providential warring of heartshaker with housebreaker, and of dramdrinker against freethinker, our social something bowls along bumpily, experiencing a jolting series of prearranged disappoint-ments, down the long lane of—it's as semper as oxhouse hum-per!—generations, more generations and still more generations. Say, Baron Lousadoor, who in Hallhagal wrote the durn thing anyhow? Erect, beseated, mountback? Against a partywall, below freezigrade? By the use of quill or style, with turbid or pellucid mind, accom-panied or the reverse by mastication, interrupted by visit of seer to scribe or of scribe to site, atwixt two showers or tosst off a trike, rained upon or blown around? By a right down regular racer from the soil or by a too pained whittlewit laden with the loot of learning? Now, patience; and remember patience is the great thing, and above all things else we must avoid anything like being or becoming out of patience.

'What sort of a conversation is that?'

Begging your patronage, Madam, he said, he's one of the best jokesmiths in the trade, a hard old artificer who wouldn't quit. But what did you say?

'What kind of a conversation would you say that is.'

What kind? Masculine, I suppose—yes, men at play. That's what it is. Don't you like it? No, you shouldn't. I once thought that he wished to write one book his wife would be incapable of reading, where he could say anything she could not understand without his having to endure her misunderstanding of it. It's like establishing a men's bar and keeping the party going forever. It's a directory of all the things men would think to say had they not been convinced by the logic of their mothers, their wives and their children that everything of the sort is out of the question.

'It sounds rather sordid.'

There you are. It is not unpleasant actually to be filthy, it is only distasteful to be forced to regard something that seems to be foul. I hope you don't mind my reading to you, but it occurred to me that that was just what I wanted to say. The rhetoric is clear, and correct. But beyond that, it's an outsize, unfettered glory of rational plays on words.

'It makes you sound pretentious, that's all.'

See here, Lucinda, everything I say makes me sound pretentious and artlike, rigorously so. I know it. I am made to say such things. Besides, I want to. For years I endured the behaviour of people who walked away from me in mid-sentence because I refused to talk about their typical dilemmas in fashionable ways, the sort of talk I would regard as a derogated form of silence, because I wouldn't endure their offensive logical exercises in fact which keep coming back like the noise of a jingle, their rubrics, their homilies, the things everyone says to defend him against himself. I was always too direct for them, or too obscure.

'Perhaps . . .'

But without, so far as I can say, having changed my attitudes and having preserved the cast of my mind in silence, I began to find that what I said when now and then I emerged from my privacy into a momentary society, perhaps at the invitation of an old friend, assumed the character of entertainment. Whereas I had been rude, now the same play would be simply charming. I noticed that my every chance remark was welcomed with a laugh and retold to others whom I did not know. By means of a logical reverse in which I played no part, I came into a reputation for wit. It was as if I had changed my name.

'So you say.'

Your phrases are becoming briefer. As you say, I know what that means. Quite unaccountably you will covalently sneeze and yawn, managing at once to transport yourself to the opposite shore of an unbridgeable ravine, and so disposed, we may each tend our sores in all intimacy until our next, or last, encounter.

'Shall I laugh?'

One cannot perform alone.

'Let us say I laughed.'

I discovered that at a word I should be surrounded by lovely women whose every amusement was my invention.

'A poet's reverie.'

Quite. A dream, and a fact. But I did not take up writing them letters, though they might have loved me for it. I reserved my secrets. I enjoyed myself. But enough; my point is that my only interest in logic, *au fond*, is that of parody, the sort of barroom talk in which one makes a series of logical remarks that turn satirical when they prove themselves by simple assertion.

'It sounds rather like masturbation.'

Yes it is, but I think you mean to say once more that it seems to be sordid. The world of the way things are supposed to be, how properly things should be done and said, the world of formulas, standards and slogans, comparing the normal and the necessary, ignoring all volition and influence, this world known to us all as THE WORLD is largely of feminine invention and masculine execution, like every organized language in which it is never possible to produce just what one wishes to say. It is a good enough way of life, but to some left-over degree, it is alien to a man who has to take himself off, repeatedly and for the same refreshment, while in the same scheme women never need to leave men.

'Never?'

Never in the manner in which I am speaking. In fact, and for what must be called a wide variety of reasons, women leave men daily and hourly. But that kind of leave-taking is always made important, even legally binding, whereas what I mean to mention is nearly imperceptible in the scheme of things as they are meant to be.

'I left James.'

Don't talk about that.

'Why not?'

Because it is another damned example, and nothing to do with the idea.

'Because it makes me sound portentous . . .'

Good heavens.

'Isn't that it?'

I expect it is. But I mean to say it is irrelevant to this series. I think it is irrelevant because for some other reason it angers me to have you speak of it. So that whenever it comes up it becomes irrelevant, perhaps finally for no reason at all.

'You mean that owing to your whimsical distaste for the subject, James, you undertake to exclude it logically. That's pretty clear.'

Yes, but at the same time it may indicate merely that I did in fact change my name, he said.

'So you did; though to remark it now makes a good example of the silly, over-subtle thought Yeats mentions somewhere . . .'

The poet surrounded by lovable women . . .

'Indeed.'

Well, did you leave James permanently, or not?

'I don't know.'

Really! We can mention anything at all, but it does seem that you invariably raise questions I have already answered. Of course you left James for good and all, as a point in logic departs from its antecedents, but since you have been educated by my example to see that affairs of any sort are rather chancy, you choose carefully to say you don't know what will happen. Very good. *Le premier leçon est fini.* Now let us go on to the subjunctive case, and beyond that to ignore all the rules. That is what rationality is—a kind of play that is not so childish.

'If it is not childish that is because one plays for keeps, as children say.'

That's the way we put it to each other, that's the story that protects us, the way things are supposed to be in history, the invention of a cause for everything. But that is not the way it is. When a child fights, people are amused. When men fought people would take fright. But fighting is no longer permitted, so fearful is fear itself become. No, in our time it is playing for the moment in the present, a mode that may be dangerously close to the way women have always done. In past time it was playing for the future, a mode which like every other is still with us in some degree so that art, always first and last, is still regarded as allusions to the future, the often cryptic sayings of the gods, the type of authenticity. But throughout and uniting every mode of human life is the great play and interplay of meaning which, being artists all, we regard as life itself, now conceivable only in terms of fact. It is the nature of man to need to find significance in our life—to invent it, for it does not exist. Formerly people trusted their gods, the supremest men imaginable, to indicate the condition of their aspiration. But now under the dominance of fact in history—every man his own god—each invents a normal story of his own to be known and admired only by himself. It is a task to which women, who formerly lacked souls, have proven to be equal.

'*Est-ce que c'est la fin de la lecture, Monsieur,* or will you read on?'

For instance, in that ballet, you remember . . .

'Thank you. I do remember.'

Well, my point is . . .

'No, thank you.'

I see. It must be lighter, isn't that it. You can't bear any reading as tight as that. It bores you.

'I am not bored, as you assume, but I do not want example after example. I'm not doing this for the joy of it. I'm not enjoying it, but I am doing it, and at one point it seemed that you might tell me something I should like to know—I don't know what—and I thought I'd be willing to endure the lot. But these damned lectures! As my mother says, it's your manner, not your words. One would think I was an imbecile hearing you repeat yourself over and over in all this talk that goes on and on—with great cleverness, I'm sure— well I've been at school, I've had that sort of thing. Must I go on having it before and after breakfast and for a bedtime snack as well! You ought to imprison a number of little boys for a few years and let them laugh at you until they pass your examination rather than wrenching my ears with this schemy apparatus.'

And what color is it. Is it blue? or may it not be slightly white. And have they any more of the same type, the type that is so tight that it looks like nothing as if a quality of white were added and then refigured for the same purpose. But as for me, my dear, give me a small number which in spite of every fashion retains its shape, its careful nonsense wherein it fairly glows. For the space being as it is, circumscribed, let the figure play in close simplicity with the color, or on the other, gayer, side, ignore the ground and leave necessity to part its play. One can't have it both ways. A line nevertheless makes its way describing the ornament as it goes, and the shape, whether broken or maintained, decides to part, and parts, and having parted is typically reformed. Parting is such a livid afterthought. I think after all I'll just take a wrap of fur to cloak my Russian mistress in, a simple jump stitch with breast point blouserie and a sort of undercut nettle with a button at the back. But you're laughing again.

'Yes, I should weep, but I'm laughing.'

Why should you weep, he said, why digress?

'I suppose laughter is more conducive . . .'

Tears being on the other hand rather more ductile . . .

'You are silly. I have always considered you to be silly. I know that you are silly, and I invariably remark that you are silly. Even though I cry, I see you as you are and say so. Yet you go on being silly and I continue laughing. It is perfectly inexplicable.'

Happily so. Still, to be silly is more important than being Cecily. I beg your pardon. I find that inadmissable.

'Nevertheless, you have once again admitted it.'

Yes, thereby giving you again the opportunity of explanation, however resolutely you decline the chance. It isn't necessary, you know, to have a subject for conversation, and it would be better if there were none than these stupid exchanges wherein we prove out to each other whatever we both know and have known and will.

'I suppose that what we are about is communication of some kind.'

Love *encore une fois*. I had a grand theory about that at one point, I wrote you a letter about it, didn't I, yes, about love and communication and bridges. Oh my god, my education, that's what you'd say, you often do . . . It was a grand theory. Perhaps it still is, but I've forgotten. What do you say, is it still good?

'It was our engagement.'

We'd only just met.

'It was the fourth of May . . .'

The letter was undated.

'Perhaps, but I remember it.'

In any case, a lovely day . . .

'Yes, certainly, and the fourth of May.'

I could have pressed an artificial rose.

'Having spiced it with a commercial scent, I suppose.'

Very likely.

'And trite—offensive in three senses.'

The third, in those days, being to the touch.

'No, not that so much . . .'

You had resisted me at every opportunity . . .

'Just so. It was your mode of importunity that I resisted willingly, the quiet undemandng presence—how unlike the rose you've just invented to represent it otherwise it was. From the first you remained with me constantly, actually there in the room or next to me as we walked in the open, like some exterior obsession, a June fly whose attention cannot be diverted from one's hair. I found it almost insulting of you never to leave me alone during the whole of that brief encounter which seemed to be interminable.'

But which ended, as I recall, rather soon after we had begun.

'I found it necessary to leave.'

No, you found it necessary for me to leave.

'And after you did finally leave, I found that letter, left like scrap on the rug. I didn't open it at once, rather I tried to guess what you would write me—I think I imagined it would be a poem you'd remembered, or perhaps only an epigraph. I was quite unprepared.'

Yes, I'd written it in advance, as I knew I was to meet you for the first time when I was sure that I should think of nothing to say to you.

'You said you wanted someone to talk to. How odd.'

What's singular about that? he said.

'Someone to talk to. How did it go—something will have to be done about having someone to talk to.'

Something is going to have to be done about my always being alone and having no one to talk to.

'Yes, something like that . . .'

No. That was it. I remember it perfectly, even now.

'It's easy to tell that you have it by heart.'

But the sentence did not occur in the letter.

'What letter?'

The letter which you call our engagement.

'Do you mean to say that after all we are not married? Of course not. But if we are not affianced, we are surely engaged in an endless series of remarks . . .'

Seemingly.

' . . . the purpose of which is not entirely clear, even to me. Do you love me?'

Passionately.

'I am glad to hear it, although I believe nothing.'

But you have my assurance.

'Yes, and that is all I want.'

Since I have no money . . .

'I shouldn't have thought it possible for one person to be both trivial and vile in the same instant.'

But once again I have for your sake accomplished an impossibility. After all, formality consists in repetition.

'This is ridiculous.'

Isn't it.

'There's an agreement.'

An agreement in fact, but not in quality. It's a disagreement expressed as consent, a not uncommon means, as when a woman during the interval in a play remarks that she finds the play thought-provoking, and her friend, who detests her, replies, Well, I'm certainly provoked, and they go on sipping cigarettes of the most fashionable type, regarding each other avidly, looking for flaws and errors of taste, or of logic, which comes to the same thing.

'It is a pity you weren't born a Frenchman, for if you had been, you'd no doubt have a lively appreciation of the failings of women. As it is you have only a keen sense of their foibles, which you remark again and again as if for the first time. How pleasant it would be to be a sheep, whose interest in everything resolves to whether or not it can be eaten, who makes no sense of images.'

A most appropriate aspiration, my dear, whether or not you like the word, for the character of a sheep is that of a woman who has nothing in mind.

'You seem to know a great deal about it.'

If I do, it is only because as a child I was a woman, as all children are instructed by their mothers to be, but unlike everyone, I undertook to remember from the list of all associations, those in which I spoke and thought and felt like a woman, memories which the process of masculinization is desired normally to confound if not to obliterate. It was the rather perverse scheme of a solitary, precocious child, and as in every contradistinction, I found myself successful. It is not bad for a boy to play alone at games of his own invention, but like every experiment, it carries unexpected results invariably regarded as unhappy.

'And often regarded as important, I believe.'

In any case, such additional memories as I have are not supposed to be decorative, though that is how I think of them. Most boys, being naturally gregarious learn the various modes of the life of men, which requires forgetting how to be a woman, almost from the beginning of their existence, so that by the time they are advanced far enough to think about it they have no possibility of remembering the matrix of us all.

'Not only do I fail to grasp the significance of a single word you've just uttered, but in addition, I detest your treatment of profound matters after so factual a fashion. It smacks of child-psychology, a scheme that is unworthy to be called a myth, even in the derogatory sense.'

Perhaps so, Lucinda, but I mean to say that man is, on the level of necessity, profoundly feministic and that every characteristic masculine attribute of god, as it were, is a learned sense which is always applied over the utile, and which, like every artificial thing, forever imitates our own biology. And it is the decoration, not the beast, that one admires.

'Apparently, you desire to recreate the world.'

It is appropriate for a woman to disdain whatever appears to be impossible.

'I merely think this bible is overstuffed with ideals and wanting illustration.'

I grant you a surfeit of ideas, at any rate, not ideals, as I lack ambition to complete the figures once described. Nor is there a lack of images, though their light often casts an unrealistic tone.

'Then you suppose realism to be feministic as well.'

Perfectly, if it is at all accurate. You see I disagree with Jews when they would explicate my nature, but in response I only propose a different formula which changes nothing, and for which I conceive no argument.

'I can see how you call your activity imperceptible. Perhaps I object to it in the same manner as when you have read part of one of my books you put it down, remarking that you find it insufficiently prurient.'

Ah yes. Women love love stories. They are their pornographies. And with the success of feminism, there comes to be very little possibility of telling any other sort of story.

'Isn't it true that your version of creation is among the minor successes of feminism after all?'

It is in the sense that every love story is a literation of feminine erotic fantasy which is always thought to be innocuous, or trivial, so long as it contains nothing of interest to a man.

'I do hope this won't become one of your vulgar stories concerning pricks.'

There! As always you supply your own illuminations.

'I have also had enough plays upon my name. I know everything about it.'

You have that kind of control.

'Control?'

You can't be excited by what I say. Immunity is a great control.

'Well, but, oh, I don't know.'

Of course you do.

'Beside, I really must get to sleep.'

Necessarily. Even her long triumphant somewhat sad and slow remonstrance is a testament of her control over his reflex.

'What did you say?'

Nothing.

(Mention *pasticcio,* and flowers.) Well, it had always already begun, I suppose, he said, the tracing of a purely deliquescent recidivist, but that I would be an artist came to my attention to the extent that I began to think of art myself and to lose my awe of other artists naturally quite gradually over a period of several years that seemed even as they passed to be many. Among other things it was important for me to have the opportunity of doing what everyone may as well call wasting a lot of time, spending a lot of time, spending it alone or with one or two friends, but I did so not as a waste of time but as what I came to regard as a means of ridding myself of the necessities of time as it is generally conceived, the necessities of chronological, artificial calends. During all this time I was doing nothing, I said that I was doing nothing, and I meant to say that I was doing nothing for which I knew a name, a convention to which I always return whenever I feel pressed for time. Or if I am annoyed by the means of transportation, for example if I am impatient at the rate of traffic in a street, my impulse is to abandon the car, not because walking would be faster, but because, without the car I could permit myself no hope of achieving the destination I had set. I do lack confidence in the possibility of planning things, and my greatest pleasure is to discover the nature of something by chance. While I said I was doing nothing, it's true that I was thinking of everything, if not at once then from time to time.

(to buy: flowers, lightbulbs, beer) I found no inconsiderable question. I had everything to doubt including time itself, and I lived
without hope that the questions would resolve themselves. (make the
bed, paint the windows) Especially at first I was completely alone and
I had no experience, I had not even a paragraph, or whenever I had a
paragraph I threw it away in the mail and each of my friendships was
in its course tried by what I had to say, and eventually I repeatedly
decimated the number of my friends by leaving them to fall unaided
into the abyss of some standard category. I always thought I had one
or two left. It was then that I began to be able to read and in my
reading of what came to my attention by chance, perhaps by the
recommendation of a friend, perhaps through an allusion in something else I chanced to read, I made up a strange collection of readings
that meant much to me, though as I continued reading it became
apparent that none of the things I admired was in every respect just,
or that in each case I should wish to take exception to whatever I even
very much admired in some or other important respect. (hood latch,
muffler, air filter, spare wheel, locks, rubber bands, body estimate)
Silently I rewrote everything. But I am making it seem as if my
reading was important, while actually it was merely something to do
because I had as I say more time at that time than I could conveniently
use as I had already rejected the pursuit of business. My real reason for
doing anything was for lack of anything else. My sense of the abun-
dance of time was completed for the first time in the midst of the
period of which I am speaking when I had rid myself of nearly all the
harassments of every sort of organization. But I did nothing still.
Even though I had time for them, for example, I read no periodicals.
  (call J.
     Willoughby
     Harvey
     D.C.L.)
But I had one friend from the very beginning of the realization of my
life. There was for us no possibility of making the choices, as we
thought of what we were doing as a series of choice, there was no
possibility of deciding ourselves in concert, but for a long time until
we had each of us laid the foundations of his life and of his art, we
arrived at the same conclusion, invariably at the same time and in
much the same way. At first we could not admit to each other that
that was what was happening for we each feared any invasion of
privacy, of solitude, which if it were violated, might easily have

destroyed the equilibrium of independence that was our strength together. By means of rhetoric we became far stronger than two. At a word we could establish a world which in the next instant we would have no hesitation to demolish. As we continued in this way, we marvelled at what had been the incredible extent of our agreement to which nothing was irrelevant, indulging ourselves then in reciprocal congratulations without end. (mailbox, wash the windows, polish the bed) At about the same time it became possible for each of us to declare, as we did, to anyone who had any interest in him that he would be an artist. The principal mode of an artist is always evident to himself so that there is no real choice in respect to type, but as the type is more limited or purer or freer from accumulations of something else, the decisions which will determine form and style, while perfectly analogous among the types, are less problematical. *It is even questionable if art can anymore be made in words.* I realize that question very fully, so much that no amount of satisfaction so far absolves me of it. At the time I found I should continue wasting time, or living to no apparent purpose, possibly forever, I remained so young that every successive limitation I imposed upon my life one way or another I considered to be a misfortune in some kind, even as I desired the limits that such a term as one's name imposes. It was much later, at the end of this formative process, that I discovered what I had already decided in a motto of Baudelaire's.

To be, above all, a great man and a saint in one's own terms. But when one's terms were to be cast as mine would be in forms not of my own invention, although I invented a complete jargon, nothing that might be expressed in words would easily dissociate from what I had to say. (*The difference between a man and a child is that a child may be obliged to undress.*) Thus my formation became the necessity of every philosopher; to find a formula so general, so inclusive that it remains unexceptionable in any circumstance. It was after I had at length come to these decisions, without having as yet assumed control in the realm I had already proclaimed, that I happened to meet Charles.

Flower. With June comes one of a number of things—whatever you wish, I suppose. But for me there is something which you would not care to know. As I say, I shall have forgotten completely by the time it is over. This is (was) the second June. Very little interesting, I know, but all the same it is the second (was at that time). I have referred to that, referring it to you and that reference is from where I

start, if you please. A long drive . . . *inconnu.* Love in the night
. . . *incomplet.* We have to establish a connection which does not
exist between a regimen of daily work and the life of our progenitors.
After all, after all! My dear sir, we may no longer share that, whatever
it was. But it is that that will occupy me as it may for what it will.
Otherwise I do not recall the second June. But enough. You know
already that I eschew a subject, now see that I shall mention what you
wish. I shall consider a great many things. But that is not the
resolution of attention. For that purpose I shall set all these things
before you and tear them down without regret, to expose my standing
fraud to the departure of your pretensions, the excitement of not
knowing. And I shall do much more, if you please. It is my own
cliché. The fact of the found object, for example—it is itself complete. But do not suppose I am writing philosophy; think rather that
this is what I do say. One fact the more. I have set myself the task as
well as any German. Do you notice the change? So much for that then
it is no explanation.

Rrose.

Daisy. Here I am dressed to the teeth in my jock with a hard-on. Now
I ask you whatever you may care to respond to. Not that you would.
Besides, you're in no position to put the question. I ask and never
mind the response. What is the answer? What is the question. I can
only scratch the surface—I maintain my superficial prurience. Crosset asks me, Would you like to screw her in the rain? As I love
walking in the rain I say, Yes, in a warm rain. That was a quick
intellectual jack. I just wanted to ask how you quit a job.

Marguerite. Here it is a rainy night and nothing to do but quote from
a review of somebody else's book. It is quite typical of me that since I
am unable to locate a copy of the review from which I had thought I
might quote, I shan't try to find it, or to quote from it at a later date
because now that I think of it I really doubt if it is after all something
I wish to preserve. Some letters remain unsent.

Even in this journalism, from which I am giving you some exerpts I
attach to letters, remaining unwritten, being kept or retrieved or
rewritten and misdirected, or resuming currency, put to a different
use, in short, all incidents convening. I too have been thinking of

questions of style which do not bore me so much anymore. Frankly, it is surprising how much I have changed, however inadmissable that may be, when it is taken into account that only a certain amount of persiflage, given the value of the same number of pages and hardly any poetry worthy to be said that it was composing everything into this pasticcio (dance) (pearl) (flower). The question of music, I repeat. But less like drumming up trade. Whatever is dear enough will sell well enough . . . it will estimate well too . . . it will even reorder and capitalize and sell out. Now you do not have free associations at all. That is what it is called. Experimental — I include mistakes but I do not intend that. Full stop. I quote. Now you are going to think that camouflage is a new word, and therefore, but I mean that I am hiding something, well, that you may think so. Why begin again? We don't know that, do we. On hearing that he had been misquoted he said that he would not unnecessarily contradict it. If you made, as they often do, a list of all the associations of necessity you would find out what it means to me as well as containing some contradiction. I have plenty of time to stop and point. I even tell stories once in awhile. Or all the associations of history. The same thing. Short sentences. One has a style of life, a scheme (oldstyle) that might be derived by the smallest inadvertence from moment to moment, everything and the manner of it — a style is expressed and retained in one's face, in a house. In a story I use the word so a lot, in a history I say which the more. Do you live in a house which cries out to your every visitor, Here lives someone who is exciting to know! Question-point. I left the light on all night. When I came back I noticed an orgiastic glow coming from the upper windows. But I felt too sick to go up and put out the fire. This will give me a couple of more pages. Do you know that? However so rhetorical such things may be, they are the means by which and the style in which I derive any notion of style I may achieve, apart from whatever else may be said. We keep on using the same words, and you could say that some words were out of date, but all that of style has to do with the what I mean.

For example, for many years he bore out the cliché that was suitable to him as an appropriately struggling artist in residence. Above his door he caused to be painted a sign:

J'ai defendu l'Artisme du printemps et de la guerre.
                                                          And these
words he hung somewhere in a suitable appropriate place where they could not be seen, and wherever they could much less be read and

understood. In due course, however, his enigma was rapproached. 'It is quite possible,' he thought to whomever was near, 'that I have as I have a few words a day. But is also possible, even likely, that they are not new forms. It is possible that I drain off my pool of remarks. It is possible that she was wrong to say so, but then it was not to me that she spoke. It is also possible that I have more to say as I do have something to express, but who shall say I have not said the things of this moment?'

Dear Sir.
The white man also killed my father, who didn't know what else to do. But aside from that which does not exist, there have been some things happen. During my unemployment which was due superficially or really to a strike, I wrote something which does exist, not your usual, or even unusual novel, nor an essay or a letter, nor a clutter of various pieces and not anything else that I now of, but still something that exists. I decided that it does exist and that I should go on with it two days ago when I allowed myself to read it for the first time. A great excitement! and now D. C. L. is reading it—I seem to want very much to talk about it, although I don't know anything to say. It has perversely entered my head that in writing this letter I am beginning to revise what I wrote very quickly and without thinking. Although I do not yet know in what respect this may begin my revision of the work, I see no importance to the connection which insists that a revision supercede that from which it may be said to come. I have a lot to think about revision, and I shall think about it in the course of writing it as I am at the moment, and I shall make no decision about revision till I have finished it. I do know that the critical controversy among men of letters which recurs from time to time in the papers obscures more than it shows. While I suppose T. S. Eliot wrong that an artist must function, like T. S. Eliot, as a constructive critic of his own work with the end to perfect the mask of art like any standard scheme of children's education, so is anyone wrong who says that the word is sacred, that the series is simply given. Such arguments proceed as usual from obvious determined points resulting only in more propaganda. Pop art will go the way of writing on toilet paper and will be succeeded like everything by nothing. But I have much yet to do with this which may become a book, not all of it thinking, not all of it writing, not all of it aging. There is for example the possibility of burning the manuscript. You

may not see that that could be a pleasant thing to do. Someone I know did, as Goethe did not, burn his first lengthy piece of writing and he reported it as a greater experience than writing a book — which then however he proceeded to rewrite without recourse to the score as I am doing now having, like Goethe, omitted the firing. Surely revision, whatever its shape, does not partake very much, as do the flames of one's typescript, in the excitement of composition, in the interest of the unknown. Nor is reading what has been revised likely to be much as excitement, however enjoyable it may be in other ways. Could there be a more excellent example of the dullness of revision than the process called the same which goes on continually in the fields of social and political history? You take any scheme by the nose and tweak it until it hurts enough for the head to turn round a few degrees to the West and voila! you've made your reputation. As a matter of course everything must be corrected a bit, as usually at the end of the process of cooking anything it is desirable to correct the seasoning with a bit of salt. And usually, though a work be advertised as having been revised twelve times, revision is nothing more than that, the addition of a bit of worry. I mean in due course to distinguish revision from re-writing and worrying a set task. Meanwhile, please allow the suggestion that revision is the type for translation. But it is in revision, to return to the current derogated condition of the word, that I derive the source of the dullness I perceive in what literary people are pleased to call modern American literature, pleased because they flatter themselves they have defined a nationality. Laa di dah di doodle doo (I hope my accents are correct). All that fiction is revised literary realism, quite unremarked by any vigorous reality, sustained entirely, and barely, by allusions to the ephemeral realities of everybody's every day, dull, drab, dead, dogged, done. I make no claims, for if I did, everything I have would have to be stolen like everything insured against accident. I have already forgotten the names of the examples that prepared my impression. Reading anything current, or even anything that is still dusted, like conversation and modern life itself, one must find it full of stupidities nevertheless required by the limitations of its author. He doesn't do dialogues at all well, does he. It is a dry climate, and even a phantastically strong prurience like mine has a comprehensible limit. But as you surely say, although you are bored, reading and conversation and art itself were hardly ever more exciting and hardly ever less. You know that verse of Whitman's. I have to doubt that the purpose of revision is to make for excitement, the reader's or the writer's, nor could it be, as for me, to make anything more perfect, for that is a process which in conscience can neither end nor be begun. But despite its dullness, the subject of revision maintains my interest in its every connotation, and it will be my interest which gives life to whatever I say next. You cannot renew any experience as you renew a machine; no more can you remake something written which to begin with did not exist.

Our conversation about your friend the onanist recurs to me from time to time. It is rather obvious that masturbation has in a sense come into fashion, for with some candor it is now thought possible to see as 'normal' any behavior in which many participate and normative relations are usually so expressed as to become the thing to do, as well they might. A psychologician writing a book I once had a look at posed the typical ploy that all sorts of itching are the same so that by means of his revision it is no worse to pick your nose or scratch your chest or your balls than it is to jack your prick. (Typically too, I expect it is still better to blow your nose and change the subject.) There appears from time to time in certain lower middle class women's magazines an advertisement for some sort of balm said to relieve 'female itch.' Apparently a proportion of unenlightened women have this horrible itch at the crotch and it could not occur to them that when they indulge it they are masturbating. Concurrently, I notice that when my prick has lain shortly in unaccustomed disuse there comes to be an accretion on the surface of the acorn beneath the foreskin, called by the Greek word for soap, an irritant of that area as it is to the tongue, said to be analogous to the wax of ears and the sandman's gift, which seems also to partake in the philoprogenitive process as a cause of my familar masculine itch. (A good joke, it's that soap which has latterly been distinguished as a cause of cancers of the female parts.) But now that it is admitted that Clemens and Gide commend the practice, and Jean Genet and William Burroughs have literally celebrated masturbation, and observant doctors lamely conclude that there are some people for whom it is best, the way is indicated in which there is nothing wrong with whoever habituates the solitary mode. It gives me the impression that I am living, said a writer of my generation amid the corroboratory laughter of the readers of that little magazine. Indeed there may be found a way in which there is nothing wrong with anybody — perhaps that is my abstracted grail.

It is clear that there can be no normal degree of sexual prurience though there is a classical subject of it. (To please Mr. Auden I pray that I have not spoken of an object of contemplation; to satisfy myself, I wonder if I quite understand his stricture.) There are so many variations in possible behaviour that any attempt to assign a value to a degree of prurience must fail me though I were to write nothing but the histories of factual pornography from now on. Value aside, there remains much of interest to be joined. It is Baudelaire's repeated observation, I remember, which associates communion with women and the necessity of sharing one's soul; seen thus, the classical relation is disenchanted to that of prostitution, as well as being supressed into somewhat awkward language, which is nevertheless my own revision. Is it finished? Yes, it is. How well I admire the poet's maxim, The true hero takes his pleasure alone. That the license which poets have authorized in the matter of solitude should be renewed explicitly to cover masturbation is not surprising. N. Berdayev is quoated in the paper, during an exchange of scholarly speculation on Shakespeare's sexual proclivities, as having written as follows: In essence the sexual act is profoundly opposed to all genius, to all universal conception and all universal creativity. Genius is through and through erotic but not sexual in the specific differentiated sense of the word.

One may notice in this connection the careful use, other than the heedless confusion, of mixed metaphors. There is always 'something wrong' with a poet or a wit, and it is noticeable that both poetry and laughter these days achieve their greatest popularity as a pastime among older children with whom, in terms of the sexual metaphor, there is always 'something wrong,' so much so that their poems and their jokes are of indifferent quality. For the adjustable artist, there remains the love story which the feministic purveyors of the stock dignify by association with the epic novel which would find too few buyers. The novelistic trade to women, communicating a heavy savor of hope to idle wives, is pursued by busy fuckers who make love at night as people do on television, just like everybody else. With their audience they comply to interlude the climax of their every history. Do you see the joycean pun? I call it a freudian slip. And all this letters of bitterness ends, without expression or remonstrance, in the sale of what remains, the secrets of little boys and other remnants of masculine puissance, the histories of the lives of artists by themselves called the memoir of a man of letters. The ladies find them hardworking, healthy and happy, or, if cursed, they are so in some classical manner which, when one, in the story of his life, has named the form and found it universal, comes to blessing by a different measure.

In addition, my research into sexuality which I have been aware of conductiong since I was four has uncovered a number of facts which bear on the subject, that of critical autobiography. Among those not generally known are these. The practice of cutting the foreskin from male infants, a custom which in Europe has been traditionally associated with the Jews, has, with little fanfare become extremely widespread throughout the world, having become standard American medical practice some years ago. It is conducted in the name of Hygeia, but has the demonstrable practical effect of toughening the sexual membrane and rendering it less sensitive to the touch. At present, circumcision is advertised quasi-scientifically as preventative to cancer, but that explanation is not ten years old. There is little doubt that circumcision achieved its Western popularity as a discouragement to masturbation, which was regarded as highly unhealthful and which was combatted on the same scale as the pox. But despite the existence of explicit, acceptable reasonings such as these, universal circumcision has a more radical source. In a predominately feminine civilization such as ours, where people live in houses, where forms of speech (e.g. slogans) carry more influence than general ideas, and where prohibitions of all sorts abound, the prime importance being shared as well by sexual extravagance as by murder, a wholesale reduction of sexual prurience is a most useful and perhaps necessary social effect. In addition to the fact that circumcision makes his prick less interesting to a child as plaything, I should say even less useable, there exists the set of customs which logically divert the high sexuality of older children by the permission of other vehicles of power such as automobiles and crude sports such as American football. The fact that older children have latterly made a great display of sexualistic modes of dance and dress, rather enforces the impression that they are not easily defeated by caresses, than indicates what such behaviour may purport. It is a very believable fact, discovered by medical curiosity, that the longer a being forgoes overt sexual expression, the less vivid will be his impression of it and the more easily will he decline to impotence in middle age, when, very likely, the fact that he can no longer get it up to work will be a source of pleasure in itself as he found that form of exercise distasteful to begin with. Indeed I believe that the larger proportion of rakes, studs and ladies' men of previous centuries were invented by the custom that parlour maids would initiate the children of their masters at the age of ten or twelve, as a result of which their lust became insatiable. No articles of the human constitution forbid the specific sexual function at any age, though the pituitary withholds the expression of love and the fullest extension of its organ until puberty. In sum, at present, the universal convention of circumcision, less honored among uneducated persons than among the norms, will toughen the pricks of the populace, circumcision being the rule of industrialized maternity practice, sexual disuse is more easily inculcated in children therefore and among men greater stimulus is necessary for arousal and longer engagement is wanted for completion, to the advantage of women who cultivate their own sexuality, with the more general result that the larger part of the population, both men and women, older and younger, is deprived to some indeterminate extent of sex.

To account for their vast increase in political and monetary power, the highly possessive, conservative, godless, feministic middle classes, personified no doubt by actual men, invented a system of human psychology which also accounted for their sexlessness, a scheme which received expression less than a century ago in a form immediately available to Jews, who had long before founded the European bourgeoisie. The scheme, being in the historical mode, quickly encompassed the entire Western world, providing the definition of modern man. Among all the sexual schemes of psychologicians, I have read a few, and in that little, excluding the concomitant reams of medical pornography, the supposition I find most useful is that which shows the sexual direction to be a function of custom. The point is rarely made with much clarity or at any length because the logic in which it is included is one of the customs by means of which most women are assured a servant. It is decided that there is, for every individual, a set erotic stimuli, which in fact may be anything at all—the saddle of a horse of the leg of a table would do—and of which the decoration of women will form the type. Among a number of functions, the profession of psychology has classified the subjects of erotic fantasy far enough to be able to effect the redirection of sexual responses to the satisfaction of its customers. It is found that the answer to an individual's erotic nature lies in the diurnal history which can be invented to demonstrate the truth of nocturnal fantasies so that the story of one's life, far from being that of anniversaries, will turn on points at which, it is convicingly asserted, the set of one's ultimately sexual associations were accumulated. The dogmas of popular culture, psychology and religion surely convene to cultivate the one-to-one relation between the sexes which, astonishingly with so large a population to control, remains effective against the natural proliferation of human events. But although for a certain purpose it is possible to place in classes every mode of sexuality, from anyone's own point of view the nature of events remains intact, despite the story which may surround it, so that one wakes to an affinity with flowers quite by chance. The revision of one's arbitrary predilections, however their names be cast, bears so little relation to the cure of sickness, its vulgar mode, that it may be called the universal human task. Manners, now seen in autobiographical form, makyth man, the individual talent that exists to be informed. So long as he dominates himself, a man may cultivate him as he please, knowing no exorbitance to anything that is quite of himself. So that I must take exception to the quotation which I copied out for you. It is entirely a critical manner of speaking, having very little to do with the way things are (a concern that is almost always sacrificed to the paltry god of linguistic clarity) that specific sexuality can be differentiated in a man from everything or anything about him. Nor do I care to be able to derive an important distinction, other than a momentary critical one, between the types of sexual expression, always assuming that their customers are pleased to use them.

There remains in the sexual metaphor, however, the question of the given and received distinctions which are recognized by us as well of which descriptive points are too uninteresting. The most of distinctions between fucking and jacking will arise, after all, even as does our own, by placing value into the scale where lovers are conjoined. All the cavillers of masturbation, from the crudest medical speculators of the nineteenth century to the most artificial amateur philosophers of the nearly present, of which the chief was D.H. Lawrence, have maintained for all possible reasons that sexual expression be reserved as a form of communication. Self-expression in whatever form is a typical point of contention among all unreconstructed anti-moderns from whom the juxtaposition of artistic and sexual self-expression will evoke guffaws and cheers. Those who take the serious mode of this conceit make the error in reverse. What cannot be understood by everyone is always a subject of general fear among those who understand it, and what cannot be understood at all will forever be perfectly suppressed as wrong. Although the definition of insanity has been quite different from one place to another and from one era to the next, there has at least until now always been some real madness of behaviour based in utter mystery, completely incomprehensible. It is nearly possible to say that the only remains of this human form are the various physical cancers, the vulgar form of madness. The classifications of psycho-pathology now encompass all but the very rarest of maleficent influences of the soul, and those rare spirits that retain their freedom are largely subsumed in art. Surely the late-blooming madness of numbers of artists in the nineteenth century, may be traced not solely to the pox but find its source as well in the extent to which their self-expression, whether of ideas or images, remained incomprehensible and unreceived. At the same time, it was widely believed, particularly in this country that masturbation, like the pox, would render one insane. No doubt many onanists thus retreated from the world. It is appreciable, though hardly, that the very pox was partly fictional. The previous European conceit was, after all, that every instance of sexual expression however divinely ordained contributed to the course of death. Poor Onan had done no more than disappoint the wishes of his dead brother's wife.

All self-expression is essentially unrelated to other people, and in some term is always near to the unknown. The unknown is the type of historical sin. It cannot be prohibited, it can only be forbidden. No historical customs may regulate self-expression, except to deal variously and at length with the few known forms it takes, for most self-expression passes unrecorded. Anyone is permitted to say, I feel sick, and then leave the room to purge, but I have never heard of anyone saying, Excuse me, I have a hard-on. It is man's curse to call significance upon everything earthly and celestial. Sexual expression seems wonderful not, it would seem, for the delightful nervous sensation it occasions, but because it will involve one with another in ways that seem meaningful, as in the convention of mutual love. I suppose that among the remarkable things a man may do, masturbation is the most nearly insignificant. Artist or onanist, all realize something incommunicable. There is a popular affinity between what is incomprehensible and what is insignificant. The considerable revision of their world in the shape of international architecture publicly acquaints the people with a style of indifferent self-expression for which private masturbation leaves them prepared. Their autobiographies make indifferent histories to elaborate a public criticism just as this story ends confounded with my greetings and best wishes to you.

I remain, Sir, your devoted solicitor, and friend; Adieu!

In 1958, at a very early age, the distinguished Jewish critic of American literature, N. Podhoretz, wrote, among other things, the following sentences published in *The New York Times Book Review.*

> —With one or two exceptions, they are not as first novels have notoriously been, directly autobiographical. There are no portraits of the artist as a young man among them, no cries of outrage against the world for its brutality to sensitive youth, very little uncontrolled wildness of expression or structure. There is talent to burn among the new writers. The truth is, however, that a novelist achieves significance by taking thought about the world he lives in, by trying to understand what it is that most matters to himself and his contemporaries from day to day and from decade to decade; by trying to determine what constitutes the uniqueness of his own period, and therefore of his own experience.

Whether the truth is or is not varnished, it always appears presumptuously at the end of the story. In the case of American letters, there is a very short history to remark. The colonial-provincial period, including Poe, Hawthorne, Emerson and Melville, ended toward 1890, having spawned a largely infertile and gothic tradition which spread its wastes through the twentieth century in the form of highly journalistic ephemera. In its way were generated a number of amusing editorial freaks, as Elbert Hubbard, H.L. Mencken and James Thurber. Theodore Dreiser was the only one of note who did not disintegrate to humor. Henry James was the earliest great American literate to leave the country. Henceforth, the major forces in American letters returned themselves to Europe where they died. For the purpose of this synopticon, the names Gertrude Stein, Ezra Pound and Thomas Stearns Eliot will represent that generation. They placed themselves firmly in the category of New Art which had been invented in the nineteenth century by Baudelaire, and among Americans they admired only Whitman and Henry James. There remained two novelists to form a third expatriated generation. Ernest Hemingway would popularize a taste for hopeless adventures, taking his stand in Paris, and later in Cuba. Another stylist, William Faulkner, put forth a monumental vision of his own country, the American South, which, although forced to incorporate with the United States, remained an English colony less Americanized than Canada for a hundred years. Faulkner's work was received as seriously by Sartre as

Poe's had been by Baudelaire. Many events coinciding, it happened that the children of immigrants combined with persons escaping from ghastly preparations for the final German war to cast by way of expedient accumulation and gravity the American matrix of International Art. There were developed no American literary masters of this style but T.S. Eliot, as a British subject, and Edmund Wilson were notable critics of it. However, poetical practice became as popular as medical practice and the writing of novels was industrialized. The masterpiece of the formative period of International Art was the atomic bomb which, by its inhuman and ecumenical pretensions, is a perfect classic of the age. In 1945, in the midst of the period I am now describing, it happened that there had come to be a larger number of Jews in in the United States than remained in any other country. They concentrated in New York, for a hundred years the artistic and financial capital of the nation. Earlier in the century, Jewish Literature had, as Gide remarked, largely confounded itself with French Literature; throughout these thirty years, what had suddenly come to be called American Literature as a result of the European prestige of Hemingway and Faulkner, came more and more into association with Jewish Literature so that at the present time, the two are less distinguishable than British and American writing is. By way of their great history of diffusion throughout Europe, it would be appropriate for Jews to to administer the International Style in a country composed entirely of European immigrants. But not only is the Jewish influence resisted in this country, but the American Jews have used the opportunity offered by their maturity to produce literary works on subjects that are of more interest to Jews than others, ranging from psychoanalysis to situations created in the Judeo-German dialect. The characteristic of Jewish Literature is that hopeless suffering is valued. The characteristic European value is the aspiration to Dominion, that is now fragmented to partial memories of all that has been lost. By coincidence, then, for the International Style, anything goes.

In the nineteen-fifties, when business in general was very good, there was in this country for the first time a large number of artists, most of whom were painters, and poets and novelists and critics, many of whom had some international reputation. For the novelists and critics, life was a race against time and money to see which would force-feed sufficiently to be able to fill the modern literary pies in the sky created by the third expatriated generation and its apologists, the ranks of intellectual communists who turned from politics largely to indulge their sexual fantasies. Writers and critics would still sniff with some diligence around all the most recently published work, including that which was refused the freedom of the press, so as to try to determine which way the literary winds were blowing their constituents. A few were earnest enough to admit the existence of nothing. The race expired when it was discovered that the vice-presidencies of literature did not yield to competition, though quite a few made some money off it. But that fashion is still followed by those who abandoned their souls in the nineteen-fifties. At the present time, as if to forestall the onset of a predictable fin de millénaire malaise, there is a new fashion of criticism that was heralded in the previous generation, for example in the art criticism of Harold Rosenberg. It uses philosophical techniques without being a philosophy of literature or of art. Ideally the critic would invent a scheme suggested to him by the common associations and characteristics of all current art and literature, wherever produced and no matter by whom, which he would use to extract himself from a cataclysm of information laid on by the sophisticated arts of publicity. Having then artificially buoyed himself in the factual sea, he will undertake to attach his scheme to the underlying masterworks of all epochs by composing the historical catechism that demonstrates his resolution. It is the journalism of the International Style, and it is by no means simple, nor really new. Although it is only a European fashion, it bears some relation, perhaps only synoptic, to the famous Chinese scheme of the Book of Changes which in turn shares similarity with the European folk-science of astrology. The contest among critics and writers is now then on a subtler scale, for it is necessitated that critics and artists anticipate each other simultaneously. The game is so complicated as to exclude most critics and artists either by way of their not being up to such synthetic tasks or by the refusal of some artists to play the revision. In addition, some critics have assumed pretensions not only to philosophy, from which the critical rhetoric has always derived, but to art as well. Thus the invention of the critical metaphor of which some of my work is one sort of demonstration. Once, not long ago, George Santayana wrote, I have been a philosopher, almost a poet. We are now upon the end of that distinction.

Sociology has come to dictate the terms of the International Style by way of its being the language of democracy, as underlaid by psychologistics in the historical mode. As part of the demonstration, we will now omit a Norn's mouthful of examples illustrating that decree. Consciousness in the International Style requires one to view everything contemporaneously. What people, or in the case of art, one person, are doing somewhere is supposed to be well related to everything going on at the same moment everywhere. Whereas the news of the day had been a report of whatever the people in town were talking about, the news of the day is now really the news of the day, and comprehensible as such. While maintaining this modern spherical awareness of simultaneity, it is superposed that something going on somewhere is related to everything else having gone on in the same place in all past time. Thus the history of the world, in factual form, escapes in an etherializing quotidian series toward the unknown past. It carries with it nuances of all that is recorded which, in this way, shows itself at one with the modern tendency to vaporize. That effect is a contribution of the previous revision of the world, defining history by politics. In this fashion, it is easily conceivable that critics have already included in their schemes many works of art and manufacture which will remain completely unwritten, and it is now more likely than ever that there is no surprise in store for us.

It is possible that one does not make friends in the sense that young people can be friends except when one is young. It is likely that one may not have friends of that sort when he is older. In most cases when those who have been friends no longer see each other often they will forget the details of the fiction of their friendship. In this connection, it is illuminating to notice that old friends meeting again after a long interval will do their best to act out a recreation of themselves for each other in anachronistic terms. Thus it is possible that old friends do not know each other, just as a man may not know his son. But unlike brothers, fathers and sons have no recourse to the play of recollection, so that paternal encounters are often marked by some of the same cleverness displayed between those who have long been slightly acquainted. By virtue of their distinctly similar memories of a certain time in the past, old friends do not mistrust each other as strangers do for they can with some accuracy anticipate each other's every move. It is quite likely, however, that among a number of friends of different periods of one's youth, a few will eventually have changed the characteristics they display in personal encounters so far that compared with the manner in which one has set oneself all that can be evoked between them are the remains of a minor reminiscence that is no pleasure to recall. This effect will be enough to destory the very source of our recognition of each other, if it does not lead them to impatient recriminations. If they are honest they may never see each other again.

But there will be others among the numbers of one's old friends who will not so radically diverge. One or two when they meet you again after a change of years will be pleased to report that they find themselves delighted to forget the past and make up the present, as when a man becomes his father's only friend. But before that, there is a possibility that two persons who have shared much may maintain an interest in each other which ordains that when they meet, however infrequently, by chance or by design, each wishes to understand what has happend to the other, if not in every detail then generally, and doing so will combine to form the series of their continuing relation, saving remembrance as a condiment too piquant for ordinary feeding. In addition, it is conceivable that the details of a youthful friendship will conserve vividly as points of allusion in an aging connection. The use of friendship will remain as a manner of definition and renewal. It is doubtful that one's friends at any moment will be much older or much younger than oneself, though one redeem a parent or cultivate grandfather. We say that the processes of fiction, of which making friends is one, do change as one gets older.

Because Mr. James Joyce is so p
ainstaking and assiduous in the
perfection and expansion of his
text and the correction of his
proof, he is tired and has aske
d for a month's rest, to which
request the editors acceded rea
dily, confident that the reader
s who derive so much pleasure f
rom the results of his unsparin
g pleas unsparing efforts and d
istinguished creations will una
nimously approve. —R.B. Kitaj

One does not want to reconsider everything that has been left out. I heard her call from the street while I was still in bed, although I had not yet had enough sleep. When I came upstairs she was already there, I knew, but I had not yet found my glasses. As soon as she noticed that I could not see her clearly, she gave them to me. Most of it is inconsiderable. There were two women in the room. I wish to preserve a short list of titles like eggs in an English pie. One asked questions, the other awaited our departure silently. I avoided making jokes, but still I affected an extravagant, ironic tone to my voice, which I enjoyed. She did not yet remember that I did not always speak that way.   *L'Étudiant d'Architecture Qui Parle*   We talked about what we saw along the way, and inquired of each other the names of the rivers and the towns. She scarcely suppressed her enthusiasm for a different part of the world. But I did not hesitate to express my love for the countryside in which we found ourselves. *Assemblage in Kit Form*   The day was gray and the climate was dry. I had not remembered her clearly, aside from the color of her voice, and her dress which was blue.   *The Song of True Freedom*   We went out of the way to visit Hale Eddy. I filled up the time with explanation as she read from the maps. I was always interrputing my stories to designate a house or a horse. Later on the roads became steeper and after a while there was nothing to buy. I said so.   *The Nineteenth Century Buildings of New York State*   She did not yet say just what she did. It was succeeded by another scheme in a matter of chance.

For *The New York Times Book Review:*

To say less than that this novel is one of the more unusual effects of the New York newspaper strike of 1963 would be impossible. To say much more than that might also prove impossible, for it is a book that does not suggest easy generalities about the young, nor does it settle down into one of the categories of literature that helpful critics have laid out for our guidance. It is really a book that speaks for itself; it is a strange book that remains interesting though one does not know just what it is.

It is covered with a photograph taken by the author of two of the windows in his house in the Wall Street district of New York. Upon the sills of the windows appear several objects, most notably a bunch of daisies. Toward the end of the book he remarks, after reciting the contemporary history of style in men's underwear, "And, if I may say so, the beauty of all such observations is that they are, like a view of daisies, facts without meaning." He is a man who, like most of us, likes facts, but he is distressed by the use to which he finds facts put.

He puts them to some distressing uses himself, as when he supposes cancer to be "a vulgar form of madness," a rearrangement of facts that comes close to making nonsense of the language. Surely this is not a book about facts or a book of facts, though it may lead, like the course of an experiment, to speculation about the nature of fact or any of perhaps a thousand other subjects.

Still, it is not a mishmash. The intransigence of the title, a phrase selected, perhaps by chance, from the jargon of some cryptic bureaucracy of commerce, sets the tone of self-assurance maintained throughout in measured pace which is peculiar to the author himself. For an example of his technique, at one point early in the first section he writes, "Concerning his brother and sister, who were younger, there was nothing more to say, and he did not follow the convention of going on about them as if he did not know what he was doing." In that sentence, as in many others, he demonstrates the ambiguities of his own position in writing the book. Or, as he puts it, he "breaks the mask" of artistic self-control in a way which he nevertheless controls. The long series of sketches, dialogues, stories, games, themes, lectures, poems, portraits and plays of which the book is composed appear to the reader as inevitable while he is constantly assured that they are largely accidental. One of the author's slogans, buried at various points in the text, is, "I traduce the informal." He is willing to use everything and anything for the purpose of undermining its irrelevance to what has gone before and what will follow. He often uses words oddly. People do not say that they traduce things. The key, here and typically, is that the French word *traduction* means *translation*.

The noted Egyptian critic of American literature, Mr. I. Hassan, has in the course of his disturbing criticism posited a "literature of silence." It may be this book is a master statement in some such genre, which Mr. Hassan admitted did not completely exist when he set forth his theory of contemporary writing a few years ago. We can get at the base of that sort of fashionable criticism, if we remark that the kind of electronic music that is to be heard from modern composers is the music of silence. From a commonly held point of view this music is really noise, which is to say, incomprehensible sound, and there is a sense in which silence is also incomprehensible sound. But in his *traduction,* the author of this book sounds out his every resource in such a way that the effect is more like a view of daisies than the cacophony of informal music. His "silence" is noisy, but as the performance proceeds though innumerable movements, we have the strange sensation that we begin to comprehend the unknowable, a sense usually reserved for poetry at its best.

The virtuosity of the writing, done in quite various styles and modes, gives the impression that the author will try any arrangement of words he can think of. There is even a paragraph or two written relentlessly in not very good French. But from time to time the reader is reminded that much has been omitted. There are a few quotations from the parts that have been left out. So that again, as in speaking of silence and noise, it is easy to trap ourselves in rhetoric (what, after all, is easier?) for it is certain that all the noises that he uses are the author's own. Perhaps the most remarkable thing about this remarkable book is that the author manages not to trap himself at his own games while he mines the approaches of every adversary, occasionally by means of a simple joke.

But although the reader occasionally laughs aloud and more often chuckles quietly as he reads it, this is not one of those books designed principally to evoke such a response. And although it is largely serious, neither is it reducible to a quasi-philosophic series of maxims. One of the words which is used most frequently in the book is the word *scheme*. Basically, a scheme is any unifying series, any process. More generally, the author sees all of man's undertakings, all history, as an infinite number of schemes that continually change in every respect. Thus far everything is completely informal, the creation of the world inevitably begins in Chaos, but already the way is indicated for the construction of yet another scheme which will clarify one's own situation in relation to everything else. The formula is lapidary and obscure, but the idea itself is not new. To the unsuspecting reader, the book seems at first to be composed of letters and other bits of autobiography, a number of selections of poetry in prose, and portions of storytelling which are abruptly terminated. But as one proceeds, one finds the author seeking to demonstrate that successive variants of a myth cannot be disregarded as irrelevant, that the sum of related tales is a living aggregate, that all elements in a complex system are related and that their sense can be derived only from an analysis of their interrelations, of the place which the unitary scheme can occupy in the set of all schemes. That is why it would not be erroneous to regard this book as a scheme of schemes.

A brief review is no place to attempt an analysis of all the interrelations which such a scheme implies. Indeed one of its implications is that such an undertaking, at whatever length, would be a simple exercise in logical fatuity, like the definition of a language that would have no use. Paradoxically it could be said that just such a language is here defined. It is one of the author's schemes or games to presume, for example, that a story, often anachronistically referred to as a history, may be composed by the juxtaposition of unrelated remarks so long as the historical syntax remains intact. What results is a "story" of the type for which a reading of all the B's, say, in any alphabetical index will yield an extreme example. It is highly tempting to cite, as is usual in reviews, one or two actual examples to illustrate this unusual process, especially as there are many eminently quotable pieces of writing in the book, but it would be completely misleading to suggest that anything short of a reproduction of the entire work could represent the style, or even the quality, of the writing as a whole. At one point the author quotes, with evident approval, part of an interview given a few years ago by the cinemist Jean-Luc Godard: "If you know in advance exactly what you're going to do, it's no longer worth the trouble of doing it. At the same time, it is I who have organized the race. We have therefore the right to quote what pleases us. Why be constrained? If you want to say something, there is only one solution: say it." But it is an achievement of his complicated and problematical point of view that this entire review is in fact a quotation from the book itself.

We ask ourselves, What is this book about? Nothing is clearly an unsatisfactory response. Most superficially, it is about what the author did and thought during the newspaper strike, and then what he did and thought about that. The book is divided in two. The second half is said to be a revision of the first. What did he do? Nothing extraordinary, from his account, except that he wrote this book. In the first half, the author is preoccupied with beginning. In the second half he is more interested in ending. But furthermore, the book is in fact divided into three parts, with titles. The first part, slightly revised, is presented as it was written. The second part, which is concerned with omission, is in turn divided, the second of its parts having been written after the entire third part of the book was in draft. With an unexpected degree of precision, the third part has three parts. It is based on material accumulated during the first year of writing, which was assembled later, and yet later completely revised. It is ultimately concerned with the uses to which language may be put; in effect it is a demonstration of various metaphors which may be construed against the incoherence of life itself. Its scheme is a complex of allusions to all that has gone before in other words. But rather than expressing a completed metaphor for life or a new mode of viewing the world, as do most first works, however tentatively, this particular return to the text represents the author's criticism of the various modes which he has disposed along the course of this most indefinitive norm of narration. In another sense it is his response to the imaginary challenges presented by artists and critics of what he calls 'the early modern generation,' most notably James Joyce and Gertrude Stein. Then again, it can be seen as an appeal to the men and women of his own time to realize their own style of life and art, perhaps by means of works bearing no apparent similarity to this book. And so on. But no matter whether his tone at one point or another is serious or playful and regardless of the author's radical distrust of the professions and the languages, it always seems that he might have taken for his epigraph a line from *Finnegans Wake* — "Oh, yes, and something else occurs to me."

Whatever construction may be put upon it, the book exists only as phenomena in series. It is, in any case, most aptly titled. Like many other books, it must be read to be understood; unlike most, this book wants to be read carefully more than once.

Mr. Castle is an unemployed victim of labor disputes who was formerly in service to the Sunday Editor of the New York Times. He often reviews his own work.

Then, a week before he would be twenty-five in a month, he decided by chance to go for a month to England and France. His friends laughed, and he said—the opportunity presented itself and so I decided to go—and his friends smiled. He threw up his job with a flourish which went unnoticed but was rewarding. He flew. Once there he would have more time and beside that there lay an excuse. Part of the liquefaction will have occurred by the time I arrive, he thought, and the rest may take place while I'm there. He was busier than ever before he left and after he got there he had nothing to do. But there was nothing he did not do, repeating as he did so the everlasting knowledge of what it was, which kept him from thinking very much about it. The police passed him politely through the port. He took a bus, he found a seat, he read the news, he gave the paper to his neighbor. Getting in, he took a cup of tea and made a call. This will be good for me, he thought. All the notices, without showing surprise, looked favorably upon any such thing. Whoever answered said that would be fine. The cat was pleased. One felt at home in England.

In the morning, he got up and came down for breakfast. The toast was cold and brittle, the air debilitating. The meal was hearty. He gulped his tea and ran for the bus with the others. Fortunately, however, he had nowhere to go. As it stopped for a light he jumped off. He stepped quickly through the gate and vanished. They gave him something to read while he waited. In a short while she appeared, trailing her coat. She said she was surprised but she clearly wasn't. She said it was too early and set the price he paid at once. When she had given it to him she continued to sell it by remarking the wrong way to make it. Then he went whistling on his way while, really, he invented his own destination. Don't forget, he had nowhere to go. He agreed to be civil. Needlessly he went by a longer way which led him past the scene of his misfortune. He smoked less and drank much. After all he was not drunk and otherwise there was very little to eat. There was something to be said for it. It was great enough, but quite short, were distance contrasted with power. On the other hand, one had words for everything. The bluish distemper of the walls clung like moss against the ground of chalky plaster. It smelt mouldy as small beer or dregs. Furthermore, nobody noticed how little it was. They said they supposed it must seem tiny but thought they shouldn't have thought so. He lost patience and chafed at the bit which insinuated itself the more deeply creating a moral gap in his wounded conscience. It couldn't have been worse. Everyone was helpful. There was nothing to do but to go somewhere else.

As soon as he left the city he found himself in the country, passing quickly by everything in sight. In due course, he came to stand before a particular house in a certain road at Northampton. He soon got used to the smell of coal. Actually he was glad to have a place there. On the one hand he made a friend and on the other he did not. Occasionally, it rained. But whatever it was, the weather caused congratulations. It was quite remarkable. He began by getting up and coming down again. As long as he knew what he was doing there was more than enough to do. Now and again the birds twittered. The fastest way to go was on foot and it was easy to walk. He would as soon have talked, and there was, in this case, something to say. There was no need to explain himself for everyone assumed that everything was understood. At that time he was able only to write one page. Actually he was never able to do it. Each time he tried he failed but he did not fail to try each time. The long vacation proved worthwhile. After a time he would take a walk. It was on one such occasion that he first began imagining things, knowing all the while that he couldn't keep it up. Once he cried for joy. He realized he was hungry before dinnertime and without being thirsty he drank a pint of best bitter beer. Now in the evenings he began to tell a story for lack of something else to do. He told it very well and one or two people listened to him tell it. They had never heard anything like it. It was not like what they imagined, and they listened as if for the first time, just a few of them. Although he would be reminded momentarily, each evening as he talked he forgot what time it was. But from time to time he rested and when he did the others told each other about each other, making indifferent stories of similar ways. Sometimes they talked to him in the mornings as well telling splendid little stories that seemed completely pointless and perfectly charming indeed. However obvious it might become that they had nothing at all to say the thought couldn't have occurred to him. He went off every day without lunch and came back later with a good appetite. He talked as if he were eating and couldn't remember what he had dined on. At length, which was only a few days, he could no longer see straight, nor clearly. I suppose he fell asleep on the floor which was where he slept there.

In England, for example, he was able to realize that to go up one must come down. The controversy was interminable and the story became endless. One or two continued to listen for as long as he told it and they had no idea he was repeating himself. He was completely unknown and his name was still good. Nobody had ever heard such a story as his and they did not know that it was not a common version. Before he said anything they were completely unprepared for it and afterwards they were of the same opinion. He wasn't able to guess the subjects of their stories, which were invariably correct, but he loved every word of them. Although they knew the answers they asked no questions. Once again he arose only to return the call. They all sat about on the floor in various attitudes of discomfort, prepared as usual to listen to the story. It happened that for a long moment nobody said a word. Then somebody laughed. He cast his nearly bleary gaze toward the unexpected premonition. Two or three more began to laugh. He had never seen anything like it. Some did not laugh at once but after all everyone laughed. It was what he had been looking for without ever hoping to find it. Immediately it became general, a word for it was found which everyone remembered and finally the story realized a fact as if no name had ever been better.

The noonday girl, this time once more all in blue, steps forth to survey her possession of Saturday morning. The lexicon is abstract, the sentence is the same, the fact is quite concrete, the poem is somewhat stolen but lively and often quoted. She sings: ratty boo, sofa sofar so, automobee, ought to be moby, sofa sofar, ever over debout, ever tin over, skit a lit day—ratty boo. The importance of digital contact is stressed, death pulsates figuratively, willing to be walking, wishing to be browner. The necessity of frequent conquests is displayed in muted cries. She nuzzles her mother who deals a prudent rebuke. She watches her eyes lift each other in surprise. Everybody follows her disappearance and the men return her glance to their work. And what would it be, what word would be the word that was found? A premonition of four parts to the last rise.

Length? What is length? More slowly; nevertheless a gradually stronger resistance to interminable recurrency, newly reformulated in long words that do excite the lower ear. Wishing to be walking, raining, seen to be talking, fighting—they dropped to give each other up. One, two, one, two to be one, two to be two. When she saw me again tears showed in her eyes then, a slight rearrangement of the parts. With a certain sum of priceless caution and the addition of a bit of force, merry becomes as marry welcomes the merrymaking out-come and income of marriage. Two, one, two to be two, one to be one. Stars silently coincide, unnoticed, known and believed. For that, strange plants bloom cryptically in the soil of custom, the darkest recess. Once freed, they would eye each other sightlessly, soundlessly, as greener flowers do. Yet awhile their rubrications stand oppressed. A vine and twine. Slowly holding arching pressing sliding, come give us a kiss, she says, or a laugh, she says, 'used for something finally deciding to go on digging doing it.' One, two, two, one . . .

With more than that comes plenty of this—speed—lack of care, a corps of passions so slowly grown to where it now nearly by permis-sion bursts to the unisexual climb of more or worse, then by this trim gorge, this stand of blood, willingly divided thrice, and added to with some abandon, now going forth under colors well-known in that vicinity and to which the beholder adds his own assimilation—it's like life—and well it is when you get to the top you return and begin somewhere else nearby a little differently, taking a chance each time, not the first, not the second, but the third, always permitting whatever happens, always with half an eye glued to the plug and something else that neither sees nor winks—it's an art—perhaps a bit more carefully on occasion, without any need of virile images to captivate the sinewy responses that flee not before the ear, eye or word but pass and repass across the irony of animals, the third a hidden adjunct of the first and willing member there presiding, the same third a source and cause of hope to come in the name of lifelike verbs.

At last, the blue metaphor to end this *inattendance*. Infantile remarks becoming momentary images transmitted back across the strand of tempo rise curiously crossed but more than ready for more words. A final remonstration. An ambiguous silence played only by that means, a contradiction, and more ephemeral the terms. There are brief pauses but the lessons prove successful. An image recurs from the text—an eye, an ear, a nose, my eye in your cheek. Not only is there heat enough but something more may be required, maintained, only to the point of expression, never over the line to the word and the others. Time, but unaccountable amounts and so on and on to the indications which prove a demonstration. This is not an attempt. It is a question of research and it is quiet, a notion of husbandry almost excluded, but further, no, father, and blank to the next occasional criticism of weight, perhaps, without that coherence but a nebulous sensation of the first point in series. (silence)

A bird, I can hear, she . . . my . . . it . . . a tiny little—it was nothing, a bit of a . . . just about to, more, there was, one tear, and he . . . by my . . . and OH! . . . it is he of be for

Tile to show being
top not a lot
for the new and more
    marks fights sings sends
    drains finds rings rends
    sights feels winds wends
    darts feints binds bends
      and and and but fire knows

          and it is of the, how to cork the bloody blue bottle to death, and so and so and so and so . . . and then, grass, warm rain, a light breeze, two whistles

It was after June when I arrived au point d'argent sur les minuit, and I was tired of talking anyway. I made my way quite without under-wear, as it was not the season for it, and as 'madame' had very voluntarily promised I found the key to my door in a niche at the edge of hers. 'Prenez garde, Monsieur de Château,' she cried with a laugh, not to fright me, and, opening the door to reveal a slice of her kitchen and half her careful face, she offered cognac to celebrate the vacancy but I demurred remarking my fatigue and supposing she was not prepared to have me accept. By means of a series of pushbuttons whose locations I could remember I lighted myself along the econom-ical hallways and up the ancient stairways toward a door at the top of the last step, the number of which was, by the normal custom of the house, one less than that stamped into its key. I could remember having been given a lengthy explanation of that fact as a sign that I had come to be, at some point, an habitual guest, but I retained nothing of the sense of it, save the assurance of 'madame' that it was correct to have it so. I regarded it as one of the woman's jokes, of which I completely understood fewer than half when she occasionally trapped me for a real display. As I let myself into the darker chamber, it crossed my mind that it could be she did not always address me by the aristocratic nickname she had applied to me which sounded such a deliciously false and appropriate noise in her ear (she had originated it as a name to call one of her cats) but when I pushed back the shutters on the street, the question left me. I had always found the rue Mazarine attactive in the rain. I gazed avidly down the dull white of its shuttered fronts opposite to their bright reflections in the silent running stones. I caught the breath of some vaguely berliner song played by the band au café du Lapin Belge below, and I heard footsteps retreating quickly up the street in the direction of the quay, but nothing moved as I stood in the light cool breeze before the window. Then, thinking oddly of nothing I could name, I left my shirt and laid myself to sleep.

I thought I had nothing planned, yet at the same time I had certain intentions, or pretentions, the more automatic of which would reëstablish, so far as one might, a set of conditions for life in a manner which I had come to expect of the place or of the people, as I had begun already to do in parrying the brief persiflage tended by the abbess. While I was not well acquainted with any historically superior mother, I had no remaining doubt that 'madame' at some other epoch would have made an excellent administrator. She gave the impression of hoarding jewels, and that she did so secretly for fear her love might destroy her fable any day. She always dressed in black and prayed at home, being doubtless of her piety. But at the same time she recommended everyone to read the novels of M. de Balzac, who, in one of his later works, had given his painters lodgings in her very house, or, at the least, in one of the houses that had been joined together by her predecessor, to whom one presumed she had been married, but who might himself have been a piece of fiction. As far as anyone knew, he had had no name. It had been in Paris, for example, that I at first began to write customarily in the mornings, a habit I maintained for as long as I had any habit of writing customarily and without purpose. I lived in another house run by a servant who was really called Sammy and who spoke rather badly (I suspected he was from Algiers though no Mussulman himself). I was awakened at the latest possible moment by the service of some coffee and milk and some buttered bread so that I had no need as I had no desire to go out until I was quite ready to walk as much as I pleased, typically to the extremities of the other quarters of the city where I would take another bit of food at the bar and return by public transportation to a central location where the entertainment of my evening might begin. Cast in a different tongue, the fitful dream of my reintegration, I heard the doors of the vehicle collide after each stop. In the metro one must open the doors—in the train one closes them. The sign, FERMETURE ANNUELLE, repeated itself. I renewed my defenses as I fell past the commercial fantasies of my half-remembered, imperfect privacy, toward the recreation of an impersonal world in which everything had been arranged by them to accord with some different logic I would appropriate. Silently, my attention rose within the stream. Surely, my sensation reached me without reason. Slowly, I remade by way upstairs, remarking the position of every switch against the dark. A movement reasserted its integrity, I sensed an intrusion due the sun and, turning away with additional pressure, I awoke to a flood of nuance. By the early light of dawn I noticed that she had placed a marguerite in a little vase on the table by the window, as had been my custom when I had a flower.

The silence had lasted. I had rested only briefly, yet without refreshment I felt eager for the day. I took a light relapse, allowing the remains of my revery to suppress itself, after which I readdressed myself in the midst of a vague glint of expectation. I couldn't tell the time of day for the clouds, which had not yet been burned away by the still dormant sun, the climb against noon. I set myself for the third of three such experiments, beginning early and defining the nature of the chance, the genres that the logistics of strangers engenders. I thought I knew no correspondent, save the casual acquaintances of commerce, like 'madame,' who, as usual, was not yet stirring when I passed without her threshold. Here, in the realistic chill of a morning so little advanced that it remained unhabituated to a greater extent than had its adverse eve, here, I say, might be found the moment of clarity indispensable for the relation of how I wrote certain books, but in effect that was not the fact I chose to make. I favored distance. The scene might take twenty minutes or less to be made, or displayed, but its purpose was not less than to encompass, including every indivision of the radiating points, some small purchases, my phantastic amusements and the lessons to be learned from a history of France. Subsequently, when I should be fully awake, and the number of effects would have increased in proportion to the time of day, I might think over what I had thought and done to make of that the rambling untidy journal which I sent to the friend who was equally alone, if not more lonely than I felt, myself. I bought a piece of bread to keep me company. My extraterritorial visions centered about the Dauphin, the nature of his education, and so on, in the midst of the shame I felt when once I realized that no matter how well I conducted myself I could not live to know more than proliferating uncertitude. Yet Charles would forever be the indomitable issue of my soul. Amiable relations were thus reduced to the level of entertainment in a movement of logic that seemed unbearably direct, though one be afforded the consolation of a life *by* Mallarmé. My tears ran in unfortunate veins. But the texture of the bread, the taste of the coffee, the smell of the tobacco, made everything I saw become delightful and expressive. At the same time it was not reduced to a solid core of meaning, not that it might not be criticized. The strange blue and white umbrellas were awkwardly untwisted just in time to catch like dials the first hot summer sun when all at once the clouds had melted. Or, perhaps it was a day not different from many others, save that my perception of it peopled the city with apparitions of them who became, at certain times, invisible. I trailed through the smaller and the open streets, without noting their names, not knowing where I found myself, unknown and subtle in correction. I desired not to remember whatever I had written, less still to translate a voluntary reconstruction. Jumbled together with all sorts of people of business, whose hour it was, I looked with pleasure into windows showing an array of equipment for the kitchen, and I examined with the delight of a man of letters the offerings of commercial stationers. I entered one such shop for the purchase of a supply of a certain style of envelope. Now after a long period of forcing myself to daily bureaucratic work, I was not sure that my habits had not changed, though in any case they had never been so regular as they might suggest themselves to be. It seemed likely that now, when I had nothing else to do, I would arise early, not having required much sleep, and make a tour of my haunts. Thus after a little edifying incoherence, I might write through the afternoon, or if I thought of a destination I might continue my promenade. On the first day in which I observed this order it was possible to meet a pleasant woman of whom I had heard and who had heard of me. Towards evening I could introduce myself to a few of her companions in the trade with whom I drank and talked and dined. Once in a while when I met her by chance, she would arrange to come by the rue Mazarine from where, depending on the weather and our inclination, we might variously divert ourselves. On those occasions, which were not quite frequent, 'Madame' would invariably shreik something incomprehensible up the stairs to the effect that although I had lost my youth, I had at least not lost my reputation.

(It is suggested to the reader that the preceeding three sections, comprising a visit to foreign parts be re-read aloud before proceeding with the sale.)

BOOK FIVE

The Further Sale of What Remains

As a scheme it was all right. In effect, however, it was tedious and confusing. That was too bad. It would be impossible, of course, to clear the air by resorting to biographical detail. No, the triumph was complete. People are always full of advice for those who have already done something. Why is it not, they ask, some other, simpler, newer, more traditional, clearer, & yes, cheaper thing? There can be no answer but that in fact it is not other than it is. That is a conviction, as in the case of a character, but it is not a misfortune. Inflation has had diverse effects that could not be predicted. I am speaking of inflation in every sense, without listing them. Why bother? The answer is so simple, so clear, so direct, so obvious and so devastating as to be unremarkable. Nevertheless, it is my profession, and my love.

Whoever you are, to you endless announcements!

Clean it up. So far, as even such a phrase implies, the narrative has proceeded in a normal manner. *Hors texte,* there are a few quotations of value, each appealing from the sense of a certain character. 'Myself,' for example. There came to be a time, when it was I do not know, in which the sort of recording I had done before no longer satisfied me. It was not a formal question, but as usual it had only formal results. There were five, 'myself' (and Charles) excluded separately. I admit that their development seemed to be haphazard.

Actually there was a justification for every move. The program is to make a chrysalis of the novel I did not write using some of the same material that I have perhaps treated elsewhere by means of fiction. Can I recall every circumstance of this decision? I cannot. In that way it is unlike a crime. *C'est de la prose libre.*

It is asexual and amoral. It is a complementary fiction to both philosophy and poetry. It is perfectly suppressed; it is not a love story. The story is missed out but the characters live on. Must there be a story? Yes, but I do not desire to tell it.

The complete set
of six characters
together and separately:
Avoid the challenge of piecing out the story.
Do not be concerned with the length of it.
At the same time, do not make it more vulgar.
All women must be one woman.
The unifying principle is contained in the words, *At the time of which I am speaking.* At the time of which I am speaking, may be any time of which I wish to speak. It is not simply the continuous present, it is the ever-present. It is not the presentation of the six; it is the formation of the one. It is the relation of one and five. At the same time, there is none of the freedom of the first book, which is perfectly simple. It is the definition by liquefaction of the personae 'myself' and 'the other,' the redistribution of the sources.

. . . It must move. Nothing may be mentioned twice. I can relieve my embarrassment concerning the materials I have so far presented only briefly. This will develop briefly. Nothing is anticipated, the life of an animal, nothing is dreamed, all comes actual: before and after is irrelevant. Although the past tense of verbs certifies historical seduction, it is too easy to use the present tense itself. I do not have in mind the integration of the 'perfect' work. We have here the invention of time. As against my other work it is formal.

Having begun, beginnings. Casting about, out. There could be a characteristic phrase or word, a namely indication, but such an other form would insinuate itself, eventually to cover this that is already too easy to overlook. In the draught it is as dead as trees. Five, They were not at all equal, Some were quicker than others, some nearer, some further from the point. It is an investigation. Of what? Here is the table: and here begins the exercise.

S-H-W-V-D

0.	1.	0	W	-1
0.	2.	0	D	-1
0.	3.	1	S	-1
0.	4.	2	H	-1
0.	5.	3	W	-2
0.	6.	4	V	-1
0.	7.	5	D	-2
0.	8.	0	H	-2
0.	9.	0	S	-2
0.	0.	0	V	-2

1.	1.	0	W	-3
2.	1.	0	V	-3
3.	1.	0	H	-3
4.	1.	0	D	-3
5.	1.	0	S	-3

15 fifteen 15

The one who is most complete is also the least lively. And there is a demonstration of the mystery of volition, as in everyday affairs. I understand it better than any other point. White moves, giving her the impression that she has been his influence. But actually he admits no influence. My comprehension of this mood of reality gives me license to apply characters in his case which do not actually pertain to him. It is the microcosm. It shows it as it is in greater things that are less clear. It is not the same thing as a myth or legend. In some term, in this very paragraph, that is my domain. He doesn't make an example. It is not what he does but that he does it at all that holds our interest. It should be remembered that he is the lover of machines and numbers; more generally, things. No poetry but straight existence. It is a unitary principle, to which everyone aspires to integrate.

White is self-conscious, he understands himself more perfectly than any, without trying. But its expression is perfectly cryptic. He never objects to any other formulation, ecept that now and again we smile. Because he knows that what he is is nothing else. This conservation has actually no purpose — in him it is a decoration, or no proof. So it would be pointless to invent a list of what he thinks. His test is always that of the right reaction. No false notes. He is an accomplished skeptic, but still it is not thought. More than anything else, it is youth. He has a sister, a mother, and an aunt; he has a wife and a daughter. Yet he has never been seduced. He has sometimes almost been seduced, like the time when he had finally to hide in a fireplace, but has never given over far enough to make that type of mistake. Thus it is not mere safety when I say he is indomitable.

In other words, it is not fear, it is character. Because it is without necessity. It certainly has truth and more than enough time . . . a cat? Yes, it is like that. His world is distinct and circumscribed in the section of his choice. The list is endless of things in which he takes no interest. He is a refugee from those he never wished to join. He is sometimes amused but he is more often annoyed. He refuses, He stops, He shouts at her. He uses politer means in other situations. His resource is anger. There is no explanation for it. He is small and masculine. To what do we attribute that fault? A persistence of detail, begot of the tongues of too many women, perhaps a certain self-indulgence, an admitted lethargy after dinner, and the inclination to let it pass denied. He does not like to be alone. He hardly cooperates. He doesn't understand other people, who strike him as rather odd. But his irony takes forms that are strange to any intelligence that would commit them. Thus we are loath to recreate the design that will necessarily became debased. Debasement is an unfortunate effect at the root of every metaphor, but as it is unavoidable, we do not brood upon it to hatch a little something else we do not intend to say. That is a type for control, and it is there one finds White's excellence. He orders things, and they come to be arranged exactly as he wishes it, more perfectly than anyone perceives. He is an artist but there is no product. And what else. This is to approach, once more, the end of a series, which is always, for me, a matter of hesitation. I would rather not set it but I must. I have had more than enough sleep. There is nothing else to eat, And finally there is nothing else to do. In truth, there are never more than two points each of which is unrelated. The rest are elaborations. Which may be delightful, and which I most certainly require (for without them everything is next to nothing) but I mean that the relation of one to one is the most painful process to compose.

0.2.0

There we have it. It is D. C. L. who, at the time of which I am speaking, most closely reproduces the 'myself' I have yet to decorate. He is actually an artist, with original products, obliging saleswomen, important telephone calls and photographs. But it is almost a necessity. He is a natural ascetic combined with sumptuary impulses and desires. He thinks in a peculiar manner that gives him the illusion that he is in control. I believe I have never done anything to break that glass. Nor is the last sentence but one an example of such a thing. Cutting remarks are not my forte, anymore. He is logical, but he overlays his system with rational pretensions that disconcert his nature most productively. There are always excesses in such a process. His is boredom. Now unfortunately there is a type for boredom that is so strong that the reader must willfully ignore it or else I will never be able to say what I have to say. He does not yawn, he does not complain, he is not a supposition of mine, nor do I care to take any liberties with the character he presents at such a precious point. Both he and White have a desire for friendship that we do not profess. It attracts him, not toward his friends, whom he hardly trusts, but rather, for example, in the direction of an Oriental philosophy which applies to anything, but also to the ignorance of women, whom he lives with and loves. There are now three. Like the cryptography that he admires, he makes quick synthetic formulas which, like jokes, expire with pauses of inattention. I mean he is taciturn but articulate as well. He does not smile beautifully or often, He is convicted in content and form. Even so, he flees from the historical point of view, perhaps with the ancillary purpose of appearing more attractive from that quarter. He will admit that he does not know how to do it. He will admit the use of numbers for their arbitrary values, but he takes no real interest in them. He relies on himself as if it was a method of explaining everything, and when occasionally he finds it lacking, he is honestly perplexed. Perhaps that is how we came to make up our combination, a performance which, at the turn of a phrase, could destory any momentary competition, which never knew what hit it. He is not always satisfied with the logical response, but he does not doubt the process. Our collusion had the advantage that he was tenacious just at the point where I broke the mask. When this is well-oiled and simultaneous there is no end to the intellectual wonders you can create. Of course they don't last, but it wasn't desired that they should; The process is perpetually renewed, and it doesn't always end in destruction either. It was always deleterious to women, however, something we eventually had to watch out for. To say it again, whimsy and irony and things like that are not natural moods for him, but he admits illogic in a synthesis like lightning. Lightning naturally divides, and there you are. He moves with grace and slowly. He isn't very well dressed, but his phrase is always exact. He does not apologize. On balance and in theory, he will use any construction which can explain his point of view, but he will rather use those that rely, as he does, on pure existence: a great color, a succession of shapes responsible to numbers, a formula of words. He is inclined to set his explanation in scandalous terms without putting any interest in the scandal. He abdicated his position in his family, which was an excellent one, for something else which he conceives as more respectable, more dangerous, more dignified and actually mystical. The mystery lies in the relationship between the thing and the event. It is too easy to say that there is no such thing: It is desired to invent it. His unadmitted moral concern serves rather to create the necessities upon which he thrives, those which, he supposes, will move him away out of perfect logical inexistence (rhetoric). He will say he is bored where I might say disgusted or enchanted. He confides, as I do not, in the barest minimum. He desired perhaps to be more decorative, but like everyone to some degree, he finds himself incapable of being other than he is, so that he sticks to fact, fortunately not hesitating to invent them, and carefully appreciates the beauty of what's already known.

The short hard fast novel must be very largely concerned with events — it may well seem to be a parody — but the events are actualities. They need not be great or very drastic events, perhaps only commonplaces presented without significance, like the truth. The Jewish novel of the type will be characterized by zany events, or wishful thinking dignified under surrealism. But the question comes up, Can there be a novel without poetry or history? We shall see. It must not appear obscure, that is easy. It must be obscure. You do have the form of the dance . . . the characters together and separately . . . the interaction of events, not personalities. Since it is impossible to make a ballet of it, I am forced to use words that are weighed down with precise ideas, but I shall try to lighten them with expressions that are trivial, empty, hollow, and invisible.

At the time of which I am speaking, many things happened of which I shall mention several. We were five, myself excluded, who would be six including 'my self.' So-and-so sat in a chair pretending to read. When I came in he looked up and smiled. There was only one person in a dusty room. It was so dusty that anyone actually coming in would feel the need of the bath when he left. Often, nevertheless, we did not bathe. The equipment for it was sometimes lacking but moreover, since anyone could buy a shower, we felt, What's the use? As long as it was only noticeable and not remarkable. Then we changed. At the time of which I am speaking, I had trained her to cut my hair from time to time as I pleased. It was not a chance that we would divide or unite without intending to. But it should be supposed that we knew what we were doing and might have told them what it was though more often we chose to be not so revealing and anyway on with the play.

0. 3. 1

This fellow, S. R., did not seem to keep secrets much, though more so than I did, but occasionally he laughed and nobody knew where it came from. He had a reputation which as far as he knew he had done nothing to deserve, but he kept on doing things the same way he always had, which was not the same as everyone else, though he often had a hearty wish that it could be undistinguished. What is the radical similarity of this and that? he thought. When it came to the question of what could be done, he professed not to know. But as I say he did know what he did while he made a display of modesty. But that time was all over. At the time of which I am speaking, he had been absent for many years. We still respected the man he had seemed to us when we ourselves had still been children. He was easily embarrassed. He was easily impressed, but he chose his impressions carefully, so it looked as if he were sufficient to himself. He has always lived alone. As he grew more apart from us, his infrequent communications inclined to a mocking style of verbosity, après Joyce, intended to belie his pretension. But he undermined himself by consistently failing to appear when promised, then disappearing when I thought he was set to stay. It is the elusive quality of words that he could demonstrate by his very uneasiness in company.

In any case, he was convicted. As an undergraduate he had continually professed the apology of art, whence sped his reputation in philosophy, of which we remained completely ignorant. But thus shining in anticipation as he waited at the light, when it broke he made the hard left into the arduous and unhistorical byway where he was taken in hand by other convicts. He doused his lights. None of them could perceive his private hesitation while they professed to know just what they wanted. He did not propose to undeceive them. The goal was their only association, and for that purpose he withstood their ribald good fun like a penalty in justice. His monkish rigor bred in them the terror natural to crowds when confronted by a solitary man. If a racehorse veered from the track it would automatically default and a workhorse straying into the race could achieve an unrecognizaable triumph. Its rider might or might not find the right words. *In the old days there was definitely the problem of free will; Now everything goes on at once.* Therefore he determined to go on with the race into which he had been born. He didn't like it. He admired horses and the pasture and the stable. Not having been able to satisfy himself by birthright, he determined on a manner of his own invention which in those circles seemed to be a hobby. He even managed a few medical jokes. His course was respected by his fellows for containing so many decorative allusions they could not themselves sup-

ply. Quietly he did things he didn't have to do. He never satisfied the
expectations of his friends, And he lost his old acquaintances. Sometimes he thought he could no longer think. He was the personifi-
cation of inoffensive cleanliness, as he had always been and as he was
required anew to be. Nevertheless he took a lover's interest in every
aspect of freedom. I wrote to him of my disgust upon disgusting
subjects, which he could accept, though I knew that my expres-
sionism embarrassed him. He ignored me, quickly, & assured me of
his interest. The suffering was part of the birthright and of the
profession. As much as if he had actually been a poet, but less
expressively. In that profession, all suffering was to be subsumed in
work which absolutely did not express what it eradicated. It is known
as suppression.

Now that philosophy is art, medicine is the only moral science
left. We are here in a difficult position. While desiring to present
everything actually, we chose at first the difficult object of mentioning aspects of a process — the life of S. R. — of which the actualities are
unknown unless they may be guessed, which we prohibit. We have
only to mention a few words typical of biography to dispel all doubts
of the subject, except our own, those which are, I feel bound to insist,
the only doubts of any value to us. It is like pain. The sentence, The
King of France is wise, expresses the relations that there is a person
who is king of France and no other person is king of France and that
the one who is the King of France is wise. But at the time of which I
am speaking, there is no one king in France, and nothing is known
actually about any such thing. So much for philosophy. But even
though I mention it in this connection, I do not know why I know
that that is not what Stanley thought. It had been a process of
education, at least at first. That is usually a process that begins with
liberation and continues in the light of liberality toward a perfected
suppression of all that is defined as unrelated to the subject. It is like
slavery. What he said was that he felt like a whore. He doubted that I
would be able to know what he said. But I did. Which is why he
added that he found my continued friendship for him a continuing
pleasure, though he hardly encouraged it, perhaps slightly mysterious since the time when we began to speak so very little and so very
seldom. Since the time when I no longer knew what he did. Since I
had obtained a license to fictionalize his life, though I refused to use
it. Sometimes I would still send him a letter but he would not
respond. Very occasionally I received a short note to assure me that he

still existed. One of them was concluded with this historical anecdote: At the height of a certain battle, Admiral Lord Nelson raised the telescope to his blind right eye and remarked in some heat to his lieutenant, Sir, I really do not see the signal. Stanley would have been an anglophile of german tendencies in spite of having to be a jew. But he did not realize his disenchantment, which is nothing like not realizing one's affinities. More clearly, he would have been a monk, for whom, within the strictest regulation, everything partakes of freedom. Charles seemed much more the saint, and had therefore to cultivate vulgarities, of which there was no doubt that Stanley hadn't any left.

I am pledged to assemble a view of 'myself' from out these reflections of my friends at the time of which I am speaking. I might say anything, of course, but honestly I didn't know what he was doing. Sometimes I thought of it. It really annoyed me when he didn't carry out his plans to visit me. I used to say that S. R. is certainly not where you think he is going to be. Now it was only that he did not keep engagements. Otherwise it had been that he stole things. At the time I didn't know that and it didn't annoy me when I found out. I laughed. He didn't think it a good joke, however. His only intemperance was part of freedom, the first part. I think it amazed him to see me say so at the time of which I am speaking. 'Now I am more confused, unknowing and sick than I gave ever been,' he wrote. 'The bad smell of this chase — god the stench. The ball-twisting, breath-searing run of it — sniffing hot and voraciously after that dark whorish recess — looking for and rooting out that splendid gilded diadem of the truth of what is actually one's own life.' And I replied, Yes, it is often like that. 'What is the importance, where is the worth of any value in trying to decide whether it is better or not to define and maintain distinctions or to obliterate them — those distinctions, boundaries, capabilities, possibilities, chances pertaining to what you have picturesquely labelled, the various forms and qualities of energy as expended or constrained?' At the time of which I am speaking, he called me Fred.

Dear Stanley, We should have talked more often, or used those occasions to speak of things slightly more delicious than what we chose. I await, without too much impatience the long letter you mention in your last note. I am afraid that my invitations are somehow devastating to the intentions of my correspondents. It has occurred to me to use some of your infrequent communications in lieu of unremembered and unknown events. So I have been doing some research in four letters I have found. 'One must realize and believe in the fact that one's personal limitations are not equal to the bounds of probability.' I can only say, We are going to be forced to realize our own limitations and it is not pleasant to think that we may know what they are. Far from saying anything unhappy about truth, we work so fast as to be enabled to ignore the question. I am afraid that too sounds impolite. You speak of a 'gradually accumulating and paralyzing disbelief in one's capabilities to know the truth, embarrassment even at the mention of the word. The word has been contaminated by association with the stars, planets and men in general—I mean the truth about the nature of one man's time in the light of his action and thought experience. What is very hard is to have to realize that this condition cannot be got at through syntax.' The truth is that the truth of one's life is the life itself. You do not have the truth about something, you just have the truth. It's true that the truth might prove rather unrewarding. It is like beauty. You are correct to mistrust artists in this connection—the best that can be hoped of them is honesty. The professor will prove his syntax which is very comprehensive. Medical metaphors are perfectly good ones. But they are not more or less true. They are not true. The disease is descriptive, but the pain, which cannot be formalized, is true. I believe that the truth neither fits in (to art) nor disintegrates. And the undesired truth of pain is not more truthful than the pleasant one of ivresse, but the words lie, and that's your pain. The truth of one man's life expires with him, even if he has transcribed his experiences, because the words to begin with were not true for his life but only for his poem. The novel arises as fact, but that's also not the truth. It is his rhetoric that alone reintegrates him with the past and future of mankind. What is dead is done as truth. The charm of the truth, chez nous, is the process by which it forever recedes, quickly becoming imperceptible, as the history of the elements departs like lightning for distant suns, never to be seen again. 'In essence, it (the truth, the sense of error, the conditions) is, almost in the terminal sense, absolute.' It is the definition of disregard.

These summaries may pain you. Please understand that I respect, even share, your disenchantment. Surely I will not anticipate the character of your sickness. Solitude works. But I must push on.

During his long silence, he told me that he sometimes banged his head against a wall. But he was more inclined to laugh and when we were together we did. These things I remark are really not events. They are even not events presented as words. As events they are nothing. It is like truth. But it is embarrassing to me in terms of my intentions in this novel. I wish in truth to invent myself. I am creating a personage that speaks. Is that all? I'm not interested in that question, at the time of which I am speaking. It's true that there is a profound agreement between 'myself' and each of my friends, but that's not interesting either. My distinction from them and my apprehension of them are the two points of interest between which will hang, when it is hung, the actual series I present.

But if anything I am too honest. He and his family lived somewhere in a big wooden house. He used to love to hear my father's house described because it sounded, the way I told it, like a little palace. He liked to go to Europe where he knew nobody. He was often miserable there, At least nobody tried to comfort him there. Once when I was in Munich I went to the largest bookstore and bought a slight volume of Blake's poetry in German. We did not share Blake, or German, or truth, or slavery or prostitution, only a few inconsequential remarks of things we noticed, laughing. He lived then in a small house in a suburban housing development to which his parents had retired, having raised their children though they still kept a shop. Once I visited him unexpectedly, to give him a book I'd found, *British Insects,* which was to become as famous between us as my old letter denouncing Paris. He was locked inside the house asleep. I waited through a terrible movie nearby. In the evening he showed me his bibles with lurid drawings in them. His parents kept their counsel in the kitchen. He had a room with his books and his bed. Nobody had any news of him. He had met a few whores who touched his heart and pleased him. And one who disgusted him senseless.

My letters to him, at the time of which I am speaking, were tirades. Sometimes they were also decorative, sometimes plaintive and some of them remained unsent. He kept them together and from time to time he said he read them again. It amused him to think they might make a book of letters. But later he found my puerile papers, as Charles calls such things, to be, I think, somewhat embarrassing. After he read my first book, in the revised version, he said he had read it several times with pleasure, and still he did not know what I might say next. Occasionally, to place the silences, he asked me about three of my other friends whom he knew slightly. But on the whole my friends do not enjoy each other. I have nothing to say about that. On the other hand, everyone knew the woman with whom S. R. had conducted an interminable though sporadic and somewhat saddening love affair. She would compose a sub-plot, if we wanted one. She was a good comedienne; she could speak weep mime dance and sing. Women did not like her. One day she took my arm and asked me what I thought of her writing. I said nothing. Stanley and she might have laughed a lot and cried together. When I saw her again she looked strange to me. Each of us knew her quite independently so for everyone except me she was also a connection with S. R. She could play the part of 'the noonday girl' if anyone would write it. She wore blue very prettily, I thought, though not often; at the time of which I am speaking she had never been seen wearing green. But why was it all so saddening? Later on we decided. I did not then know what it was to live as vividly as they did, apparently, live, expressing 'great' joys or sorrow to the curiosing world. At the time of which I am speaking I supressed such aspects of my own life into letters to S.R.

The real doings of any man are perfectly mysterious. The logical rationalizations of his actions—the excuses to be told to women—always point away from the mystery toward a central fiction concerning his life at the time they were made, such as the way in which and how strongly he may be said to love her. The best men make these excuses without shame and gracefully, at the same time not for a moment believing or defending what they say. To make objections is correct but crude, and more often very likely rude. In defense of honesty, I sometimes find myself in such a rudeness, because I notice that for the sake of sincerity people will believe their words. I would give no excuse. For, in this vulgar age, how is that fact to be distinguished from any other? The nobler course is to persevere, which is what I do in any context where 'the public' is not a party to the fiction. I cannot trust a universal formula for society. The mystery is found out in every man as the grace of a surprise. A man who will do nothing unexpected is not a man, and he has no secrets, and provides no obstacle of any sort. This point is not something new nor is it something else. It is perpetual and himself most nearly. It is the source radically opposed to fact, that is to effect. It is the source of resource. It belies the study of phenomena as radically unsound. It is the necessary association with eternity. It cannot be apprehended, it can only be forgotten, like a fact.

I have had a whole pot of coffee, yet I do not yearn for 'some-

thing else,' except silence. That is prose. He said that he had had
nothing but coffee and wanted nothing but silence. That leaves out
the point, which is, however, incommunicable. That is paraphrase.
What is the peristyle? A certain part near something. All fast prose.
It is like love. It is not just a device. The reintegration of substance
and denomination out of histories. Everything by intention of course.
But the effect is unintended. That cannot be explained away. It is like
laughter.

S. R. understands much well enough to say that it is nothing.
The classical memorandum: *Ce ne fait rien.* He seems slightly quaint,
like a German phrase that is not all-embracing. This is not rich it is
simple. Now at the time of which I am speaking, whatever it is to
which I must refer (back) is unclear, but it is not any more difficult.
His letters become a rarity, and surprising, therefore, not unwel-
come; I read them again for the first time within the protection of a
couple of years. It is safe to say there is no correspondence. Safe? It is a
dangerous situation. Nobody knows what is going on when the
microphones, or the supply lines, fail utterly. We say something has
happened. It could be nothing. We hope so. In a story an inconsequential matter is not remarkable. There is always something to
which to return in Proust. It only remains to invent a consequence
which is always psycho-logical. *The morale of the workers is disfigured
upon a ground of trivial events.* He is busy disregarding anecdotes.
Nevertheless silence. We believe there exists a wavelength to which
we will not tune, except to hear the silence late at night only slightly
and incomprehensibly interrupted by inefficiency. One-way mes-
sages. 'Can we not say things more easily? No, I guess not.' The
trouble continues. You could forget how he looks. We still believe it
is nothing. But how is that possible? Somebody will come up with an
answer. Cannot we ourselves invent a conclusion? Nothing easier: as a
result of his immersion he took on another character he did not like
any more than he had liked the period of waiting for the event he
would create.

If only he had a little physical idiosyncrasy then I would have
him. His hat, even, but like everyone he wears no hats. His hair is
cropped so as to be imperceptible (I think I remember that it would
have curled). In hiding he was predisposed to red clothes (that is not a
joke) like a hunter. Now his tweed is in perfect stripes only a little too
narrow (in that it is like every modern tweed), his trousers are of a
good quality soft material that has no name and no color, and his

shoes — he must wear shoes of some sort . . . but he has a small nose and freckles. They are not very noticeable. He is, at the time of which I am speaking, thinly, what would be a full face looking a bit low, but he does not seem hungry. Sometimes he experiences hunger as others of us will walk for hours, as they say, for pleasure. To fill it out — often he did not eat. More often he did not sleep. Thus he invented extra time in which, so far, he chose not to weep. 'But again, Demosthenes, consider; can not a fervent truth be multi-dimensional? Let us leave off and consider all of the above merely time-space ramifications of the Given Continuum. I demand a rococco finale: The Fool has enough foolishness to despair; only the Wise Man can tear the veil of existence with his laughter.'

Thus to begin, S. R. the unknown man, suspected of wisdom and fraught with doubt, convicted in certainty and certainly in love. At the time of which I am speaking, of which I shall try to mention several. I who had admired him began after his fashion to admire me. I am quickly flattery. I mean praise. I aggrandize but I don't seek. Anyway things changed. In the short hard fast novel I invent myself. I said that before I understood the stipulations of the license. Let us analyze. There are five distinct persons *and myself*. However that may be, it is all myself. Unless I invent it, I don't exist. It is the development of one character. I must be sure not to name it. Without this effort, All references when I, my, myself and certain he's occur, will refer only to 'something else.' The quintessential process subjectifies objections. It is not my purpose to make things as clear as that; Thus it is not a concordance. But it arises from such pretensions. In a sense, I am attempting to include breaking the mask into the mask itself, something the rigorous application of which I should detest; at once too clever and too flagrant a deception. These six characters do not fully develop 'myself'; the license permits me to add to the sixth all those aspects which do not find themselves among the five. Only the sixth 'myself' is not actual. The five participate in the defense of truth. The sixth is purely coincidental. It is not the clearly dreamed character Lafcadio of Gide, the pure wish, the straight hard and fast. Surely Lafcadio, no less than Genet's Divine or Huckleberry Finn, was a masturbation fancy; but I would not leave it at that point, which is much too clear. I am bound to add aspects of a more generalized day and night dream in a series of increasing realizations, the villain of Barault's Enfants de Paradis, Ray Gosling's hard hero. Then for type, Lennon, McCartney, Harrison & Starr, and coming all the way in at Lee Oswald. One perceives immediately that these phantoms are not recorders of their way of life; when they do write, they have nothing to say. But like Proust, Joyce, Beckett, Gide or Stein, I am of and without the 'literary' world, and for me the 'myself' of this letter is more often than not fantastic. United at this point are the audacious, the Truffaut etc, Arrabal, those who appear not to hesitate. It is there that I combine with the fantasy, though of course, it looks like something else. It is there, and not in the literary modes, that my reality will be found. . . . At least for now.

0. 4. 2

In May of 1872 I was awoke by a breeze carrying the savors of a time, eight years ago, like a bird, a certain smell, however, that I associate with nothing else, and I was quick to remember what and where it was. Quickly I cast myself

Oisive jeunesse
A tout asservie,
Par delicatesse
J'ai perdu ma vie.
Ah! Que le temps vienne
Où les coeurs s'éprennent.

back to the time before the beginning of the story whan I had no thought of character, when I lived in sheltered comfort in spacious rooms provided with dust laden rust colored carpets, rooms fitted with the old brass lighting fixtures I loved to furbish in my solitude. I had no notion that there would be no story, nor of that denial. My *fête de la patience* was, as I remembered it, unnumbered by events. I knew only one, now the oldest of the five, but slightly, And I had no occasion to remark the figure eight, or the second of the six, or the fiction by which I would amorously redraw my fate. It reminded me of the endurance of Charleville, eighty-six years previous, recovered just this morning. At the time of which I am speaking, I shouldn't have thought so.

But how? The character was undeveloped, but I must say, it thought itself complete, on the outside anyway. Well, there was no realization of the nearly necessary task of inventing destiny. That sounds great. No, but partly on account of certain pressures that happened to get applied to me at the time, and partly out of curiosity brought on by idleness—for my studies did not intrigue me and I longed for I knew not what that I assumed appropriate to another age—I began at first to write an apology for the upper middle caste. Even then I saw the possibility of inventing my inheritance, though not yet of choosing it. You would say that eight years was not a long time, but only one with the point of view of God would deny that dignity to 1872. I was then attracted by the ease of summer, by the integrity of animals at leisure, by the life afforded, as I thought, for patricians' sons. I had not discovered that it did not exist. I was in fact inventing what I thought I could admire while I thought that I recorded it. At length I permitted one or two of my friends to read what I had seen in strange illuminations. I desired to question correspondents. I had as yet read very little, I was not yet accustomed to reading, and I valued the opinions of those who had.

One of them was someone I knew in connection with a theatrical production I had undertaken to organize. He happened to live nearby and we passed from time to time and nodded. Later I discovered that the plants he kept then had died of neglect, as he returned so seldom to his apartment, having devoted himself wholeheartedly to what turned out to be a most complicated theatrical affair, of which, at the time of which I am speaking, I heard only a few isolated rumors which I scrupulously ignored. He wished to consecrate himself in favor of another with all the thoroughness for which women have been distinguished. That fact, in combination with his generally most pleasant manners in which he showed up perhaps only a bit too self-effacing, had earned him the gratitude of a masculine aggregation which could not appreciate the character of its pleasure. From what I have learned in the course of a long friendship, I think that the time of which I am speaking was a happy one, for him. He was perfectly engaged then in what he did for those he loved and they returned his reward. My own devotion to something else at that time was apparently as complete as his, but it was radically different than his because I thought I knew what I really wanted, which he has never been entirely willing to decide. I may have been wrong, but never unsure. My own efforts would result in achievements on my own head—perhaps ruinous in the case of great mistakes—but that was the type of excitement I sought. His work was very much the labor implied in love, continuous, almost uneventual, never finished. I wanted what was apparently forbidden me; he did things that other people found unpleasant so as to please them, and it did. He was successful at first when I was merely audacious. It must be mentioned as well that in those days, as later and even now, he knew everyone, and his name, by his virtues, was everywhere familiar in the restricted but wide-ranging associations of the college. He was such an obliging creature, at once gracefully childlike and attentive, at the same time as he was a man of cultured tastes and opinions, always too tactfully and never gratuitously expressed. He was never referred to by other than the invariable full form of his Christian name.

Over the years, I have had several occasions to mention his name to those who, it might be expected, would have forgotten it, and I have found that they retain there a pleasant, even fond, association, though some of them express contempt for his great friend and patron. The mistake was that they prejudged things categorically. At the time of which I am speaking, he existed in the shadowy periphery of my life, reappearing incidentally to disappear as thoughtlessly, for my part. He was perfectly respectable, yet exotic with an English manner tempered by a Christian upbringing and Southern associations. Women's hearts were opened to him in a perpetual invitation to create the lovely images of grace and charm which the old books had led them to desire of men. I see him in a pilastered drawing room, inconspicuously well-dressed in green and brown, taking a glass of sherry with the grandest Dame whose eyes sparkle like her beads in the allusive candlelight of gentle laughter.

At the time of which I am speaking, my great friends were all of the milieu into which I had myself been born to associate the sons and daughters of eastern and midwestern merchants. Those of whom I have chosen to speak, however, the great friends of my later youth, were reared in differing assocations. The second, third and fifth each have in some term connections to the Southern culture, though except for one, all their parents had originated elsewhere. The same three have since abandoned the profession of english christian faith for nothing of the sort. The first and fourth are jews from northern cities, and they like all the others have long been abandoned by their faith, now reduced to physiognomic crypts and the remains of legendary cleanliness and the imperatives of the immediate family of women. We fled the South. I still love to see the Service. We may return Orthodox. I will have him Baptised, but not circumcised. We bought a house in Boston. It is not important.

0. 5. 3

Aye, Davy, it is sex, ain't it? Everything takes on its own pallor, even that. You don't know what it is at the time. You couldn't care either. It hits you now and then, when it's so good you almost laugh, but we don't do that. You keep looking around, out. It's not really a sport but you joke about it with the boys that know psych and sleep private. You've got your own cot too but it isn't the same. Keeping up. The clothes are the thing for awhile. A triangle of lavender at the neck to cover what shows of the ageing chest, a new shirt, hand pressed or unpressed, a certain shoe, slightly heavy or very light, and the youthful cutaway to the coat. A certain style. Cut to the thigh. Look at that! But the eyes, that's what I really like, and the hair I always notice, and the voice, It isn't sweet. She calls me by my last name. I always fall in love with the blonde hair, but I take the black every time. Except the first. That was not a mistake, but I didn't know, and to tell you the truth I don't know yet. At the time it was almost like love. She didn't understand what I was getting at. I got her to the point where it annoyed her that it wasn't like the movies, and then I showed her what they don't show. I didn't do it the same way. I knew what I wanted but not how to do it. I wouldn't try, though, just make it. It was OK, it wasn't much, a little summer, out in a boat, a few beers later on, stars and like that. One night she sat in my box with the boys, very dark, a lot of laughs, a wood fire, and later they said they admired my decision. That was the last I saw of her, not a bad thing at all, one of a number. I would never insist.

It's my own business, alright, you can bet. Still it was White's too at the time, and I knew it, and we shared it. That's hard to get across without the wrong idea. I'm not even sure what the wrong idea is. You do not have these two or three boxes like certain rooms with names on the doors. You just have whatever you do or don't do. One time I said to him, To hell with the danger, I'm not a great faggarty crumb that makes the walls come tumbling down around our shattered preconceptions. And he told me he knew what I meant to say, though what he said was that he didn't. The great thing with him was keeping it up. He had more respect for the danger of changing the words, the forms, of the gaff. His family would have been more satisfied to see him make the break so they could be sure of the trouble. But he always stopped short of the definite answer. If you let it in, you could be convinced that it really was your mother, and then where would you be? Back in the office screwing yourself. I was pushing it another way, which was alright too, my style, but I think it was harder for me. I got a bad case of the superficial pox, and fell in love unattainably with another damned married woman, and by the time it was over everything changed. I swore off that. His story was, you took it easy, even if you had the quickest draw on the block, and more often than not it worked right. At the time we were living in a place which had the ugliest women we had ever seen on land. Taken separately and together, as we took them, imaginatively, every evening on a stroll. Everyone was out of town. Or else engaged. And otherwise highly aged or less attractive than the boys. Eventually we flushed them, separately, finally using his scheme, but it had been a relatively boring hunt. We got drunk, exchanged impressions and played games, like in those plays you see them write for two men on the stage. Walking down the street, I found out that the young men eye each other, and if you're with a girl you'll notice that the young women do the same with the girls, and let nature take care of herself. That is not how it is in Italy or the movies, except for the women, who are much more desirable.

There were other subjects. Architecture, for example. That had been the beginning. More generally, how do you do things. At first we wanted something you could see left over. We talked about it over gin. We thought we wanted to do something in a certain way. Perfect. The trouble was I lacked patience and he lacked charm so we thought we might build it together. The discussion became interminable, and it is still going on, or the echoes of it do. Finally, at one point we started out to make it, separately at first in different cities, and then it happened again that we both gave it up, almost at once, as if it were part of a plan, for the same reasons in our different ways. You can't do what you want. Not in that way. Well, it was not just the same, but surely it seemed that it was. Despite all we went through he never came to understand how I could do everything at once. And I never had a good view of how he could bear to do nothing. In the end we shared a taste for decoration that was so firm that we could exchange remarks about it for two hours straight without stopping or thinking. When we did we laughed. That was usually when the gin runs out. I'm not going to talk about the car.

There were the right pants, and for other times the blue jeans that you swim in to make them a perfect fit, and the colored T shirts, keeping it above-board and visible, and a certain type of collar that our schools had taught us not to wear. We could have had the jargon too, but that was for the children, who, if we used their words, we mocked. It was just at that time that the high bourgeois culture finally collapsed, having been sustained only by a safety pin for over two and one-half generations, when it rusted out. We didn't applaud, we didn't know what had happened, and we wouldn't have listened if anyone had been there and said so. They didn't know it either, our old friends, but they called us turn-coats. A nice historical point, I have thought. I went out and sold all my good old clothes and got nine dollars and fifty cents, which in case you are not aware of the cost of things is nothing at all compared to the price. I came to know all about the qualities of corduroys, as a practical matter. One winter I almost froze over.

White bought a motor cycle, although he hadn't the money, and his aunt, who was lovely, wasn't however inclined to let such things pass. If this was the story that you think it may be, I would have had to have bought one too. But I didn't want that. We never were the same. We had these few things, that meant everything, to share, and we did that while it lasted. And we knew it was good at the time, a surprise. We went together as far as we could go without regrets. One time his sister took me aside. They had this lovely little house in a beautiful old section of the capital. Once I gaffed him he was in love with her, but he knew that that wasn't it. She got the idea that it was only him that wasn't the same anymore, because she knew him better. I must have looked blank for a second and then of course I switched to the charm. And also she was married to this charming scholar, so when I went to see them, the old guy (he had a son my age) and I exchanged the lot of ironies, and they also drank gin, it was all in the family, but I never could really express anything to her because all I had to do, what she wanted, was to put my old face back on and assure them that everything was all right and would be forever. Why fight? It is not a revolution, though there are still many who will say, Oh yes it is.

That was before the great pop stars. We still liked jazz, but at the time we started to turn it off. What I did was give away my records and the player. After a few months of silence I bought the radio. It really took the women to bring us into the music, which was sex in a different form that they liked just as well. It was all right too. You had the idolatry before and knew about the equilibrium, but we had to have the break before we could change over. You see there was this difference. Those who had never had it when you could still have had it as it used to be (who you knew, the right cloth, the free drink, the well heeled marriage mart) did not get this intermediary stage where you were seduced by Art. They moved right in because nothing had happened to them. It looked as if a lot of them did, though, when comparitively few of those who took the veil had the name like Adams, but they were the ones who had just been set up to make it as newly come in by the old way, the ones who had been handed a few big advantages in the schools, and had been shown the solid silver, and had been welcomed by the noise of death, though it didn't sound like that.

Hi. We dropped our names. A funny little mouth, she had.

I'm an actor, okay?

Sure, why not?

Show us how they do it way back home.

Are you nuts?

Sure, baby, a little jag. Why not?

That's more like it. How's your chip?

Great, thanks. And yours?

Silly, he don't even know what's a chip.

But I do.

Funny man, a real troll.

Do you walk?

Like a car.

Permit me to rescue your highness.

What did he say he did? Oh yeah.

Let's cut out.

What's this?

Alpha Romeo, Italian.

I seen them around. It's bright. Say, where you going?

Out.

I always go by Downley's now. They got a cute box.

That was your sister was with you?

Her? My sister! I don't believe it.

Okay cool it.

I shouldn't laugh a bit?

What color d'you call that?

Pumice, it says here.

Straight?

You got some sense of humor, alright.

You know what pumice is?

Yeah, for your nails. You a college kid, then?

A year out — it didn't work.

The same with my brother.

How do you make it?

Type and file.

Good job. Around here?

Doctor's office.
Take my pulse.
You move in quick.
Go ahead.
It's too fast. Any cardiographic history?
No thanks.
What about the mumps?
You're quick enough yourself.
Is it in the movies, then?
No, no.
Not the tube, I never seen you. At the disk?
Forget it.
I guess I can know where I'm off to.
Look. I got a full chip. What's the discussion?
You start something, you have to back it up.
It takes a long line. You drink?
What kind of question is that?
Pardon me, lady pumicelips, but I'm not out to buy an argument.
Hot too, huh?
And frozen solid if I want it.
I guess that's what you meant. You can park it now.
Here?
They never tag them, not a bright one anyway.
It's a party, sounds like.
I always keep my friends close by.
Teach us the new way, would you?
Why not? It's the same. George is great—look at that.
D'you mind if I don't change clothes?
What a troll. Dansez, M'sieu!

Later we smoked, catching my breath to keep it up, passing it around the community of peace-loving rebels, all full of themselves and abandoned by language. From India a lovely vision, thanks. Or was it Araby? I forget the poem now.

This is the question of types. Actually, you break just at one point, it doesn't matter which. In U.S. it is often the length of hair, controversially, with both men and women. What's your position on length of hair? The answer gives the type. We went to the longer hair right away. It makes me look like a kid. I'm not supposed to like it, am I? she said. But she did. It was her relatives got to her with the dividends called help in return for no sex in the daylight, and so she left me. It was a big joke for her to light a cigar; when it came to the hair they knew I meant business. Salesmen became belligerent to look at my neck. White went to a beard. Soldiers shoot when they see one. *There is a substitute for everything, we learned when we could talk.* The substitute is always better for the types. Less commitment. College women dream in Freud's fastidious terms. Less beauty. Lascivious merchants gurgle and wink. Less grace. Perish the prurient thought to get on with the prescription of money. Will you step up the apples and pears? And have a cup of you know who? Take from the muscular stomach of a bird the number of people worth knowing in New York and I equal the remainder.

The types are mechanics. In the old plays, you had, aside from the people that moved, the mechanics, the people that seemed to move. It's good for a laugh, but you can't think about it — there's just nothing there. They fill it out and cut the tension off sometimes. But nowadays, there's nothing but that, to hell with the plays, in our own life, eternal mechanics, each in a little different way still, certain ones to certain machines. Try saying something unexpected to them once and see what you get out of them. The wrong laugh. Life is the factory over and over again. Am I kidding? It's not worth betting your life anymore. That's what we moved out of. More than one-half of those who thought they had moved out at the time later found they had just taken on a new and different role, the dear terms. Whether or not you have a permit for change what's the difference? You get to sit down while you do it slightly better. I made my own way up to linotype chief. Cheers, sweetie, good-bye (fat chance of that, if you know what I mean). The trouble is that if you don't simply move up and you really move out, there's nowhere to go. The mechanics are now sophisticated. It is very well publicised too. When you leave utterly, you're out the daily bread and you can't be forgiven the use of the sky, the last right. Oh, there are still a few ways to go. The prince of the lost realm teaches history at Rheims, and yawns. Yet there's the unlikely job. The free lance at a hundred bucks a throw, or maybe ten. Be a hustler, but it gets to you, a gamesman on the move, take a job for a minute, my address is everywhere. You win it away, without your name. The other standard is art. You have to have one idea expressed in one style *pour épater l'ex-bourgeoisie* and leave your ex-soul with the fashionmongers. If good that lasts ten years, like a movie star. There is that possibility too, part of the same thing, a little more or less severe. You pick up the banjo and bingo, but at any rate it isn't easy. You can also be a handy-man if you can do it, or an inventor, but there is a machine for that too. We understand the mechanics of any situation, and we are not therefore afraid of them. But may there not be something else, excusing my diction, Please? Help comes in the form of the university grant for the graduate, a free psycho-analysis for the idler, the military service for the militant, the home-made movies for the imaginary. They fall out of school & take the film from the floor. These four ways point away from all the little sins that thus get reformed by the closest approaches to nothingness we have ever yet named. Not for me, it will be a cold day, in May.

Good-bye to that too. White and I left it alone and together. It's true that we both were in a more or less good position. What of it? Everyone is in some position. Let them make of it. Stuff doesn't just arrive, you have to order it. Both of us turned first to our personal life, set straight, in both cases a wife, some possessions, he kept the same house and I gave mine up, but it wasn't mine to begin with. White bought a car. I was able to get a long trip which was good, an exorbitant waste of time. I didn't do a thing but take the next meal and once in a while the next train. One day Charles showed me Rome. Then it was the job from hunger. At the same time, I built the house. You must know one thing. Without that, it is a child, and cries out and is solaced and broken in. It isn't the quality of reality, it must be what I wish. For animals there's the truth only; for people there is only art. It keeps coming up. So I thought, why not? From the center, A letter, *Et cetera*. For White it was harder, and I didn't do it with him, so I wouldn't know quite. But he had more to set in place, and more interest in the things, i.e., the whole story before he could begin. Art as such went out with the buildings in modern style. Eventually it was numbers and the new kind of job where the top man has placed himself to hire equals whom he doesn't begrudge, and nobody else understands what you do. Both are a type, but only from the other side of the rotary glass. From where we see it all, it is me.

I like shoes. I pick out a new pair with the greatest care, and if I don't watch out they won't fit. I walk. In the shop they aren't tight, but later they may be. Mostly it is the way it looks from above. Just right. When I'm eating something, it's almost unnoticeable that I do it a certain way. She almost said I would have made a great dancer, but she knew that wasn't right. This is not a different style, it is only a different character. When I sit, my hands are somewhere. I don't always notice it, but when I do, they are. One is under my knee, and I can see the thumb at the side. I love to dress, but not the first thing in the morning. I always dress somehow. My walk, which I do not remember ever being different, is noticeable. My performance at the typewriter attracts everyone's attention. It is not automatic. Dactylograph. I have sensitive ears. When they test them, sometimes they used to test them, they cannot believe I still hear the voice but the answer was right. I don't like noise. I have a certain kind of fountain pen that is no longer made. It is not out of date. I use a certain kind of ball point pen and a certain kind of yellow paper which is not the same as before, and which is almost gone. It is not old-fashioned, it is no longer sold. I put the butter in a special dish that holds just one-half pound. I have two great black L. C. Smith & Corona Typewriters Inc., number 8, one with pica type and this one with smaller type. With one finger, very quickly. I still have to watch out. Because if I forget, I won't be doing what I think I want to do. Because what is not a story does not write itself. Just remarks, No. A character. The idea is to move quickly. The idea moves quickly. Without a slip. I shall only apologize once. It doesn't rhyme, either.

She gave me the bad news. And slammed the door. On my back. I had already left. Straight cut. If I wanted to know what I had said, or how I got this passage across I would, just like any other reader, have to take the book down from the shelves and search for the passage, and then read it. It would be finished. There has been a movement and nothing will be quite the same again. She does everything to make it not to change, not this, but that. But not enough. I do not disagree. I insist.

0.6.4

He neglects. I wrote to him in the capital. I said I didn't understand what the hell was going on. That was last night. This last summer, I said, whatever was it all about. I do not seek gratitude. Some of my friends have the names of kings; Therefore, they have to be princes. I said I do not like to be used. I said I didn't know how he could use me without my permission. But I got the sense that he was doing it all the same. With that sense, in most cases, you can only withdraw yourself. Or you can use the users. But with old friends, it is no longer a question that I like them. It doesn't give a damn. He said he was going to send me a letter which as a matter of fact he never sent. And then he interrupted his silence to let me know that he might one day send it to me. I regarded the possibility with indifference. He got the impression that I regarded him with indifference which was not exactly true. Under my influence, years before, he had got the idea that he could write. Before that he had only known that he was smart. His old girl gave me a job in order to have news of him. But I had none. They had used to be noisy and I had told them to shut up. Shouting was the way a life could be conducted, but not with me. She was disappointed. He had another friend too. Then he fell in love with the guy's sister. But he and his sister had always been in love, so that it was, once again, a *ménage à trois,* but a different one. His dependencies are complicated. But his taste for fact and competition are astonishing. He was, or would have been, a Marxist, so that he became, or would have become, a Freudian. He said, first and last, I don't believe in women.

I had known him years before. He was correct in believing he was not the same as the others with whom he compared himself and that he was not the same as he had been. If she and I were really in love, then it was safe for him to hold onto me. Or, if he and she were really in love, then it was safe for him to be in love with her. So he thought. What if she made things a little harder? She was very photographable and now more determined to succeed than he had been for years, but the affair was highly involved and she understood more of it than perhaps she admitted to herself. She had certain desires. This is not hearsay, it is fiction. It was a tough thing. Two generations of women, and the next as well (though he thought his seed was no good) conspired to silence that which was extremely articulate but would choose nothing to say. One evening he entertained me for two hours with extempore poetry, though he didn't know it. I was drunk but it was lovely. His citation in my favor mentioned courage in a way I could only understand because I was then his friend. But perhaps I had mentioned it to him, I don't know, Cocteau, but he was always making me compete with him. What about this? And that? Too often, I drew the blank; No interest. I wished him well, and I don't think I gave him any advice.

But after I have heard so much about it, and the way such practices are misused in other countries, how is it possible that I can concern myself with the denunciation of another personality, however nameless? I protest that that is not what I am doing. I am seriously engaged in constructing 'another' for the purpose of contributing aspects of 'himself' to the 'myself' I create. His life, at the time of which I am speaking, is the major factual contribution to 'my

own' which, without his, at that time, could in no way be said to
exist. Then is that not, I respond, the very sort of use to which in my
construction I object? His use of me? I must allow that, logically, it
could be said to be. But there is a separate logic of every intention.
And in this novel, in which 'I' have the clearest sort of intentions,
which could not possibly be more frequently expressed, the logic that
ought to be used is the logic of my intention. So, you see, first of all, I
am granting my use of aspects of his life to which I am, speaking
strictly, not entitled. At the same time, in the second case, I am
distinguishing between that use, which is fully documented, and the
derogatory uses, secretive, allusory and half-hinted by means of
tangential remarks, to which I believe he has latterly put his own
representation of myself. I believe that he has cast me in the part of
'the illogical,' a place where, I quickly concede, my own present
position in regard to him is founded. For I find nothing about him so
objectionable as his misuse of logic itself for no other purpose than to
provoke so-called illogical remarks in me. It is logical for the illogical
to contradict the logical, as Corneille remarked.

There is no doubt, briefly to begin, that I was trained in logic
used for victory. But, from a very long time ago, I was more strongly
attracted to skepticism, which is not generically illogical, but which
fosters, incidentally, an attitude of doubt regarding logical rigor
equally as it would doubt everything else that may be argued. I am
not claiming that I myself was perfectly skeptical, or even ironical, a
more artistic form of the same thing. Nothing could be further from
the truth. But it is true, that in relation to this prince, I found myself
engaged alternatively in perfectly logical exercises, and other exercises intended to demonstrate a skeptical position toward such logic.
I am sure that the company will appreciate the exasperating effects of
all such discourse without any further proof. In one of our endless
arguments taking place as recently as two months ago, I interrupted
myself to tell him Flaubert's charming story of the chimera and the
sphinx, which I here repeat. A sphinx, such as the famous stone of
Egypt, firm upon the sands of time and place in the eye of the eternal
sun, observed or thought he did, a chimerical shadow play. This gay
and almost inexistent subject having thus amused the stone for the
lifetime of a god or so, the sphinx, in his way, desired the fleeting
creature to transport him away with her, or round and about at least,
as he had nowhere to go. The chimera cheerfully would grant the
stone's one wish, but when the sphinx arranged himself upon the

shadow, she was crushed to nothing. But while the sphinx denied himself the pleasure that he thought he sought, the chimera, which had not escaped her fate, was nevertheless apparently not beneath the stone. Her existence had been perfectly denied, but everywhere he looked, he saw the same agreeable fancies lurking in the very rays of the ruthless sun. The monolithic principle remained triumphant, and the charming truth continued to be manifest. We are here dealing with the question of proof and guilt. Those are, I know, two separate questions, but unless they are adequately conjoined at this point in the narrative, I should be forced to endanger my old friend's position as the fourth in series.

The logical principles which 'the fourth point' sought to assume were those that would destroy, momentarily at least, the principles (not necessarily illogical) which had been the basis of our association. If it is granted that there should be less noise in the city, it is too logical to assume that it is desired for silence to be ordained. It is a matriarchal plea that not only insists on the virtual supremacy of the eldest son but would exert all influence in the direction of the nature of that being, so that, at once set free and bound around by the limitations of his mother tongue, he wallows lovelessly in rhetoric he cannot even understand. There is no judgement contained in these lines, save in rhetorical terms, which cannot move. But in a quicker sense, and sensation is quick, I became forced to conduct my part in a dialogue of which only my friend could hear both sides. He mediated, now taking (I an assuming something) my position, now that of his solicitor, whose attitude was more fortunately guessed for being at least somewhat more stylized than my own. No doubt his desire was to prove one of us wrong, a project he could never have accomplished had I been more patient than I was. For none of us, if there were really three, would play the sphinx. Yet he kept on trying me in this way, one certain to lead me through this facility to make an almost public denunciation, or a direct insult upon the intelligence he never doubted.

At the time of which I am speaking, I had as yet done no more than propose schemes to him that were radically other than what they appeared to be so that in the midst of his refutations I could only resolve to laughter and report to him that I did not exist. Logistics aside, however, the situation was complicated by the dependant character of his relation to me at the time, not that the dependancy was exclusively from mine to his, but the balance did so list. At the same time it was passed off as equality, sometimes with the aid of rather elaborate artifice on my part. I desired to draw forth the princely character which he unwittingly would hide in ignorance. That, in turn, was disguised as modesty, an ingenious tactic, I am sure, but one which I found to be a detriment to himself and its awareness of itself. Indeed everything seemed to be other than it was. A spirit of compunction pervaded the convoluted syndromes we had made to fill the space between us, latterly becoming phenomena only slightly connected with either point of origin. The debate was always about 'something else' but we could never agree even that it was, and we hardly began to identify its character until now. As always, I reject the aid of clichés. By the use of analysis he sought, not truth, which I believe cannot be seen in that manner, but proof, to which the technique was equally unsuitable.

But clichés sound more like accusations than speculations do. People found him aparently confused. I thought to say that he was obscure was more illuminating. Except of intentions For all anyone knew, the cryptograph of him described by my fictional antagonist would agree with mine. Except I had no answers. He wanted answers and he was under the illusion that could not invent them himself. He thus found it essential to discover a way which would lend the necessarily invented answers its own truth. I always accepted possibilities where he excepted them. He was always concerned about my apparent indifference to the promise toward which I graduated, one point at a time, as much so as if it were a promise which in fulfillment he would gain the benefit. I took that as flattery, but it had the effect of delaying what it ostensibly hurried, though I made no complaint. It was almost that he expected less of me than I habitually gave. He responded with what I have called ignorance. As when a woman long unmarried comes into the habit, when certain things are mentioned, of saying, I wouldn't know. Of course nothing has ever lived up to my expectations of it, all of which have I think by now undergone that change, except 'myself.'

The intellectual hard and fast is rearrangement. I isn't that but this. Sincerity is out of the question. You have to be sure. If you know what you want to do, everything fits in, like a surprise. The moving hard and fast is also rearrangement. O.K.: the right place at the right time. But I invent it by being where I find myself. I shall do it. It is like a story. Nothing is irrelevant. It moves, It runs, It works. But it doesn't worry. It could stop. They wait for me. I move in and do something. Nobody knows why. It is not a secret, it is unknown. They are not unhappily surprised. Indeed they are highly pleased to be in trouble, however they complain. It pleases me, I do it. For what? For nothing. Sometimes they are unhappily surprised, and still they are pleased. They do not want the trouble to stop. If it stops it is ruined, it is dead, their lives are nothing, but there's no possibility of that in truth. The rich man no longer rich who never had anything else is no longer even himself. But nobody has really ever been in just such a position. The degenerate star. Regeneration used to be popular. Now abdication is. There is always something. I refuse. *Je me tue.* The intellectual hard and fast is no respecter of facts. It eats them. Assimilates. Uses everything at once as if everything were 'myself,' which it is. The moving hard and fast is no respecter of ideas or persons. It embodies them and moves. It is a villain or a hero, but not just any hero. I move in and do it. It changes things, like fate. It doesn't change fate, it moves like fate. Which is just as much an act of love as an act of death. We love death. It is a character. It is not merely a character. Merely a character is a caricature, accumulation, repetition. *Having done one thing, one can do anything.* The novel inside the novel has yet another interior mood. It is I. *Je me tutoie.* Or, it is intuition. That is great with the hard and fast. It is not violent, It is more like wit, *in spiritus sanctus.* It is not reasonable. At the very least, it has the excuse of amusement. But if that were all there was to it, nothing would ever get done. At most, it occasions the suffering of others in toils of one's own invention, even as oneself. I place myself, that is 'myself,' in the way. As a character of the hero. The decoration proves it. The intention disclaims it. The affination of events and words. There may be a great deal of noise about it. There may be an international denunciation. There may be a scandal. There may be an examination. There may be a conviction. But I have already left the place.

I quote 'myself': When I did form a specific intention, I preferred to carry it out on the spot, or else, to defer its execution by means of a completed revery, into the indefinite future, or to oblivion. Thus I had a great supply of extra intentions, things I would be pleased to do if any occasion for them arose, which I did not regret having not yet done. I contented myself with the probability that the combination of all possible moments would produce a sufficient variety of occasions to suit my most general plans. But to prevent me from getting into habitual moods in which I would usually do things that bored me, I used, in addition, formulas of prejudice. For a long time I said, I never go to the movies. I was known for my distaste of all museums except one. I never watched television. I refused to read newspapers and magazines. Or I rejected sweets, except in the morning. And I refused to play any standard game. And I did not choose the shortest route. And I did not know how fast I went. And I ignored the price of things I did not want. At the time of which I am speaking, whatever I said, the sense I most disliked was any feeling of the sort I had when I was rushed.

Now at the moment, at the time of which I am speaking, I felt beset by an entire catalogue of things which would change in due course, and the sooner, the better. It is a period of transition in which transitory matters subsume all one's life, in which even questions concerning means of transportation may, as they invariably do in my family, assume a primary importance which they cannot serve to justify, then, at such a time, it is just the thing to resort to an essay in simultaneity, a consideration of everything at once, which it is my custom to attempt by way of a letter to whichever of my friends is closest.

0.7.5

To D. C. L.:

Beside the fact that I wish to see how my typewriting looks on this page, it occurs to me to say a few things about our various appreciation of some of the sayings of David Jones,* and some of the differences are those between you and me, and some of them are those between visual things and things self-evidently of process. The 'process' of painting, although I understand it only most generally, is a strange one to me who only makes visual things such as photographs or drawings capriciously, as a diversion. When I come to think of painting or other principally visual forms of art (leaving performances aside), what always impresses me, of course, is the strangeness, the otherness, the existence of the object in which all process is utterly cryptic. The familiar effect in which such a word as 'cow' or 'brick' may disintegrate itself from its meaning upon close scrutiny, is the nearest I can come to an analogy in language for the strange quality that a painting always has for me. The most particular thing is also

---

* 1895-1974. Welsh painter, engraver, poet & critic. Roman Church. Selected essays: *Epoch & Artist,* Chilmark Press, 1963, New York. Lived in London.

the most abstract. I should not be interested in dragging in to a consideration of this effect such a process as is said to take place in the mind of the beholder to create the effect he calls beautiful. For although there are many processes round and about painting, such as the processes of art history, transport and reproduction, to name three fairly 'objective' ones, it seems to me that the great thing of a painting is just that: the existence of a certain facture which is not a name and to which names are fundamentally irrelevant, though they may be informative or decorative. I am much more at home when I am speaking of process, which may be how I am attracted by the criticism of Harold Rosenberg who is also at home when he speaks of process. I am very likely, for example, to think of any piece of writing as an excerpt, in several ways; an excerpt from all writings of the same tendency whether of style or content; an excerpt from everything written by the same hand; an excerpt of everything that went into and comes out of the moment in which something else is chosen. Or, I say, it is about everything taking something as example.

I am not inclined to force an analogy at this point to associate writings and paintings with process, although as it happens the analogy lies directly to mind: It is quite pleasant to suppose, in the words of one painter quoted to me by another, that 'on this earth, repose is caused by an accidental obstruction in the movement of matter . . . it is an error to regard such stoppage as primary . . . the pictorial work was formed of movement, is itself recorded movement and is assimilated through movement.' I am in no position, nor would I be, to deny such a view of things, and indeed it is very congenial to the sense I get from my pictorial hobbies. But I am always caught short by the thing itself, a thing which, except perhaps in a few special cases, does nothing to me that suggests it might be otherwise. I don't mean to set that as the exclusive character of a painting, it is shared by natural forms and by perfect artifacts. I think it is the character of process to suggest that it is at any moment of its existence one of many similar things which might have been chosen (that is my special problem) but that ideally every process as a whole suggests every other process. The analogy which I would prefer to make between painting and writing is the less convenient one that a single entire process—for ease a short poem but equally Finnegans Wake—exists, not so much at each of its points but rather at all of its instants taken together, in the same way that it is obvious that a painting exists. It is of the most difficult analogies, because just as it is obvious that a painting is there in front of one, it is entirely obscure that the given process exists because of the limitlessness of its suggestions, the way in which it is an example of everything. I use analogies, here and elsewhere, because I find them to be the best indirect method for transmitting experience. It is worth pointing out that the analogy I shy from is the one that puts painting into the context of process, which is natural to writing, while the one I prefer puts writing in the context of thingness natural to painting. In the one, process is the greater good (to be old-fashioned), in the other, existence is.

Of course none of these points is quite true. To begin with, I think that one who is at home with process will be quite likely to admire things as such, and it just as likely if not more so that painters in this age when process is the true reality and is thought to be, will successfully associate themselves with process in many ways.* So one notices the analogy of the analogies. It is hardly surprising that my interests exhibit the contrariety that Mr. Jones observes in all personal interests. In addition, what interests one in any process is the continuous midway between rather arbitrary births and deaths on various levels. The memorandum which is accumulated notes of the process of a certain business concern is a good example of the found-object sort because it happens that it necessarily describes its own process, in much the same way as action painting is said to do but better. A legal document, of which the best example for my purpose is a constitution because it is composed almost entirely of names, is a much more 'objective' or formal sort of found-object characterized by process because its process accords with an utterly conventional form that is referred to only briefly in the final article, that of amendments. Each article has as its subject, not 'everything,' but a certain conclusion of another process; for example, the quartering of troops in the domain of citizens. Seen in this way, a constitution is among the things an artist may find that is similar to a poem that an artist may make up. A memorandum is likely to be admired, if at all, for its

---

* Even when difficult, if it is fashionable to associate things with processes, it will be done. The art critic of Les Temps Modernes who reviewed the work of Roy Lichtenstein was moved to mention the 'fidelity to process' of the artist in reproducing a frame of a comic strip, one of many, originally produced by a crude printing process which the artist imitates in the process of making his picture. The action painters and the critics were romantics of process, so for them pure process equals reality—the illegible memo.

process alone, and if it is then it is not very poetical. In an age such as ours, constitutions become vague and tentative shadows of their models—one need only take a look at the Charter of the United Nations Organization to see that—and a poem, however conventional or not will have to lose the thingness that is characteristic of names, which become uninteresting end points, except to the extent that with great tenacity a poet such as Joyce or Jones manages to include everything in the poem. Joyce is the type for such a modern poet (Jones seems too exclusive, but the 'better poet') and he is so generous as to include in his poem a very large selection of words from other languages as well as an innumerable amount of word-assemblage, which is perhaps his art, his 'idea,' his move. At any rate, he succeeds to create a peculiar poetical process that in itself exists as a whole. That is what all the talk about literary 'form,' which is so confusing because it confounds processes with visual objects, resolves to.

We live, it has no doubt too often been recently observed, in a prosaic time, but even the prose is not much good. Writers and ordinary folk who do not know Latin nevertheless write in a shoddy vulgar semi-form of it in which the meaning of 'anticipation' is lost in a way that 'brick' can never be for us until there is no such thing in the world. It is not only tiresome, it is high stupidity to have continually to buck up against a worthless amount of supposed cultural imposts and inadequacies. One's annoyance at these effects often gets expressed by being shouted to the far walls which leads to further harassments, none of them new but all of them increased and also debased, like echoes, or like the effect made by huge signposts composed of reflectors or 'electric' paint, those idiot boards by which we are to be directed through the 'federal highway system,' that is, the land. It is much more pleasant to ignore the nonsense and be a poet of nostalgia, or more especially to be mute as a painter, and they are quite lovely occupations and quite possible 'in our society' where one's paintings can be informed by procedural technique, I suppose, and where there are more people than in all Rome who will be pleased to read your verse. But any process is naturally an ephemeral sort of thing. A memorandum is immediately incomprehensible to those it does not concern. And for type in process, I should choose the dance directly thrown away.

The types for performance and for objectivity will bear no analogy that I can see. The stupid one would be to say that the process of a painting is its continuing existence. But even if it can be thought of in terms of process, every sort of painting is not very prosaic, not very amenable to the way of life and art that we have, such as it is. Even George's illuminated paragraphs cannot be seen to move. It always remains that, for us, a thing or a name is strange. For me, however, that otherness is still the condition of aspiration, in the sense that it used to be said, among writers, I believe, that all art aspires to the condition of music, to that formal clarity, that perfect exposition. I desire to make a poem out of a conundrum of processes, some of them actual, some of them metaphorical, and likely what I make up is a bad poem though it be ever so many ideal processes perfectly conceived and printed, yet a poem is what I wish though I could not write a good poem should I try. Mr. Jones is a very good poet in the course of which he deplores as I do my vulgarity but as he suggests in his preface to *Anathémata* —things made over to the gods—'It may be that the kind of thing I have been trying to make is no longer makeable in the kind of way in which I have tried to make it.' He cannot quite believe that while I cannot help believing it and at the same time I know that art of ephemera—the realism that conspires against me but in terms of which I find myself—is no good art. The record of anything I happened once to associate in train is simple history made over to my successors to forget. The Drapers' Company may have kept their books for centuries, but our much improved procedure fires them automatically after seven years. That is what is unsatisfactory about this prose; That is what is unsatisfactory about this music of noise; That is what is unsatisfactory about this motion picture. It is fashionable to lack interest in what can be thought to be eternal because of its impossibility, and I am party to that fashion. But I cannot quite believe my words.

Nor is that any more satisfactory. One ought not, I believe, to enter an alien concept such as eternity, and directly leave for church, there to admire the great history of symbolism. Not that it would be unnatural to do so, and that such an exhibition is of the nature of man I surely endorse. But at this moment I find zeroing in upon my brain, numerous and diverse sensations that I must cauterize. The dictionary suggests to me the bible.

Now the Spirit speaketh expressly, that in the latter times some shall depart from the faith, giving heed to seducing spirits, and doctrines of devils;

Speaking lies in hypocrisy; *having their conscience seared with a hot iron;*

Forbidding to marry, and commanding to abstain from

meats, which God hath created to be received with thanksgiving of them which believe and know the truth.

For every creature of God is good, and nothing to be refused, if it be received with thanksgiving;

For it is sanctified by the word of God and prayer.

If thou put the brethren in remembrance of these things, thou shalt be a good minister of Jesus Christ, nourished up in the words of faith and of good doctrine, whereunto thou hast attained.

But refuse profane and old wives' fables, and exercise thyself rather unto godliness.

For bodily exercise profiteth little: but godliness is profitable unto all things, having promise of the life that now is, and of that which is to come.

This is a faithful saying and worthy of all acceptation.

For therefore we both labour and suffer reproach, because we trust in the living God, who is the Saviour of all men, specially those that believe.

These things command and teach.

Let no man despise thy youth; but be thou an example of the believers, in word, in conversation, in charity, in spirit, in faith, in purity.

Till I come, give attendance to reading, to exhortation, to doctrine.

Neglect not the gift that is in thee, which was given thee by prophecy, with the laying on of the hands.

Meditate upon these things; give thyself wholly to them; that thy profiting may appear to all.

Take heed unto thyself, and unto the doctrine; continue in them: for in doing this thou shalt both save thyself, and them that hear thee.

Among the derogations of our time, the case of religion is most typical. Everything to which it is desired to add a certain unattractive anachronism will be described as being 'religiously observed.' Even I, who had much appreciation of it, rather shudder at the thought of Salvation in any form that is not my own. I too would sooner mention horseshit than thanksgiving. In the strictest sense, it is now possible, as Saint Paul remarked, to dedicate one's life to anything whatever. There is no fragment of any active language which is immune from profanation, nothing is unsusceptible of becoming god for a moment of the process, though least so our old classic God. Christ is done for as a magic incantation, but the word lives through our disenchatment as the expletive of a surprise, and to hell with Moses. In this relatively hopeless situation, some people, indeed many, perhaps almost all, will find themselves content to worship and pray by way of scrupulous fidelity to the 'in our society' process, which, they must contend, is all there is. In this revolting manner, all life and art becomes, for these abject subscribers, an endless process of allusion to objective facts that have no meaning, save that they are available to everyone. It is this detailed banality, or, if you wish, sophistication, that derogates anything that could be called style or literature in this epoch. In the living language, I am constrained only to remember what Dristan 'means,' and also to speak of Lucky Strikes, even if I do so for the most personal reason, that as I write I always smoke a cigarette that bears that name. Of course I am free to cultivate the dead, but what good is that? Pure decoration, my dear, mere rubbish. The Queen in the play by Le Roi Jones called The Baptism is a type character of this time and place, a man very much like me, of equally ephemeral crudity and charm, a disgusting creature, never-the-less 'of God,' who like me, 'believes' he is the only person onstage at the moment with any appreciation of high style at the same time as his behavior is utterly informal. That that reference to an unknown play will be lost on all but a few of the very few people who have ever seen it or ever shall, and by whom it will be soon forgotten unless, as cannot happen, it is constantly recalled, is a decent example of the momentary processes I notice. My point is that mammon as god is a detestible triviality which, in a phrase of David Jones, is debilitating to contemplate. Still, even though I might, I would not for long or categorically divert my gaze from its fascination upon the process of the sale.

Even if we should one day make it to come true that All men are created equal, it will still be, as well, that *Manners mayketh man*. It is fine to realize a thing in such a forceful way. But a statement of belief impresses upon one some responsibility, for instance, of behaving otherwise than might have been his lot if he could have chosen, as might be, some other mood or myth. And from respect to my responsibility, I willingly ignore the 'high standard of living' that is or would be mine 'by rights,' and I willingly live in a certain way that has a tendency to undermine the happy confidence of soul-less women that they have triumphed o'er the hearts of men, and, altogether, it seems to me that I behave as an artist, or, that is to say, after the

manner of men of all time.* And in doing so, I subscribe to all the
current formulas which pertain to art at present: I believe in the value
of oblivion; I believe in the operations of chance; I believe in the
analogy of analogies; I believe in the displacement of distinctions; I
believe in the process of the moment; I believe in the truth of the
private vision; I am party to the unknown; I believe in the speed of
light; but as an artist I especially believe in the nature of man *sub specie
aeternitatis* which is the Holy Ghost.

Were either of us suddenly asked to consider such a problem as
the creation of the world, you or I would be likely to say, 'Well! That
is rather lovely, but it is imponderable (it is boring) (I can only do
what I can do).' People who can habitually talk about such things
certainly have none of our interest in understatement, in the limitation of our profoundest concerns to the very minimal, perhaps for the
sake of clarity and order at home, in our own minds. Such extravagant
visionary sayings appear somewhat insane from our domestic viewpoint. Rather then speak of the Eternal, or the Beginning, or the
End, in any connection whatever, we will reply politely that what we
do is simple and gratuitous, that at least it has nothing to do with the
demands of other people, and that we cannot conceive that it could be
related to the requirements of old or new God, though we can
appreciate the analogue. Yet I have already gone so far astray from the
least of all possible ways to cultivate our garden, that I may as well
add a bit to our discomfort from the rarified condition of the upper air
(as our cabin is unpressurized), by remarking here that the nature of
the life of man on earth forms the type for the conception of eternity,
the only process of which we regret to speak.**

There is one sure way to get a laugh in the theatre these days,

---

* 'But then I have reflected that, as St. Paul and the Christian fathers held, women
are of their nature without souls, that they commonly receive a soul from some man
and that Muriel Agnes had been shut off more than is common from male,
humanising influences.'   Rayner Heppenstall in *The Greater Infortune.*

** *Ethics,* by Benedictus de Spinoza. From Book I, of God. 1663. 'By eternity, I
mean existence itself, in so far as it is conceived necessarily to follow solely from the
definition of that which is eternal.

'Existence of this kind is conceived as an eternal truth, like the essence of a thing,
and, therefore, cannot be explained by means of continuance or time, though
continuance may be conceived without a beginning or end.'

From *Ethics, Book V,* of the power of the intellect, or of Human Liberty. 1675.
'Whatsoever the mind understands under the form of eternity, it does not understand by means of conceiving the present actual existence of the body, but by virtue

and that is by mentioning God. I have stopped joining in the general derision since I noticed it, just as I miss many occasions to mention, for example, Shakespeare or Freud, not that anyone dares to laugh at those august abstractions. I believe that there is something, to which we refer as Man, that is worth something. To think so is not very exciting, it is not glorious, nor yet charming. It is such a thing as one would prefer to avoid having said; it is now rather disquieting to me to have the vivid remembrance of the sectarian motto by means of which my mother would reassure me as a child when I was sick: Man is Spiritual, not Temporal. *** But rather than feign ignorance of these effects, I find that some such saying that remains to me by accident is the very least that I can say, as I cannot omit to greet our old and older Friend, as I pass by, though where it used to have the wonderful scent of mysteries defined, His slipstream now reminds me of the sweet smell of death. And then comes the haunting, singing commercial, What do you mean, Mean, I mean, Mean, What do you mean?

Unfortunately for the great cause of explanation, I see what I know as being self-evident. All about man is his tendency to Lethargy, if you will, his desire to forget all of his associations with the force from which his very existence depends, his unique will to power through fabrication. There are, I presume, a numberless amount of processes for the formulation, in every conceivable form of artifice or metaphor, of this impulse which is man's nature. And all these conformations refer to the idea of man himself in his excellence being as they are expressions of I am god, like the rationalistic slogan, *Cogito, ergo sum*. There is no sort of delusion that can be prevented by means of remarking such a fundamental phenomenon, and, definitely, anything that may be derived logically from such a point may

of conceiving the essence of the body under the form of eternity.

'Things are conceived by us as actual in two ways: either as existing in relation to a given time and place, or as contained in God and following from the necessity of the divine nature. Whatsoever we conceive in this second way as true or real, we conceive under the form of eternity, and these ideas involve the eternal and infinite essence of God.'

*** Mother informs me that the text I loved is called The Scientific Statement of Being by Mrs. M. B. Eddy, as follows: 'There is no life truth intelligence nor substance in matter. All is infinite Mind and its infinite manifestation, for God is all in all, spirit is immortal Truth; matter is mortal error. Spirit is the real and eternal; matter is the unreal and temporal. Spirit is God, & man is his image and likeness. Therefore man is not material; he is spiritual.'

be proved to be false. Indeed and in fact and in many other ways, the conception itself, however natural, may be denied or forsworn. There is no way of establishing this truth so that it has a degree of certainty even approximate to that which we at the moment entertain with respect to the speed of light as a perfect limitation. It is like a useless fact, or a piece of higher art that has no necessity outside the artist's life. It is hardly illuminating to know this, it is really important, it is even time-honored, it is not even interesting, but it is there, here, in me. It is the occasion for any confidence, it is the means by which I except myself from everything else, so that I may continue, refreshed, in the creation of something else again; in it waits the possibility of any choice: it is all the law and the prophets.

But having indulged myself in that bit of prophecy, I think it well to point out again that the heresy I make bold to mention is extra and super de luxe, in a way that was successfully formulated by the Christians as 'someone else.' Or, in our fashion, I say that I write only when I have nothing else to do. We intuit ourselves, and each other, so to do something for the satisfaction of our desires, and, perhaps, for those of others of whom and which we cannot know. At last we know how unseemly it is for men so young as we yet are to limit our intentions to what our fathers have allotted for us, though we thank and bless them, all. By the example of each other, we make ourselves believe that some men will continue in the immemorial tradition that we choose, forever, even if we get a little jealous of our domain from time to time and keep looking in the newspaper to see if anyone is thinking of quartering his technicians there. By way of this really unwarranted confidence, we contrive as is required more or less vulgarly to associate ourselves with eternal process and existence.

And now to God the Father, God the Son, and God the Holy Ghost: Amen.

0. 8. 0

The embarrassment is always settled in terms of movement. Now that is not a psycho-logical statement. It is a quick answer. But wait for the interpretation of the dream, if you please. Then on with the play. It is like in the old days. Consistency was desired and achieved in preference to some form of insanity for which there is a name. It came to me, or, 'I' added it to 'myself' (in the sense of attraction), by way of D.C.L. That is not the stylistic influence, but the actual. It appears, perhaps, out of order. But remember that I have here to describe an order that is only actual. It is like the weather. It was often called 'inspiration.' That is a good joke that goes three ways, but never mind. Reading leads to writing as much as the other way around. More so, really, because it is only assumed that the experiment leads to the lecture. Often that is not the case at all. If you think I am setting up another paradox, please ignore it if you can. At the time of which I am speaking, we were both moving out of the sincere mode which is so straightforward that it seems to be a fraud. I found it dull, except at certain points, those occasional misplacements we called wit.

And leaving the fifth, we come back to the second point, to Don Juan in disguise. At the time of which I am speaking, he returned, incognito, from London. Maybe I could have recounted the biography of it, but I really had no idea of what had passed with him for life there. One day he showed up. I was not too surprised to see him. It was pleasing. At that time, one got the impression from him that he understood everything that might be done or said, and because of that one could feel that one understood him, which was often not the case. As soon as I had come to know him slightly, it seemed as if I knew him well. So much so that the first time he killed himself, the priest, who meant well but was a busybody, came to me and said, What can we do for him? It surprised me for a minute. I had then no idea that he needed my help, nor that in future there would be occasions for me to offer it.

At the time of which I am speaking, our friendship had strengthened unaccountably. By then I had already tried to end it, at one point, which had only drawn us closer. By now he was one of my dearest friends, though I knew almost nothing of him. Without asking any favors, he suddenly moved in towards the center of my life. He had again endured a shock which brought him, if one can believe his great friend who rescued him, or had him saved, for diverse reasons, just beyond the point of death. It had thus become necessary that he once more rearrange the elements of his life to make it viable again, which he was in quite a good position to do. But the change had to some extent rearranged for him his own conception of himself, so that now he was unsure as to which of his many friends would assure him of their loyalty. He retreated to the home of his grandfather until he should settle things sufficiently again to live alone. And then he stopped to visit us. Someone I did not then know had already called me to tell me he was in town.

He was, he said, determined for the first time on establishing himself in an independent manner, but he was as yet quite open to any suggestion as to just what that manner might be. Needless to remark, I hadn't any. It was soon after I had started to establish myself, you recall, and that task was, at the time of which I am speaking, only barely conceived. Its character would change, at least in color or some other nuance, several times before it could be named. I liked what I was doing but I couldn't recommend it. Nor would I, and to others, what I did seemed then like nothing. At any rate, for the first time in several years he was not completely busied with all sorts of engagements, and he had time for the first time in some time to think, and I realized that I did not actually know him, so I asked him what he had been doing. In the course of his grand disillusionment just past he had become a slight figure in the literary world of three different cities, and to begin with, he told me what he had found out. He was quite a storyteller. He evoked little scenes with the greatest economy, like the novelists he admired, in such a way that one immediately saw everything, not as it was indeed, but as he would have had it be. His treatment was a little sketch which the audience invariably filled out with historical details of prejudice. The story, which could not have been written down, thus fulfilled the dreams of both the teller and the told. At the time of which I am speaking, I would very much have liked to hear what he would say to a question about me from someone not known to me, but I never did, and the time of that wish passed.

He took refuge in his stories. You see, once he had heard something of someone, he made that fact, that person, that story into his own domain. To this day I am not sure that I have heard them all. Indeed, I venture to hope I have not. Rather in this way, he came to have many friends, many of whom were in some way connected with his great friend, from whom, at last, he fled in despair; from whom, I should say, he had originally fled repeatedly, only to revive his interest as a result of every interruption. It was his classical mode, to flee, and until later he couldn't realize that people no longer behaved that way. You have to be chased to make it work. He hoped for, indeed believed in and depended on an eventuality he couldn't name which would unite him so strongly with his friend that a bond like that could only be invented and retold, it could never have been lived. He made things be more difficult. Perhaps it is there, at some point in that sentence, that he and I would make our encounter.

I value his stories, but surely our association did not spring from such a wordy source. Whatever he thought, he had a hard time putting words to it, something than which I found nothing more natural to me. The maddening thing was that if one chose a word to help him out, as I used to do, he accepted it as one might a present of fruit or flowers, disregarding their type and color for the nature of the gift. Of course he could have distinguished among the types, he was too well educated not to. When I suggested honestly that his acquiescence was too facile, he took another course, calculated to please me, of wondering if my proposition were the right one to apply, so as to satisfy my objection, he would slightly disagree. He had not the right effect, though I was often more polite, and it concerned me that he would find other ways of agreeing with me, actually against my will. It is really complicated, but the simple answer is that I did not want him to do whatever it appeared I might want him to do just because I said so. For a time I quite gave up offering any opinion which might indicate what his ought to follow. It is not a pedagogic principle, but it is related to one. It was meant only to be salutary. He had to cultivate an actual desire, and no one else could make it for him. I daresay it didn't have much success, but at the time of which I am speaking, our meetings were likely to be distinguished for our silence. It was boring.

Going back to the question of necessities, I didn't know what his were. He overlaid his necessities with the apparent desire to please his friends and the covert hope that he might yet save himself. It is like the Christmas tree, which by then has no roots. He cast necessities aside and covered the result with ornaments very pleasant to behold. I don't think he had much to eat, except at a table especially provided. But he had the greatest inclination to sleep of anyone I have known. He would then often doze in the middle of a reading, which was often what we did to pass the time, the better to decorate his images, I supposed. He didn't need more sleep. You have to distinguish between need and desire. They are incomparable, no matter what the lady says. Somehow I had more need of him than he had of me, which in truth was actually unusual, as much so for him as me, though things might very well appear to be different than they were. With him, necessities were forgotten, while desires were manifest.

To his annoyance, occasionally he lost a friend. Sometimes they accused him of lies, their quick solution. He arranged things to suit himself as much as any artist, with the difference that he did not always know what he was doing. He made therefore unintentional mistakes, some of which could with justice be called lies by the people they affected. Often they were regarded, rightly, as a lapse of memory. His life included a vast amount of allusions to the lives of every other person he had ever known, a countless number with whom he kept up a tenuous relation, always open and about to be renewed, even if he forgot the name. The extent of his search for he knew not what may be what almost did him in, or a more particular fantasy, though he was no poet, but the time came, of which the time of which I am speaking was but one of several, when it was always up to him to begin again, bereft of some illusion (which, I did not know), to build himself upon the base that receded ever more quickly behind him, time out of mind. Then he needed my help, and I gave it in some fear that part of my existence would depart with his.

The formal point is this: that fear is one's quick response when it happens that elements of truth or life and necessity or culture coincide at a point from which one's interest is deflected, whether that boredom or any of the requisistes are quite realized or not. This formula has an actual source, if not the one I have just described in application, it is not a theory, no plot, no poem. Thus it happened that at moments of his extreme embarrassment when he was most frightened, I came to tell him a story that would relieve him, however slightly, like a pill. I didn't get it ready in advance, but when the time came I knew that it was right. At the time of which I am speaking, I was not as practiced as I am now. The story was as endless as the story of the annoyance it resolved in response to other desires which if described would not make sense.

With that great friend, who was really not 'myself' at all, he had constructed an actual world that was nevertheless so imaginary that for it to continue to exist required himself to vanish. He would decide upon his own way to die and do it. It seemed too logical. Both right and wrong. His solution was to disappear successfully, but not to die. It had its imperfections, but there could be none better. His friend called me one morning to say that our friend had gone. When I returned the call to report that all was as well as could be, the man gave me the repeated impression that he had a rose on his coat but it was piece of dark silk in his pocket. That is not a fraud but a disappointment. I could then see what had happened by my friend. Nobody knew the actuality of his experience, but I saw that he resolved to hope in the face of every likelihood that it would shatter, making him the spitting image of his progenitor, for whom there could be no hope and no such desire. They used to use the metaphor of Faust. To counter that, my friend and I maintained between us an obstination for the actuality of every thing, despite an increment of fanciful images used to decorate the worst. What is it? How does it work? Officially, I put in against secrets. But in composing American letters, among all the other things that one may do, and apart from what we all must do, I notice that something does not happen, and probably it has no name. Mies van der Röhe, in America, once said that his constructions were practically nothing at all. Jeanneret, who began by changing his name, could only say to Harvard, *Il faut avoir du courage.* If this metonymy looks obscure, it is nothing like so dark as the reality it changes. One must have a scheme from the heart. My dear friend, who seemed so unlike the heroic myth of love, lost his heart to the highest tower, which in turn had no other name. Mine, at one moment now past but still remarkable, could be set with 'the tradition of the new,' a striking phrase, a formulation of the American hegemony in art, where, at the time of which I am speaking, the most formal things are arbitrary and every classic is a foreign object. The most important question is Why? all the answers belong to What? and every real interest pertains to How?

True that the inexorable quality of the convention of time has long been authorized in poetical practice, as well as in numerous private illusions. But only think that beyond the ultimate practical limit called the speed of light we place the contradiction of the necessity of time, just like the promise of heaven. It has interested me to see if I can work at writing, because it has been one of my prejudices that what I do is not laborious, but rather a sort of formal series of illusions whose only comparison to work is that it consumes as much time. It is part of this *lavori in corso* to permit oneself to waste it without a question. *My work is in part a record of how I wasted so much time.* Now it is precisely every form of waste that I abhor. In such a formula of tension one can always find the source of beauties, but it will not yield a beautiful way of life as such. Very occasionally, then, I refresh myself by doing indeed many things together, acquiring and replacing lovely things for the perfection of my surroundings. Or I throw a charming party in the evening. But I know by experience that the harassment of the water is much worse than any benefit I get from cooling off, and so I rarely swim. It makes such a profound activity as respiration into something more than a matter of course, as a sickness might, and it irritates my eyes; And in just the same way as all the artificial emergencies of every business do, it makes continuous motion both necessitous and meaningless. My answer to the question of an alternative to slavery is to play at the derivation of a metaphor for my experience, something which cannot be applied generally, something useless except for my own purposes, which cannot be understood therefore in any other manner. Happily it is always necessary to sleep, not to waste but to destroy time wholesale, And while clocks do not sleep they continue in labor according to our system. Secretly, I admire a stopped clock, and I love her who makes it run again. What Charles said was, Some gifts have genealogies, some have descriptions.

0. 9. 0

We return you now to S. R. From the heights of familiarity we drop back into the unknown, complaining only a little because the man does not reveal himself at once. No, waiter, I am not writing a novel. The speed of the drop changes our minds. Quickly we desire nothing more than to bury ourselves. Usually it is suggested what ground will be used for the entrenchment, but I leave that to the reader. After all, this is not a satire. It moves out. The motion is reflected at the back of our ever-changing minds. Then it flies out of our mouths in the performance of the moment. Its act is to vanish. We remember nothing but that we had a good time. The hard and fast will only aggrandize if described, a different kind of pleasure, I am sure. He knows it but he doesn't do so because he knows it. That's just how he finds out. Actually there's no difference. But when it comes to nonsense he shuts up. The point is to be a sense of movement, of direction. It doesn't take many forms. It goes on until it stops. A chance remark of which everyone makes game and nobody remembers. We spent all our money. Let's go. It needs a city but it doesn't have to be a pretty one and anyway there are no rich uncles; if she had to be a bitch she didn't have to bet her money on him but just go on to make a funny story without agitation that was less to her than simple information. If you want a light, you strike a match and put it to it. You don't think about it, That's how accidents occur. You do have to take that chance. It was a mistake to light the candle in the wrong place. That is not accidental. Who could tell you, the cops? Preferably yes, says the safety. However they know less than you. There is no doubt that no more laws should be passed. And those already on the books should be manipulated to arrest the depressing tendency of thought. We do not always drink, and we do not always think before we break the mask. The thought moves too, and that moment will no more continue than will the action you might mistake for one another. We do it anyway. For a long time he didn't do much. And he never told one what it was. Whether he did it or not was left completely unknown. There was not the slightest difference between one thing and another. He loved it. And furthermore since he was always alone the question of a moment could stretch into an eternity. You know, if you go to a movie alone, are you there? He didn't care to be a critic either. This is also not an imitation. There are innumerable mistakes. It doesn't matter, it's fast and that's the price. He got so damned mad at me that he wouldn't say a thing. Probably it was some accident, something I said, I don't know. I thought I would call him up and tell him that I loved him no matter what I said but that didn't work because he didn't answer. He prefers silence, he always has. If you don't know, I can't tell you, is the way she puts it. It really annoyed me that I couldn't get through. They say you have to respect both time and distance. Maybe so, but I liked it more the other way. It's an essay in ignorance, not an accusation of any kind. I am willing to apologize, but only if it will get things moving. Is that why an apology is handsome? It seems to him to be no use undertaking the impossible. I feel the same way about what *can* be done. The thing would be to get us both to do the same thing at the same time. We have to leave that to chance, as they now call god. I cannot do it, I have tried. There are influences, but I am not thinking about them and it is certain that they are not such an ill wind that they have a specific color telling you from whence they blow, as you used to be able to tell where old bricks were made because of the color of the clay which was different in every place. Now they do not exactly use any clay in it and the color is faked so that in ten years it will probably wash away revealing nothing we don't know already. S. R. showed nothing and promised little so if he should do anything it would be good, I figured. I wasn't burdened with a profession so I could afford to be more pretentious. The scientist who philosophizes has it made. And so things went. I use that phrase a lot, and I would use it more often if form didn't follow function as it does, and I mean that you couldn't possibly sell all the words that would be required to convey the entire eventuality of each and every moment of even a single life in process. Some have tried and still they left out almost everything. You see what I mean with Dreiser. But Stanley wanted one word only. You might as well find something else to do. If it comes to

where you can't do something although you try, you probably have
the wrong thing in mind, an accident, no, a mistake. There is no
remedy in that form. The same with trying to name & cure a disease.
You have only to begin anywhere at all and go from there to some
point where you'll probably see your old idea in a new form and then
you use that. It sounds simple. The point is not to dwell in it. It is
called action, both in jargon and in English and in French. It is not
the opposite of contemplation, it is something other. The invention
of events induces waiting, she said, but she was bored. Alright, yes,
To death. It's true that civilization requires slaves, but whatever they
tell you, she doesn't need our own time. She wanted to recapture it
but we want nothing more than the opportunity of throwing time
away. No, says the safety. Mais oui, say we. If you think about it
things are getting worse. If you don't, things are the same as ever,
which you can bring around to your thinking if it makes you feel that
much better or results in an epigram, but which is not a thought and
should not be part of your thinking if it doesn't have a good use. If
this is like a lecture, it is half a conversation, missing our correspondent. With a little more work I could have said nothing in the same
form at the same speed with the same apparent necessity and the same
obvious gratuitousness, but I had an end in view which was to say
some of the things I would have said to Stanley if I could have at the
same time as I said them to myself, and in this way to continue to
invent this 'myself' I keep on referring to, and to entertain a moment
longer the 'you' I speak of as often and invent just as much.

That is perhaps a gross illusion. They say that the recollections
of great men by other great men are worthless because the one is
always talking about himself. Thus about the author they are sometimes marvellous. Bad artists always admire each other's work. They
call it being large minded and free from prejudice. *But a great artist
cannot conceive of life being shown, or beauty fashioned, under any conditions
other than those he has selected.* It is only about things that do not
interest one that one can give a really unabiased opinion. Without the
least justification, one engaged in the invention of oneself will use
materials availed by the reflections of oneself that one's friends present, so violating their privacy and preventing the restoration of their
integrity after the operation. However it is not cruelty to anyone. The
justification of a character in a novel is not that other persons are what
they are, but that the author is what he is.

At the time of which I am speaking, there were only a few notes
left over from whatever we had at one time shared. We lived together

like congenial soldiers for a time, and suddenly the war was over. That is always the great experience of those who have it, and those who live through the war in extreme youth or in exile are often jealous at the thought of having missed it, and later on they make up for the war they lost out on by tremendous works that stupefy the ruined powers of the soldiers they admire. Afterwards, there was a certain exchange, on a decreasing scale, of visits and letters and promises, and then it came to be that I no longer knew where or whether he lived. Among them, I have one ghastly letter written from the beautiful city of Genève, which Janet transcribed for me on the typewriter so that I could read it, so strongly had his misery affected his hand. 'What can be done and what cannot be done,' he wrote, 'is the least important thing I can possibly consider — it is, in putting the problem that way, a little like wondering about god. It is a consideration of such remote and *impractical* proportions — it virtually and with no effort precludes talk about success or failure. Those two are indefensible terms for me — wailing wall words which imply for the user an experience of some use, worth, exactitude.'

Aside from the writing, which is all I am thinking about as I work, something happened. Our cat died while we were in the country. She began languishing somewhat a few days before we left, and while we were there she grew markedly weaker, and one evening she lay gasping on the floor, and died, naturally as all animals do whose lives are not the objects of art. It was the most saddening event I can remember. We buried her at night in the ground behind the house, happening to lie nearby to a fence that encloses a pasture in the next field. All the cows, ten or twelve, gathered together quietly at the nearest part of the fence, their heads and necks across the topmost rail, looking at us as we dug the hole. We thought she had been bitten by a rat. When I was small, whenever I was sad, I became at the same time angry to think of the devastation of things, of tools or pets or toys or machines, that had been lost, or left in the rain, or which no longer worked; and about people, and animals, their time and the life of plants and animals being naturally and remorselessly wasted and rusted and ruined. Once I got out of bed and went out in the rain to place a bucket over a seedling I had just transplanted. More usually I found that I could do nothing at all about it and I felt bad and cried myself to sleep. I felt the same after the cat died, and I still think of the cat like that, and the destruction of buildings in the cities, and the deterioration of automobiles, and the disintegration of families, and the debilitating effects of disease and disuse.

0. 0. 0

'The fourth point' replaced in the tenth post becomes, momentarily, the source of everything abstracted, and, with a supernumerary interruption (like a quotation) it will presently resume the past when it becomes the twelfth as well.

Now the fourth point is not a name.
    It is not only a typographical convention.
        Nor can it be recalled to the senses as a color.
            It is the principle of logic carried out beyond the rules.
                Neither can we demonstrate a more than curious connection.   It adds to nine what cannot be taken down as a reminiscence.   Not to say, of course, that it cannot be reformed to parts.   It takes its position as an artificial resolution sevens.   New work in this field rarely defines arithmetic formalism.   It seeks by means of analysis to yield a lifelike series which can be reapplied,

like a story, to construct one's own life in terms that everyone will understand. I have many objections to this method. But most important, the technique fears laughter. The witty observation, thus robbed of grace, becomes unlaughable. It begins, Nature does not laugh, (nor did God), therefore. . . . One quickly turns the century* page in some hope that the exposition will become more lively in its second act. But no; how annoying it is. People of course still tell their jokes at work, but it is possible to notice that ordinarily their senses are not quickened by the industrial process but by old things that are irrelevant to the life in which they find themselves. Is there a symbol here? I believe that has been so well thought out that the question will eventually disappear. At that time we may have something more to say about it. Any discussion now will invariably produce wasteful disputations in the realm of factual distinction. I am proceeding gingerly along tender lesions. At all events, the modern liberal anti-German humanist point of view gets into serious trouble when it attempts to assimilate scientific technique. It becomes a soporific like masturbation. Why do you do it? The answer is called a rationaliza-

---

* In the manuscript of this book, which was called NO ANTICIPATION ALLOWED, this expression appeared at the beginning of page 300. FTC

tion which is like a lie, applying a fasified syntax that no more gratifies the subject than the object. It is as evident that the only resolution yet to have been invented and generally applied is to have the trouble explained away by translation into psycho-analytic terms. It works at the very minimum, I am sure. People who think that they want to die can be persuaded that life is worth living. They leave the regenerating auspex under the new delusion with a lifetime guarantee. But although we are glad of their redemption, we see nothing interesting in the flight of these happy men & women. Nor do the analysts, whose regard for the patient ceases when the evidence procures no more grief for them to latinize, a process that is therefore most usually protracted. Now when one looks above and beyond the minimum, you still find people using the high implausibilities of asexual economic science, substituting dollars for doughnuts, without a thought that the performance of a special sense is ludicrous. The language is remorselessly mercantile throughout. It is here, and not in the lower depths, that the synthetic process will find its goal.

There is no shortage of rhetorical sythesists, but what they say has already been programmed for them along the lines of certain great critiques which perfectly anticipate each movement of the process. There can be no actual synthesis that doesn't rely on wit. The performance by demonstration (what is badly called experiment) is a deadly bore. The historical resource usually is that the basic critique was formulated in such a way that it had to go directly out of date. Right away the elementary principles are adopted into the process of education forcing the elaboration of their origins into the anachronistic mood thereby giving larger generations of scientists enough work to keep them busy. It is scientific realism, the drastic process of revision. It gives to abstract conception the impression of movement and improvement, just like its visual representation will, by means of optical trickery and gadgets everyone may play with. (please yawn)

Literary realism, on the other hand, works to assure the continued success of the commercial metaphor through sex. Social realism is a minor aspect of it that had been attached by those factual intelligences who are content to describe the informal proliferation of events by means of photography and mirrors. These self-immured slaves succeed as well in capturing the evacuated imagination of the public (which does not exist) through print. By their own count they win the world-wide election without alternative. There always used to be fantasies about what would happen if the slaves came into their own. The Saturnalia, it is presumed, directly guarded against just such an eventuality. *Now we know.* By means of pure phenomenology the world series of events is transmuted into the absurd boast that slavery is abolished. Historically, that is true; that is, linguistically. The literary realism of the Roman Church and, finally, of the Constitution of the American states, has formalized the aspiration. But there is no satisfaction because it is apparent, though not remarkable, perhaps, that we have merely concretized another fantasy, as we began by doing, and that slavery dignified as labour, remains the preponderant way of human life.

The demonology of Europe is expressed in American propaganda and realized in American life. It is useless to consider our experience under any other form. In this way, for example, it is quickly seen how the science of psychology, which was developed to be a legitimate causality alternative to economics, has been brought in to reconcile scientific and literary modes, an undertaking to which its rhetoric is unequal, to say the least. In other words, the substitute for money has been logically over-extended to be used as the profitable substitute for God. Thus is language pejorated in medicine to the style of a disease. The industrial malaise could have been captured as well in the Marxian reconciliation of democracy and history if it hadn't scared the conscience of what was left of the upper class, forcing the syntax of education briefly to reassert its aristocratic temper as a penchant for reviving old distinctions. Thus too, it can be seen how ten, which should be perfectly solid, becomes twelve, that is utterly flighty.* And it is at that point, when we come to it, that the English abandon their pet names for numbers, resorting to a system of enumeration, albeit not the scheme ordained at the 21st point. The French, more clearly, changes once at sixteen. This is not a description.

As a concession to history, I shall finish up here and then go right into the recount, the last review of the five in final order, but omitting the numerical details suggested immediately above and below. You will then get part of the disintegration, or, if you prefer, liquefaction, while the rule is still in force. The regular interruptions will remain unannounced from here on. *This is the way the world begins.*

---

* In English feminism you will note the predominance of the dozen and the facility of the decade. See too how easily twelve becomes thirteen, a number that is apparently prejudicial to women.

There is something to every century, more or less. Everybody knows when it is time for a change, and they change. In every century there are three generations, since quarters are inhuman divisions. They say a man has three score and ten years to count. At the age of twenty-five, a man has more than a quarter of his life. A hundred is only comprehensible by tens. Ten is good for a single fashion of address; people do not remember more than ten years together. Nobody knows just when the change comes to them until afterwards, and even then they are somewhat wrong. I am pleased to count myself among the last generations of men in this century while I am still young. I can imagine that I shall see it to the end through a few more revolutions without the harassment of finding myself unable to comprehend the movements of men who will be younger still. As I know from the experiences of some of my contempories, it is most distressing to be actually young and then to get oneself in the preceding generation. One feels torn as between two equally foreign parents, and becomes old early. Every ten years there is a new generation of people who are in their prime. Rebellion is hardly the point when it is out of the question. People who are thirty years apart in age cannot in truth understand each other, for they were born in different lands. A classic beauty can be recognized after thirty years or so; before that it must remain one thing of many, however outstanding it may seem. There do not remain, of course, ten years left over, in a man's life, in the fiction of a century. We can believe 100 because it is incomprehensible. The determination of thirds is not a matter of fiction but of intuition. Ten is a fact that everyone knows. I may revolve with the fashions three times over, but then as to the newer way I must stop. These motions are not propelled but operate by consenting impulse. How do we know? We agree. *On the point of becoming a man one has stopped to look at the field and the forest. One meets there the people one will have to know.* We congregate about the periods. It is nothing to speak of the exact middle point, but between this and that, something happens to me that makes me smile. I love it. They say all fashion may be insignificant. So what? We who are young now have two generations of us behind us. Shall we be the advanced rear guard? It is an honorable position, like every other, and it is more problematical than most. We have all of us spun ourselves out of the damned nineteenth century, and the smell of the sea refreshes our drowning. A prefiguration has been offered. Our time renews itself in France where it began. That rich patronage will hardly condescend to notice what it cannot admire, but as we have left all our timidity in time now past, we quickly uncover her disregard like a dropped glove used to be. We live in the Anglo-American hegemony, incorporating many more influenzas than there are types of winds. Our catch-point is process and we make only problems; we are unfamiliar with answers, all of which in fact we may know. As the third of three we are congenial with our great fathers of the early modern generation. For what, after all, is our own American past? A couple of crude anecdotes that must be told in stale phrases, a few events that were but points on which the lives of a few states-men turned, pointing nowhere

He does what is done in many places
what he does other
he does after the mode
of what has always been done

that we can see. Mr. Williams to the contrary, there is no American history that has not already been forgotten in advance, just as there is no American language, and only the barest and most necessary functions of an American civilization to keep us going. If we still lived in Europe, we would need such things of the past, and we would have them. By us, these things can only be researched and museum'd for our entertainment. Our choice has always been to invent and realize techniques, of which the cultivation may remain to European hands. To Mr. Jones, who retains all these things we do not miss, our behavior was somewhat amusing, and vaguely reprehensible. To Miss Stein, who lived through the beginnings of the American hegemony in France, our nature was of course her nature and she knew herself as well as any native has ever known his people.

At the time of which I am speaking, something happened to occasion a trip to Cambridge for the purpose of visiting White. Since I had first known the place years before it had been for me the epicentre of a certain world away from which I moved not in space but indeed, in time, but which, like the other, maintained itself without my collaboaration. I wanted his opinion. I valued the adjustments he made for every consideration. His estimation was always just because he was, as near as could be, disinterested in the subject. It could not have been said that he needed the things which he accumulated. Just so the agent does not want the contract he negotiates professedly. In the basement, for instance, which to begin with was largely occupied with a useless old furnace, there was stored a large selection of all the

things he had ever acquired aside from anything to do with his car
which had a room to itself. White had become gradually enmeshed in
a form of life which had begun as his own invention. As it continued,
the mood more and more assimilated to itself certain conventional
elements, like formal decorations in a tradition, so that at the time of
which I am speaking, the story of his life had come to resemble that of
many other men, though the storyteller has to make the facts unique.
Meanwhile he quietly preserved his idiosyncrasies. White has a keen
commercial sense. But it is not sales, wherein his desire for profit and
his sense of justice will confound him. For example, he buys all the
food. From the outset of the convention we developed of exchanging
gifts, at his suggestion he became likely to find for me tin cans which
had the decorative advertisement for the contents lithographed to the
metal. This kind lasts a long time and will remain very bright if kept
dry. It will be thought that purchasing today necessarily concerns the
purchaser with money, but that is not the case. I began giving him
tools of which the use was not apparent. At the time of which I am
speaking he purchased an entire household of miscellaneous items.
With a certain exception, he loves things not so much as getting
them. He taught me how to shop. His interest in his machines,
however, was to have them in perfect working order. Moreover we
agreed between us that neither would we drive certain kinds of cars. I
always knew something about how to take it apart if only to clean it or
make the margin more exact numerically. I am inclined to love the
thing; he to the process of attainment. He accumulates things the
way a voracious general reader accumulates books, taking as much
interest in everything as a cat fancier does in each of his cats, a certain
amount but not the devotion of a connoisseur. Knowledge is strangely
beneficial but it can get to be too much. For him it is the process only.

In his profession, they have got it down to two types: the
straight series and the comparative charge. Among these there are a
victorian toffee cutter, a colonial sealing iron, and a modern wire
stripper. I once gave him a good electric sound amplifier with which
there was something wrong. It took a lot of time, but finally the
thing was better than it had ever been because in addition to its being
fixed I rigged it up to cast a decorative pattern of light in front of it.
He was married to a young girl somewhat smaller and younger than
himself and they had a child who, at the time of which I am speaking,
was a little girl growing rapidly. Their house, which they intended to
outgrow, was at that time an accurate measure of the world in which

they moved. In addition to this careful accumulation of things to which by an ingenious arrangement of the parts the small space of the cellar was somehow sufficient, there were also several electric powered woodworking machines which, in a world larger by half than White's, would have occupied five times the space they had. When he had more than enough time, which had once been quite a bit of extra time quite often, he frequented certain shops in the poorest section of Cambridge where he lived at the time. In other words, there was the thing itself at a certain price (whether you knew it or not) or, on the other hand, many similar things with peculiarities at various prices.

We exchanged visits from time to time. Such times were always reminiscent of those when we had been constantly in each other's company, when that was still permitted to us, not that we told the story well or often. Although they were for the most part old-fashioned utilitarian objects, the only use he made of most of them was from time to time to take them out to show them to his friends who were always interested in his things. After a year which was for both of us very eventful and divisive, he had dropped everyone he didn't like and he had made one or two new friends and he had married his wife and he and I reconciled ourselves to the turn of events. Although one did not then as now know what might happen, and White would be the last man to predict the future, he arranged his life from moment to moment to his own satisfaction. Beside a taste for decoration in every sense, we shared together the root sensation for which to be recovered is the word abstracted. We were never circumcised. Of the five, he was the only one who remembered me in this respect. At the time of which I am speaking, for example, I had long since completely learned to read and to regard books with complete familiarity, while with him books which as a young man he had used to cultivate pornography had retreated into the far distance, the intervening haze of which might be interrupted momentarily when we met again by chance or by design. That purchase he had made already and with repetition so that its logic was inexorable at the same time as it remained unliterary. It turned out to be a brilliant purchase, providing him with an endless store of curiosities, many of which he liked while he didn't need them. He recovered the entire investment by selling some apparently worthless junk, and he hired a small warehouse in which to keep his extra supplies. It is just there that his acquisition becomes uncommercial and fulfills, by another substitution, a profound desire. In that way too, he was at length encouraged to adopt a profession which concerned reordering in abstracted terms whereby electric impulses represented the statistics of all commerce. Now at the time of which I am speaking, the number of his friends had increased to the point where he could surround himself in Cambridge with people who understood the limits of his hospitality, who respected his wishes and depended on his character while they could joke with him about the rules that he enforced and they enjoyed.

The courses of my life and his departed from each other as quickly as they had once come together. In consequence, I permitted myself to fictionalize White's life had not events done otherwise. In another context I had done the same with him as I am now doing with myself, except that for myself I have no name. But all anyone could ask me was how much of it was true! I could only reply that I didn't know, and my reply was invariably quite rude. For in order to answer the question, I should have had to destroy the form of this little book over which I had brooded for such a long time to give it some elements of poetic unity; and the actual parts, even if they were not ruined in the process, would be scattered and deranged so as to make the whole as incomprehensible as it had been to begin with.

Because it seems to me that there is always a simple explanation, though perhaps not the one that everyone repeats. I doubt that what cannot be explained simply could be explained at all, and that is the alternative. I may, of course, inhabit both spheres, as Master and Viceroy or Vice-president, but not at once.

From the nineteenth century all explanation is forced into the progressive mood, of which the critique will doubt the desirability of necessary supercession. The physician of our own time, by addition, contributes schemes to control the change, of which a nuclear reaction is our high classic, alas one that is inconceivable in terms of all experience, because it is presented as a devastating revelation, like news, and not as the invention it must be. Our ordinary classic of the type, the electronic computer, misunderstood as well, will disregard the types, in order to be able on a moment's notice to remember them as facts. We have now got to where we satisfy each other that we understand the numbers that concern millions of persons, dollars, pounds of silver, food, fuel, gallons and the like.

My heater produces, in a measure, 35,000 British Thermal Units whenever I turn it on. At the moment my thermometer registers almost 19 degrees Réaumur. And so things go. I nearly mentioned the cost of time. But it never occurs to anyone that one knows too many people (though one may say something else in just that way) because one never does anything one cannot do though we may do things we were not sure we would be able to.

And it comes down to the question, *Did he do it?* Which right away suggests to us that there are other questions in which we take more interest. As soon as the investigation can be begun, they quite overlie and, indeed, outshine their source. We find along the course a continuous series, always more or less rhetorical, of answers to be ignored, or used. Cannot the modern world charge be met in a clearer way? The strongest indicator of which is the anti-locution that hides the characteristic individual, nearly dead, about to be reclaimed by a new visit. Sighs the visitor, 'There haven't been any new motivations in 500 years.' Can't our situation be suffered with deeper penetrations? Does prose, to enjoin an ugly time, have to be ugly itself? or clumsy? Is there truly a correspondence between the thing wrought and the wroughting? A *likeness?* Is it that way? Or does it come to be the light and dark it is by virtue of the torque which throws it somewhere else?

One of the ways by which it may prove to be impossible for people to do something they want to do is that they find they have not enough time. It is a famous limitation that has been noticed and recorded over and over again in every epoch, all of them European. As the population of the known world increases, at first by straight evangelism and then by leaps and bounds, there is a concurrent increase in the amount of time there is. Nobody personally has any more time, just as a statistically anticipated length of life alters nobody's life, but there is simply more time that cannot be related to the proliferation of clocks, or mirrors. And every one does something always, for which our languages provide. While never ceasing to bless a certain sumptuary idleness, we of Europe, wherever placed, have looked down upon a nameless inactivity as disgrace. It is a crime in cruder, a sin in finer atmospheres, but we rescind your grace at first by shouts and then with tears. While searching for just the proper game or pun to play upon it, we come to recognize ourselves insisting that *thy* eternal will be done. Never more stirred than by a dusty paradox, it makes us, as a paradigm, to find a word that fits the name that understands the orthodox. Replaced by right opinion freely published as described, the evil thing turns out to be an action to be tried; And time, now seen turn in and out, and multiply, resumes, under this other name, antiquities of doubt.

> While never ceasing to bless
> A certain sumptuary idleness
> We of Europe, wherever placed
> Regard a nameless inactivity with distaste.
> A crime in cruder, a sin in finer atmospheres
> We reject that beauty now with shouts, then tears;
> And searching to manipulate just the proper pun
> We see ourselves insisting, Thy eternal Will be done.
> Nevermore stirred than by a dusty paradox
> We deem a word to set the orthodox;
> Replaced by right opinion freely published as descried
> The evil thing turns out to be an artist to be tried;
> And time, now seen turn in and out
>   and multiply
>   resumes, under this other name
> Antiquities of doubt.

For what, after all, is our own American story? One remains a child for ten years longer than nature has to have, and those who have reached a certain age are provided with the time and money but not the will with which to become children again. No period of adjustment is occasioned by the famous 'increase in the complexities of modern life,' for there is never any change in that respect, that people cannot perceive a vaster prospect, except in their computations. Eventually each one finds his integer which, because of the crowd, is usually not anything like what he might have wished, as a young poet, to do. And suddenly we find that art—and it is also the art of doing nothing—is a popular formality by means of which to pass the time. But I admit that there are days when I have wished to be a common laborer if only to have something to do that day.

Just in time he wrote to me unexpectedly from the capital. Without that I wouldn't know what to say next. As usual he politely suppressed his anger, but I wasn't sure what he was leaving out. Maybe he had found in what I said an accusation. What he said was that I placed him into competition (of his own invention as mine was of mine) and that he did not enjoy the sport. He didn't say why & perhaps he couldn't have known; he said it was nothing, which was a

well-written resolution. He thought, he said, that in fact there had
been no designs, no purposes. He knew what had happened but he
did not know how it works. At the time of which I am speaking, the
designs, his and mine separately and together, have been abandoned
like films already made, only to be replayed on occasion or even
accidentally destroyed. It stopped being made, but to say that was
nothing would be merely accurate and not a full view of the affair.
But permit me to quote from the letter to which I may refer again.

Thus was begun the pretense of needing a rest, which I had for three
or four weeks, or perhaps more. But the pretense had ramifications
which were not but should have been obvious from the beginning.
That is, when one pretends to do something, or be something, in
some sense more than he intended he is. But he is in a different way.
Because his being is transformed and modified so that it is only
possible through the pretense, though he is aware that the pretense
and the pretension are in some measure beyond his control and will.
Pretending an interregnum in friendship therefore alters the association not in the exact manner a real interregnum would, but perhaps
in a more drastic way. There are most of the difficulties of a real
interruption plus the difficulties attendant to the knowledge that it is
an interruption that you have willed and used to experiment with
something. In this way both the pain and the guilt are greater. And
the knowledge that the experiment has gotten out of hand and is
beyond the reach of will becomes a terrifying presence. And the how
of reversal becomes a grail. Reversal was attempted in late August
and September, but its onset was too close to my departure; It had
not proceeded to point where its own momentum would complete it.

The dignity of a prince can be protected as well by his intelligence as
by the uses of his other powers, as his advisers will classically remark,
having no powers of their own. I dictated a generous response,
demanding nothing. I did not care to use the professor's metaphor
myself as I respected the style in which he had caused it to be obscured
among the sentences.

   Thus far in the recount, the first is stabilised and isolated at the
center of his world; the second kills himself off upon returning to the
capital, affecting silence; the third—but we have yet to reach that
point of this analysis. *Who did it?* That is the question that must
haunt these papers far beyond their factual termination in the type for
modern after-life. 'This dying,' he remarked later, 'is often disap-
pointing in that I have lost some people I liked very much along with

those I wished to lose.' In what relation to the realities can that be placed? We have been trying for some months now to find or make an answer to the question. We are prepared to disregard the impetus of jealousy and that of its obverse, ignorance. By elimination, for reasons that are so good that anyone can guess them, we leave ourselves with no resort at all. But it is like being uncovered on the endless plain, indecently to attract attention, as it is unlike being run up a dead end. And the imperatives prevent our recovery by way of any operation. That is very hard to accept, as our experience will not authorize the product of our imagination. So we bury it. Even if the body has a name that we must also call ourself, even if every natural inclination points in a livelier direction, even if the experiment has succeeded by every other standard, we must terrify the source. In so doing we act in the best tradition, and thus provide a further metaphor that lives.

Then there was S. R. who was remembered for his infrequent letters and his ever promised never seen visits and the occasional telephone calls to Philadelphia. And who was somehow an imposing eminence for me but no one else. Perhaps because everyone else knew him. It really went too far; to the point where he had become (as, to another incarnation, Babe Ruth who hit 714 homers in his career plus 15 in World Series Competition) my ideal. Which was ridiculous because my idols were usually people with whom I had some actual association; and by then they were an anachronism at any rate—you were my last. So I was always, in your domain, comparing myself with an imagined Stanley, to whom I always came off a bad, imitative, second best. Which brought to mind images of occasional letters from another and lesser school by the hand of another and lesser medical student. Besides, the wild letter apropos of nothing (but no less enjoyable for that) is not my style. I plod more towards the irrelevant essay about the only vaguely interesting subject left.

Among other things, it saddened him to think that he could no longer make me laugh, but I don't think he knew   (Was it his fault? or mine?)   how well that fitted into the story I was telling. *Analysis is the renaissance of lying from debased analogies.* At the time of which I am speaking there were many points at which we refused to agree with each other, which made it interesting. Like old friends we relied on allusions to the past. In his case there was the difference that the past was constituted entirely of points of actual fact, and it was great with him always to be correct in remembering these facts, which is to say any facts he had ever noticed, which were for him so like events. I really wanted him to have the day, as any victory gave him so much pleasure, so that I adopted the custom of objection only when my acceptance of his advice would have led me to take positions I could not hold, in which, for instance, what followed would have made an end. In return, he continued generously to regard me with the slightest deference, perhaps as it was when certain persons of higher rank had a friend who was, officially, below them. At the time of which I am speaking, the courses of our lives (he said our spheres) had radically diverged; he was on the point of making decisions that he said he had already made which would estrange us even more than the accidents of birth and life had done; I had already taken those changes for myself.

It is quite agreeable to suppose, with David Jones, that there 'occurred' sometime as recently as in the course of the last century, a Break with the past which, as time passes against that indefinite event, makes it decreasingly worthwhile to mention or allude to anything that held any sort of meaning for people living in the world before the Break.

What was always remembered has since been forgotten. Latterly the doctrine of change by chance, based in what we call the Break, has been reimposed back upon times and places to which it is irrelevant. Reviewed, the darkened epochs assume an industrial glow whose history extends no further back than that of the idea of mass production. This revision has had diverse effects, among which, chiefly placed, we find the disappearance of the arts of decoration and the domination of the arts publicitaire.

I cannot conceive my task as the remnant of a bone I cannot quite grasp. For I cannot satisfy myself that I shall be able to make game of anything at all, no matter how ephemeral it is, knowing that my word remains secure. There is a clear exorbitance to anything in view if it would allude in any way to other than itself.

I vouchsafe a word, however, by leaving it to present it as it will. At least, your response is part of your biography; for everything is part of mine. But it remains that the name of anything is utterly without meaning, unless, as may happen, I managed to tell you what it means for the moment in which I use it, at the same time as I insist that what I am is art.

It remains that the name
of anything is utterly
without meaning,
unless I shd. tell
you what for
that moment it means. But I
                    reserve my own right
                              to mention anything at all

THAT MEETS YOUR EYE

                    Sorry . . . to allude to everything
                              that exists for me
                              and when I can
                              I will conserve more there
                              than meets your eye
                                        if that is the phrase.

    Such are the technicalities of my decision to explain nothing at
all. Or, the only necessity of explication de texte . . .

                    But it has no necessity.

                    Explanation is the luxury
                    of continuing a moment longer
                    what is forever past.

One can scarcely put the question
                    Which James?
                              for it has no
it has no antecedent. That is a fancy word, and the whole of the reading in its every moment will concern itself with establishing
                                        James
for that moment alone. Aside from all that, which is not concerned
with events—I wish to reward both the pedants and the libertines,
equally—I have some patriotic responsibilities to what I know as
mine. For the fact that everything may be not much I can think of no
suitable apology, except, perhaps, that in making such a suggestion I
have already done it. Shortly no form of discretion will seem possible,
as even now none is.

He was very sweet. He is lovely and it pleases him to be so, but sometimes it would please him more to be otherwise than that. Like us, he pretended to be shocked by a scandal. It was a genuine and durable pretension, the effect of a desire unmitigated by harsh realities and unconcerned with any malice. Short & sweet. Nevertheless they also said he was cruel. But it wasn't a type. That was their story. It was most obligingly helpful and ready to be used. This can be boring or embarrassing but it was never thus. He played his part and then he fell out, down, beside, within a tree (*P. araucaria excelsa*) kissing the ladies, one by one in turn. He fell down beside a tree, handing them over the harsher, the spiny and resilient branches of the tree, first one, then the next, until he tripped. The former forest of the floor accepted his head with unaccustomed grace as if it were already the cradle in which that desire would die, uncounted and lost in the woods, the well-written centuries, the perfectly enigmatic terminology of fears. The ladies aided by dutiful husbands flowed quickly toward the spot, their skirts shrinking as they ran, to make a cup of tea, a super dinner for the best of guests, with medicinal perservatives. But he was up again before they counted ten, hardly dusty and only a bit subdued by the manner of his accident. After they brushed him off—only one needly point stuck in his thigh (*Pinus sylvestris*) —he went on with his act automatically. (I) was out of the country (the question). We did not make fun of him. We made nothing of him. Why do you do it?, they replied! It is the influence of another hack writer you can't stand to read. Hang it up and let go. He did so, repeatedly, never quite getting the effect that gave him back the sense that he was wanted there. When he believed, at a very early age, that love is not divine, it broke his heart. We do not speak seriously in that manner anymore. Unfortunately I do not know Latin. (You have neglected his education, the avuncular salesman said when I was a child who visited us rarely and who was quite good-looking.) He had moved away, into the purer air, I do not know correct term, away. A simple division is much too clear. He had a nice place there. But he was so sensitive to the heat and the darkness and to the sky and its inhabitants. I think he does not like animals. He never kept any with him. At the time of which I am spkg. . . . boredom. He had that, he knew how to cheer anyone unless he was not up to it, then he slept. He was often alone in the air with his names. Taxonomy. He liked absolutely everything he liked, almost everyone. Cruel! Demanding, rather. They meant that he wanted

more than his parent could possibly give, even if she had not been
hindered by, what was it? He assumed his own way which was neither
here nor there though everyone who tried tried to place it one place or
another. But to get back to his heart, it could not have been stouter.
He got himself into it and it got him out. His lifetimes lasted hours.
Then newly refitted with the right old attitudes he went about setting up another final abdication. He was far from guilty, he was
actually as free as birds. Or fish, clad in a brand-new shiny black
bathing costume, who will not drown. Safety aside, the power of
suggestion is not all that it is said to be. A suggestion at the right
time eliminates that possibility. Thus they will call it ill-timed. It is
an escape; that is what they do not like about it, although they really
do like just that. It takes one into the purer air to relieve one of the
impossibility of doing it, and the responsibility of being there, which
sinks into the horizon like a boat. It was all to be so domestic, really,
with sliced peeled tomatoes, tiny peas, and a simple kind of meat,
beer of a certain sort, everything set for a certain time, which would
be customary, to dine with a hundred and fifty close friends. His wit
snapped unexpectedly like surprising allumettes and not seldom
induced a silence he might fulfill with a personal request. The question was, would anyone do for him what he would do for anyone?
Nobody could. Each thing proved its own limit and fell out, only to
be nursed back into a semblance of respectable doubt. No poetry but
solicitations. *I am speaking of anticipation, which he encountered early,
and stole, and bestowed with love on the next person he saw.* It was like a
mythical creature that does things people cannot do so that everybody
may. That is what it seemed like, but from the point of view of the
myth itself, it does things so that it may be enabled of impossibilities
itself. That is not a popular viewpoint, it is artistic. Having done all
that, he had nothing to do, and nothing to show, and no business,
several trades, three professional licenses, and post cards from all over
the world. He was strong but he could not give her his life. He was
bright but he could not intuit her being. He was sad to say that he
could not assume her tears. He left her. He made it seem to her that
she had done it so that she suffered satisfactorily. It will probably be
thought that I here cheat the reader of a story I could tell. Not at all!
Since he thought of nothing in terms of words it was not so difficult as
it may appear to show that he was victimized by his own choice,
which one, he could not have said. He knew only what is actual, and
that his love was well received he had no doubt. He had no doubt of

any actual performance and I am not his critic. But he was afraid that he did not know just what he was. He was afraid that he would have nothing more to say to them. He pretended to be impressed with age, but he was afraid he didn't know how old he was. He was too practiced an integer for it to seem ridiculous or pitiful. The least last moment, even just as he was about to be exonerated of his duties, and raised into the heights of whatever nameless place he could desire, might be one too many. Assuredly he did not do it either, even though he seems to be so innocent and unassuming, & weeps so beautifully, & sleeps so often.

The tyranny of style in art, for example, has been condensed so as to transform it into a force being exercised on the scale of personality. There is no demand that any artist emulate another. There is a penalty for that. There are two penalties: the legal, and the important personal one that allusion is wasted on the young. The rule now requires that an artist imitate himself in each ensuing work, performing for the press a station break that is guaranteed by the maker for his lifetime in return for what can not be called eternal fame. There is scant difference between completely refusing to believe what happens, and utterly accepting all the news as is. Every day is new. But by the fiction of tradition, even that of the tradition of the new, each day must be made to seem as much like the last as yesterday was like the day before. Fortunate it is, then, that the weather still surprises us and in spite of every safety, the changing weather still makes good metaphors for our volition in this most over-populated age.

TTSABASTILAGOBIOBAMOTOROTFE. .ntefneoelagfdrrdssttodesdhe

Since his painting hangs as if forever at my back, I comissioned D.C.L., the In the first scheme, the last A and in the second, the only A, refer *landed artist, to compose a drawing as an information of my remaining* back to the same A which thus, by chance, unites the two anagrams *remarks concerning which he is the subject. Doing that, what follows as an* with their sources. *illustration is what he calls*
                               A Decoration for Any Book by David Lee.

[The typograph should always be adjusted so that it looks as good or better instead of being a mechanical one-to-one reproduction of the first edition. Even orthography is not truly as constant as friendship seems to be.]

THIS DECORATION WILL Be printed in accordanc
E WITH THE TYPOGRAPHYx of the book. the spa
CE OF A VERTICAL UNITXx is equal to the spac
E OF THE UPPER MARGIN.x the first three vert
ICAL UNITS BELOW THE Upper margin each havex
THE MAXIMUM NUMBER Of lines of print which
A UNIT CAN HOLD. THE Fourth and fifth each h
AVE TWO-THIRDS THAT NUmber. the sixth unit h
AS ONE-THIRD THE MAXIMum. a horizontal unitx
X IS DEFINED BY THE RIght margin. if the mar
GIN IS LESS THAN ONE-Ninth the width of thex
X PAGE, IT EQUALS ONEXx horizontal unit andx
X THE TWO UNITS BESIDEx the margin have norm
AL CAPITALIZATION, WHIle the third, fourth a
ND FIFTH ARE WHOLLY CApital. if the margin i
S GREATER, A HORIZONTAl unit is one-half the
MARGIN. IN THAT CASE,Xx the first three unit
S HAVE NORMAL CAPITALIzation and the fourthx
X THROUGH SEVENTH AREx wholly capital. if b
Y RULE A SPACE OR POINt occurs at either lim
IT OF ANY LINE OR NEXTx to the common limit
OF THE CAPITAL AND NORmal parts, an x is place
D THERE AND THE SPACEXx advances. this decora
TION WILL BE PRINTED In accordance with the t
YPOGRAPHY OF THE BOOK.x the space of a vertic

AL UNIT IS EQUAL TO THe space of the upper ma

RGIN. THE FIRST THREEXx vertical units belowx

X THE UPPER MARGIN EACh have the maximum

It may be seen why it is I mention eternity in this connection. Although it may not seem so, it is a question, very largely, of communication, and not a question of design. Real numbers do not enter into it. There is, however, an imperfect correspondence between one type of thing and the other type which he has situated in this illustration which I read by force of will. Every possible remark will not make it one bit clearer. The grace of god passeth all understanding, yet we do understand what we meant when that was said by way of such examples as the one which illuminates our nearly perfect friendships. What you do see is the contrast between stasis and progression shown in the text and in the arrangement of the type as reproduced conjointly. What follows is a reading of D.C.L.'s disposable concordance left to me for other purposes.

The Book of Changes *(I Ching)* distinguishes nicely between form and content in a hexagram entitled as Pi, or Grace. The image recommended to illustrate grace is that of fire at the foot of a mountain. In such manner will the superior man proceed to clear up current affairs, but he dare not conclude controversial matters in this way. In the lower trigram, the dark or yielding line informs the situation and in the upper trigram, the strong or light line provides material, and so on. The lower portion of the trigram represents clearly defined rules of conduct, and the upper, those that are firmly established. The strong element is equated with love as well as content, and the yielding element with justice as well as form. The judgement given in the book might be paraphrased to say that logic and tradition do not suffice to deal with what is extraordinary. *I Ching* eschews the dualist without foregoing the distinction by means of the perfectly inclusive mode, what the Chinese call *Tao,* which reduces all questions to one: What is appropriate to this time?

The Oxford Dictionary quotes Beaconsfield as having said, 'Grace, indeed, is beauty in action.'

Revision is very often a matter of lectures anyway. Shall the ending be happy or unhappy. After all, it was not so much that the story ended unhappily, but that it did not end. The novel had both a program and a message. The ship cleaved the water with a slight noise of cleavage. It was possible for readers to delight in an exposition of the element of chance, one of the bases of the program. They might even come to believe in chance, the obverse of the world of their daily lives in which they necessarily assumed that causes had effects. It was that fact that readers remarked most often when they thought about the novel, though not in every case. The program was so skillfully carried out, so smoothly and naturally transcribed, that for many readers it would completely disguise itself as the story of a vivid love affair, ending with a shock. By this time, readers of novels were of course accustomed to unhappy if not yet to inconclusive endings in the books they read. It came as no surprise, then, that the primary technique used in this particular novel was continuous dialogue, which would, as he said as he was writing it, rather write itself. The technique was suited perfectly to the process by agreement and to the message by perfect opposition. Let us go on awaiting events, he said. Nothing is so harmonious, regular, logical and mathematically exact as events, once they have happened. What sort of things will they be? What does it matter? Already we know it's not raining, and that it's the first of May. And so things went, one after another, rapidly on until it stopped.

The events in the story, which was told continuously forward in time, and at the present in respect to place, he had drawn from events very like them that had occurred in the course of his life, so that he was writing, as he thought he should of things he actually knew. On the other hand, he had never, before writing it, experienced the very process of which he wrote, so that the facts in the book that had been drawn from his own experience came to be completely imaginative, even to him who knew more about them than he could say. Perhaps the only point invented entirely for the purpose of the novel was the final one, which did not seem to be an integral function of what went before. He had never questioned that the ending ought to be other than it was, neither when it occurred to him or after he had put it down and could read it altogether for the first time. Perhaps he had been momentarily and pleasantly surprised. Still, anyone who could write at all could have substituted an ending which afterwards would seem to be the inevitable and necessary termination of events. However that may be, for this man who had only written a book, many things came true on the twenty-fifth anniversary of his birth.

There was one question about the book itself. Everyone who read it experimentally raised the question in one way or another. It looked to everyone as if, after he had finished the book, the author had kept on writing, but writing a new and different book instead of concluding the one on which he had been engaged for months. It seemed there was something after the fact, so to speak. Some were said to feel that it was a pretentious and didactic essay tacked on but irrelevant to anything in the book itself. It might, someone said, be used as the basis for an introduction to the popular edition. Others noticed that there was a stylistic change coming right after the final event. Some of them thought that it was the best part of the book, by which they meant to say that it was the one quite distinctive feature of the book, and that made it more exciting to them. All this was news to the man who had done this thing. Such remarks were usually conceivable to him when mentioned by his friends, but nothing of the sort had occurred to him though he had thought of nothing but his writing all year long. Certainly, however, he had no doubt of the relevance of the final passage to every event he had mentioned. When he had made it, the thought crossed his mind that it was a natural conclusion of everything, particularly the sudden death of the girl in blue, for which no explanation could be suggested. It seemed to him most appropriate, he said, because after the last surprise of several beginning with the first, one could not leave the reader cold. Things would be different with both the writer and the reader after the experience of so particular a series of events, however precisely drawn. He couldn't believe the suggestion of one of his friends that he had gratuitously indulged himself in the composition of philosophical stupidities based on what the story had unexpectedly revealed to him. Anyhow, this is the paragraph that caused the furor.

Having begun by knowing, as somebody said, that sex is an incident, I came finally to understand that sex is a secret everyone keeps. It is, like every other, an unsharable sensation. That it is a secret is a way to say that it is interesting, and in that way it remains interesting to the end, when it is certain to remain unknown. All lovers, however practiced, remain completely inexperienced. It can be said in many ways. There is a tension in each of us between what we think we know and what we cannot find out, and the resolution of that tension, the beauty of it, has to be certain knowledge, even including what cannot be found. The sexual pretension cannot be remembered and attempts to do so imaginatively can only cause, if anything, a repetition of the actuality. Even the horror of her death could not drive from my mind the knowledge that our life endowed in me. Nor was it simply easier that she had died, leaving me no uncertainty that the story itself was ended. Sexual ravishment is the distinctive source of love, and despite everything that two people may say and do in love, each one keeps a secret completely intact as the secrets of two strangers who, on meeting in the street, incidentally inquire the time of day. To love is to play at any one of a great number of things, none of which could be quite believed in any other manner, and it is a matter of guessing after every secret which cannot be known. In the past, all arts seemed marvelous for the way in which they appeared to be so completely organic or real or significant or meaningful to those who experienced them by making or partaking of them, while the processes of life itself seemed figmentary and enigmatic and unsound. Two people have only to appear together on the screen for everyone immediately to assume that they are of course 'in love,' or that they are 'at war' or otherwise cooperating in some art that will in some term make sense of life. It has been the fate of this century to fight the last, a fight enlivened by the fact that we conceived weakness in ourselves, a fight continued on and on in terms that we find foreign to our experience by virtue of the fact that the Nineteenth Century has gone out of actual existence to remain with us always, a syntax that vibrates within us, like the too vivid remembrance of a bad dream sometimes will. That time must have been a great one in which to die, and we, the successors upon its death have been left with an existence as fitful as was theirs, to be entertained by more nonsense than all their schizophrenics could conceive together. The meaning of our Break with the past may be to realize as fully as can be that the life processes themselves, by metonymy and without metaphor, may be converted by means of history into works that are as real and as exact as works of art that were admired before. For eighty years we have searched with unparalleled diligence among bits of old-fashioned architecture of time and place, looking, mistakenly, at home, for other ways in which to make our lives, I might even say, for some manner in which to go on at all, and very few have found a way of it and fewer still have come forth to show what they may have found among the wreckage. To share a secret in fact requires common experiences of the circumstances which produce it. Hence the freedom of the press. But in this epoch, as perhaps it may be everywhere forever, to know what one man knows one must be that man. It is not surprising that nobody in time past told secrets with impunity as later on they have now come to do. The systematic violation of a prohibition, the preoccupation of so many in this present time, leads to ritual, unfactual observance of the prohibition and has been, among other things, a source of the lamented prostitution of the language and the dispersal of the meanings of our words. There remains for an artist to demonstrate the unknowable and the meaningless in a sort of art that is no less organic and real than any life may be made to seem, or than any other art, and which works itself wholly out of history, time out of mind. Though their machines may have no taste for it, people always love a dreadful surprise. Our foolishness is purely realistic, as you see.   August 7, 1963.

Qu'est mon néant, auprès de la stupeur qui vous attend?

From this point on the story might perfectly well proceed at its former pace. The only thing is that if I allowed it to do so either I should have to cover dozens of pages with my own private reflections or I should have to make a violent effort of the imagination to present all that happened from somebody else's point of view.

That of Charles, for instance.

For although I remember almost every minute of my time with the clarity called 'as if it were yesterday' I was in fact living inwardly, feeding myself on phantasies, to such a degree that when I presently woke up I found that I had got left behind by my own action and that the other actors in my story were so far ahead of me that it had already ceased to be my story in any but a purely technical sense.

At the time of which I am speaking, for example, there is a cement strike and contractors are reluctant to stockpile stone. On the other hand, a letter to Stanley was a rather different sort of thing.

Mais ce n'était pas permis.

S.R.: I am sitting in the sun or the shade of trees. Forms of inanimation and of life. I am able to see a dog which can be tied up and watered, quite willingly. You may be in the same circumstance.

The wind and the noise of trees, a form of silence, and of stillness, and so on. Seeing something and trying to say it. Not being able to say something you do see. The possibility is to demonstrate what you do see, not knowing what it is and failing to invent its name. It is a momentary aberration. Perhaps it is something and it may be nameable and that is a condition of aspiration. May we see all our schemes as divertissements. If I may say so without suggesting an achievement, If I may say so without commanding histories, If I may say so in the wind under the trees on the Fourth of July.

I have been reading some propaganda for freedom by J.-P. Sartre. It is strong veal. You are a romantic of freedom who has been educated by yourself to see that there is no such thing. It is like love. That is how I could conceive the impossibility of philosophy. But in practical American terms, the capability for philosophy and for everything must be kept open. Practical schemes ignore possibility and are finally ideal, unfactual and exclusive. At least they are not dogmatic to begin with. It is unimportant that A.E., the modern artist, will say that he thinks commercial signs and signals to be beautiful. Which is not to say that they may not be.

To say anything one exaggerates approaching dogma by the back way and, occasionally, deciding one's own truth however polemical it may seem. I carry on. You admit the possibility of stopping and you would die for love as well as for disease.

'It happens very often that a man has it in him that a man does something that he does it very often that he does many things when he is a young man when he is an old man when he is an older man.'

Nothing defines: Which is not to say everything else.

In *Finnegans Wake* it is an evocation of the artist as an old man, an old journalist, say, who plays on his reputation as an old-fashioned raconteur in such a way and so continuously that everyone must agree that he's better than ever, not older by a day, and there's fire in the old boy yet. Here's your brandy and your cigar, Sir Winston, now make your sign. It is the ultimate in being able to do something and then doing it.

My birthday greeting: But there have been always some among us who have known to do something well, and who have as a matter of course gone on to do something they could not know and would not. May I be there.

Many of the jokes in *Finnegans Wake* are like automatic garbles occasioned by writing quickly—in that suggestion, there is the entire language in all its history—or by typographical errors of which the first editions of the newspaper for every day offer hundreds of examples. Joyce is the great exponent of the great modern cliché, the slip of the tongue, but he reaches the heights because he has no interest in the sense of the cliché, being unintentional truthful revelations, middleclass mistakes. His plays are more delightful and suggestive than the mistakes of our newspaper's machines even though, no more than they, could he consciously 'use the device.' He acted as an honest artist who had the interest of an amateur in words. But he had not always been as free to choose anything that came to mind as he apparently felt toward the end of his life.

The fame of an artist always exceeds his expectations, dues, intentions and even the worth of his works themselves.

Presumably as a form of entertainment, a hobby from all this attention, Joyce let drop some remarks which indicated that an industry of literary realism could be founded upon his books, the sort of establishment once provided, for example, by Babe Ruth. It is part of his amusement to try to engage the wits of his admirers, and even his own, so that people try in all seriousness to make sense of laughter and evaporation.

The book is a demonstration of the efficiency of success in modern art. People like to be led to be dead to die quickly and then go to bed.

I think it likely that he took a journalist's delight (his defenders may now leave the room) in everybody crowding round him to hear what secrets they could, and he had some, the secrets of everyone, and that he was glad to tell what he knew was only that he was an artist, and not a critic, however much he wanted to be famous.

On the other hand, when they took *Ulysses* seriously, he must have had to redouble his hopeless laughter. 'Loud, heap miseries upon us yet entwine our arts with laughters low.' If he lived to see the aftermath of Finnegans appearance, he must have been additionally disillusioned, though perhaps he was by then too blind for that.

Having in him so much of the storyteller's faith in the possibility of laughter as the only satisfactory response he was party to an undisclosed movement that was able to obscure all romantic agonies if only for a moment by means of an hilarious excessive realization which has since become more popular.

The literal possibilities of sadness seem greater only to the inexperienced, and the young.

Nevertheless he kept at it without dropping a stitch. It is equally unpleasant to read a whole joke book or *Finnegans Wake,* though I'm sure one could do both. Gertrude Stein set out to write a book in which she described every psychological type there is, and after writing a thousand pages, she saw that it would be possible to do it, and so stopped. *Finnegans Wake,* a much better book, is one that has been written after all one's intentions have been fully realized, a senescent lingering over the possibility that one had not indeed accomplished what one had already the reputation for having done, trying to do once more the things that one had done before. That is like Proust.

While it is a vast compilation of one man's mind and its effects, a generous legacy deserving all gratitude, it is only haphazardly unified bits of historical and local gossip.

It is somewhat an extensive parody of *The Anathémata* by David

Jones, which is to say, among other things, that Jones is the great artist that Joyce, with his talent for publicity, was credited with being. But as the original of *Finnegans Wake, The Anathémata,* appearing twelve years later, could only be seen as drawing obscurely upon Joyce's coup.

Joyce recognized for all men that finally he could say anything at all in whatever language got his fancy or in none. It would be lovely to compare his final effort with something or everything by Dreiser, but I can only imagine the conditions which would receive the juxtaposition with laughter and the right response. Besides, the married scholars haven't time to read so much.

I wrote this all together as a tirade but revising it I broke it up.

If *Finnegans Wake (The American Tragedy)* were shorter, it would be nothing. As it is, we find an imponderable object of which the best that can be said is that it is really there.

Or, the book is like a demonstration by investigation of all excess wealth. After all, what are the possibilities of extended parody? Boredom, and the limited esteem that will be granted to gross effort. I could read about 60 pages of it with lively interest and remarks. It is not that I don't know what it means, I know perfectly well from the first page what it all means and I reserve for it a special regard I save for dead people who do not die. I do not wish they would. It is a tender subject.

What is so interesting about beginning middle end that leads one to confound them? It seems to me self-evident to ignore them all, a remark that dates both him and me into differing popular literary schemes. He wrote in terms of his popular scheme, achieving the desired effect (as critics must stupidly remark), and he was great like Babe Ruth. If I can understand the impetus for making a home run, can I appreciate the desire to make more than one?

Shall I deny the heroism of the heroes of art and games?

I do not mind what people do if they will not require my attention in all the events that occupy the press. *It has now become the game to bore the reader while trying, probably without success, to interest the writer.* My remarks concerning old man Joyce are aortic, prejudiced, simplistic and bound wrong by every critic before they were conceived. I make no accusations. It is like my royalism, it is like my insistence on the measure of a man. Whatever cannot be formulated so as to seem impersonal must be wrong. So am I.

The popular scheme also provides us with some possibility that all time will end, realizing on earth the old fantasy of the Death of God, as it is supposed to at the end of each millennium, repetition making each succession of the fantasy both more credible to modern ears and radically different in its effects.

When Lee Oswald remarked that he found Russia to be incredibly boring, I knew he was an honest man. And his is a case of the technique of the popular scheme, which can be summarized in the paradoxical phrase, quick death. To achieve a reputation in the popular scheme, one must either affect excessive sincerity, which has nothing to do with honesty, or do something that will necessarily be misunderstood. I cannot believe that there could have been much hate, evil or any rival theory of realistic information in Lee Oswald; Neither does it strike me as at all credible that James Joyce was centrally concerned with formal artistic problems. Both of them did what they did.

How am I to hold onto positions that are not those of all authorities on every subject that gets my interest, nor yet the simple opposites of what is universally believed? It is not even permitted to ignore the chatter, which is the simple occasion for my disheartenment, and it is surely a question of freedom. To do it as one wishes, indeed, is the definition from which the publicity deflects in horror of the consequences. It often seems to me, and now, that I cannot but do what must be misinterpreted so far that the obverse and the reverse and every other facet of any reading will be irrelevant to their source. One can always apply for a poet's immunity, a license to have lived vainly in a democracy where everyone did something else, *But what is the difference between being entitled to be insane and being forced to be famous?*

STUPIDITY TRIUMPHS!

The Final Sale of What Remains

From long ago, the Prince has written to me that he is sinking, and that he lacks volition to save himself. Perhaps this message will be the means by which I can cast myself back to the time I need to find once again; perhaps out of this echo of a still dimly remembered exchange will come an image for this life which aimlessly recurs to me. He says that desperation might be an apt word for his condition if only it did not connote so much vitality.   (pause, change voice)   It was a summer and it is a fall in which there was little rain charac-terized by invariably beautiful Sundays. Less often now I would take a stroll for it happened that I was largely occupied with household chores which lay to hand readily awaiting my invention of them. It doesn't annoy me that I spend so much time in this way and I usually find the work to be encouraging, not that I need courage especially. There is a great deal of variety to it, and I cannot tell you any routine which might as well describe it. I move haphazardly in and out of doors, up and down stairs, from one thing to another. Usually I find it amusing, and it is rather more difficult than anything else, to do several things more or less at once, concentrating on each of them only momentarily, as you might cook dinner, but with nothing so definite as the meal to come of my activities. From time to time I think about what work remains for me to do, and, truthfully, I think that after I have done one or two more jobs around here I shall hole up for the winter once more and do nothing. It gives me a feeling of freedom that I enjoy in contemplation, and as I remember, it doesn't frighten me because it almost never happens that I do nothing when there is nothing left to do. Something almost always comes up even if I lack the will to take myself to the pictures, or the money. For example, my dreams asleep become much longer and more entertaining. Or someone will call up, if I have a telephone, or I shall meet someone in the street whom I either did or did not know before, or someone will suggest to me that we make a movie, or else something else. It is a familiar unpredictable series of events which I anticipate almost with resignation in my manner. Let's get out of here. After all, it is usually always I who shall give the life force to any such adventures, so let it leastways not be me who starts them going. I have lots of good ideas, but so do they. Let come what may, I am here, as I used to say.   (pause, change)   Recently a few people have left me one way or another. In most cases I was glad enough to see them go, even when their leavetaking was almost imperceptible until one day I noticed it. The Prince left me very obviously in stealth, by the back way on tiptoe. All the while I have been entertained by my interest in an art movement centered upon what they are pleased to have called dancing, though it extends to everything that can be thrown away. Before my eyes they reinvent all movement, every tone of voice, and music. I also did a little occasional criticism for them, which they enjoyed, and for the literary press, which it did not. It is so natural that everyone not a critic despises critics that it is easy for one not a critic to practice criticism to spite them. But one not a critic writes pointless criticism for he is too aware of the point he is making not to admit that it is unutterable. Besides, exercises in tastefulness, no matter how banal in execution, are at last of little interest to one in whom there is no use for criticism.   (pause)   Which is to say that once we got outside into the air into which dusty leaves were falling with a certain noise onto the pavement and silently into the river where they did not fool the seagulls, all that we had thought to say was forgotten even as it had not been said, and we contented ourselves in the climb toward Christmas by remarking pleasant architectural details as we passed along the way. It was a beautiful Sunday in three months of beautiful Sundays and that meant that then the sun shone with a brilliance ordinary for the sun and delightful to behold. We noticed points we had not noticed on buildings we had pased every day for more than a century if time could be counted. I was fond of retelling to my friend how the carriage rods which assured the congruity of the walls of these old brick buildings were often attached outside with a decorative star cast of iron, and whenever I happened to see one or more of these stars, I would fondly recount the occasion of its placement as if I remembered it from life. It was as if the grime in which the painted buildings stood neglected could be ignored by way of natural light. From time to time, when we passed one of the six very oldest buildings which had been converted to other uses, I would try to imagine them in their original conditions complete with horses being drawn up in front and women fainting. I was all right when it came to the architecture, which perforce came first, but in imagining their actual setting, I would always trip myself up over references to inauthentic motion pictures I or someone else had seen. I was especially bad at the horses even though whenever I have seen horses I have always looked at them very closely and tried in that way to become familiar with them, taking every opportunity of doing so as it is a city in which these strange animals were somewhat still in use. It was one of our pleasant pastimes too, to see if we could find any signs that people were living still in these buildings which were supposed to have been deserted long before. We were not alone, for looking out of our own windows from time to time I would see people passing by and looking up with interest, even curiosity. I had not just the same defect as many of them who could not have imagined what sort of exotic literary life went on behind the ancient glass in which the clouds waved by like flags, but I too should have been pleased to meet at least for a moment the fugitives whom I could thus detect, though they lived, as we ourselves lived, in near complete obscurity.

(change)   Our life at that time was not entirely represented by a series of photographs such as those with which I have presumed to amuse you. Indeed nothing I might say at any length whatsoever including very shortly would serve me any better to let you know me as I then was and as I should become. Indeed if you are reading carefully it is only you who know me as I am and everyone else, myselves included, is much less certain of this knowledge. Indeed you know as much as can be known and I have it in my power to keep you so informed.

The next day it rained for the first time in many days. I was then reminded of the leak in the roof which never occurs to me when it is not raining. Paradoxically, it is only when it is not raining that such information would be of any use to me otherwise than as a simple exterior harassment of which there are very few, I think, in the course my life has taken. Nowadays we also keep a small rat full of garbage because the rat was clever enough to gnaw a tunnel up the asbestos insulation that surrounds the flue from the water heater to a point beneath the sink where it is inconvenient for me to stop his exit. I should have to take down the sink. I think that Fuzzy is a good name for a domestic harassment such as a rat which is circumspect enough to have done that and to disappear and be quiet when we are near the sink and during almost all the day. Of course it is given to you to think that I am being facetious with all this language, and that really, as you would say, we shall quickly set about poisoning the rat and stopping up the hole, if we have not already done so. That is my wife's view too, and she thinks no name would be good enough for our rat. But although she has every opportunity of buying poison short of being able to afford to see a movie, she hasn't done it yet. I am not sure it is even on her list. So it is that we live with our rat, and that is an example of how we live with all the things we happen to have with us now. Our plant lives in the same pot with two weeds, the seeds of which we apparently imported from the country with the dirt. They are both quite attractive and very different from the house plant and from each other. Even I expect that in due course we may at least place the weeds in other pots so that they do not endanger the life of our little fruit tree, but it is by no means certain to me that we will ever do that. I remember from a child how difficult it is to transplant weeds, even though many things which seemed difficult to me then now seem simple, or uninteresting. Anyway the rain made the usual pleasing noise on the roof which surely seemed louder to me when I as a child slept beneath other roofs. It also made a pleasant noise as it hit the street pavement when I went out to walk in it. As I stood by the river, I was too far away above the surface to hear the rain confound itself with the greater water, but I could see a little turmoil at the surface which I expected, and I enjoyed being warm and wet. It is often said, usually by people who do not know what they are talking about, that life at our house must be like living in the country. What they scruple to say is that they wish they lived in the country, or as we do in the city, and they stop themselves from that embarrassment by the simple convention of compliments to houses in the country in which they are very practiced.

After the rain stopped, I went out to buy some underwear. I looked at all the underwear in the display windows of all the haberdashers and men's outfitters I passed in several sections of the city. I saw a great deal of underwear, I suppose all the different kinds that are sold in the city, made by several makers and offered at various prices. It was just at that time that the manufacturers had all introduced a line of completely elasticised briefs designed to girdle men's loins probably the better to fit them to the vogue of very tight fitting outer pants which could not be worn by fat men at all, but to which, it was implied for the purpose of sales, slightly sagging bodies could be adapted by the use of such an elastic sheath. This innovation was most prominently displayed, but one had a view of the other types as well. The oldest type still sold, familiarly called long johns or union suits in the form of loose fitting light woolen coveralls, and its improved modern version, heavy knitted cotton shirts and pants held fast by elastic bands at the waist, the ankles and the wrist, both of them used strictly for warmth during winter sports or outdoor jobs: Several versions of drawers, or boxer shorts as they have latterly been called, the most traditional sort being full-cut, baggy and extending almost to the knee, now available only at the most expensive shops, and the popular type, being similar but shorter and less fully cut, either attached by snaps in the front (the kind called skivies in the Navy) or held up by an elastic band: And another type of shorts, of knitted cotton covering the upper thigh (called midways) a modern version of long johns since with improvements in heating arrangements warmth is seldom what is desired of underwear: Then a very brief version of the classic drawers in broadcloth or silk, fitting very tight and appearing, from the manner of their advertising and the types of shops in which they are sold, to be designed for homosexuals who do not wish to wear the briefer models and who take pride in the neat appearance of their underwear: And finally a large variety of different sorts of briefs, all being similarly made of panels of light knitted cotton sewn together with elastic tapes which hold the garment tight to the body at every point, covering only the buttocks, groin and the prick and cod in a pouch.

These briefs are considered by men to be the most modern, the most popular, the most vulgar and the most erotic of the standard types of underwear now in use. In the garment trade, the term briefs is also applied to what everywhere else are called panties for women. With the popularization of outright sexuality among women, men's briefs are often bought for them by their women as presents. Although there is a certain lewdness to remarks concerning every sort of underwear, the term briefs is always euphemised by the substitution of a brand-name, which, before the war was always B.V.D. (itself a cryptic indication), most usually now after the war, Jockey. Aside from elastic belts for athletes and silk straps for dancers, and little caches-sexe for Frenchmen, briefs are the most restricting and least bulky of all the types of underwear now sold. Their chief effect is to hold the prick and cod close to the body whereas naturally and with the use of shorts the sexual accessories hang loosely and swing about as the man moves around. Medical men have determined that the testicles do not function efficiently in the production of reproductive cells if they are as warm as the rest of the body has to be, for which purpose, it is admitted, the scrotum relaxes to let the balls be somewhat cooler. In a variety of natural situations, however, such as in cold weather, or swimming in cold water or during sexual activity, the cod involuntarily gathers itself closer to the body in an effect that is simulated by the supporting pouch of briefs. I do not know that this in any way impedes the reproductive process, and I know of no popular legend that supports the biological claim. However that may be, the well-known and unadervertised erotic character of these pants can be used to account for the proliferation of nuances in style among the products of the various manufacturers. Like all erotic responses, this character varies greatly from one man to another, as much as does the exact size and normal disposition of each man's genitalia, so much that for example, in some medical schools, the prick and cod of every student is routinely photographed to provide a gallery of variations to be leisurely and scientifically inspected. For the purposes of this history, however, there may be classed two general types of briefs: That which is fuller cut, an elastic band hugging the wearer at the waistline, and made with a relatively large pouch for men who desire less support there or whose cods are rather larger; And that which is very brief, its elastic gripping below the navel at the level of the hip bone, having a less fully articulated pouch for men who want their functions drawn up tight or for those with rather smaller sexes to be contained. At the same time as the second type is known to be more likely to prove erotic, it also protects the wearer from the embarrassment which may attend an incidental hard-on in the street.

In the history of the nether garments of men in European culture, however it is told, there invariably remains, in every category, a division of type. In the usage of Americans, both types of whatever garment may be mentioned are still in use in some respect. Generally speaking, for example, Northern European tailors, of which the greatest are the English who invented the classical styles of the nineteenth century, of which the American business suit is a scion, will construct their trousers to be long in front as well as relatively roomy in other respects. In classical Northern dress, therefore, it is only appropriate to wear drawers underneath if one is to avoid the slight discomfiture of trousers that are too roomy in the crotch. But even if, as is current custom among them, the trousers are fitted rather tightly, the crotch is always designed to allow the prick and cod to hang in front. Jockeys or shorts may comfortably be worn in that case. The more restricting briefs were probably invented to be worn with the products of Southern European tailors, who typically make their pants in such a way that the fly appears to be part of a tight band that joins the back seam to bisect the garment rather clearly, forcing the prick and cod to be worn more or less to one side or the other of this band. Among Spanish men, for example, there is a convention that the prick must be worn on the left, although that is also its natural inclination since the left testicle normally hangs rather higher than the right one. The famous California blue jeans (the name is surely French) are constructed in the Southern mode, as are certain of the trousers advertised in this country as 'continental,' though not all. The sources of this division in style are very obscure, but it is recorded that in ancient times men wrapped their loins in one of two ways: either they cinched an hanging cloth at the waist to provide a simple skirt as is often done with a towel by anyone today, or they would wrap the cloth up and around the middle parts in a manner much the same as babies are now wrapped in diapers. I would suggest that these customs, the first recorded in Saxe, the second in Gaul, might well obtain, at the very source, in differences in the typical size of sexual equipment of the various European races, being, especially at first, larger among larger men and smaller among smaller breeds. The Nordics and the Iberians, having been relatively well isolated throughout their history, still typify this trait. The Russians, the Germans, the Slavs, the Italians, the Greeks, the French, the English and the Americans (the former less the latter more) display the unsettling effects of cross-breeding which, for example, has caused someone to record the saying of a British physician during a military examination, The larger the man the smaller the penis.

In more formal scientific explication, it is recorded that at the onset of puberty, the gonads release a supply of a hormone known as testosterone which not only causes the male sexual characteristics to become fully developed, but also regulates the extension of what are referred to as the long bones, including the digital ones. If these laws operated mechanically, it would still be true of everyone that the larger the man the larger the prick, and there would never have been so much popular interest generated in the subject to begin with. To my knowledge, there are two natural effects which always or most usually bear upon the question of the size of pricks. The novelist, Lawrence Durrell, has recorded the appearance of a character with a hard-on 'twice his size.' The implications are several. One, that authors being in general impressive persons who do not have much interest in what they are about, are also those inclined to having larger pricks at nature which when stimulated do not become much larger than they are. Artists who, on the other hand, are less recorders than inventors of their time, tend to an highly expressive mode, which, it may be, does imitate their most private physical character. To a T. But aside from such unworthy speculations, anyone may know that the extreme variety to the limp size of pricks tends somewhat to be equalized out by the ratio of erection, which in my case, for example, is at least one to three. There remains to remark the second natural fact I promised, which is that a man's cupped hand provides a space which is just sufficient to contain his prick and cod in order to protect them when he is frightened. And if I may say so, the beauty of all such observations is that they are, like a view of daisies, meaningless facticities.

By the time I got back from my jaunt, the meeting of the art movement was underway and the question of dinner had already come up. Excuse me, they said, rather often, if they chose to differ. Later they shouted at each other without apologies. One might have wished, as I did, for a good British chairman, if one had any experience of that sort of thing. You see I once had a card to the Oxford Union where they also did a deal of shouting, but there was not a moment of the debate in which the red-haired chairman did not have the control of the meeting at his fingertips. Of course in the art movement they would have preferred to have no chair at all and no meetings of any kind, but however romantic they become, they cannot escape the experience of having been suckled amidst the great American institution of student government, and when there is any doubt of who's in charge they will return to it as if to nature. The meeting went on and on and everyone restated what had been put better in earlier versions of the meeting. Had they resolved at last to have no more meetings, there would have been a cause for mutual congratulations. They do not consider that if there were only made an opportunity for everyone to get in their two cents' worth, then the meeting would be over. For it is always maintained by the chair that it will be able to decide by some convention that the committee has accomplished something, and that becomes the end to which the fiction of the meeting will pertain. If as usual it is not well-chaired, much of the latter portion of the meeting, usually the larger part, will be consumed by the chair's attempts to speak a sentence which expresses the accomplishment, and the less said the better. The end will come when there is nobody left in the room with enough guts to delay the departure of everyone a moment longer by objecting further to the formula last proposed by the chair who, if it can still remember its exact words will repeat them with as much assurance as it has left, nod its head in resignation and at least allow everyone to laugh wthout trying to give them the impression that their laughter is a waste of time. But aside from all that which entertained me well enough, I liked the art movement because the people who congregated about its periods were not children. Many of them were very often joyful and playful but when as usual they had something to do, they did it, they did not plan it all out and wish for the day when they might be enabled of all miracles. I am always fascinated by children and by a fire and by the sea and by animals and by the television when I see them and what holds me is that strangeness in them that is just as continuously mobile as the familiar course of my life. A fire and the sea are the strangest of all the moving things. When I was a child I remember deciding to remember what it was like to be a child, and I do remember that form of life so that children are less strange to me than they are to everyone who has forgotten it, who has none but the standard given and received memories one does not know. If I had nothing else to do I suppose I would be glad to spend my time bringing up children, but I can't imagine a form of life that would leave me nothing else to do. Perhaps you will get the idea if I invoke the convention that I am self-employed. I must object, however, that men who are self-employed usually behave toward themselves like an employer would, giving themselves standard things to do that can be had for the money in any kind of shop. You can't get what I have which is never for hire nor for love. For as often and as variously and as loudly and as beautifully and as cleverly and as finally as I may tell you my secret, it is still my secret. . . . . . I am so newly come into the shape of a man that I should rather call the certainty of all men childish than dignify the child's estate by returning pleasantly away.

All alone with the best reception

    All alone with more than the best reception

                There is no story to tell.

If, as seems likely, we shall call them then do not forget it. In the rain it will be necessary, but remember not to. On the other side there is something else that is not the same. For all you find only to discard, there is something else, an hour. A year, however, is not the same thing as many, many hours, it is a different system. As before we knew what to call out as a reply, and as before we remembered to maintain the same name for something to eat, it will have it as before. We had an intimation of the worst possible reflection. But was it not still somewhere as we knew it and remembered it in every way? Why not, they replied pianissimo. In a second time, and in the last inadvertant reflexive action, whatever is apparent may be only what remains. At Christmas time we gave away a speech, on the last day of the celebration, the day after the last day. You may speak, dear sir, of anything, gladly invoking the choice in which there is no choice. I have no more to present than that. One time is as good as another, whether you are young or older. But when you have that which is so clear, why cannot you tell us what it is? Thank you very much indeed. Our lovely time was not a moment longer nor too short. It is just in this way that whatever we have with us is continually disguised anew once more and rightly thrown away again as if it had been for the first and final time. The sale continued on by means of statistical events, purgatories, repetitious pleasantries, cheap decorations and confessions until the very last minute at which like a signal the whole operation changed to strip the works of green. It was an activity of astonishing duration, drawing everyone together, and one for which patience would be no substitute. With that as a commencement, whether or no you like the word, let us turn somewhat reluctantly back to context.

For it must be, as it is to all of you, that something that has a certainty that while it is not especially hidden for any purpose, has the elusiveness of trees. Whenever there is or may be said to be anything particular it may, nay it must, be known to exhibit to us a certain degree of clarity, like an image. Here again, however, it is almost important to turn yet another moment away from the center of the argument in poetry in an attitude that is something like fear of the end. There is the direction of something in the necessity, say, of a formula. Clearly it is only something that is nothing for which there are several common expressions. Very occasionally there is only one known way to make up a formula. One may as well detect, in that occasion, the root impulse for saying anything, if I am not becoming too formal.

I often want now to imagine an unexpected event happening at an unexpected time. My disgust with literature when it is not the object for criticism, which is a different sort of enjoyment, is I suspect their propensity to pad out weird time schemes with real facts, or to organize facticities (perfectly respectable and sufficient to themselves) through the low crafts of killing off the current names of those facticities (an easy task considering the diction of authors themselves) and giving a blithy credence to the formerly somber necessity of [attempts at] personal transcendence.[1]

In that necessity one may well detect the root metaphor of any saying. The nearness of something, to assert a convenience, is altogether other than that from which I have so far abstained. The character of distance is really intended to represent a spatial alteration, as was graphically achieved in oldtime perspective. There, here, now, then and so on are possibilities for a vague degree of limitation. The detectives (critical or political) of this effect are quick to explain the joke besides setting up historical perquisites. As a convenience, I may say that I have now explained the joke away. If we may turn to a passage further on, I want to assume your confidence, if possible, by means of the customary warrant, plotting the line carefully and filling in with accurate details, even though my next remark be also unpredictable.

There has to be the barest certainty, hasn't there? The skeleton of branches is to be presumed whether or not the proof is noticeable. There may be a lengthy quarrel, for example, about my diction, but I shall take no notice of it if I can. Perhaps it is the sort of performance at the sight of which some laugh and some do not. That will permit us kindly to be asked many amusing questions and some stupid ones, but I should be allowed to deny it if I can. Here, as in speaking of trees or anything else that has a name and may be known, I must insist on a matter of convention. The lines run together in parallel inorganic courses to represent my verbal poetry as best I can. True, I must simply continue this extension. I must hereby show it as it is. I must do what I have thought to do in a way that neither deifies its sources nor makes nothing but facts and rhetorics of my yellow leaves. Now whether or not a tree is visible is what is rightly called academic. If it is a tree at all is another matter and insisting that it is

[1] Charles, *The Puerile Papers II,* edited & introduced by F. C. Castle, 1966

will be just as pertinent as some such moral question. If there is any
necessity for which I must make allowances, it is that I am doing this.
It has been shown and admired that one may proceed well along in
this manner, and that such a process is not a chance. The die will give
no reason for it, neither any more against, especially if it is, as it often
is, a matter of pronunciation and denunciation. For it is the tree, or
whatever you choose to call anything, that is lucky enough to be
something somewhere sometime.

Furthermore, and this immediately complicates the moral question by tossing in the furies of the dead and hibernating curiosities,
we propose that the rewards of idleness in the part of any man to play
the proverb of his time will justify themselves to him in replacement
of the very word. An assertion, cutting the surface of this contexture
with a smile, would be frivolously made. An example, the usual
resort, is invariably diverting. It was pedantic, though sometimes
fashionable, to present the allegory of anything quite realistically
with attention to the details. If a red bird hath a leaf, six toads
a-humming, who comes there cried the sentinel, and so forth. Any
sort of stiletto may show its own delightful quality, sharing that as
well with others, without becoming other than its name implies.
Any certainty might be founded simply in a style of tastefulness to
the dictation all more ready to perform by having been historically
convened. But as I say, it doesn't matter. It has often been observed
that mice living in churches before the war looked skinny, for lack of
anything to eat.

'Failure in communication results in the bizarre if not the ludicrous.'[2]

I shall venture one more demonstration, if I may. By now, you
must be prepared to doubt that there remains any rational impetus for
me to dress the window of my desires with another display like those
you have, I assume, already read. But still you ought to be able to
agree that there is some worth in something else. Perhaps both of us,
if I may defy my medium to such an extent, continue in the hope of
something that can be anticipated. Yes or no, I should prefer not to
think of it that way. It may be that for a moment I can bring myself to
your service. If I can, I shall then have made something obviously
useful and done so by intention. Let us be anachronistic. Survey, if
you will, with your customary mind's eye the breadth of the gamut

[2] The Times Literary Supplement, p. 745, 1963

from *aei* to *zie* and the height of the range from the *sea* to the *sky,* and select out of all there is nothing but the questions that can be implied by the following words: social, economic, historical, scientific, philosophic, artistic and technological. As we already know, there is almost nothing that will not come up into some prominence if the right kind of scrutiny is applied to it. It is supposed to be a baffling milieu in which to try and think, for at the same time as anything may be thought in it, and even believed, there are many equal objections to every possibility. Because it is impossible to think in the most general terms for long, the conventions which we salvage for use in reducing the scale of life to something comprehensible make universal thoughts seem unwanted and strange.

The general character, Boss (sometimes called vice-president or viceroy) is presented in these passages as antipodal with that of Hostess (who goes by many names with as many functions) in only one respect, namely the contrast between desires manifest as obligations to other people and those that exist as invitations to satisfy oneself. On the left, one finds the poet classically surrounded by (or surrounding himself with) desirable women, but these are really disinterested Lesbians attracted to a muse. The droit, being the 24th part of a mite troy, is therefor brought around to undervalue the character, Boss (editor, croupier, etc.). Thus set up, numerous subsidiary paradoxes spring forth. By the use of alchemical measures from antiquity near infinitude, the poet also suggests the electronic atom with its infinite possibilities while withering his opposition to a word. But the reduced forces are also those which he himself (director, guide) inherits. The islanders congregating to one side bear, it seems rather carelessly, the blue banner proclaiming 'OM-PL-FW', the Organization of Minimally-Paired Left-Footed Words.[3] On the other hand, or rather 'foot' as the animal is disguised, the droit appears as a diamond needle radiating invisible electrons that captivate automatic floating spirits, including those of poets, and gently but surely accustom them to slavery. That the point should radiate rather than receive these magnetic sums is a stroke of genius. The chief fault is that all these images combine only in an exalted paternalism, under which the aspect of welcome far outweighs that of filial responsibility.

My dear Father, I wrote, have been thinking of writing you for several days recently, but I don't know what I shall say. In a certain

---

[3] The letters will also suggest omni-plural-sex. Cf. op. cit. Charles p. 293.

sense, I have perhaps already understood with you whatever I might have to say now or anytime, but what am I doing if I omit saying something that I want you to know. For sometime we shall not have every opportunity to say things as I have now, and then a terrible feeling of wasted time will come over me in waves like nausea is said to come. That feeling will come again anyway, no matter how much I have said, nor how well I am recovered.

As it happens, I have been sleeping quite a lot, yesterday and the day before, and I have been dreaming about people we know. The dreams were about me and some of the people we know were in them. The dreams were most delightful, quite colorful and in them I was young and gay and careless. In the one I remember most clearly, everyone we know was in a fine house from which the carpets had been cleared for some sort of ceremony, like a wedding, which gave everybody an opportunity to get dressed up and stand about smiling at each other. I found myself impatient with the whole affair, as usual it entailed a lot of waiting for various aspects of the convention to take place, and I went about making amusing and even outrageous remarks, leading on a few other youngsters who felt the same way. We ran through the house sliding across the polished floors on white throw rugs the way children slide along the sidewalks covered with sleet. Everyone pretended to be put out with us, as we were old enough to know better, indeed hardly younger than I am now, but they were really very charmed and pleased and I was immensely happy. At the end of the movie I stopped some child who was waiting to be in the ceremony to ask her whose house it was. She told me two or three times, but I had never heard of the people even though I was entirely in my element and I surely knew everyone who was there in Lockport.

I am not one who supposes that dreams need to have any unusual significance, and I almost always enjoy my dreams, even the bad ones I sometimes have just after I go to sleep. What I want to say, perhaps by telling you my dream, is that I am glad you brought me up in the place where you had always lived and where most of the people there had always been and would continue, a place with that kind of permanence. And I am entirely grateful, if these words mean anything at all, that I am of a family so well connected and known in that place as ours is, largely because of what you have done, but also because of others in the family, what you all have done. I expect I shall always maintain associations with the place.

Some time after I had, at the age of eighteen, left off living there, it occurred to me to realize or imagine that when I left to go to college and on from there to make my life such as it is, I had off-handedly abdicated from such a position as Crown Prince of that place. Though I did not regret doing it, I came more and more to value seriously who I was there and what I might have done from that position. Of course it is true that I didn't like most of the people I found there very much, but I didn't turn away to find many more congenial people elsewhere. Neither is there much more opportunity for me to find here or anyway some convention of life which would suit me better, though I didn't know that when I started out. Very strangely, even to me who is so familiar with it, it is given to me to make my own way somehow that I now and then more or less clearly understand. You have founded me so well at the source that I cannot say there is any question I may have chosen an unsuitable style of life.

I am in the process of ignoring two or three different vocations, opportunities to engage in standard callings, one of which is a very good chance, so to speak, to be a publisher of books. It has always saddened me to have to close with more or less force such doors which have kindly opened in my way, for there is no reason why I should not do such things as are offered very well. Although it is a great cliché, I know you would be immensely happy in my success as something or other, and believe me I should like you to be pleased. I have to say it never occured to me to have to explain who my father is, or who I am. I have never known the answer, but it does not seem a likely question.

From time to time it amuses me to imagine a commercial résumé of the life of H.R.H. Edward Albert, Duke of Windsor. For 1936, the entry must read, King of England. I have been writing out my life for some time now and it is possible for you to imagine that an item in some such future résumé I shall not have to write will be some great thing. Among my sadnesses, of which this letter is an expression, the likelihood that you will not like what I write or how I live is a shame like wasted things, my renunciation of the throne having taken place already when you thought I was still a child. Please know that there is no reason for it, and no better way, and I say so with love and sadly.

We expect to be with you for Christmas at home.

[signed] Cork.

I felt sad. Sad as the wind in the trees. A sad oak. (the sadness of borrowing) sadly I sand smooth the shaved surface for an S curve of mistakes & omissions choosing strangers a missionary mildness sorting out the parts I still stand singly I sigh "it was a subsistence substance silently sought or summoned from the recesses of success" that is the sources of excess through signs and symbols the sice toss and a sibylline sale to recross a standard crystal glass where shining sightlessly my lass saw her silhouette amid seven stars of which six soon knew the solitude of perfect darkness

From the top of a tree where it often lay, my mind wriggles free to go forth upon emission to more or less astringent foes who felt, as I did at one time, that all in the every point of each semi-circle of wood could be known to the satisfaction of most of my contemporaries. Slowly then, I emerged upon the sands where it was generally shown to be true as a right that something should be done to forestall that which could have no other choice than to become lighter. We dropped some things, by the way, in a storm. The allusions that had weighed us down were nearly all then taken up for middle class museums where they were kept at the right temperature and prohibited to smoke. Neither was that more clear than any fig, dried without the leaves, might appear all squashed and strung up in a naturalistic bunch of which one or two was only a part, a very small strawberry, one of a quart to be picked from the vine. If I had had my way of the affair, I think I should have driven the entire truckload of them to the dead end of the road at the river's edge and then activated the tilt mechanism to make a one-way chute to where from which they could never complain of again. But if it had been done in such a way as to provoke from me and from my brothers of every variety who were all corrected as to the season of birth and the necessity of it, then I should have cheered, shouting, All right! Go ahead! Light the candles and twirl the chandelier! Let's get on with whatever it is because it's high time for something to happen. A story, say, of 400 pages with 400 words to each leaf, an allegory of life on earth at my house of all places, all peoples, all ways, a ledger kept at Romany to be reëntered into from time to time with a sense of lightness to the touch that belies the real weight of the book.

What with all this talk about narcotics, I quite feel like the theatre again after so many memories of past Presidents having been compiled and serialized locally in such dull way as to fascinate my awareness upon the ill effects of using almost any kind of paint that is available because of the fumes which could kill a man and did, in fact so much so that I thought the audience tonight was terrible though not as bad as last New Year's when that guy brought his mother and his sister to that party where they served no drugs. The kinds of recording that one can do by recording what can be heard and seen inside or outside of recording sessions is essential to know before one can embark, if that is the word, upon a life of recording everything one heard or knew or thought he heard or knew or recorded at will and quite disregarding the chance effects that any particular recording may have on that factor of the brain and of the blood which responds to recordings when they are properly arranged. Finally, I thought, it would be desirable, as I always in any case felt, to do anything, whenever possible, short of extending the life of the play, to alleviate up to the high water mark all pressure of whatever sort upon whoever felt it, not to say that I approved of the knowledge thereby acquired, so that everyone, including myself and my friends would be free to think as they usually and even preferrably thought that whenever two or three of us would gather together in some tavern or other, we might allude to anything any one of us had ever said, and it would be the same, almost, as knowing without doubt that what could be said would be said, except, of course, that we no longer had any right to be certain. Because willingly or not when the whole story was fed back to me that night at the party we found insulting I could not tell where one period began and the other ended. It was the sensation that we were being pelted with pieces of oranges and perhaps even tomatoes from the rear which made us make them take the primrose path they were laughingly to take quite without thinking of the cause of their misfortunes. For if anyone could have known at the time of that meeting or at any reading whatsoever that there would never again be anything like it in the world or outside anywhere, well we would have behaved differently, believe me. We would have had to say that we knew the end of the series and thus provide them with a good oldstyle occasion for applause. However out of habit that had been cultivated originally for that purpose we persevered through the storm and whatever else may have happened as if it were really nothing.

For while it is easier and easier to compile long combinations and ever more curious strange juxtapositions than which nothing stranger is remembered except for the information that describes the life of every day, nevertheless the forms of the feeling can be reassuringly made known to everyone without the matter of it getting in the

way. As a formula for dogmatists that was pretty good, but I preferred and I still prefer when there is any occasional choice to work
from life, so to speak, by way for example of going out into the field
and plucking a green straw of grass which by the custom of the
country one sucks. Neither less nor more of the green feeling I call
sadness, subtly bright like a rainy day — it is merely reflected — would
give me any sensation that might have the pain of a cinder in my shoe
or a smaller particle beneath my eyelid. For history, I reflected, was
never concerned with these things which I had at one time chosen to
call the apples and pears of my life any more than it would ever be
concerned, not that history could be personified, with the other
golden fruits in dehydrated form I ate for breakfast in those days. The
extension of anything is not concerned with the purity of the idea
itself and always results in more or less boredom that can be
anticipated (but not known in advance) given only the scale of the
proceeding. He always replied with a little information touching
upon the insidious effects of burning any kind of dead vegetables near
any living organism, saying that he would rather wait outside if it
were not for the rain, or the impossibility of the perfect chair, or the
noise of chewing made by any careless eater which I myself detest
unless I am eating too. Neither is the sadness of being certain an
infallible guide to words themselves.

My dear Prince, I wrote, I am not at all sure that religious and
sexual concerns may be well equalized, but I should like you to see
them, momentarily, as metaphors for simple life or truth or process.
It is a man's great shame not to be able to accept life as it is, the way
all other animals do, but to require an artificial convention to be
construed against what he must regard as a meaningless series of
events to form a way of life. Or, one must choose something to believe
that appears and feels sufficient to become the meaning of the process
of one's life.

What are you doing? they replied. Only to discredit us, they
asked, What do you think you're doing? With an absent smile and a
muscular clasp they exclaim, How do you do!

In the form of my name and address, we recognize the remains of
the convention of personal influence which, historically spoken,
reached its heights in such phenomenal beings as Buddha, Moses,
Aristotle, Christ, Mohammed, Caesar, Charlemagne, Thomas,
Shakespeare, Descartes, Goethe, Napoleon, Victoria, Wagner,

Baudelaire, Stalin whose inventions resulted, among other things, in empires, languages and religions expressing a desire to embrace the world. So much for advertising.

The condition of sexlessness is quite normal among all civilized people compared with the life of their tomcats. The comparatively high sexuality of people under twenty, of members of the lower orders of societies who have nothing else to do, and of all those who may be regarded as relatively uncivil is in some degree what leads on all those who are more civilized to form a collective determination to subdue these unruly beings, whether the intention be accomplished by history, education, welfare legislation or devastation.

It is the common man's pleasure not to know any more of the meaning of life than can be expressed in a few simple homilies and it is his curse to desire to know the meaning of life as fully as anyone may. It is his shame not to encounter the meaning he may be led to expect in one form or in another, a shame of which he is more conscious the better educated he becomes, a shame which he is almost always capable of keeping secret because his awareness of it at the full is always dim, fleeting and occasional. Thus he is inclined to grief at funerals and weddings. When a man can no longer keep the devil's knowledge to himself, he must be classified as an insane and be forcibly subdued or benevolently changed. The extraordinary man creates or finds a metaphor which expresses what he has learned from life and thus contributes, in his turn, to the general cultivation of the soul of man, and, having done so, maintains his particular distinctions, or dies forthwith, or sickens hopelessly.

The notion of freedom, so utterly uncongenial to every system of personal influence, has become the common coin of the known world in our time. I too believe in freedom, but in itself it is no way of life. The dominant fashion today prefers an historical-sexual approach to the problem of meaning, but, perhaps originally, permits the continued existence and cultivation of every other mode of life in which anyone has any interest. Organized critics and hired snipers will severely tax dissension, to be sure, but the defectors may also harass the greater body of opinion in a free-for-all of various slaveries.

I have to point out what you already know crushingly, that human life to be believed must be seen through metaphor, and this occupation is ultimately of the order of invention, for it replaces not something that we might know, but only the nothingness we call life. As you say, it's true that a full prick has the power of moving men's minds. Sexual activity is wonderful because it is a lifelike sensation shared by everyone, more or less, which may associate us one with another in ways that seem to be potential of meaning and composed of truth.

Like every other possible metaphor, the historical-sexual job is precarious because it consists of ephemera and shows a tendency to disintegrate at the popular level. It was no dim mistake that the people of Europe in the middle ages were not permitted by their rulers to be learned to read. The great increase in populations through the various revolutions engendered by the fantasies of slaves and mendicants has generated a large class of persons capable of under-standing & propagating this most basic metaphor, which has its source in everyone's experience, for no system of personal influence can any more extend to the ends of the earth.

For many people, indeed almost all, it would appear that there is sufficient significance in the story of their own lives cast always in terms that have sexual implications; And the continual repetition, reconstruction and review of that history towads a hypothetical, inexistent *finissimo* usually known as happiness substituting in for death is more than enough to occupy their minds. Surely I have not enough information about them universally to apply my entertaining theories of poetry.

But I suppose that the sexual metaphor cannot be as successful as other ideas presumably have been (there is no way to know that everyone in France believed in God during the tenth century) because sex is, as I like to say, too near to the bone, to reality that is no king's raiment and can have no meaning.

It is the greatest possible experiment, and one that has so far always known defeat even as no influence has ever yet quite ruled the whole world, to put an idea to the test of everyone's experience. Indeed there is scarcely an idea that could be formulated in such a way. In those days there went out a decree from Caesar Augustus that all the world should be taxed. For an idea to be believed it is necessary that everyone concerned have some experience of its source; at the very least, to be made aware of it as fact which in our time almost passes for belief. At the same time as roads and bridges can everywhere be built in the American style we hear of the worldwide acceptance of the utterly impossible conception of freedom, some-thing that is not a great Western idea but the appurtenance of many ideas as many different people have built their bridges.

It has been the delight and the success of abstract ideas that they can be reformed and expressed in endless concrete metaphor. Go and tell it on the Mountain that our Jesus Christ is born! To abstract things out of life is not at all as attractive and most people cannot even do it, nor can they understand what those who do it are about. People like Job who seek the meaning they must somehow find or invent by going through the very eventuality of life will end in a timeless depression of racial dimensions from which even genocide is no escape. Old-style painters and modern journalists take pleasure from endless description of lives, and people like to look and see, but their portraits form no occasion out of which people in general can, as they must, take heart.

With my best wishes for thy continued Health and Good Cheer, I remain, dear Sir, very truly thine Apostate and Friend.

[signed] T.

The first thing I did one particular day was to get up somewhat later then I often did and go downstairs to meet an appointment with the garbage man Angelo Barretti who was not yet on the street, he was late. I had taken a holiday to use up my guaranteed sick pay and I had chosen that day because it was my birthday. Instead of picking up the mail on my way, as I usually did, I took it out of the mailbox and sat down on the stone loading platform next door in the sun. There were a few things that day, including a check for twenty-five dollars and greetings from my father, and a piece of blue legal paper dispossessing me of my house in lieu of $1,300 arreared rent which I did not owe, an event that was to have taken place no later than two days since, according to the paper. I went back upstairs to call up my friend who didn't answer my ring. Then Angelo Barretti, the licensed carter, hailed me from the street and I descended to speak with him. I showed him all the rubbish to be destroyed; he gave me a satisfactory price and technical recommendations. We saw only one rat. He seemed affable but he was soon on his way, declining coffee. Then I remembered I had forgotten to eat breakfast, which is usually the first thing I do when I am dressed. I ate something, some cherries, and I made a pot of tea. I was somewhat preoccupied with questions of garbage removal since I could not leave everything to Angelo Barretti. Right away I had to buy a large can with a tight lid and one day I should have to transfer half of a full tin keg of lard in which, perhaps, a rat had died, into another can so that we could get it out

without spoiling the steps with grease on some subsequent Tuesday
morning. But above all that, in what was for me a rather crowded
morning, there was the question of the legal notice. First it is necessary to figure out the exact meaning of the prose, which is easy, then
you have to invent an accurate story which fully answers why such a
meaning should now be desired to be committed to my care. That is
always much more difficult and highly conventional, so much so that
usually it is a good idea to engage one or two lawyers who, given all
the facts and knowing all the rules, will be able to suggest the motive
which one quite rightly presumes to lie at the root of any legal act. Of
course such critics will often, even preferably, disagree and it is
possible that all of them may be correct and that they are all wrong,
but it is certain that in such cases they do not have as much interest in
the matter as do those named in the document. They spend the first
part of the interview getting one to trust them, not at all an easy task
considering the strength of the literary conventions they thus
attempt to thwart, and then they tell you in a minute what they can
do for you and how much it will cost. The price is higher if there is
more revision to be done and more action to be quickly enjoined. The
cheapest and very often the best solution will employ endless delaying tactics of one sort and another for even at law it is still true that
people will lose interest in things that are indefinitely receding into
the future. Besides all that, I thought, perhaps I should have to buy
the house which I didn't want to do, although I like it very much. In
all such affairs of a certain magnitude your wife will be of no help to
you as an adviser, unless you yourself are helpless, because her resolution will be quickly to adapt herself to the clearly expressed wish of
any man. She may weep briefly and begin packing up the things of
the world to have them moved somewhere else which guarantees that
nothing happens there and costs us all my time.

Then, as quickly as anyone could say a thing, the fall was down
around upon us. That season opened with the bang in which *haute
couture* was denounced from practical magazines that had sold out
long before with the advent of winter draping a shadow in the form of
brisk nights and crisp days over all the leaves and wherever there was
any grass. People prepared to alight, speaking in figures, dressing in
greys and blacks and white, showering the pavements with the refuse
of their minds. Life became businesslike. Sheaves of paper were permitted to disperse, scurrying through the streets in an effort to keep
aloft on a light wind from around the corner. The very paving stones,

where they were still exposed to the freedom of the air, tightened up after an expansive summer in accordance with a perversion of scientific law. Manicured lawns trimmed their unseen toenails. Subversive animals made up their own brand new fur wraps and so innocently prepared their present slaughter, some of them more expensively than others. One or two hundred-thousand dirty leaves fell from a tree and all of a sudden it occurred to me to think of all the trees in a different manner. The dear turkeys were fattened systematically, to be eaten twice before long. You were made aware of the speed of time by means of constant remarks and shortening the work week. Tempers subsided and the seasonal crime rate declined. The pattern of arrests was deliberately changed by reassigning all the forces to unfamiliar precincts. I actually bought a slightly chipped white porcelain bowl to go inside a cuspidor for thirty cents and began to use it as an ashtray. American art threw back its front gate and held open court with the people. Moths and mosquitoes and other remnants of the other season expired abundantly. Racehorses met for the last time in lucrative convention, pitchers were tirelessly described on the point of taking one step backwards in the middle of a crucial winning streak, the purification of milk went on as usual in a collusion of all dairies both in favor of and against the real interests of the people as a whole, and business at the *bureaux des postes* picked up again. Of all this nothing could be seen. On the surface of appearances the electric light flickered dangerously close to the bubble of truth wherein lay all the laws each by each from the number to the last mouldering away most high. Autumn is as cruel as its converse.

It's a very good/book/pen/play (nice day) / Wenny pas day *
cinny doe beo / / nen clei cerlipan fir de lily * ene / (3/4) / figtue su
meito phinwe orgu / enepas Wenny vlor bwyler decile / / Vlor
elebiticam soronoe obtu / sin forlito horbelae ene beal ene byl bor-
difor sin forlito orgu / exegesis et coloribus non disputandum est /
nix ciea nen dimetea * fertin martues Wenny sin dux / / nen clei
cerlipan fir de biby ene / (1/4) / Wenny pas vay cinny deo boe / / *
　　Je pense / et les vents / si non * sol fa la / Mes choses sont fini /
s'il faut que du soir / / Les enfants encontrent les murs et le ciel / où là
sur la table la couverature / / Si pour les contrats du café midi / un
entrecôte ni cuit ni garni / Il defend des arts et la grosse chanteuse / il
s'arête ici pour l'on s'amuser / / Bien du fin / je reviendra

I find a lot to mind in this world if you don't mind my saying so
and I shan't take a minute to explain to you what's on my mind on
this perfectly wonderful day here under the stars in the absence of the
moon where we strayed briefly over the lunch we had brought with us
to the big new outdoor barn where we strayed briefly over the various
kinds of the foods and of the insects that will collect in such a place at
night as well as the slightly different ones that come to the big new
outdoor barn where the cattle are daily plugged into the system of
feelings and textures and sounds and feedings and where they eat
what we thought they fancied, mostly hay nowadays, and where we
can sit in the slightly scratchy remains of fodder and hay and straws
eating or drinking whatever we have with us as we do not like dried
grasses for that purpose, sitting there ever mindful of our duty to each
other and to ourselves and its awareness of possibly expressing to each
other at least if we could for just a minute know it and say it in all this
privacy while doing some homely task away from home and its
terrible associations whatever we thought as we ate from the lunch
she had made freshly in the morning when the sun baked everything
it touched to become some ashen image thrown back to us to make
into something to say that will turn everything to gold except for the
hay and her hair and the cattle are lowing. We left it all alone crying
out to us and to all of us please to check the race of nights and days
upon the stones and over the mills and through the swamps and floods
and rains and wells and pipes and sinks and drains for the freedom we
held in check today, tonight, tomorrow and last night which left us
timeless in the inky light of washable dusk where the late rose
bloomed and the night died slowly and we crown each other for a
moment that would be resumed if it were told. Whereupon there was
in the East as a great noise a wind that rolled over a terraced hill and
cut through the air like a weed; and the bears feasting on the vegetables ripening along the third tier were thereby filled with tremendous
desires that rose up on their hind legs and shot forth from their locked
jaws as definite as starlight by which to lead them on the journey
outward toward infinity, leaving us anxious and thunderstruck down
by the waters where we made hasty work of graves: now in the world
and out of everlasting value I fly gnatlike toward the fascinating
burning filament, the moment, the now, the new, the current
flowing swiftly and imperceptibly through and around the rocks of
our times past, undulant, lapidary, solipsistically defunct where once
flew the river of my emotions like blood pounding the arterial shore

the roof of my mouth a palate of milk warming on my wrist the root at
my midriff a print of each digit the muscle of the hair two eyes for the
other one and teeth the better your face, and tongue the faster your
voice, and sniff the cooler your nose and twinkle do your toes and ears
and eyes   please hide me

Roughness / I glued the lock into place / she was twisted /
nothing happened tonight / Pray sit down. / cattails give off the
smell of burnt umber / May I sew you to another sheet? / ce ne fait
rien / never, no, never, she said / / Finally, Willy ate it all up. /
striking a gong rich / it was known / I fed the cat liver / the pad, and
she erased it / pour four tablespoons / my hand lay along the counter
/ Sharpen that knife! / silver dioxide. Do not consider / / beginning
once more now / of which nothing is known. / a matter of confidence
/ / if there were anyone / a ballpoint pen / neither he nor she could
make the tape / say that again / it was easy, she cried / laughing
silently / say that again / black on rye / end of a pot of fire? / three
tries will do / a teardrop and a coffeepot / color of nuts / final, but it
was / bark

Either the silver candlestick was protected from being covered
with drops of red wax by the bit of newspaper with which its recepta-
cle was lined, or the candle, presumably one left after a celebration of
Christmas many years ago, was too thin about the base to stand
straight by itself. In either case, it continued to burn and to cast its
peculiar glow about the room and to let fall its excess wax, most of
which piled up on the paper which extended in a circle about the
candelabrum to the size of a medium grapefruit. It occurred to me
that it was draughty. The candle flickered and went out.

As a matter of fact, she was saying, I have red candles tonight in
your honour, my dear.

The two of them looked at each other as if in complete agreement on some hard determination, and, one might almost have said,
in love. His name had escaped me. I thought it seemed a quiet
evening, the more so because I had anticipated having to endure a
crude blast of fresh air if I came to the gathering. She had rung up to
ask if I would help to entertain her charming friends who spoke no
English or was it French now I forget a little here. As a matter of fact,

she was saying, it had proved to be a quiet evening. But she was very happy to be at home once more. Thoughtfully I cultivated these pictures as an object for contemplation.

There was no mistaking the fact that they were guests. As usual some of them were seated in various postures on the carpeted floor itself. They were almost surrounded by casually disregarded books, half-finished drinks in simple large glasses, and ashtrays, pocket-books, toys, and sleeping cats. From my point of view they seemed not to be a group of any sort, but rather solitary youngish men and women with most of the typical characteristics, one style of hair, another sort of dress, a lovely high-heeled shoe and so on. They were perfectly attentive and absolutely quiet. Even the occasional remarks of my hostess to her guest did not disturb the quiet. There was no conversation and no music; one heard only slight noises from the city outside and only now and then a remark of the sort I have mentioned, disassociated, private, not anything one would stop to listen to. Being in the room at that moment, I felt a sensation of completion and cessation and satisfaction that makes me drowsy. Indeed it now seems to me as I think about what I saw there, that the evening was composed by means of invisible partitions that separated guest from guest as a pair of lovers are soon separated from their friends only to be reunited more strongly with them later. Each person in the room seemed to show a friend's discretion for every other. The atmosphere was such as to suggest to my lively imagination that everyone had already left, forgetting to take themselves with them as they went. The drinks and books cast their mute suggestion of an entertainment about the room in much the same way as actors' properties on the sets of elaborate plays will suggest somewhat half-heartedly to the observer of an interval in a rehearsal the action of the story they are intended to embellish.

This evening, for example, it struck me as rather curious that although I had only recently entered the room, no one on the floor or in the chairs had acknowledged my presence in any way. Perhaps it was true, after all, that I was not there. To ascertain my presence at that now vanished moment, one would require to know if anyone else remembered me, but then, who were these people whom I say I saw? They in turn would need to know my name, and to have retained it after all this time, or at the very least be able in some way to conjure from the details of my description as I then looked someone of that appearance whom they did not know. At any rate, the hostess would be of service if only the detectives had any way of knowing who she was. And the fact that I thought I knew who the hostess of that occasion had been would be as irrelevant to the truth of the matter as milk must be to grass.

Because of the dramatic effect of the overhead lighting in the room my face was quite obscured by the shadow of the ceiling. At first I simply turned toward the sideboard and poured something from a bottle into a glass which was conveniently placed, and then I tasted from the glass a slightly bitter wine. Carrying my glass in one hand, I stepped forward into the light and made an inconsequential remark to the first person whose gaze I happened to encounter. His face looked in my direction as if I had attracted his interest, but he did not make a sound. I took a place on the carpet with my glass where I could rest my back against a large green winged armchair with serpentine outlines in which nobody was sitting just at present. Some of the books were open and there were also other papers here and there that seemed to have been used as I was accustomed to having used such things. I had no thought of taking up something to read. I studied all the faces in the circle of the people and the things like furniture. Once it occurred to me that the whole thing might be a familiar dream in which everything was almost as it might be in fact. I had not much interest in knowing if it was, and I was certain that the drinks and the people were as real as I was despite the half-formed possibility that they were just set pieces made up to benefit my own still play. And then, with all the direction, necessity and tightness of a sexual movement, or of an artistic technique, but with no such form, winter enclosed us.

(L'hiver nous enferme.)

He began to write his second book sometime later the following day. 'you were good to wash the dishes last night' she said from above as she began slowly to descend the wooden steps the color of gray paint 'good morning to you'

Her eyes he thought were particularly bright to match the light which flooded the room blindingly through five great windows on two sides of the hall, for she had been crying to herself all night. She took a few steps across the ageing floor boards toward the white porcelain cooking stove in her unripe-cherry-red dressing gown. She lighted the flame by turning a knob at the edge of the appliance, then bent low to the level of its surface, squinting in the morning light to adjust the heat over which she would warm some milk in a bright blue porcelain pan with a long thin handle to it. She took the milkpan from its tiny brass hook on the wall next the stove, and she opened the high white porcelain refrigerator opposite the stove withdrawing a quart bottle of milk and then slamming the door of the icebox shut, rattling the wires of the electric toaster that stood on top of it empty. She poured milk into the little pan and balanced it carefully on the three points of the grate over the fire holding it lightly by its handle to keep it from tipping over as it might. She straightened up from these adjustments and gazed across the room to where he sat at the other end looking back at her, his whole head above the back of the stuffy squarish chair against the light, his body and his face in dusty shade.

'good morning' she said. He nodded his head and turned to be able to see a tall houseplant in its pot of red earth, its large oval leaves drooping slightly like the ears of some kind of dog. He shifted his legs from the red tufted footstool and stood up. He walked to where the plant stood on a low birch table where also stood a dark green two litre wine bottle half full of water. He grasped the bottle by its neck and dumped the water carelessly about the foot of the plant making it muddy where the dirt had been slightly parched. The noise of the falling water quickly ceasing, he righted the bottle and carried it to the tubby white sink behind where she stood before the stove. 'I forgot to get the coffee' he said. He turned a knob which let cold water run into the wine bottle from the spout that was fitted with a noisy mechanism to infuse bubbles of air into the water as it ran. The bottle overflowing, he turned off the water, leaving the noise behind, and reached for a fuzzy yellow bath towel which hung on a peg over the sink, and then he wiped off the botle and dried his hands with it. Her voice, when she denounced his mistake, had the color of fresh instant coffee. 'go and get some, why don't you' he remarked as hotly.

She took the milkpan off the stove and set it on a little table next covered in hard red plastic. Then she turned about and sat down on a small bentwood chair, covering the yellow flowered print of its round seat, and setting her arms on a long broad thick board table opposite the sink. She picked an unused cigarette from the debris in a large round orange pottery ashtray near her left hand and, having fixed it in her mouth, lighted it with a stick match she drew from a small wooden box lying nearby on the table.

'or you might just have hot milk today' he said. He rehung the towel and replaced the water bottle, walking the length of the room to do so, and then turned back, beginning to gather up a large assortment of newspapers and books and magazines which lay strewn about on the threadbare pinkish or reddish somewhat worn carpet covering over the floor at that end of the room. He folded the publications up and separated them into three piles which, when he had sorted out most of the things, he put each in a different place, the books on the floor by his chair, the magazines on an unsteady unfinished round maple table nearby, and the newspapers beneath a step of the stairs at the other end of the room. 'how are you' he said.

'oh all right' she said. She reached for the handle of the milkpan on the other table a little ways from where she sat and brought it over, then pouring the milk into a large low white cup fluted on the outside and making almost no noise. She let a spoonful of fine sugar run into the cup of milk and then she stirred the mixture with the empty spoon. She met his glance when she was about to take up the cup. She picked instead her cigarette from a notch in the tray where it had nearly burned out. 'it doesn't matter about the glass' she said. 'I've broken several' she said in a tone that sometimes would make him smile. 'It must have been a tall one, there are lots of them, at least ten' she said, looking past a stopped brass clock to where there were clean dishes stacked upside down at various angles occasioned by natural forces and their shapes in a pink rubber covered wire rack on a counter next to the sink.

'yes, at least ten' he said, reminding himself as he spoke of her remark.

'is there anything for breakfast? have you eaten? what would you like? some pancakes?' According to their custom she prononced the word as if it were spelt differently. She squashed the rest of her cigarette, took a drink of her milk, and stood up to set about making breakfast in the usual way from milk and a powder contained in a printed red and white cardboard box. First she did one thing and then another and another and at last she set before him a white plate with a small stack of flat brown cakes on it

Which having prepared with butter and maple sugar syrup in a certain way he ate with a steel fork that made a certain sound whenever it happened to touch the plate. When there was nothing more to eat, he stopped and laid the fork on the table. He stood and went back to his chair, taking up the book on top of the pile he had made, and she sat at the table correcting a list of the groceries that she wished to buy that day. At one point she asked him if it would be agreeable to have certain kinds of foods on certain occasions, to which he replied that it was. Another time he asked her how much money remained in their checking account at the bank, and she told him. Later on, when she had gone out to do her errands in a relatively small car painted green with a canvas roof and brown plastic upholstery, he fell sound asleep although to all appearances he had done nothing to be tired of.

And that is my story for the Year of 1963. It so happens that, among other things, I simultaneously conclude a little cryptic affair, of which, since I am naturally generous in many ways, I shall say that at this writing I use the last of a ream of cheap yellow paper I have been using for everything for nearly a year. It is a kind of paper most usual to certain professions, though it is going out of style with them, a kind I have used before, and bought in great quantities, and refused, but which I have never sold, if I may be excused.

I have spent the evening in a most old-fashioned way by sitting for my portrait, or, more sincerely, by sitting in my chair and having my figure included in a painting of the scene. I, in turn, photographed the artist, my sister-in-law, an art student, from where I sat. As I waited through the process, I was entertained by a reading of Hamlet on the radio, and I was permitted to read about in a few books which lay nearby (as my pose was that of a reader) and my attention was diverted in several ways quite pleasantly. I scratched my head, and renewed the position of my arms and head and tried imperceptibly to ease my ass. She works quietly and politely forbids me to see what she has done. There is a sense in which I had nothing to do.

American time, as I have no doubt remarked before, promotes repetition of the sort that prohibits the pursuit of stories while employing a foreign language in which nothing is said unless a story be told. Such a choice brings forth the universal tragedy of the apparently eternal rehearsal of nothing to say as if it had never been said. The sort of repetition of which I speak and of which everyone here is so familiar that it has become unnoticeable, has nothing to do with incantation, the stylized song, of which memory no longer implies the fact or the fancy that was its source. It is only a matter of convenience that one's own name does not ordinarily change through time. Even so, whatever it is that makes one remember the name as long as one lives is more a memorial act than a matter of course. And so it is with the retailing of stories that anyway are not stories, nor even secrets. The history of anything remains completely forgotten, though there is no lack of varying opinions on the subject. For as much as there can be no classical photographs, so much do all the stories remain fixed and taciturn.

The story that cannot be recalled in every crude detail even as it is recited perhaps for the first time in history is a puzzlement that in America may lead the viewer to suspect that someone is out of his or her mind. For remedy of which one may apply to one's neighbors, both familiar and strange, to confirm one's unfounded hope that it is the story that does not exist, and that one's life is really a lie.

> A regret, a single regret makes a door way. What is a door way, a door way is a photograph.
> What is a photograph, a photograph is a sight, and a sight is always a sight of something. Very likely there is a photograph that gives color. If there is then there is that color that does not change any more than it did when there was much more use for photography.　　　　　　　　　　Gertrude Stein, circa 1913

I find among my scripts one which indicates that on December third I addressed to Charles a version of the edited remarks here recorded.

Along with the 'exchange of winnings' which we know to be conducted honestly, there lies also the complete possibility of fiction which, having realized, we go on to speak of a certain style or manners and very soon the landscape is becoming formal. By means of the wherewithal you folded in a pocket and forgot, a smallish garbage plot may not become so smelly, and the bears we love to watch at food there can be tamed and lighted and assigned. In other words, when from one hand come things that allude to the controls the other will itch to lead a stravaganza. Or, the exorbitance of winning ought to be a midpoint among many occasions for senescence, each of them a partial memory of all that can be lost that way.

Each thing (name a noun) in the course of a style is a profusion of an owner's right. Each notice, in the sense of the moment it informs, makes a list that is perhaps less easily recorded. One's treatment of the whole series can be completely playful only when it is already known that the resource stored is so great as to exhaust the combination of every possible suggestion twice and still remain intact. Otherwise there are the potentialities of simple excessive figures like unlimited and unknown popular success, and the minimal affinities of necessity, relationship and certitude at last. So it is in the case of my laughter which sometimes finds its way up the wrong sleeve in an affair to which we shall never return. While there can be an untouchable marble rigged up in every provincial museum, and we might as well agree to that, the literary fact of each theory of knowledge is the sort from which it must be compared. When such undertakings become a celebrated cause, something worth something will remain.

> For several years before 1946, Marcel Jouhandeau had represented and for some ten years more was to represent, the kind of writer I should have liked to be. What I mean is that I should have liked to write, from day to day, simply about the moment and its concerns and any past matters which pressed on the memory, the prose being merely careful, transparent, exact, easy on eye and ear, varied only by the variety of the mind's approach to what it scrupulously dealt with; utterly shameless, wholly personal. That it was quite impossible is due to the rigid formality of British literary customs. The novel and the diary without dates cannot flow into each other here, and I had long been sickened by the contrivances expected of a novelist.
>
> Rayner Heppenstall, circa 1963

From the greatest provincial capital ever yet built into the earth, the repository of the unfilled wishes of all Europe and all time, the city-state of impassioned serfs and willing pensioners, the seat without a government to which the plenipotentiaries of all Princes are well come for conversation, the perverse reconstruction upon a new found island of the Duke's inland home town, the only county where everything is drawn together to be redistributed at once by sale and where only nothingness is priceless, I set forth upon my guided tour.

In company with the 'exchange of winnings' which proceeds at various speed, never greater than a mile in an hour, there races headlong and forthrightly the complete possibility of invention. Fiction remains possible to us only so long as we can certify the character of reality to the structure of the sentences in such a way as to render allusions to the essences described immaterial. A clear solution, I should say, offers no explanation. The example of a prose poem is an occasion for reading aloud. Thus a certain kind of effort answers the inclusive movement, an obvious set quotation excepting those of other significance with a purpose to conserve intentions. To introduce the question of belief will change the mood, approaching philosophy once more from the direction of the poem that is spoken honestly.

Here at the culmy point of the harbored island, we find, docked down and ferried back and forth, an only just unrealized democracy and nothing but crudities to dine on. Wandering through the snow in deserted streets by starlight and its imitators, I turn the corner to encounter the yellow blinking sign of magic and ivresse with music. But once inside the signal that I run toward, I am reminded only of the discordant shouts and groans of drunken seamen at the bar, the sordid equality of purpose after midnight which a small white cat tied with a silver bell enlivens. Elsewhere there is very little time, a statistic of waste, a type of knowledge, a degree of mass, a continual occasional discouragement, a locked and overbolted door leading to a public void, and no morning, noon, or night.

If you want something, see, don't measure it. Above all, take your time and make it work. It is healthy to expect the worst, at least at first. But that is like a medicine that she teaches you to use, a little precaution against the cold that never hurts; don't count on it. For example, they will tell you several good ways to insure your hold on your lease, but there is no guarantee that you will like living there. In the long run, you will do best if you can bring yourself around to not caring whether you make it or not. But that way is tricky and if you're very young or very old, I'll say what my old lady once told me, namely, you can't afford to be careless until you have more experience. She is a great faith healer and speaks the truth, though except for that you wouldn't like her jargon any more than I do.

Anyway, if you find yourself nearby to something you might like, take a good look and she'll probably look back. That will take a minute and clear the way for the next move. If you say something, say anything you want to say. Do not rely on things you heard other people say, including me. Poetry will only work if you are French, which is unlikely. The chances are that if you ask for something it will be handed to you, but there is a right way and a wrong way to do everything. Never put yourself in her position or you will surely fail. It can happen that you are one of those unlucky bastards who never makes it anyhow. If so, you probably have no interest in improved techniques and it's quite unlikely that you would have read along this far. But if you are convicted that way, the best you can do is want what you're supposed to want and spend your time trying not to hate what you get.

Don't throw the glassware out of the window. These babes are recalcitrant but they learn fast if you give them a solid opening play and keep it going fairly quick so that they don't have time to think. They will think anyway so don't provide the opportunities yourself. Like it's also best to get along at the office or get out. Getting along means going forward and up as well as in, so at the same time you get older and deeper and higher. It's the only real sure thing: both death and taxes have no reality.

It is confusing to consider happiness at all, so don't. That will take care of itself, as they say. When the time comes, figure you'll be able to do it. And don't grudge the boss. Make a few cracks if they're really funny, but never believe it or you're screwed. So if you want to do something, do it, but be sure that it's the right thing at the right time, and it is always right to bluff the object or ignore the obstacle. If you have lots of time and nothing else in mind, you might, for example, try rewriting this book. It could take you up to a year. It has taken me two.

Lately I've been very busy on all three levels. It has been a bit too much for me, if you really want to know, but once in a while I don't mind building up a backlog, because when things slow down again you know there's always something left to burn. Perhaps there isn't enough time in the day, but I'd rather not bother with that little ploy. Because now, except for cleaning up the mess, I'm finished. It's not an unmixed pleasure, but on the whole I love it.

Besides that there is my wife, half a dozen friends and a few acquaintances I like. I also have some relatives who, like my friends but if possible less kindly, have taken up the little task of anticipating my future for me. I must disenchant them. And then there are a lot of real problems and some artificial questions like the hot water heater, a couple of trips out of town, getting 2 copies of a letter made, practicing to learn to speak, wash my hair and have her cut it, talk to the cat, interview the editors, getting the car in good shape, make the pictures and return the negative, fix the phonograph, rehanging the vines, making some more money, a letter to my father, buying some beer, a trip uptown to order things, a letter of thanks and everything else.

L'hiver nous enferme.

Romeo Alpha — Alpha Romeo

I

I AWAKE FROM MY DREAM in a revery of past successes with somatic tears and imaginary laughter to find an intention forming on my brain of writing some sort of apology as to form and style in my writing as I have been doing it for nearly three years. I wish to re-member it.

In composing these little books, I have never been much concerned with their relations to any historical, commercial techniques of communication, nor have I been moved by other than personal impulses. Of course I have at the same time admired other things that have been written, as I have not hesitated to demonstrate in the book itself by means of quotation and parody. And my attention has been drawn from time to time by things that are not myself, nor even mine. Somebody has remarked that man is the animal who loves to go abroad looking at the world. I find that a pleasant formula by which to distinguish ourselves because it isn't very exclusive — it doesn't insist on tools, or metaphor, or intelligence, or fire — at the same time as it is self-evident. It is not a profound distinction, but I find it charming. That is not a state for which anyone but women can easily apologize today, so much so that to all appearances people now would search about them only out of necessity, and not from desire which has always been our impetus. Love and desire are one. Today we see where those two words exclusively denote to us, love for a woman or a man and desire for sexual gratification or its substitute. A terrible point — I believe we have come as far as possible toward making the sumptuary nature seem to be necessitous. One has not far to seek for the reasons in which this alteration thrives; but when we turn the page eagerly to set our doubts at rest, we find that the reasons are not interesting. You will have noticed already the common example of paradoxical eclecticism in which a person presented with an incomprehensible fact or effect invariably remarks, That's very interesting. Of course they would like to say that it is not at all interesting, but their education has taught them to dissemble. These well-known rationalizations will be forever with us, but as for me, I do not desire to know them. In fact, I already know them. I desire what is nowadays often called 'something else.'

It is significant that we have no name for what is not reduced to the level of necessity, but it doesn't mean very much. Like every other answer, the answer to that problem stands in plain view a mile ahead, and so I shall ignore it. But I repeat that I desire to make things for which there is no ready form of name, except, back on the level of necessity, my own. Now 'romance' for example is another of the words that has lost much through the devastating effects of increased circulation. Since it means nothing, I can hardly use it at all, but perhaps I may persist momentarily.

As I go about my inventive tasks which are really, as we all know, pleasures in disguise, I often give in to the desire to redeem words according to their root meanings, the original metaphors they formulated. Sometimes I do not know what they are and sometimes I redeem them to my satisfaction, but falsely, that is to say to the sorrow of etymologists who know Greek and Hindi, but I keep at it because I only please myself, and that by putting a word where I please. It is a simple pleasure, to be sure, it is even decorative, a word to which we may return. A romance is something foreign, something strange. The syntax of publicity in which we live permits us very few examples of anything that is quite strange. But in terms of politics we may in 1966 notice the case of China, which, at one time did have a culture utterly different from our own, and which, in our time, has been made into the sole forbidden and prohibited province from the publicitary arts. If I may say so, the case of China responds only to our primitive *need* for something strange, which, on this scale, is always something hated, rather vaguely though it be conceived. From what little we do hear of them we can guess that what is going on there is really the success of our European propaganda to equalize the whole world, though it is being done there in a manner at once more polite

than our own, and more effective. In any case it is not very romantic. I
am sorry to use that word just now because, even if I could, I have not
yet delimited the sense of it sufficiently to exclude the stupidities we
invariably associate with the word 'romantic'. I am obviously seeking
to establish at the outset a primary distinction between desires and
needs; I am really seeking to re-establish it, for there is no doubt that
it inheres in all of us.

If it were to be remarked, as I occasionally will, that a romance
was at one time an Italian story told in France, they would reply,
That's interesting. Unnecessarily speaking, there is no special affinity
between what is strange and what is incomprehensible. *Our impulse is
to familiarize the incomprehensible, and to cultivate the strange.* Thus we
would enslave the Africans, one way or another, and, if we were
English, maintain in all absurdity that we are distinct from France.
In the universal pejoration of this epoch, we are able to pride ourselves on having decided that the invention of God was an inferior
necessity with a purpose to explain human nature and its limitations
for 'prescientific' minds. A careful consideration will show, however,
that God was a creature, beg pardon, of desire. We will not have to
bother to recount the forgotten histories of the ancient gods to
demonstrate how fundamentally uninteresting the modern view of
currently untenable beliefs may seem to be. We have only to discard a
number of objectified conceptions (than which nothing is easier
thrown away) and, with the air cleaned up a bit, look about us
ordinarily. We will see fantastic details whlich had been rationalized
away. We will find funny-looking things that please us, and will
juxtapose experiences that a moment earlier would have seemed
incongruous. Anyone who dares to watch through the night for dawn
to come will see a good example of this effect when by the early light
he sees his habitual surroundings transformed into 'something else'
which has nothing to do with the optics of refraction or with the
psychology of fatigue. Or, if one is not too busy at that hour, it is
possible to notice quite unusual effects in the gathering dusk that
have nothing to do with the cliché of a beautiful sunset. Since we are
certainly rational, we will remark at such rare moments that all such
effects are really those details we never noticed yet. And if we have a
scruple left, we will crush the impulse to photograph the rarity
without a second thought. To all those who are satisfied by the
anti-image that these romantic experiences are mere psychological
symptoma, there is nothing more to say, for we would permit

Scrooge to persist unchanged so long as he likes, though his story, like the lives of most of us, would remain untellable.

In other words, I wish to make a gratuitous assertion of what to me is manifest. I have no interest in redeeming the souls of those who do not dream, so scared are they of symbolism. In composing this book in my spare time, of which, by design, I have had more than enough for the purpose, I have put down whatever 'occurs to me.' If what happens as a result is radically strange, as I think it may seem to be, that is because the roots of all human experience have atrophied alarmingly while the distressed and plastified vegetation lives on, if that could be the correct expression, under the dignified forms of phenomenology. Elsewhere I have spoken briefly of two effects which concern me dearly; namely, literary realism and scientific realism. They are two principal effects of the modern ascendancy of the science of history in every human thing. If we had a sense of order we would ordain History to be Queen of the Sciences, just as our predecessors ordained Divinity. But we don't want hierarchies, and so we don't have them, except in some vulgar remnants like the conception of The Boss which we must constantly divide with a view to infination.

Gaston Bachelard has made one or two statements which recur to me at the moment. In his book called *The Psychoanalysis of Fire,* he remarked that the prescientific mind will select a great subject and concerning that go on to write a little book. In the same little book, speaking from the point of view of a scientist he said, The less we know about something, the more names we give it. Whenever I recall that observation, I am invariably reminded as well of the commonplace whereby people give a variety of names to whatever they love; they speak succesively of 'my little hobby,' 'my trade,' 'my profession,' 'my love,' 'my life.' I will even sometimes say 'my little life.' In making a series of statements whose implications would discredit the scientific bases upon which our culture has latterly rebuilt itself, I feel bound to remark however that all of us do share this ground, whether we know it or like it or not, and I who does know it would take no view that is foreign to the scientific matrix. Indeed I would consider it impossible to do so. What is incomprehensible in scientific terms is incomprehensible to me. I very much appreciate many incomprehensible effects, but I do not understand them any more than does anyone else; that is, not at all. We have only to notice the inability of our most talented cartoonists to communicate to us an image of some completely other form of life in order to realize the nature of incomprehension. We can conceive of such things only abstractly; if we wish to *imagine* a god, we are constrained to see someone human.

The possibility of abstraction from life has been evident to us since the forgotten times when the first languages were invented for our pleasure. Toward the beginning of the late *Sale* there occurs a sentence crudely noted after the manner of the earliest scribes. This sentence *p. 147 —l. 14* reads, For the manufacture of the curious mixture we have many resources especially games I read in a book or wrote. I only left out the vowels, but they had no sentence structure and they did not separate the words. It was extremely cryptic but not highly abstract, a type of cliché for indicating sounds that were perfectly well known to those using them, as a modern business communication or legal proceeding is easily reduced by stenography to a few special signs, or the way our machines can store any and all information recording only electrical signals of two types. These games whose nature we can recognize in the convention also of verbal clichés, have as one of many purposes that of ridding our minds of ever vaster amounts of concrete manifestations, latterly including the realities of our common languages, to leave room, as it were, for a tide of anti-images under the form of abstraction. Thus in lieu of war, we cause combats to be staged, our plays and sports, at which we are content to watch, and we kill each other off through 'accidents.' In this form too, we invent the scientific revery which has proved so successful at reducing to nothing the hitherto chaotic features of our life and thought, though we have been using it for only a relatively short time. Such dreams have yielded up abstract manufactured objects by means of which people may at last achieve the ignorance of suffering for which we have always yearned, our anti-animistic urge for destruction and finality becoming real not in any imitation of a manifest principle, but of our own abstract invention of 'atoms,' for which dust is no adequate image.

Speaking for myself, I am sure I do not desire the end of the world. That is as liberal a statement as I can make. I cannot say that I desire to prevent the end of the world from coming to pass. Although it is possible that I am wrong, I think I hardly need to make a case for the attitude that reversed desires are not desires. I believe that all desire is simply affirmative. What those who would profess the reversal of other desires really seek is 'something else.' I would consider it wrong, or else simply accusative, to insist on any particular name for the reality out of which springs the impetus for controversy. At the same time, I am disposed generously toward those who would and do give a multiplicity of names to the romantic mood. I accept them all. For example there is nothing strictly 'unromantic' about the scientific way of life. The study of knowledge under History is founded in a desire to render every occurrence comprehensible. A disease is not fully defined until, in any given case, it can be utterly prevented and also completely cured, just as for God it was already supposed that all cause and effect had to be perfectly familiar. The trouble is that the comprehensive scheme we now use is basically unfamiliar. We do not understand our scientific laws. They are very successful, but they are not very good. By means of them, the larger part of everything in which men once took the profoundest interest is denied to exist except for madmen. The scientific mode explains everything *away* rather than truly comprehending things. Those who can still suppose that after all I have said I wish merely to insinuate myself against some of their clearest convictions will now accuse me of 'using rhetorical devices.' Although I am disposed to ignore that claim along with others that I am not just now mentioning, I shall not use the historical device of saying that such defences are outside the scope of my article. I shall respond by saying that I use naught but rhetorical devices, worn out old bits of language that have absolutely no life, for the purpose of communicating to anyone who reads the generic reality of what I am about. *If I could I would let anyone who wished inhabit me.* As it is, I force myself with pleasure into a lengthy explanation of what I know, for in this abstract form, I should never be able to explain myself, not even to demonstrate my inability.

In the presence of such assertions, a question immediately occurs, even to me, of the necessity of my undertaking. How does it happen that I . . . etc. Before considering such matters carefully, I may say that without doubt there is no external necessity, no prohibition at the root of my work. It is my privilege never to have received such a great insult from 'the world,' real or imaginary, as would require me to avenge it and vindicate myself. In such terms it would be more to the point to say that what I do takes place by means of inhibition, that is, by acts of omission whose necessity is wholly internal and thereby more or less under the control of my conscious or unconscious desires. Without wishing to develop yet another discreditable rhetoric, it is possible to say that the third point in this series, exhibition, most nearly scores the question, perhaps going somewhat too far in the outside direction. Thus I could say that this book, which was entitled as a prohibition, nevertheless places itself somewhere in between journalism and rhetoric.

If one were to read, as I am afraid I have not, the chapters in the encyclopedia on journalism and rhetoric, I expect that there would be very little information which could help one to follow the scheme suggested in the last paragraph. I have associated, by juxtaposition, on the one hand the words journalism, internal and inhibition, and on the other hand, rhetoric, external and exhibition. If I desired to make my meaning perfectly clear in this connection I should be forced to begin writing a different essay at this point.* But that is not my purpose. For as clear as a thing may be made to seem, just so much does it distinguish itself from every other thing. Any manifestation is, of its nature, perfectly clear to those it concerns. The King is dead. Long live the King! Now I am not against the clear definition of events however they are presented and I admire and often make use of various sorts of clarity (which in our day comes to be an abstract thing rather than just a quality of actualities), but I believe that whenever techniques of clarity are pursued at all well in explanation, there will be created a necessarily abstract scheme which must dissociate itself from all the suggestive aspects of the dream that was its source. While I would make no attempt strictly to represent the revery, which is always unintelligible despite the testaments of saints and heroes, it is my desire to include in the work itself various aspects which formal realism had to disregard as being inconsequential. It is just at this point in the process that I ally myself as well with the great Christian tradition of self-consciousness.

It is not my purpose to define what I am about so clearly that it becomes uninteresting. My point is that if I made here a scientific program of 'results' I should end by firing the whole work out of which this essay is the final product. Speaking more artistically I should say *The end is an afterthought.* That particular form of words has never occurred to me before now—it is part of the process of this essay—but the reader of my book will notice that what the sentence formulates has been on my mind for some years. As a child, I was never able to rid my mind of the patent inequality of the terms in

* Whenever I think about it for a few minutes, I can always come up with such a scheme for describing the book that has very little to do with my intentions. I am always going back to the first one mentioned here *p. 2, l. 8* namely that the thing is really a conventional murder mystery of the type husband—wife—lover. Although it is only a joke, all books are some such thing.

Aristotle's principle of composition; the beginning and the end seemed too short to be ranged with what went in between. Out of that childish impression, which in my mind has always retained the greatest clarity, I, as a young journalist, sought, among other things, to explore the possibilities of writing which entirely omitted historical details, since as I say elsewhere they are all uninteresting end points, or which used such details in a completely decorative manner. My daily record would then present everything quite of the moment in ways which all formal scientific and literary history must discard as useless. As I had several other intentions and ideas to try, my work does not completely suppress historical details, or always render them decorative, any more than it really reproduces any moment of my existence. *The work is quite imperfect in any particular respect, as it was bound to be for the lack of any singular intention.*

One of my readers chanced to ask me when he had read an early part of this edition what I meant by remarking the 'eternal influence of Cézanne.' At that moment I no longer knew exactly what had led me to set that phrase, but I could say that I had it in mind to notice that Cézanne, having invented the modern conception of two-dimensional space, had become indispensable to the history of every modern artist's work, since everyone thenceforth more or less adopted his convention. In the same fashion, the name of Baudelaire is always associated in some way with that of every considerable poet since his time. Thus, and in many other instances, I also remark the 'eternal' influence of the nineteenth century. I should like to add, for example, that it is now decided by psychologicians that schizophrenia *p. 48 — l. 6* is a genetically inherited character and not so much an environmental effect. My critique of this disease, characterized by the famous aspect of the divided personality, would set its invention in the nineteenth century where one finds also a dominant syntax of division in all things with a source in animal symmetry. Schizophrenia is the result of a failure of the synthetic function of the mind. It is cured either by consolidating identity in whichever part is considered more authentic, or by the fragmentation of both definitions to permit the subject to reconstruct herself anew, or by a combination of both techniques. A weakness for dialogue is symptomatic of it, and in general forms the schizoid character insinuates itself against all schemes that are unitary or indeterminate. It must be obvious that the *explication de texte* going into every such allusion would have to be three times the bulk of the work itself. And

beside linguistic notes, there are quite a lot of anecdotes concerning
the composition which in themselves would make a formidable history, though perhaps not an interesting one. Since, for example, I did
not wish to decide arbitrarily what to call myself as author, I once
looked through the first book to find out which version of my name I
had happened first to mention   *p. 30 —l. 7*   and I was glad to be able
to settle on that one for this work. But I shall not continue in this
vein. I have other projects in mind which as Goethe, who is always
quoted and never read, remarked, 'would take a lifetime to complete.' Before I resign myself to other things, however, I wish to
make a subsidiary essay into my idea of decoration.

As the ones who love to go about looking at the world, people
who are basically makers of things, creatures of desire and not of
necessity, have always made pleasant things to look at. Often in the
past we dedicated the things which pleased us most of all to God,
knowing without doubt that things which most pleased men would
gratify their genius. Even now there can be no doubt that people are
still doing what they have always done. If our mood is that of novelty
for itself including all our famous innovations, it cannot and should
not be denied that our pleasures are of the same order as they have
always been. Even if it can be demonstrated to our satisfaction that
every classical idea of beauty in any form has come to be eclipsed by a
cataclysm of abstractions in the form of basically meaningless words
(with the exception of the female nude which in most cases, however,
is used as a rhetorical device), even now there can be no doubt that
people will create analogies and metaphors for the purpose of sensual
gratification, however far removed such subjects of contemplation
may seem to be from good old trees and shepherds in the field and
plates of fruits. I am never more pleased, for example, than I am by
my appreciation of a well functioning machine of good design such as
the typewriter I am using now or the automobile from which I have
just alighted. But I take it furthermore that such terms as 'one
million dollars' which is nothing like the Romanesque altar piece it
represents for us, do gratify sufficiently, though perhaps not fully,
our classic metaphorical desires just as people in the old days loved
looking at the altar of their church as if it were 'something else.' Now
we find it vaguely embarrassing to gaze upon what is necessarily a
certified object of art, and to piece out the silences we explain to each
other how to see it. Formerly people could familiarize themselves
with the truly incomprehensible nature of God by means of a retable,

or whatever it was. Today we distinguish ourselves from the past by ignorance of art, from what is merely 'strange' by cultivating it as we might a rare weed within guarded mausoleums. Our genius seems to be expressed more nearly in contrivances that will wash our dirty linen for us or effectively produce electric imitation of the most beneficent outputs of the sun. This situation in which we find ourselves is more comprehensively artificial than that of any previous human life. But I must insist when the amount of people in the world is properly discounted for, what goes on here is neither generically different from nor more complicated than the life of our ancestors. It is quite simple. At the same time there is also an ever vaster accumulation of factual differences which is making it more and more obvious to even very young people, such as myself, that the quality of life today is strange to what it was. Although I am young I am in the curious position, through a variety of accidents, of being one who comprehends both styles as well as an intermediary range of modes. I sometimes say that I can remember very well the turn of the twentieth century as well as last New Year's. What is strange to me, the subject of my romance, is not only things that are very old, the forms of nostalgia or homesickness from which all but liars suffer these days, but it is also things that are very new, the forms of desperation or hopelessness which all modern artists must experience, though if they are scientists they need not express.

The French psychologist Charles Baudoin in his collection of aphorisms under the title *The Myth of Modernity* has pleasantly called our attention to, among other things, various aspects of what he likes to think of as our taste for the 'clean sweep.' Under this name he includes such factual diversities as total warfare, Swedish furniture, urban renewal, simplicity in dress, and the decline of the lyric mood in poetry as well as bureaucratc tyranny and a remarkable scheme called 'the rectification of brooks.' The list of good examples is really endless. I would like to add another whole category, namely the combined effects of 'the disappearance of the arts of decoration and the domination of the arts of publicity.' If it is not actually impossible, it is nowadays 'prohibitively expensive' to cause anything to be made in any but the simplest and least interesting manner. It is true, of course, that our complicated machines incline to the baroque, but we obscure this character by means of relatively formless 'streamlined' housings that win prizes and sell electric typewriters. All that one hears in the publicity about 'lost arts' is intriguing nonsense, like a care for some kinds of animals who have lately disappeared from the earth. If we really desired to make anything in any way at all, we would make it, for never before have so many people had so much time to do as they please. We apply ourselves rather to a mess of commercial distractions and factual distinctions and find time besides to consider seriously such an abstract problem as death with a view to understanding it in terms of a search for the secret of life, the source, the essence, the 'gas' of life. It is my proposition that we have substituted an appreciation for abstracted and often perverted linguistic forms in place of the gratification our forbears derived from looking at abstracted actual forms in decoration. And I see this effort as a principal turning point in the great European change-over from ignorance to stupidity *en masse*.

The only art necessarily preserving the aspect of visual decoration, which I value in any form, the process in which a decorated surface will always be produced on the industrial, even ecumenical, scale that we today so much admire and powerfully demand, is printing. You are blind to lovely murals and faded tapestries while your eye is entranced by every product of typography, lithography, photography, cinematography and, coming completely up to date with the irretrievable image of the moment, television which is so radically debased that it cannot call itself 'electrography.' I think it perhaps needless to say that when I speak of decoration I do not refer to 'good design' as things are deemed which participate in the class rhetoric of contemporary art, but I am not so sure as to be able to omit the remark. By decoration I refer to spaces which would be uninteresting to look at if people had not placed marks there, for example, this bit of paper I am filling up with characters of the greatest interest to myself.

Those who are confirmed nostalgics will now remark with incipient tears in their eyes or from haughty professional poses, as I sometimes find myself doing, that the Aldine printing faces or Garamond, my all-time favorite type, can be proved by all the rhetoric at their command to be better than most recent inventions along those lines, and that the whole history of modern art has not shown so excellent an architect as, say, Sir Christopher Wren, not to mention others who were greater and so and so predictably on. Others of us, hopelessly modern, turn from photography with a shrug and live simply between bare white walls (elsewhere they are green) which if anything seem to be appropriately abstract.

The graphic arts have two peculiarities. That which qualifies them as arts at all is that they are unnecessary. We could not live as we now desire to live but if necessary we could do without printing. That which disqualifies them as higher arts is that they can produce no classical forms, they can only reproduce the classics of other genres. That is, the products of these arts do not describe the process by which they are produced. Every photograph is equally classic for every other. These are the types of exclusive definitions in which I take some pleasure as a rhetorician but which I would prefer, in the best interests of my art, not to make. I steel myself, however, to insist that these arts inevitably and in every form always allude to 'something else.' It is a long hard road back through the age from the cinema of truth to classical romanticism, as our advertisement would lightly put it, but we have at least opened the way.

Whether any such path will become well-worn is a matter of indifference to me. Such resolutions, as far as I am concerned, exist only for the moment of the process it takes to grasp them and let go like each of innumerable posts along an incline by which one could raise oneself along. A critic throws away her definitions, as a dancer abandons her gestures, only to renew them. But it remains, even after the 'final' sale, that a decorated surface attracts my attention and holds my interest, and the better it is the more I like it. The printed surface is always decorated for some other function, however, many exceptions may be cited such as the 'Egyptian' types once cut by Fred W. Goudy for his own amusement. While I concede that printed forms, and, through metaphor, words themselves, have effectively substituted for decoration the appearance of it, I absurdly maintain that this debased and impermanent tradition does not satisfy me, that I still seek the images of old in architectural details of every sort, these strange, meaningless signs of a previous cultivation of the human sense that are left to us only to be ignored and indeed obliterated as soon as possible. I am reminded at this point of certain historians' devasting logic to suppose that Søren Kierkegaard thought as he did because he lived in Copenhagen where the weather is foul and the company worse. Nevertheless, even if it was his limp and his love life, I would say that my nostalgia of decoration, as an example, is metaphorical of I know not what and what I do not desire to know, to name, or of what I would vaguely term the poetical impulse I find within, not wishing to put a finer point upon it. I would add that this metaphor is wholly explanatory, abstract.

But although I cavil away at them for not being as good as I would have them if I could, I embrace the sophisticated arts of publicity under their two generic forms, rhetoric and printing, and by so doing I will create what scientists may call a synthesis, or artists say invention. With almost the desperation of the cinemist who causes one camera to photograph another which is taking pictures that have already been shown, I wish carefully to combine all I know to make a better substitute than any other for what I cannot know. And because I am literate, I attach myself to literature by writing a novel, a romance, a guidebook to newly sundered linguistic realms about how to write a novel. Yet having forgone somewheres the history or plotted story which is the form's distinction, and elsewheres the poetry of character which is its source, I either disqualify my work or extend the limits of the type. Actually I do not care what what I do be called. . . .

L'effet de la science est d'ebranler les certitudes
et de confondre les principles les plus manifestes.

II

AFTER THE PICARESQUE PHASE, when it was still desired to reform
the epic, the forms of the novel, by then thoroughly cultivated, had
been graduated into a few classic types; the heroic novel moving
toward the psychological study of personal character then coming
back in on itself to reveal the personality of the author, principally
either by means of exoticism (romance) or the history of disenchantment. Disenchantment is analogous to explanation but it is similar to
education. You got the story of how people realized themselves. It
was a popular and useful art setting up paradigms of good and bad
behaviour and opinion from a criterion of success and failure. The
straight romance, being more artificial, had you assume a realization
to begin with, usually in terms of an evil character. All these basic
approaches are still effective in literary art and will continue until the
death of history, even if 'the novel' folds up tomorrow.

As a matter of personal taste, I have never been much attracted
to classical epics, even those originally composed in some form of
English. They strike me as being lugubrious, not an entirely bad
fault to have, but tiresome. I have always, however, loved long
books. During the composition of this work, for example, although I
was omitting things left and right, I was repeatedly depressed by the
thought that the book would be too short. No doubt that is one of the
sources of this essay, my 'book the seventh.' Any explanation, as I say
elsewhere, is also a continuation though on another scale. The admirable thing about very long poetical works is that they are practically
endless. One gets rather lost in them—but that's like life—one can't
remember everything. We have here the substitute for a large
number of notes to the text which are like signposts by which it is
intended to give the reader an impression that he could find his own
way if he tried. For instance, I should have liked to mention that I
first encountered the phrase 'lineaments of gratified desire'
p.95 —l.14 in a contemporary novel, and where I ran across it again
in Joyce and again in Blake. Instead I'm being like the doctor who
says, You feel lost, eh? Well, so do I. It is a consolation. And unless
you have something like a completely original disease he's thinking
(in the realistic mode) about his dinner or the hangnail of his left
thumb. I often feel (something) and if I get into a good conversation I
can stimulate myself to express it somehow though I don't usually

feel just that way then. It is like other things, but some are more important.

At the outset a few years ago, I made up a list of people whose books I had admired in any way at any time I could still remember, 'to cover our tracks and my nudity' as I gaily said then. Actually this list *p. 2 —l. 40* was to indicate to me the readings by which I had been influenced up to that time, some of them school books, most not, but all of them well-known standards of composition or at least books raised high on the tide of publicity which has transformed literature during the last hundred years into a frank competition for the attention of the press. Not so long ago, I made up another list of the authors whose books had moved me during the time of the composition of this book. I noticed that not all of them were writers and that a large proportion of them were French. About ten of my old favorites reappeared on my new list. The longer I pondered the two lists whereon appeared 120 influential names, the more I felt constrained to add other influences that seemed to have been forgotten, as well as another category of credit, several of my teachers. I concluded that I could never do justice to my forbears by any such means. Further along, I mean to indicate those from whom I have actually quoted at any length beyond a phrase in order to relieve that specific debt. Here, I shall console myself with a word of thanks to those artists I admire who are more or less my own age. In most cases they are not the ones to whom I owe most; but there is a special delight in recognizing oneself in the works of other people one may not know, but might.

In no intentional order, then, I have: Bernardo Bertolucci for his lovely film about stupidity called *Primo della Rivoluzione*; Rosalyn Drexler for her play *Home Movies* in which she reclaims the fact that 'we all have weak eyes'; Fernando Arabal for recalling my attention to the remarkable charm of solitude; George Deem, with whom I sometimes drink, for the perfection of his paintings; Fred Herko, who is dead, (or Rudolph Nureyev) for his vivid romantic mood; Jean-Luc Godard for his films *Vivre Sa Vie* and *La Femme Mariée* which show all the right attitudes in a coherent manner; R. B. Kitaj for his unpopular juxtaposition of literature and painting; Joyce Carol Oates, a childhood friend, for her novel *With Shuddering Fall* which demonstrates the masculine principle; Charles Webb, a college friend, for his novel *The Graduate* which demonstrates the impossibility of writing a good novel; Jon Silkin for insisting on the poetry of process, however imperfect it may be; Edward Dorn for the reinvention of artistic criticism; John Arden for the translation of poetry into action; Lee Oswald for his honesty.

There remain to this uncompleted score three of my contemporaries whose examples I cannot so easily dismiss.

Ray Gosling is an Englishman, a little younger than I, who comes from Northampton, went to school in Leicester and when I last heard, in 1966, was in Nottingham. By chance, and I mean luck, I read an essay he wrote called *The Importance of Hogwash* printed in a little magazine from Leeds. That was more than three years ago. At the time I had not yet seen anything else in which someone my age was saying things as I knew them to be for us. I inquired about him from a friend who was then in London, and received a copy of Gosling's autobiography *Sum Total.* I was thus literally encouraged to go on with what I would regard as my education. At the time he had a talent for publicity which led someone in London, either wit or humorist, to call him 'the Byron of the Midlands.' I have heard almost nothing of him since 1963 when he finished publishing a series of various apologies for what he did in 1959. Anyway he remains with me as the type for (my term) the intellectual hard and fast. A trip to Nottingham in 1972 yielded no trace of him.

Yvonne Rainer is a dancer, a few years my senior, who has spent the last few years working in and about an ever-changing group of artists associated in a dance workshop patronised by Judson Memorial Church on Washington Square in New York. It happened that I first saw her perform the night before I began writing the letter which became the first pages of this book, though the dance to which I there refer was not hers. Later, I found the program dated February 15th (1963). It is hard for me to say just what I admire about her work, but I would say that it is more her writing than anything else. She uses words in her dances. I think that is not why I like them, but I could be wrong. From time to time she has found a way to explore the formal possibilities of movements that have no meaning without insulting or neglecting her audience. When I asked her, she sent me a copy of her essay *Some Thoughts on Improvisation* from which I have quoted the slogan, Regret garrotes the imagination.

I think I can say that the form of my book would not be what it is if I had never heard of Alain Badiou. On the other hand, this book was already conceived and largely filled out when, in September 1964, I happened upon a notice of his book *Almagestes* in *The London*

Magazine which I found in the offices of *The New York Times* on the last day of my employment by that institution. This notice, which immediately pleased me, was largely a paraphrase of the publisher's announcement (Editions du Seuil) from which I shall quote the first period:

> Ni roman ni essai, mais oeuvre littéraire (l'éclat de la langage, la richesse des notations visuelles et sonores, l'invention sans fin et l'élan du discours n'appartiennent qu'au poète) et expérience de pensée (au croisement des courants marxiste, existentialiste, structuraliste) Almagestes est le premier volet, consacré au *langage,* d'un triptyque dont les deux autres parties seront consacrées à *l'homme* et à *l'Histoire.*

It was some months, and I was well along with this revision, before I could get the book from France. That summer I had, in answering a question, referred to my work as a 'three-in-one book.'

I cannot say that I have 'read' Badiou's book in the same sense as I can say I have read most of the books in which I happened to take an interest. In that sense, *Almagestes,* like few other books, has to be considered as 'unreadable.' But I have read about in it a good deal and I have made, somewhat laboriously, some translation of a few difficult sections with which to amuse myself and some friends. From what I have thus gathered of his intentions, it seems to me that despite innumerable differences in our ideas and attitudes we share a determination to show everything altogether or, if not that, then to make a complete demonstration of one thing implying everything else. Along the way, in both cases, there are also numerous and diverse polemics and jokes and masks. If such an aim is taken with literal seriousness there is no doubt that the thing cannot be done, even by means of collaboration as it was attempted by generations of writers of the Bible, who nevertheless succeeded. Both of us, I suspect, will get into trouble with the authorities at this point, because they would find it 'unnecessary' to do more than retranslate the old work, putting in modern analogies and scientific figures, and leaving out old words. Speaking for myself, I find it undesirable to do even the necessary minimum. From what I hear of the modern Bible it must be much worse than the ancient one. It was bound to be so. No modern cathedrals have any of the excellences of the classics of the genre even though with prestressed precast concrete it is now possible to cover much vaster spaces, such as a whole baseball park, to form convertible places of entertainment that bear no analogy to places of worship. There have been as many technical innovations in poetry as in static structure; but the applications of purposeful technique in both cases and every other has not changed, even slightly, the human desires which the arts of composition satisfy. We have radically changed the processes by which those satisfactions are achieved. Therefore, even as we ridicule the new cathedral, we are not making up a better Bible. Bible it is — the word means book — but it is no good analogue nor any substitution, nor even renewal: it is something else. And playfully, since we are so young, we cannot resist trifling and tempting at the symbolists and metaphysicians who would destroy our doings into historical categories that are already filled up and sealed.

By comparing or associating myself with Badiou, I do indulge to some extent in self-aggrandisement; to what extent I am not sure. I think that the deployment of his *langage* is more formal and more extensive than mine is here. He can use, for example, aspects of the late war in Algeria and such things as I would disdain (but we have had no war here for a hundred years and none in New York for more than 150) as well as parts of philosophies and mathematics of which I am largely ignorant. It would appear, indeed, that his book and this one are phenomena as far from similarity as any two European novels in existence. But the form of them, that is to say the intention, is the same. The differences between them are due in part to the differences between the cultures in which we find ourselves; and then they are due also to the differences of experience, of inclination and of taste between each other and so on; that is to say, however, they are mere factual distinctions that we each cast decoratively and in a synthetic manner upon one basic formal aspiration — the epic poem.

As she becomes more familiar with me I find that my wife is more often inclined to voice an objection to whatever I tell her by saying that I do not really know what I am saying. She is resisting my information, 'for some reason,' as she will say. In my turn I always add that it is for some other reason than that I do not know it. She never resists the advice of her doctors, however, who tell her much the same things as I do, but in a different way. She who has never bought a piece of fruit except on special commission from me has, on the recommendation of her doctor, taken to bananas and golden apples in place of pastries from which she was inseparable before. I do not have the logic for the game. I am seldom introduced to people who are so ill-mannered as to try to force me to admit that I do not really know all the answers. At the same time, I am quite willing to admit it while not doubting my ability to inform any situation. I actually appreciate her point, however, for I often doubt that others know what they thoughtlessly repeat. Indeed I am often certain that they do not comprehend their facts at all. It has recently been mentioned to me that there is an overflowing shortage of engineers. Sometimes these things are on the point of being charming, but by such means people are suppposed to concern themselves, as cannot be done, with such things as engineers in general. The logic of relations as exemplified by the world-famous theorem of relativity has been invented to crush all such domestic objections on an ecclesiastical scale. I believe it has by now succeeded as far as history is concerned. In a democracy within a republic such as we have here today, it is highly scandalous the way good-looking people can get their way of a world that is supposed to be blind to charm. Believe it or not, I could write a book about paradoxical eclecticism (Badiou's phrase) in our society, but it would be a different book. Besides, it is already available in *The Foundations of Modern Art* compiled by Amedée Ozenfant in 1928. I mean that despite all our useful suppositions, there remains a level of realities which I call 'performance' that necessarily goes unrealized though it affects our actions and our beliefs.

Having congratulated Ozenfant on his prescience and Janet Belle for her perspicacity, I am left with the question of whether I know anything of the epic and, regardless of that answer, whether my book participates in anything of the sort, however it is defined. I am veering close to burlesque but I continue to control the course. A good performance is the triumph of fraud. There is no telling how such successes may be achieved. I have recently had a man ask me to hand him a pair of scissors in such a sincere manner that I thought he must be asking me for something else. That is a perfectly rhetorical sentence of a sort that will be seen through immediately by zealots of every persuasion. Nevertheless I have the audacity so to undermine it because I know that many people, including readers, have had just such an experience which, unless it is somehow recalled to them, they ignore or simply fail to notice at all. No matter how I additionally interfere with that remark, I have some confidence that in it I have scored a communication point. It is much harder to apologize for fraud than it is to apologize for charm. That formula, like every other, contains its own solution.

The epic is its own universe. All at once it embraces everything known to its creator, often including things that must be, strictly speaking, unknown. *As he reviews his lengthy revery the poet will perhaps discover things he did not know he knew.* And in terms of fact, it is all misinformation because these worlds do not exist in fact. They are neither merely fanciful nor merely factual. There is no irrelevancy to it. It is the only totally encompassing form. Is it circular? Of course; and square and without dimension. But still it is not all or nothing. The epic poet is incapable of mentioning things foreign to him, for everything he touches, however lightly, is instantly and wholly incorporated into his design. It follows that his task, like Noah's, must devolve into a process of sorting out the whole world. His only invention is to make a repository adequate to hold whatever he desires to save. If he can, he may even borrow or find the form cast off from some other purpose. The intention is inclusive but the process must set limits. The actor who is playing drunk attempts to walk the line; we would say that if necessary he could succeed (since he has taken nothing but cold tea) and thus fail the part — but he staggers and desirably succeeds at fraud. We would only wish there were some unpredictable manner for displaying so much truth. It is for this romantic reason that we do not imitate the moves a camera may record; nor would we show emotions of which people are actually incapable.

III

There's only one slight difference between
   Me and my epic brethren gone before,
And here the advantage is my own, I ween,
   (Not that I have not several merits more,
But this will more particularly be seen);
   They so embellish, that 'tis quite a bore
Their labyrinth of fables to thread through,
   Whereas this story's actually true.

ANY EXPLICATION is bound to lose some readers for a book, as will more, if it is good, the text itself. And in this argument, which I now close, it is made clear enough what purposes I have and how I desire them not to be mistaken. 'Yet a word!' gasps the expiring hero from the floor and goes on with a valediction that fills five pages more. In truth we would go on forever. But at length we realistically cease, only to reappear in printed forms. It would be pointless for me here to condense the themes and notes that would permit me, when asked, to recount in a minute what I have been doing here. Raymond Rousell, before dying, wrote a paper he called *Comment j'ai écrit certains de mes livres* *p. 200 — l. 12.* Perhaps one day I shall have to do the same thing, but for now I think I have made enough suggestions to that score. Here I have only to incorporate the end of this book, and to that end there remains the pleasant task of mentioning those who have unwittingly helped me.

Though they knew not what I was about, my employers during the period of composition supported me in such ways that the work would have been rendered more difficult without their aid and, indeed, might never have been begun. Namely: The Newspaper Guild of New York; The New York Times Company and John McCauley, Dan Schwarz, Lester Markel; Andrea Service Corp. and Richie Zimmer. Those who have held the property I occupy in Front Street at Old Slip, a small warehouse built in 1836, have also helped my cause. In particular, The Famous Three Bears Corp. and John Economo; Harold Kreiger, agent for the previous owner; and Messrs. Allen, Melvin and Charles Fergang, the present owner and his sons. For my friends, whom I shall not name, all thanks would be inadequate regard.

Plagiarism has come to be, in this literal and commercial age, a worse offense than libel. For that reason it is my duty to make a note of the fact that I have lifted several sentences *p. 124 —l. 13* from a review by Sarel Eimerl of the autobiography of David Garnett published in *The Reporter* magazine March 1963 to represent the journalism of autobiography. But all legalism aside, what is esteemed in art is its originality. The same character is regarded more handsome still in science. For every source an author notes, his own value is diminished by that much, so that inflation, under whatever name, warrants him to claim with modesty that his work is all his own. On the other hand, I would be pleased to mention, if I could, every source that I have touched in passing and to fill out every allusion with a note. Very early on, I decided to forego the use of footnotes altogether, a promise I later occasionally broke. But to satisfy my pedantic impulse, it pleased me from time to time to go back over what I had revised and remember where I had gotten this phrase or that name, or explain my use of certain words, or add to my case in favor of such and such a point. Although this great list makes entertaining reading for me, I found that it would please me more to dispense with all such academic mechanism. I am in some doubt, however, that the value of certain of my remarks will be at all apparent even to the careful reader. It is unfortunate that it has not been my mood to treat of those tirelessly repeated allusions that form the demand for literary glossaries. Where I recommend 'that verse of Whitman's' *p. 177 —l. 39* no other authority can direct one to these lines from the third verse of his *Song of Myself:*

There was never any more inception than there is now,
Nor any more youth or age than there is now,
And will never be any more perfection than there is now,
Nor any more heaven or hell than there is now.

At various points in Book Five I have dropped four well-known names without integrating them into the text. 'The name like Adams' *p. 222 —l. 40* reaches back to a sentence or two from the diary of John Adams, the second President of the United States, where he records his dream that the third generation of his family should have leisure to indulge in art. When I say *p. 228 —l. 30* 'I don't know, Cocteau,' I am reminded of the story which was recirculated at the time of the death of that publicist of modern art to the effect that when he once saw an advertisement for his ballet *Parade* with sets by Picasso, it occurred to him to think that Picasso, in turn, was by Cocteau. The Drapers' Company *p. 234 —l. 21* is an ancient association of liverymen in the City of London who published their medieval records a few years ago. 'Mr. Williams to the contrary' is an allusion to an attempt of William Carlos Williams to recreate a usable American history in his *In the American Grain p. 256 —l. 14.*

On page 257, I have reproduced a photographic print of the painting *February 1964* by George Deem. It was made at about that time in oils on canvas at the size 30x40″. It was the first of his series of calendars. At present it is owned by the artist's agent The Allan Stone Gallery of New York, through whose permission it is reproduced. Incorporated in the painting is the artist's reproduction of a landscape made in 1875 by George Inness (1825-1894) which is now in the Metropolitan Museum of Art.

I want to mention my debt also to *The Oxford Universal Dictionary on Historical Principles,* third edition, 1955. It is the authorized abridgement of the great *Oxford English Dictionary* nevertheless having over 2500 large pages.* These dictionaries are radically different from all the American dictionaries because it is their purpose to be a comprehensive record of the history of the use of words and their sources. It does not tell you what to do, it tells you what has been done. Using the dictionary with discrimination, one is able to ignore the vast accumulation of worsened connotations which in the last hundred years has obscured most of our words to the point of insignificance. It never sets itself up as the substitute for one's own command of the language, but it informs one's intuitions in a manner that is always rewarding, and occasionally even charming. Thus, for example, it can be known that the word *reward* is a medieval garble for *regard* so that lively attention directed upon an object is also that thing's reward. The article for Dictionary ends with this quotation of Ralph Waldo Emerson: Neither is a dictionary a bad book to read . . . it is full of suggestion, —the raw material of possible poems and histories.

Notes in whatever form are impelled by a real or imagined incompleteness to the work as a whole. I am in no position to claim that my work is either wholly my own or perfectly itself. The quality of truth is here revalued and that of culture disinherited. While I do

---

* In later editions it is titled *The Shorter O.E.D.* but as the preface indicates it is a much more inclusive book and hence 'universal.'

not say the same old things, neither do I say anything very new. It is perhaps an ambiguous point of view, or even trivial, but that is not its difficulty. My afterword is almost finished.

Throughout the text at many points I have reproduced the words of other people whenever I wished. Very often in setting these quotations I have refrained from making any indication of their nature. I have made them my own, occasionally to the extent of rewriting them somewhat to suit me better. I now want to redeem these sources otherwise confounded with the process that is described. To begin with there is a list *p. 13 —l. 30* of some sayings that are among my old favorites. The names of many of their authors appear listed below in other connections but these do not: G.B. Shaw, Robert Browning, E.B. White, Noel Coward, Dylan Thomas, Fred Waring, M.F.K. Fisher, W.H. Auden, Lewis Carroll, Heraclitus, Robert Frost, W.B. Yeats. I do not mind if people dislike what I give them to read, but I take some precaution lest the whole history of the sins of other authors be counted on my head as well. Abandoning caution at the end, I give you now by page and line in the order of their appearance the dead letters of my stars, my lights, my predecessors.

I would declare with Mallarmé that, *'Tout, au monde, existe pour aboutir à un livre.'* What I have drawn altogether is, at base, my own experience. In another form, it is the experience as well of everyone who reads it. Its source is all my youthful revery; I give it out for no purpose not already fulfilled; I make it over to the gods with no Anticipation of my reward or theirs.

And here, Critias, I said, I hope you will find a way out of a difficulty into which I have got myself. Shall I tell you the nature of the difficulty? —By all means, he replied.

Does not what you have been saying, if true, amount to this: that there must be a single science which is wholly the science of itself and of other sciences, and the same is also the science of the absence of science?
—Yes.

But consider how monstrous this proposition is, my friend; in any parallel case the impossibility of it will be transparent to you.
—How is that? and in what cases do you mean?

In such cases as this: Suppose that there is a kind of vision which is not ordinary vision, but a vision of itself and of other sorts of vision, and of the defect of them, which in seeing sees no color, but only itself and other sorts of vision: Do you think that there is such a kind of vision?
—Certainly not.

New York, February 28, 1966

TABLE OF CONTENTS

On the dustjacket: *A View of Daisies,* photograph by F.T.C.
On page 17: *The Florence Hotel,* New York, 1965 by F.T.C.
On page 257: *February 1964* by George Deem, photo by L. de Caro.
On page 315: *The Author at the Age of 25* by Edward Volkman, 1963.

GRATUITOUS POSTFACE

by Paul Valéry

At the age of 70 in 1940 when Paris was occupied by the German army Valéry published a play called Mon Faust. *About a year after I finished writing* Anticipation, *when my son Jesse George Frederick was a small baby, I was invited to a reading of* Mon Faust *in English. I was amazed to hear some of Faust's lines in this otherwise unproducible play and I copied out some of them as the following gratuity. February 15, 1967*

¶ I might write my memoirs. On the other hand, I might compose essays on subjects of great variety. But I don't want to, it would bore me to do it. Besides, it seems to me to be false to try and separate thought, however abstract, from life, however it may be lived. So I have decided to take all my observations, speculations and theories as they occurred to me and set them into the fairly remarkable story of my life, my relations with people and things of the world. ¶ I want to give the strongest, the most penetrating effect of sincerity that a book has ever given. That cannot be achieved if one shrinks from any of the horrors, the secret humiliations, the distressing experiences—be they true or false—that a man can remark in the course of his life. There is nothing too vile or too silly to lend the ring of truth to an autobiography. ¶ It's a curious business, distributing the gifts that chance brings me to a crowd of people I don't know. ¶ I want to create a great book, I want it to be an inextricable blend of my false memories and my true stories, my ideas, such as they are, my intuitions, my well-conceived hypotheses and deductions, my imaginative experiments—all my many voices in one. It is a book that one could begin reading at any point and leave off at any other. Perhaps nobody will read it, but anyone who does will no longer be satisfied with any other book. I want it to be written in a style of my own invention, a sensation that will glide with marvellous ease from the bizarre to the commonplace and back again, from absolute fantasy to the most rigorous rationality, from fiction to prose to fact to verse, from the flattest platitudes to the most fragile ideals. It will be a style that embraces all the modulations of the soul and every leap of the mind; a style like the mind itself that occasionally returns in upon itself to what it expresses just to feel that it is the thing that expresses it; it will do its best to demonstrate the living body of the speaker asserting itself as the will to expression, and then show the sudden awakening of thoughts startled that they could have been identified for the time being with an object even though that identification is their essence and function. ¶ The greatest minds give me ample precedent for borrowing freely from them all. ¶ I want this grand work to rid me finally of myself, of myself in every form and sense of times now past, of the self from which I already feel so detached. I want it to render me evanescent, disencumbered forever from anything that amounts to anything, both from what is common and from what is noble, and then, with my mind free, my hands free, I shall make my way to hell, a transient who has abandoned his luggage without caring what he leaves behind.

A Substantive Index

The first edition consists of 1000 copies in paper covers, 400 clothbound copies, and 100 copies specially bound, numbered and signed by the author.